Reading the words of this
wide range of laughter, te
put it down! Alan Mesher
LIFE. I learned more from this one literary masterpiece, than I had from years of studying metaphysics. I look forward to more!
Stewart A. Swerdlow, world renowned hyperspace intuitive and best selling author

You have created an irresistible character in Tenzin. I wish I had his phone number when I needed a bit of comforting myself.
Maureen Baron, Vice President and Editor-in-Chief of Penguin Books and the New American Library, retired

Your story holds so much promise to entertain, to reveal, to educate and inspire.
Susan Schulman, literary agent, NYC

You are clearly a talented writer, there's much to be admired in these pages.
Eleanor Jackson, literary agent, Markson Thoma Literary Agency, NYC

Alan's writing is both poetic and powerful. This story, as it moves from the present to the past, weaves a tale of love and loss, and runs the gamut of deep archetypal emotions that all humans share. It will leave an indelible impact upon you. The book is a must-read.
Dawn T. Clare, Harvard MBA, Clarivoyant Advisor and TV Host

The Silent Steps of Grace is a beautifully written and powerful story of spritual triumph against all odds. There are many important spiritual truths revealed throughout the narrative that will resonate in your life and inspire you to action. I highly recommend this book to anyone looking for an engaging story that can transform their lives.
John Randoph Price, Best Selling Author and Chairman of the Quartus Foundation

At its heart, this is a novel about love. Not the love sold to us through Hollywood movies and greeting cards, but something far more profound: the love that generations of spiritual seekers have sought and that Mesher weaves into a compelling global narrative that spans the twentieth century. The novel's central character, Tenzin, is the sort of irresistibly wise friend that we all wish we had. Reminiscent of Aldoux Huxley's, Island, this novel is a must read for anyone seeking a radically different perspective on the world in which we live.
Dr. Bidhan Chandra Roy Assistant Professor of English Literature, CSULA

OTHER WORKS BY

Alan Mesher

Journey of Love
The T Zone
Just Who Do You Think You Are?

To Regg,
Best wishes for a wonderful life.

All best,
Alan [illegible]
9.17.2013

THE SILENT *Steps of Grace*

THE SILENT *Steps of Grace*

A NOVEL BY

ALAN MESHER

The Silent Steps of Grace

ISBN 978-0-9660295-4-3

Published by Oversoul Communications
www.oversoulcommunications.com

Printed in the United States of America

Library of Congress Control Number: 2011944327
Library of Congress Subject Headings:
Visionary & Metaphysical- fiction
Spiritual Warfare - fiction
Tibetan - Fiction
Wisdom - fiction
Buddhism - fiction
Good and Evil - fiction
Reincarnation - Fiction
Secret Societies - Fiction
Human - Alien Encounters - Fiction

Cover Design: Cathi Stevenson Bookcoverexpress.com
Interior Design: Gwen Gades Beapurplepenguin.com

Dedication

For all who seek a better life and a better world

Acknowledgements

I wish to thank my long time agent Arthur Fleming for believing in this novel from its inception. Arthur is an honest man of high integrity whom I am honored to call my friend.

Many thanks to Maureen Baron, Vice President and Editor in Chief of Penguin Books and the New American Library retired, for her excellent work in editing the original manuscript. If you are a writer searching for an editor Maureen can be contacted at: www.bookdocs.com/editors/mbaron/

Many thanks as well to Michael Mann, a fine writer and accomplished editor, who did an outstanding job of editing the final version. Michael can be reached at apavaritavarsa@gmail.com

PROLOGUE

A person is not a thing or a process but an opening through which the Absolute can manifest.
Heidegger

Divine Grace has many faces. Not all of them are kind. Now and then she is benevolent, sweeping down in the guise of an angel to rescue the terrified petitioner from overwhelming danger. This is Grace the Redeemer, answerer of prayers of last resort, dispenser of mercy, bringer of blessings. More typical is her role as the stern, exacting teacher who drops unexpected challenges into our lives to see whether we will rise to the occasion or let our weaknesses destroy us. This is Grace the Transformer, who purposely refuses to intervene on our behalf, leaving us to save ourselves.

If one day Grace should glance your way in her cold, implacable manner, prepare yourself for hardship and remember this: her tests are premeditated and well conceived. Their purpose is to move you farther along the path to Divine Union and spiritual ecstasy, whether you understand their function in your life or not.

Despite the burdens she brings, Grace always appears at the perfect moment. We see only what we desire. Grace sees what we need. We think of ourselves in terms of the body, when we are really a soul clothed in flesh. Grace understands the duality of soul and body; she sees the soul's hunger to evolve; she recognizes the obstacles in the subconscious, the overhang of past karma, the shadows of unresolved fear and anger, and the cloud of self-doubt that prevents our progress. Her mission is to quicken our evolution, even if we don't consciously want that growth or are unwilling to go to the trouble it requires.

Grace is the x in life's equation, the one variable that can never be controlled. She sends no notice of her coming and does what she pleases when she arrives. Her sole purpose is to transform our lives and stimulate our growth. She cannot be deterred from her work and is fully faithful to her mission.

CHAPTER 1

The Chosen One

TIBET 1925

Tenzin Osun had been different from the start. He was the chosen one. When he was no more than a seedling in his mother's womb, his father, Naljor, would place his hands on his wife's belly and let the love that filled his heart flow into his unborn child. In those moments of direct contact, the door to the Infinite magically opened, and both parents found themselves swimming in a sea of love that was charged with ecstatic power.

What effect this daily transcendence had on the fetus, no one could truly say. There was no objective way to gauge the immediate reaction or chart its long-term consequences. Tenzin certainly had no capacity to tell his parents if he was aware of the love they were transmitting to him or if he felt the ecstasy they felt. Nor did this really matter to Tenzin's father. He was neither scientist nor researcher. He was convinced, however, that if he could bring the power of the Supreme Being into the equation of Tenzin's birth, his child would be blessed with a great deal of innate wisdom and consciousness.

To Naljor's way of thinking, if he watered the seed with love from the time it was planted, the child would grow to be strong and vibrant. Tenzin's mother saw no danger in trying to bring the Infinite into her child's birth and embraced the idea. When, she thought, had love ever hurt a child?

So, every night, from the time his mother knew she had conceived until the day of his birth, Tenzin's father would rest his hands on his wife's belly, chant the names of the Buddha, pray that his unborn child would be the incarnation of a high lama, and recite stories from the lives of the great saints of their native Tibet. In this way, by deliberate conscious intent, Tenzin's mind and soul were imprinted before he was born with stories of Milarepa, the flying saint, the teachings of Buddha, and the great doctrine of the Middle Way.

As a young boy Tenzin seemed quite normal, not at all saintly. He loved to exercise his imagination. He had a soft spot for animals, particularly his dog, and he liked to invent stories of great adventure and conquest. Then he would assemble his friends and his stories would become the basis for play battles. All the children in the village wanted to be included in his mock war games.

Tenzin possessed great charisma, a penetrating mind, and a quick sense of humor. He truly cared for the well-being of those around him and was strongly centered in his being. This powerful combination of attributes made Tenzin the undisputed leader in his circle.

One day when his mother had gone to help her sister in a neighboring village, Tenzin stole the plants she had been growing in earthen pots in the back of their home. He knew that these plants were very special to her. She had raised them with great devotion, intending to plant them in the flower beds in front of the village temple when the time was right. When she returned and found her plants missing she was nearly hysterical. Tenzin had trouble keeping the smile off his face, but managed to look downcast and concerned.

"Come, Momma," he said. "Let's take a walk. You'll feel better if you hold my hand. I'm sure the thief will be caught and you'll get your plants back."

What a wise and caring child, his mother thought, so old beyond his years. How lucky I am to have such a son. She took his outstretched hand and they walked together through their village, taking the long way around, coming at last to the temple.

"Maybe, you'll feel better, Momma," he said, "if you stand by the flowers that are already here for a few minutes. Then we can go inside and pray for the missing plants."

Tenzin spoke with such sweet innocence that his mother suspected nothing. He guided her to where he had planted her flowers the day before, in just the order she had grown them in her yard. She stood before them, still lost in sadness, not yet comprehending that they were hers. That recognition took a few minutes more. When the realization formed in her mind, she did not know whether to be angry or amused. Her sparkling eyes said humor but the tightness of her mouth and clenched jaw suggested otherwise.

Tenzin waited out the passing of the storm inside her, not knowing which way she would turn. His heart beat loudly in his ears. He felt her fury at him rising, and he wondered if taking her plants had been such a good idea after all. Then she looked at Tenzin's smile. She saw the pride he had in his actions, and she knew she could not be angry with him even if she tried. His love completely disarmed her. So she held her son against her and laughed. Then she made him vow he would never do anything like that to her again. He promised that he would not and went on to do other things that were equally mischievous and kind.

Tenzin had another side to his nature, one that made him very different from the other children in his village. Sometimes, though not often, a mood would come over him. He would grow very quiet and want to be alone. At those times he would walk into the forest, down the secluded path his father had shown him when he was younger, climb onto his secret rock in a clearing under a large tree and gaze at the Himalayas in the far distance. In these moments of reflection,Tenzin's mind would churn with timeless questions. What is the meaning and purpose of life? Why are we here? What was the purpose of my life?

He didn't know any of the answers. He was not yet ten years old. Still, the questions burned, waiting for the time he would be ready for them to come forward and absorb his full attention.

Even at his young age Tenzin instinctively knew that without the reality of a Supreme Truth and our link to deity, no ultimate meaning or real importance to life could exist. Life was not only to be savored; it held a hidden significance that was as yet beyond his grasp. So far, his whole life experience had been in being loved and loving in return. But something else lay in the distance, something more than this. Something he could sense but not yet touch. These moods fell upon Tenzin like clouds that obscure the sun and darken the land. When they passed it was as if the clouds had been shattered by a brisk wind. Light and warmth returned to his soul; only then could he leave his rock behind. But the moods invariably returned, creating more ferment in his soul, sending him racing back to his rock time and time again.

As he grew into adolescence, the restlessness grew with him until it became the driving force in his life. He knew that he must experience Truth first hand. Knowing that the Buddhist saints of his religion and many of the great Tibetan lamas of his country were enlightened and had intimate knowledge of the Supreme Truth did not satisfy him. Their writings inspired him. They had charted the topography, created maps of the mountainous terrain all would have to climb to attain a wider vision.

Studying this rich and varied material shaped the restlessness of Tenzin's nature into what it had really always been, the overriding theme of his existence. He no longer thought of his feelings as a passing mood, but rather as the inner prompting of his life's path. He thirsted for a direct experience of the Supreme Truth. He wanted to know what all the great ones before him had known, feel what they had felt, realize what they had realized. Second hand truth could neither slake his thirst nor empower him. He wanted to climb the mountain himself.

He was only fourteen years old, but he was already finished with the normal life.

When Tenzin turned fifteen Naljor did the inevitable. The time had come for his son to meet his destiny. He brought Tenzin to the Tsurphu Buddhist monastery in the mountains two days travel from their village and released him to the care and teaching of the great lama who resided there.

Just outside the gates Naljor embraced his son for the last time. He told him of his ecstatic experiences fifteen years before when Tenzin had been growing in his mother's womb.

"I have always wondered," his father said, "If you felt my love and prayers back then and what effect they may have had on you. Now I know. Those prayers have brought you to this gate. The seed has grown into a mighty tree, and now stands tall and true. It is time, my son, for another kind of learning, a learning I can't give you. But this much I do know. Freedom comes when the Divine light penetrates to the core of your being. When you fuse with that energy you will attain the liberation you seek. You are here. Work hard. Realize your true self."

"I will do my best, Father."

"You have always brought your family great joy, Tenzin. Go as far as you can. Let nothing stop you, no matter what befalls you. Perhaps your destiny is to conquer your Self, to overcome adversity, and to attain liberation. But it will not be easy. The spiritual path is neither for the weak nor the shallow. It is the most difficult and dangerous path in the world. Fame, worldly power, and wealth are far easier to attain than the consciousness you seek."

"Yes, father. I know."

"When doubts come and tests confront you, stand still inside yourself. Keep your mind clear. Empty it of the turmoil and conflict that fear always produces. Do not act hastily or you will act unwisely. Be patient! Remember how the Buddha overcame the evil of Mara when he sat under the Bodhi tree. He ignored it, gave it no heed, remained absorbed in the infinite light of Supreme Truth, and won a great victory over the forces of darkness. Move forward when your soul nudges you, when the light guides you, not before."

"I will Father. Thank you for all you have given me. I will never forget your words. I will never forget you, or Mother, or my sisters."

"We gave you what we could, Tenzin. It was very little, I'm afraid. "

"You gave me all I ever wanted Father. Your love. Your time. Your wisdom. Thank you. Those were precious gifts."

The time of words was over. Only mutual love and respect remained. The love that had been given with conscious intent fifteen years ago now flowed from heart to heart, amplifying their connection. All was in balance. They embraced as father and son, soul to soul, older and younger, but equal and eternal in the divine. The circle was complete. It was time to move forward. A new beginning lay beyond the gate.

Tenzin walked the short distance to the monastery wall. At the gate he stopped briefly and turned back. Then he stepped through the portal into the world for which he was made.

Naljor stood before the closed portal knowing that his son's life would now move in a different rhythm and into a sphere beyond his reach. He was proud of Tenzin, certain of his true calling, knowing he had done the right thing by him.

The great shock of his loss now hit him. Tenzin was gone from his life. A vast, dark emptiness swept through him. He walked slowly down the steep hill to the field of stones. A wail rose in his throat while his tears flowed without restraint. He cried for the two days it took him to walk home. As he approached his village he took a deep breath and forced his tears aside. He could not let his wife know how much he missed his only son. She would need Naljor's comfort now. The light of their lives had moved on.

CHAPTER 2

Beyond The Gate

TENZIN WAS EXPECTED. Just inside the door, a silent, young monk with close-cropped hair bowed stiffly. He wore a simple red robe. His face was an impenetrable mask with blank eyes that focused only within. Nothing in the monk's presence offered the opportunity for connection. Tenzin might as well have been standing in front of a statue. The blood fled from his fingertips; his stomach tightened. "Can this place really be my destiny?" he thought.

The monastery seemed cold and austere. The young monk remained as unyielding as the thick stone walls that encircled the courtyard. "Are they all like this?" Tenzin wondered. He tried to mirror his escort, conveying nothing, hiding his feelings. He bowed stiffly in return. No word passed between them.

The large courtyard was nearly empty. Three monks, dressed in the same red robes as his escort, were busy sweeping the stone floor. Their stiff brooms whooshed back and forth in unison, gathering dirt and debris into tidy rows for later disposal. They focused on their work and did not talk and joke or acknowledge Tenzin and his escort.

With each step across the cold stones, Tenzin shrank deeper into his shadow. Could he survive in such impenetrable, austere silence? Had he made a serious mistake? His body screamed at him to turn and run, to find his father, to leave this nightmare behind, to return to the safety of home. Instead, he followed his escort across the courtyard.

An invisible wind swept down the stone walls of the monastery and ruffled his robe. Though the lack of human warmth disconcerted Tenzin, it allowed his more subtle channels of perception to open amid the deep silence of this place. His breath caught in his throat as he became aware of the unseen reservoir of power that pulsed in the courtyard. Whatever occurred in the silent life of the monastery produced a palpable concentration of energy. It was alive; it was everywhere. Tenzin's body drank it in, just as the leaves of plants drink in the sunlight. His soul had been starving, hiding a secret longing for sustenance, not knowing what that sustenance might be, but knowing that when it arrived he would drink deeply from it.

That time had come.

At first, a pleasant, tingling sensation washed over his extremities. Then the energy spiraled in toward his center, flushing his entire body with heat, filling him with strength, restoring his confidence, and removing his doubt.

The power, however, didn't stop there. With a mind of its own, it reached into places his body didn't know existed. Wave after wave swept through him, each more intense than the last, each drawing closer to his core. Sweat broke from his brow. Rivulets slid down his back. Tenzin thought he might faint, but he remained silent, choosing to conform to the austere code of behavior he had observed. He focused on the discipline of taking deep, slow breaths, and maintained enough control to take one more step, then one more, and not pass out.

At the far wall of the courtyard, they ascended stone stairs to a balcony that ran the length of the wall. Tenzin steadied himself on the sturdy wooden rail polished smooth by an endless stream of hands sliding over the centuries.

His companion, while silent, was not stupid or unfeeling. He had observed Tenzin's labored breathing, the sweat on his forehead, the dampness of his shirt despite the cool day. He saw the slight tremble in Tenzin's hands, but said nothing. Instead, he acted as if he were unaware so that Tenzin might save face.

When they reached the top of the stairs, Tenzin looked back across the courtyard. To normal sight, the drab courtyard was just a stone surface surrounded by stone walls. But Tenzin no longer saw with normal sight. The power flowing through him had burst through the secret seals that limited his perception, and the energy he had sensed in the courtyard was now visible. A shimmering, golden light suffused the entire monastery. Each stone was alive, pulsing with a luminous yet hidden magic.

Tenzin's guide pointed three doors down from where they were standing and motioned that he was to go in. He leaned forward once more in a stiff and formal bow. Tenzin bowed back. The ritual was complete, the first dance between the two young men over. To Tenzin's complete surprise, the young monk smiled and clapped him on the shoulder. Then he turned and walked away, leaving Tenzin to take the next astonished, solitary step in pursuit of his destiny.

The door revealed nothing, suggested nothing, offered no clue as to what waited on the other side. Tenzin stood in front of it for a moment, collecting himself. This was the start of his new life; he wanted to make a good impression. He believed that how we seem in the beginning determines who we are in the end. He knocked. A gentle but commanding voice told him to enter. He opened the door. An older monk, thin, bald and bespectacled sat in a chair behind a wooden desk, engrossed in study.

Tenzin's eyes adjusted to the dimmer light in the monk's chamber. A vast intelligence lay behind the wizened face. The old monk's piercing eye's studied him intensely. They missed nothing, yet they overflowed with an innate kindness.

This man, thought Tenzin, is a cross between a lion and a deer.

Instead of being intimidated by the scrutiny, Tenzin found himself wondering what the old monk saw inside him. Somehow, he sensed that whatever it was pleased the monk.

The storm of energy Tenzin had encountered while crossing the courtyard had passed the moment he crossed the threshold. A warm, comforting energy now seeped into his core, and he realized that it was coming from the old monk. The man seemed strangely familiar, but he was unable to find the reason why he felt that way, as if the answer had been locked away in some secret vault in his soul. But one thing was beyond doubt, Tenzin was aware that he knew this man.

"Please sit down." The old monk pointed to a chair on the other side of the table. "I have followed your life for some time," he said. "Your father is a close friend of mine."

"That is strange, sir. He never mentioned you."

"He was not supposed to. He was my student. Nobody knew about our arrangement. Those were my terms. When he was a young man he wanted to come here and become a monk, but his father insisted he marry your mother and lead a normal life. Naljor loved his father, and out of devotion and respect obeyed. Your father never regretted his choice, but the hunger for consciousness runs deep in him." The monk fixed him with his gaze. "As it does in you, Tenzin."

"Yes, sir," said Tenzin. "That's true."

"It was simply your father's time to have a family. His soul needed that experience. He had spent too many previous lifetimes as a monk. In the growth of the soul, balance is everything."

"I never thought about my father as a monk, sir."

The old man laughed. "That's because he's your father. But through his lifetimes as a monk he had come to believe that he could only find enlightenment if he were celibate. He needed to realize that a wife and family need not keep him from his goal. You can find the Supreme Truth anywhere. He needed to learn that loving his family was not an impediment to enlightenment but a vital part of his journey. However, he wanted to make sure that you could make the choice he never had, to seek enlightenment without being encumbered by external demands and with all of your energy, if that was your wish. You are here, so I assume this is what you want."

"It is, sir."

"I taught your father how to enter the consciousness of the forest and mountains and animals around him in meditation. Your father mastered these techniques easily as he had learned them in other lifetimes."

"That must explain, sir, why animals, even wild ones, always came to him. His fields yielded the best crops. Everything he touched thrived. People in the village would bring their sick animals to him and he would touch them, or hold them if they were small enough. They often improved. The animals loved him."

"Your father has the gift of unconditional love. Animals have an innate sensitivity about who is angry and mean and who is open and loving. They felt your father's compassion for them and knew they had nothing to fear. Your father can enter the mind of an animal and know what it is feeling and thinking. He knows what is bothering it, where it hurts."

"He often spoke to me, sir, about what the animals were feeling. I tried to learn too."

Tenzin studied the floor. "I wasn't very good at it."

"The secret, Tenzin, is to align your soul with what you seek. When you resonate at the same frequency, what you want is yours. All doors that have to open will do so. Your father lives this. Someday you will, too. Be patient. This kind of learning takes time."

"Yes, sir."

"After you were conceived your father visited me. He was certain you were going to be a boy. He hoped you would be the incarnation of a lama. I looked into your nature and instructed your father how to quicken your development. I would not have given him that instruction if I did not feel your destiny was to enter this life."

"Thank you, sir."

"Now you are here and I can see you burn with the desire for the Supreme Truth. Your yearning is so strong that you have no choice."

"It feels that way, sir."

"What did you experience when you walked across the courtyard?"

"I was overwhelmed. At first I felt empowered; then I felt weak, nauseous." Tenzin looked away for a moment, then met the old monk's eyes. "After that I felt afraid. I was afraid I would lose control and the other monks would laugh at me."

The old monk laughed so deeply that his belly shook. "Ah, Tenzin," he said. "Only the special ones feel the power in that way. You are ready for this life. If your energies were dense and less sensitive you would not have noticed anything out of the ordinary. It would not have affected you at all. If someone had told you there was power here and that power could open your third eye, you would have thought they were crazy. Yet that is exactly what happened to you, isn't it? Your third eye opened. I can tell by the light pouring out of your forehead and the brightness of your eyes. What color was the energy field in the courtyard?"

"Gold, sir."

"Bright or pale?"

"Bright, sir."

"What color is my energy field? "

"The same. Around your head there is a great deal of violet."

"Do you ever remember seeing colors around people or places when you were younger?"

"Sometimes, but not often."

"Your third eye opened today because you had developed that faculty in other lifetimes. You needed only a brief encounter with a higher, more powerful energy field than you had previously experienced. Most of the monks here would give all they possess to open that center. The energy in the courtyard cleared the emotional blocks in your body so your spiritual energy could rise and awaken you. That's the heat you felt rising in your spine."

"I wondered what that was."

"Most people are very blocked emotionally. Their unresolved issues prevent their Kundalini from being active. Kundalini is the spiritual energy that resides at the base of your spine. When you activate your Kundalini correctly you evolve rapidly, establish soul contact, and expand your consciousness. However, it is imperative to remove your emotional blocks before you attempt to activate Kundalini. If you activate Kundalini before removing your blocks, it could enter the wrong channel and make you seriously ill for years, even for the rest of your life. In extreme cases it might kill you."

"That's terrifying, sir."

"Life is terrifying, Tenzin. That's why it's important to do things correctly. The right preparation leads to the right result. When Kundalini lies dormant, growth moves at a glacial pace and requires lifetimes to accomplish what someone with a correctly activated Kundalini can achieve in a few years. Before today, the time wasn't right for your Kundalini to be active. You had not released your blocks and there was no one to guide you if you had. The fact that it opened here, on your initial contact with the power in the monastery, is an important sign."

"I'm sure you're right, sir. But it was scary. I didn't know what was happening."

"It always is. You seek enlightenment, you court peace, but you reap the whirlwind." The old man chuckled. "Not what you expected, is it? Kundalini is a fierce fire that threatens your very existence."

"It certainly felt that way, sir."

"Consciousness comes when least expected. Not when you want it, or when it is convenient for you. It comes when it's time to come. It always changes your life. At first, the change may not feel very good. In fact, it may seem to make your life much worse. In the end, it always makes it better," The old man craned his head and looked out through the high window in the far wall at the peaks in the distance. "Remember what I am telling you, Tenzin. It will be important to you later."

"Yes, sir."

"Your father's wish came true, Tenzin. You are, indeed, the incarnation of a lama." He waited while Tenzin digested this information.

"Do you know who I was, sir?" Tenzin said.

"You must discover that for yourself. I will not tell you. When the time is right you will know. That will come later. This time," he said, "I'm the teacher." With that the old monk's belly shook so hard with laughter that Tenzin feared he might fall out of his chair.

"Yes, sir," Tenzin replied. But the import of the Rinpoche's words passed far over his head.

"One more thing, Tenzin. Your first challenge will be to turn your restlessness into a deep peace. Peace is the ground we must cultivate if we wish our soul to grow. Here we work in ways that help us develop our special gifts and talents. That way we move in harmony with our nature and deepen our peace. Peace is the basis of all expansions in consciousness. Few have it, so few advance."

"Yes, sir."

"I'm glad you've come. Go downstairs and enter the big door on your left. You will be shown to your living quarters and given the monastic schedule. Every morning, after breakfast and meditation, you will report here to me. We will study herbs and healing. In the afternoon you will perform your monastic duties. In the evening you will pray and meditate with your fellow monks. We start tomorrow."

"Yes, sir," said Tenzin. He bowed in respect.

Tenzin tried hard to control his emotions. The slight smile at corners of his mouth gave him utterly away. The old monk saw everything, revealed nothing. He, too, was happy. The young man had returned as he promised he would.

Thirty years before, in this same monastery, the monk's older brother, Trungpa, had taken ill one day with a high fever. He lost consciousness and sank into a delirium that no herbs, prayer, or healing could reach. For days he burned with fever, drenched in sweat, lost in some far place from which no one could bring him back. On the seventh day, he sat bolt upright in his bed, suddenly lucid and back from his journey through the gates of hell. He called out at the top of his lungs for his brother. The fever had left him weak and frail. He was a shadow, all bone, with sunken cheeks and too-bright eyes that burned with riveting intensity.

"Little brother," he said, even though Doezen was the taller of the two. "I have been diving in some dark, putrid place reliving old wars, killing and being killed. I thirsted for the blood of my enemies, put prisoners to the sword, tortured those who committed crimes against those I fought for." Trungpa pressed his palms to his eyes. "I loved the killing. I was a mercenary, Doezen. I killed for money. I was filled with bloodlust, swept up in arrogance and madness. I acted without heart or compassion. I loved war. I loved power. In later lives I was the victim. I fell into the hands of my enemies. They tortured me beyond belief. I have been on both sides of hell. This fever is no accident. It is karma, a gift to cleanse and redeem the dark stains in my soul."

"Trungpa, you are weak. You need to save your energy and..."

"Shh!" his brother commanded. "I have seen the future. Listen carefully. Another war is coming, one that will reach this monastery and end our way of life. You will be here when it comes. But I will not survive this sickness."

Doezen remembered that moment as clearly now as then. He could still feel his brother's eyes burning into him as he foretold the future.

"But I will come back and find you, Doezen," Trungpa said. His fingers pressed deeply into the flesh at the back of Doezen's neck; his eyes locked into Doezen's mind. " I will incarnate before this war comes. I promise you, I will come back. You will know me when you see me again. But I don't know if I will recognize you. That was not shown to me."

Trungpa unclasped his mala, the string of prayer beads their mother had given him. He had worn it since he had entered the monastery. He passed the mala to Doezen. "This is yours now. Remember me, brother. Remember what I have told you."

"But Trungpa," Doezen said.

Trungpa did not hear him. He had fallen back on his bed, depleted by his final exertion. Doezen had no way of knowing if his brother's words were the product of the delirium or of truth. There would not be time to find out. His energy spent, Trungpa lapsed into a coma. He died the following day.

Some sixty-five years had flown since Doezen and his brother had come to the monastery. Doezen had been four years old, his brother nine. An avalanche had taken their father while he crossed the mountains. Their mother, shaken, alone, and overwhelmed with grief feared that she wouldn't be able to provide for her two young sons or survive the coming winter. They had little wood, and less food, and the snows would soon come. So she went to the abbot of the nearby monastery and asked him if the monastery would take her boys. The abbot had known her husband since he was a young man and thought well of him. She told the abbot that she could go to live with her sister and her sister's family in a small village several days journey from the lamasery but there was no room there for her boys. The abbot visited with the children, saw merit in them. He understood the terror in their mother's face and agreed to take them in.

From the time they arrived at the monastery, full of fear for their future, and grief from losing both parents, Doezen's older brother had been father and mother to him. At first the two boys had clung to each other, sad, stoic, and in shock. But the abbot and other senior monks had nurtured and loved them, made sure they got lots of attention and time to play. Gradually, they learned to love monastic life because of the monks who loved them. Many years later, Trungpa, the older brother, became a Rinpoche himself, a senior teacher, possessing a deep nature and much wisdom. When the old abbot died, Trungpa accepted more administrative responsibility. Trungpa was charismatic, revered by his peers, a good organizer, and honest beyond reproach. One day he would surely become the abbot. But then the fever struck.

So long ago, thought Doezen. He stood now in the doorway and watched Tenzin descend the stairs until his head was out of sight. Thirty years since Trungpa's passing. Now Doezen was the Rinpoche and head of the monastery.

Time, he reflected, is a circle. It doesn't move forward in a line, event following event, detached and disconnected, so that an event that took place thirty years ago has no connection with an event that happened today. Time curves until the perfect moment arrives for the past to return and complete its purpose. The real business of time is redemption. Trungpa had kept his promise. What was next?

CHAPTER 3

Going Home

TENZIN FOUND THE big door just as the old monk had described it. He put his ear against its old timbers, hoping to learn what to expect on the other side. But the massive door surrendered no secrets of the life it sheltered. Silence seemed to live at the heart of everything in this place. Tenzin breathed deeply, collecting himself yet again, and opened the next door into his future. What he found on the other side hardly surprised him. Nearly three dozen monks worked at various tasks in absolutely silence.

He paused and watched from the shadows of the vestibule; a heavy bell hung on the wall just behind him. Then he heard the first human voices other than the Rinpoche's since entering the monastery. From a chamber somewhere off the far side of the hall came the unmistakable hum of monks chanting. Many voices combined into a constant, low-pitched, repetitive sound. The power of the rhythmic chanting calmed him, and he enjoyed a moment of comfort, for once being neither intensely scrutinized nor deliberately ignored.

The spell provided a brief interval in which he could step back, let down his guard, and assimilate his new surroundings. Like many similar moments, this one arrived unexpectedly and disappeared too soon. No sooner had he begun to feel comfortable than the bell began to ring. Harsh peels reverberated off the walls in the vestibule.

Shock waves crashed through his nervous system. He turned to look behind him. His new Rinpoche stood in the dark shadows of the doorway, ringing the bell with great intensity. The monks stopped their activities and looked toward the alcove. They bowed first to Doezen and then, almost as an afterthought, to Tenzin. They, too, seemed shocked by the disruption to their routine.

"Brothers," announced Doezen. "This is Tenzin, the young man I have told you about. He is here to join us."

Doezen strode past Tenzin into the hall. Tenzin followed with uncertain steps. The monks formed a circle around their teacher and his new student. Doezen introduced each of the monks to Tenzin. There were thirty-five in all. After each introduction, Tenzin bowed to that monk in silence as the monk bowed to acknowledge him. All the new names slipped through Tenzin's mind, like drops of water between his fingers. He stopped trying to take in any more information and, to his great surprise, he began to sense with each bow the essence of each monk.

He read their varying degrees of centeredness, clarity, warmth, and honesty as easily as he could read a book. How unique and different each one was. His heart, which had always been large, seemed to have grown eyes and ears and nostrils. Names ceased to matter. He no longer even heard them as they were spoken. Instead, he listened to what he felt and responded in nuances that were neither verbal nor physical but touched each monk's inner essence.

With each monk, the feeling in Tenzin was similar, yet unique. It was similar because of the love that flowed from him to each of them and unique because each monk's essential qualities drew from him a loving response that was specific to each of them. The result of this simple and austere ceremony was far deeper than he expected. Tenzin bonded with his brother monks in a place that required no words or gestures. He had taken from each of them a packet of energy and made it a part of himself. And he had given each of them a packet of his energy in return. The equal exchange promoted in Tenzin a profound sense of belonging.

After the introductory ritual had been completed, a senior monk named Ishan deftly touched Doezen's arm, waving him aside. They retreated silently to the back of the hall. The rest of the young monks gathered around Tenzin, talking and joking. Soon the hall was filled with the animated voices of young men; their laughter echoed off the stone walls. One might have thought Tenzin had been with these monks for many years judging by the ease they shared in each others company.

"He has come back to us, hasn't he?" said Ishan. "Just as he promised. I remember what your brother said before he died. It seems like yesterday. I always thought he would return, but I must admit . . . as the years passed . . . I almost forgot all about it. Then, when I saw that young man, I knew immediately who he was. Same energy, same eyes, same intensity and depth. You must have known right way."

"Yes."

"It is clear that he has no idea of who he is. This is a test for you too, is it not? You must be patient. You ought not to tell him. It would not be in his best interest."

"I agree. But if it is a test, it is a small one. If I were an impetuous young man, maybe, but I learned long ago to accept what comes and not to fight the current. Everything will unfold in its own time as the Supreme Truth intends, not according to my demands. My preferences are unimportant."

Ishan's eyes were smiling when he spoke. "It appears you have found your center at last."

"So it would seem," Doezen said. A half-smile illuminated his face.

"Better late than never," said Ishan, slipping the needle in deeper.

Doezen didn't bite. "It is a blessing to be free of fear and ambition. It's why we chose this life, is it not? When we were young men we were filled with hope and ambition. Now we enjoy knowledge and experience. The Great Way has become part of us. We are living it. It is no longer a hope or dream, like it is for the young ones. Look at them. So eager, so filled with life, so wanting attainment. Each with his own struggles and tests to endure. If we are lucky to live long enough we will see who succeeds, and who is broken on the rocks of adversity. I pray daily that they all find the strength, will, and love to overcome their tests."

"Do you remember what Trungpa said just before he died?" Doezen asked.

"The prophecy about the war?"

"Yes."

"Let us hope it doesn't happen."

"But if it does, we must follow our soul, no matter the personal cost. Agreed?" The two old monks's eyes locked on each other.

"Agreed," said Ishan.

Gales of laughter interrupted their conversation. The old monks turned to see Tenzin holding court, a young lion of considerable power regaling the monks gathered around him with stories of his family and friends from the childhood he had just left. Tenzin had already won the acceptance of the other monks.

A wide smile lit Ishan's face. "The young lion has returned to his pride," he said. "The others recognize him as one of their own."

"Not only as one of their own, Ishan, but as their leader. See how they love him already. He has done nothing but greet them. Yet look how they admire him."

"It's quite phenomenal, isn't it? If we didn't know the history behind it, we might be even more amazed. But we know the link that ties past to present," said Ishan.

"Truth is stored in the soul, not the mind," said Doezen. "Without the soul, we see only with the mind and can't perceive the connectivity of all things. We see things in isolation rather than as parts of the whole. Separation is an illusion. Physical sight does not translate into wisdom. When we see through the eye of the soul we see the truth. The right thing happens when we let go and no longer need to control the outcome."

"I have always found it puzzling that so few learn how to let go, Doezen. All you need to do is purify the mind of negative emotions."

"The world does not see things as we do, Ishan. Worldly people rush to get ahead of each other. If they are not rushing, they feel insecure. They equate freneticism and stress with success. Acquisition is more important to them than spiritual attainment; they ascertain their self-worth by what they possess and give no thought to their inner life. They think that to have is to be, when the truth is just the reverse. To be is to have."

Ishan chuckled. "You are describing a world that is upside down."

"What do you think? Here we have spent a lifetime letting go. They have spent lifetimes spinning webs of karma they will have to unravel in future lifetimes. Because their values are different and their vision narrower, they waste their opportunities for real growth. When they die, what can they take with them? Not the money. Not the power. What is the point of this life, Ishan, if we leave it empty and incomplete inside? If we do not heal the gaps in our being while we are here, where will we go when we die? No place happy or permanent, that's for certain. Lack of wholeness only guarantees our rebirth. The turning of the great wheel of earthly life will continue. The lessons will have to be repeated. Karma will have to be faced. In my mind the richest man is he who has attained consciousness. That is the only thing that cannot be lost. There are far better worlds waiting for us than this one."

"You make an elegant case, old friend. But we are here in this monastery living a special life. Our traditions, our religion, and our community, all reinforce and support our values. Ours is a unique and special situation. What would life be like for us if we were out in the world, without any of this to guide and support us? Would we be any different?"

"You pose an interesting question, Ishan. One that is not within my experience. I cannot answer it. "

"Nor is our way of life in their experience. How can you have a change of consciousness without the right environment to support and encourage it? If you can't alter someone's experience, how can he learn a different way? Most people don't want our way of life."

"You are right, of course. The future will bring great and unexpected changes to the world. There will be tremendous upheaval. People will be forced to change their ways of life or perish. We can only hope that out of the future suffering a new consciousness will be born in the world. A dark tide will sweep over the entire planet. No place will be left unscathed. Of that I am certain."

"What makes you say that, old friend?"

"For the second time in this century a world war rages. We are safe for now because we are not important to anyone. But there will be more wars. There always are. The ancient texts speak of this time and the times to come. But the most important reason I feel this way is that Trungpa has returned. He has come back to fulfill a purpose about which he knows nothing."

Doezen put his arm on his friend's elbow and led him deeper into the hall, farther away from the crowd of monks around Tenzin. He needn't have taken such precautions. Tenzin and the young monks had forgotten that the two old monks were still there.

"Ishan, what I am about to say must be held in confidence. It must never be spoken of in the monastery and we will never speak about it again. Do you agree?"

"Of course."

"I believe that Trungpa has returned for an important reason. His spirit is very powerful. The world will need him. He hasn't come back just to fulfill his dying promise and see his younger brother again. I don't need his care anymore and he would know that. This place is only where he begins. He has returned to re-established his wisdom and prepare for his future."

"If that is true, he has chosen well. I could not imagine a better teacher for him than you, old friend."

"We shall see. I hope that you are right. But we have been indulging ourselves too long. Look at the young ones carrying on. If we don't bring them back to their work they will soon forget all the discipline that they have learned. The work of years will be wasted. Young Tenzin is a bad influence on them!"

Doezen slammed his walking stick into the ground, but the hidden smile dancing in his eyes suggested something else as he emphasized his point to the assembled monks.

CHAPTER 4

The Power of Doubt

MOST PEOPLE TOUCH joy only once in a great while, if at all. For the next decade Tenzin lived a life of routine joy nearly every day. He was doing what he was meant for, learning to live in harmony with his nature and developing his gifts. Even the part of his life that consisted of routine — work, meditation, chanting — kept bringing new insight and growth into his life. He was never bored. He was far too busy growing.

His environment, while regulated and controlled, was highly stimulating. He didn't have to be there. The question of leaving, in fact, never entered his mind. The monastic life offered him what he had long desired. He felt inspired, touched by a higher power. He loved and respected the elder lamas, particularly Doezen, who had become his teacher and mentor. Indeed, he had come to revere Doezen as deeply as he did his own father.

He never knew Doezen to shirk his responsibility or be less than truthful. He was strong and sharp when necessary, gentle and kind the rest of the time. Nothing escaped him. There were no shortcuts. Everything had to be done the correct way. When Tenzin's youthful impulse to do something quickly, and therefore imperfectly, superseded his developing judgment, Doezen would point his finger in his face, and admonish him in a strong, authoritative voice, "The short way is the right way," he would say, "no matter how long it takes!"

Doezen's deep wisdom was extracted from a lifetime of experience, observation, and study. He doled it out to his young charge a little at a time. He was very careful not to overwhelm his students with what he knew, but to give them just enough to whet their appetites so that they would always want more.

Once, in the early years of their relationship, Doezen took Tenzin with him to a nearby village to visit a woman who had never had her period. She had recently married and was desperate to conceive. The trip to her village required a four hour walk. Doezen was preoccupied and inwardly absorbed. He spoke not one word the entire journey. Tenzin had learned not to interrupt Doezen when he focused his attention inward. Tenzin simply mirrored his teacher's behavior and maintained his silence.

The woman shared a small, two room house with her husband. They visited briefly with the husband, then Doezen entered the bedroom where she was resting. Up to this point, Doezen had only allowed Tenzin to assist him when he treated people with physical complaints, not emotional ones. Under Doezen's training Tenzin had become quite adept at physical diagnosis and treatment with herbs and teas. This time, Doezen brought Tenzin into the bedroom with him.

The woman was bloated and in a great deal of pain. Doezen instructed Tenzin to place his hands on her ankles. He then knelt over her, stroked her head and spoke in a soft, soothing voice. With the young woman more centered, Doezen shifted his focus to her lower abdomen, placing one hand under the base of her spine, and the other hand over her ovaries. A surge of heat flowed out from Tenzin's hands into the woman's legs. The room pulsed with power, and two pillars of red and gold energy rose behind Doezen like ethereal fire. Energy poured down from those pillars through Doezen and into the young woman.

While the energy poured through the woman Doezen instructed her to breathe deeply and make sounds from her throat as if the source of those sounds came from her pelvis and ovaries. She choked and coughed out short, little moans with great difficulty. Her difficulties did not discourage Doezen. The power continued to pour into her, melting the blocked emotions trapped in her ovaries. Her legs trembled. Soon she began to scream and kick uncontrollably. Doezen pushed her on when she showed signs of weakening.

After some time, the screams stopped and her body quieted. The pillars of energy behind Doezen now became gold and white. Doezen gently placed one hand over the woman's lower abdomen and the other over her heart. She seemed transfixed; her face glowed. Tenzin watched in awe as her soul, immersed in gold light, rose out of her body.

A few minutes later, Doezen withdrew his hands from the young woman's body, ending the flow of energy and concluding the treatment. With no more energy to sustain her out of the body experience, the woman's soul settled back into her body. The negative emotions that had clogged her reproductive system had been released. She was now in balance; freed from the trauma that had troubled her.

Tenzin realized that the woman's trauma had separated her from her soul. That separation had contributed to her suffering. Somehow Doezen had opened her, removed the obstruction and reconnected her to her soul. He had achieved all this without surgery, loss of blood, or drugs. Just a simple laying on of hands. Yet both the process and the outcome had been profound.

Doezen waited a few moments for the young woman to reorient herself. "Yeshi," he asked gently, "what happened when you were a young girl?"

"I was eight," she said. Her eyes looked into the distant, painful past. "A friend of my older brother took me into the woods to pick flowers for my mother. She loved fresh flowers. After we had entered the forest his face changed. He became a monster. He threw me down and raped me. He said if I ever told anyone about it he would kill my mother. I never told anyone." Her eyes returned to the present. She looked at Doezen. "Until now."

"The trauma is over. There will be balance in your life from now on," said Doezen. "You will have three healthy children. Two sons and a daughter." Then Doezen did something Tenzin had never seem him do before. He bent down, cradled the woman's head in his arms and kissed her gently on the forehead.

"Rest now. A new life is coming."

On the long walk back to the monastery, Doezen described the preparations he had taken to heal the young woman. "Thank you for respecting my silence, Tenzin, and for not interfering with it during our walk to the village. I was working with her inner self to bring her buried memories to the surface. That is why it proceeded quickly once we got there. She had been prepared inwardly, although she had no knowledge of it."

"Rinpoche, how can that be?"

"The soul, Tenzin, functions in ways that are hidden from the mind. For the mind to glimpse the soul it must be quiet and at peace. Only then can the soul enter. That, of course, is the purpose of chanting and meditation. The Buddha said that the thoughts of the mind are like pearls strung on a necklace. They shine and capture our attention. When we let go of our thoughts and turn our attention to the space between them we glimpse the truth. The truth exists outside the thought process.

"The soul exists outside the conscious mind. Who you are is not found in your conscious mind but in your soul, for that is where your truth lives. To live your truth the mind must serve the soul. Most people's lives run counter to their truth. Their mind leads and they never see who they really are. They never find their soul. That young woman's mind was absorbed in her suffering. Suffering keeps the mind stuck in patterns that exclude the soul."

"Rinpoche," said Tenzin. "Did Yeshi see her true self when you healed her?"

"She had a taste of who she really is. Sometimes the Supreme Truth gives us terrible experiences so we can realize better things later on. Don't ever forget that, Tenzin. In Yeshi's case she had been raped in her last life as well. The unresolved emotion from that trauma, lying dormant in her body, attracted another traumatic rape experience in this life. She is now free of both traumas. She is whole again. Sometimes it takes a negative to clear a negative."

"But, Rinpoche, couldn't the healing of the past rape been accomplished in a gentler way, so she wouldn't have had to be raped again?"

"You have to be aware of what hides inside you if you are to heal it. Few people are conscious of their past life issues, although everyone has them. It takes a bright light to reveal an obscure trauma. The Soul sees things from a much wider perspective than does the conscious mind. When the kind of trauma that young woman had to face is transformed, one experiences a great leap in wisdom. What once divided us now integrates us. When we heal our pain we move higher in the light. Our highs get higher. Our lows also get higher. That's the evolutionary journey. The farther we go on our path, the more joy we will eventually experience. The key to the ascent is to remove unresolved and unproductive emotions. Wholeness and integration come before enlightenment. There is no other way."

"Yes, Rinpoche."

"I've always thought that whatever happens is best, Tenzin. But it's up to us to make the best of our circumstances, to learn from what has happened and go on, no matter how cruel things may seem at the time. Look at the beauty that has come out of this young woman's experience. She is free and will now have children. We were the instruments of her healing. Our reward for helping her is that we feel light and happy. We allowed ourselves to be used for a higher purpose and it lifted us up. When we are truly open to the Light, everyone benefits. If the world sought love as much as it sought power, few of the problems that plague humanity would exist."

"Yes, Rinpoche."

"This kind of work brings great joy, Tenzin. The world is selfish. It functions on the belief that we are all separate and disconnected from each other. Most people pursue money, power, and fame thinking it will make them unique and happy. However, that behavior is the real sacrifice because we lose contact with our real self when we live like that. Greed is a curse. To serve others is actually a very selfish thing as it serves the real Self in all of us. Think about it. What we did nourished the truth in you, me, and that young woman. We served the Supreme Being and we were given exactly what we needed for doing it."

"It is true, Rinpoche. I feel wonderful."

"Remember what I am about to tell you. Regardless of what happens to us, we agreed on the soul level to let it occur. On the soul level we make our choices based on their potential to aid our growth. That is the only consideration, not how it will affect us emotionally or physically. Whether or not we know it, the soul controls a great deal of what we experience. Since the bridge between the soul and mind doesn't exist in most people yet, they are unaware of what they have chosen to experience in their lives."

"That is a difficult idea, Rinpoche."

"Tenzin," laughed the Rinpoche, tapping Tenzin on the shoulder. "I am old. I know what happens when things get difficult. It's one thing to listen to and digest the truth when things are calm and life is normal. It's another to remember it when things fall apart and fear arises. When that happens you will forget what I have said. But you must remember to remember it! One day your ability to remember this truth may be the difference between life and death."

"You are scaring me, Rinpoche. What do you mean?"

"We do not find the true meaning in things until we understand emotionally what has been said intellectually. Concepts and principles must be lived and digested before they become wisdom. The truth ripens in its own season. Since you don't yet have the emotional understanding, your job is to remember these ideas. They are seeds. Plant them deeply inside you. They will blossom as you grow. That is all."

The Rinpoche quickened his gait, signaling an end to the conversation.

Did I tell him too much? Doezen thought. Can Tenzin handle this difficult wisdom? Will he be able cradle it inside him until the time comes to use it?

He had dark forebodings about the future and strange, inarticulate fears for Tenzin. He couldn't give these feelings shape or define them, but he was wise enough not to dismiss them. In the only way he knew, he was preparing Tenzin for the trials ahead.

Their conversation had slowed their walking so that they reached the heart of the desolate plain that lay between them and the monastery at dusk. The most dangerous part of their journey was still in front of them. Jagged rocks, haphazard outcroppings, and deep, ice-lined crevasses threatened their safe return to the monastery. And now a moonless sky was rapidly turning black. In trying to prepare Tenzin for the future, Doezen had left them both unprepared for the present. The irony of the situation was not lost on him.

The rocks were piled everywhere, with no rhyme or reason. Deep chasms lay where least expected, making it extremely difficult to navigate in the dark.

They already had been walking among the rocks for the last half hour. Should they turn back or go on? Only a few minutes of dim light remained. Should they retrace their steps and wait until morning before resuming their journey, or walk across the plain in total darkness?

There was a bit of the gambler in Doezen and he hated the idea of turning back. He wanted to press on. He called to Tenzin, who was walking a bit behind him to catch up.

"Tenzin, we have to make a decision. We can turn back now and cross the plain tomorrow morning or we can continue on and cross it in darkness tonight. It could be risky to continue on in the dark. Would you like to go on or turn back?"

To the young caution is boring, adventure appealing.

"Let's go on, Rinpoche." The sparkle in his eye was unmistakable, even in the dying light. The Rinpoche permitted himself a brief, unguarded smile.

"Very well. We shall press onward. Stay close to me, Tenzin. Follow me step for step. Walk exactly where I walk. One misstep could mean death. You must stay alert and focused. Send your energy ahead and feel where the danger lies. Pay attention to what your intuition tells you and to what you feel. If you stay centered and unafraid you will feel where the crevasses are. Stay centered and it will be easy. If fear overtakes you all could be lost."

Tenzin followed the Rinpoche step for step, as he had been told. While they still had the light he could see where to place his feet. The routine was simple. But when the sun left the sky and the darkness enveloped them, the matter became entirely different. Tenzin now had to sense his way. He stepped in the wrong places; he twisted his feet on rocks he didn't think were there; he even fell a few times. Tenzin began to think that this wasn't such a great idea, after all. He could be seriously hurt. Before he knew it, he had fallen into a quagmire of fear. Doezen slowed his pace and spoke gently to Tenzin. He talked about the monastery and his friend Ishan. This settled Tenzin somewhat but he was still agitated and out of balance.

"Tenzin," Doezen asked. "What do you see up ahead?"

Tenzin's eyes were focused on the ground ahead of him. He was trying desperately to place his feet exactly where Doezen had placed his. He didn't bother to look up. "I can't see, Rinpoche. It's too dark."

Doezen's voice became firmer. "Look again, Tenzin. What do you see?"

Tenzin looked up. What he saw made him gasp. "Rinpoche, there is a light coming out of you! It's lighting up the ground in front of your feet!"

"That's right. Now stop worrying. You're like an old woman afraid of mice. You've lost your center. Fear has overcome you. What have you learned from this?"

Tenzin continued to stare at the light. "Fear is my enemy," he said.

"And where does fear come from?"

"From within."

"Next time when you face a situation that kindles your fear, you must make a conscious choice. If you decide that fear can't control you, it won't. But if you let it take you over, you will lose your center as surely as you have tonight.

People who give into fear always stumble and fall. How can it not be so? What is out of balance breaks down. Therefore, face your fear and retain your balance. Acknowledge it and say to yourself, what of it? It won't stop me. It will only keep me alert and vigilant. Then your fear will pass and your center will prevail."

"Yes, Rinpoche," said Tenzin. He looked at the dark ground for a moment, then raised his eyes to watch his teacher's light.

"Remember, fear is not a tree, a leaf, or a boulder, Tenzin. It is a feeling. Feelings are fluid. We control them in the same way we pour water into different containers. Water always conforms to the shape of its container. If we forget to be vigilant and conscious, fear will soon ignite our emotional body and take control of us. Our emotional energy will conform to the shape of our fear. But if we are vigilant and dismiss our fear, it will settle down and remain a minor wave of no consequence. This exercise keeps us centered. Whether our fear turns into a wave of no consequence or a tidal wave of tragic proportions is up to us. We are responsible for what we feel. Never lose your head and get swept away by fear."

"Yes, Rinpoche." Tenzin was feeling somewhat better, though still embarrassed by his failure. He looked up again. The lights of the monastery lit the top of the hill in the distance. He would not soon forget this place. He had not known such fear since he had crossed the courtyard when he first came to the monastery. Even then he had retained more control than he had mustered this night. He wondered how he would be able to face Doezen tomorrow after failing so abysmally tonight. Had he lost the respect of his beloved Rinpoche? He couldn't abide the thought.

Doezen interrupted his internal dialogue, "Stop it, Tenzin! Practice self-control!"

The words pierced Tenzin like bullets. He was repeating his mistake, just after he had resolved to never do it again. How subtle the mind was and so difficult to defeat.

"Relax, Tenzin. You are young and want immediate perfection. It takes time. A great deal of time. Mistakes are opportunities to take corrective actions. By learning from your mistakes, you will become more conscious. We can't grow without failure. All attempts at mastery fail in the beginning. When a baby learns to walk, does he walk perfectly right away and never fall? No, he falls many times before he masters walking. You will fail many times before you master yourself. It is expected. So what."

"Yes, Rinpoche."

"Learn to relax your attitude toward yourself. The Supreme Truth doesn't expect you to be perfect. Why should you? The Supreme Truth loves you in spite of your faults. Remember to accept yourself, whether or not you are perfect. Love is unconditional. Do not put the condition of perfection on it. If you do so, you will always be tormented and never find what you seek. Learning will come easier if you don't pressure yourself to be perfect from the beginning."

They had reached the monastery gate. Food, rest and safety awaited. Tenzin couldn't wait to fall into his bed, close his eyes, and bring a close to this night of lessons.

CHAPTER 5

The Dark Sky

IN 1950, THE threat of war hung over Tibet like a heavy shroud. After a period of diplomatic intimidation, the Chinese invaded in October to "free the Tibetans from the burden of an enslaving feudal system." The Chinese destroyed six thousand monasteries and killed hundreds of thousands of people, if not more. As the invasion progressed, reports of terrible pillaging at other monasteries arrived. Chinese soldiers burned holy books, plundered religious treasures, forced monks to fornicate with nuns, and then executed them. Entire monasteries were put to the torch. The news from the outlying villages was no different with many reports of burning, killing, and raping. With every day the threat to the monastery increased. The monks knew the Chinese were coming. They knew they would not be spared. The senior monks prepared as well as they could for the destruction that would soon be visited upon them. Holy books, religious treasures, and relics were secreted out of the monastery and hidden in safe places.

Tenzin's worries extended beyond the walls of the monastery. His village and family were near Chamdo in the east, closer to the Chinese invasion force than he was. He had received no communication from them in weeks. He didn't know if they had escaped, been killed, or were under Chinese martial law. The fates of his family, his country, and his monastery were in the hands of forces beyond his control. He could do nothing but wait and worry.

One evening, when it appeared that the Chinese would be at the gates of the monastery within a few days, Tenzin was summoned to Doezen's room. He walked along the high balcony overlooking the courtyard. The great Himalayan peaks loomed in the distance. For several days he had had no contact with Doezen. Doezen had rarely left his chamber. The senior monks had all joined him there, planning for the preservation of the monastery's treasures. Whether they lived or died was now in the hands of the Supreme Truth. They could prepare for the inevitable and accept their fates, nothing more.

By the time Tenzin arrived, the other monks had left. Doezen waited at his desk in the same place and in the same chair as he had during their first meeting. The light was dim, but that did not prevent Tenzin from seeing the deep lines of exhaustion etched upon his face.

"I have missed seeing you these past several days," Doezen said. "But we are at war now. Everything has changed. You heard what happened at other monasteries?"

"Yes, Rinpoche," he said, his jaw throbbing. Defiance served now as his only bulwark against overwhelming sadness.

"Tenzin," Doezen continued, "You are not a warrior. Not in this lifetime assuredly. I know the spark burns in you, but you are more valuable to Tibet alive than fighting to your death." Doezen's eyes looked upon the person he loved most upon this earth. "You, and others like you, are the future of Tibet. You are young and full of promise. Our national treasure is not our books and our religious art. It is in young monks like you and the light you embody. One day that light will be very important to the world."

"But, Rinpoche..."

Doezen raised his palm. "I have loved you Tenzin, as if you were my son. If I am guilty of anything it is of being partial to you. One day you will be a source of wisdom and strength to a great many people. If you remain here, all of that will be lost. The Chinese would never let you live. Therefore, I have prepared for your escape."

"But Rinpoche, I cannot leave. There is my family from whom I have not heard in weeks. There is the monastery and there is you. This is my life. I cannot go, Rinpoche. I cannot. Too much depends on me."

"Too much depends on your going, Tenzin. Use your head. This is no time to be driven by emotion. Would you throw away what you have learned and destroy all that you have become and have yet to become? That would be so much waste. If you stay and perish, all the knowledge and training that has been given to you will be lost. You cannot protect anyone. You cannot save anyone. You are powerless. You will die. Your death would only serve the Chinese because it would help them bury our future. It is not your time to die, Tenzin. You must go. This is not an act of cowardice I'm sending you on, but a mission that will require great courage on your part. For a time, you will find living far more difficult than dying."

"But Rinpoche, what of you? What will happen to you? Come with me."

Doezen shook his head. "I am an old man, Tenzin. I have had my life. What happens to me does not matter. I am not afraid to die. Life and death are of the same cloth of creation. Each inevitably turns into the other. I am much closer to my death than you are to yours."

"But how will I ever know what happened here and what became of my family? I cannot leave without seeing them, Rinpoche."

"To attempt to see them would mean certain death. The Chinese are in their village. Other units now march in our direction. Reports indicate they will arrive tomorrow. I have held you back as long as I could. You must leave tonight. I am sending Nawang with you. The two of you are to go to India. I have written to my friend Emily Chase, who lives in Los Angeles, for assistance. Several years ago she came here to study. I was her mentor. We developed a close friendship. She will help however she can. You are to make your way through the Himalayas to Delhi. Contact a Mr. Sean Wilson at the American embassy there. He has a ticket and visa for you. You will go to America. Someone will write to you about what happens here. You must go now. We have packed food and clothes for you."

Doezen used his arms to help himself stand. This was the most difficult moment of his life. Death would soon sweep across the field of stones. His older brother, reincarnated as his student, would leave him once more. They would never meet again. Doezen was a realist. He knew the end was near. Only one choice remained, one true way to go. His heart knew that he had chosen rightly for Tenzin and for himself. Each of them must now embrace this time of final parting. Tenzin must move to a different life; Doezen must move beyond life. His place was here. He had no regrets. He was not afraid of dying or in the manner of his death. Whatever was, was best. He had lived by this truth. He would die by it. He had no anxiety or fear for himself, but he did feel a sense of apprehension for Tenzin's future.

I have not been pure enough with him, thought Doezen. I have allowed myself to become attached, and so I worry for him. I can't help him if I am worrying constantly about him. Still, Doezen admitted to himself, if I had to reprise the past, I would love him in the same way.

He prayed that Tenzin would find his destiny in America. Their relationship had finally come full circle. The student must now strike out on his own. Doezen opened his arms wide. Tenzin moved into his mentor's embrace and felt the last strength in the frail old arms as they held him.

"Remember Tenzin, no matter what happens in your life, it is an opportunity for growth. As long as you are centered, the Supreme Truth will be with you. When negative emotions surface, clear them from your system and regain your center as quickly as possible. The road ahead will be difficult, but it is your road.

You have the strength to overcome every obstacles that you will meet. Use whatever comes your way to quicken your evolution. Everything that happens in life is fuel for growth. Do not forget!"

"Doezen Rinpoche, I will never forget you. I will never forget this place or my family or Tibet. I will never forget. I Will NEVER FORGET! Not now. Not Ever."

Tears moistened Tenzin's cheeks. The two men clung to one another for a silent moment while the sun set in the window behind them. A loud knock shattered their last moment together. Nawang burst into the room, breathless. "Rinpoche, I am sorry to intrude. But Ishan ordered me to come for Tenzin. The Chinese have been sighted nearby. We must leave immediately."

"Ishan is correct, Nawang," answered Doezen. He released Tenzin from his embrace. "It is time. You must both go now. Take care of each other. Remember that wherever you go in the world, you are ambassadors of Tibet. The Light must not disappear from this world. Remember who you are. Keep your head high and your center intact. You are the future."

"Yes, Rinpoche," both young men said. They were subdued and scared, facing into the harsh wind of a bleak future.

Doezen reached behind his neck and unclasped the strand of prayer beads, the mala, which he had worn since he was a young boy in the monastery. "Tenzin, I have little to give you to help you on your journey. Take this mala. It will not shield you from the wind and cold in the mountains, but it may remind you of your core identity when you most need to remember where you came from and what you represent."

"Rinpoche, please, I cannot take it. That mala is a part of you. It carries your energy."

"That is why I want you to have it."

Doezen kissed the mala and solemnly placed the beads around Tenzin's neck. Summoning his remaining strength, he ordered them to go. The young men walked out of Doezen Rinpoche's room for the last time and closed the door behind them. Their hearts were breaking but they appeared cool and detached as they walked along the balcony and down the ancient stairs for the last time.

When they reached the courtyard, Ishan gave them their packs and travel instructions. They were to cross Monla Kachung into Bhutan and from there proceed to India. The journey would be difficult and dangerous but it was the only way to avoid the Chinese. Ishan embraced them and bid them make haste. The hour was late, the moment full of peril. Chinese patrols had just been sighted on the field of stones beyond the monastery. Every moment counted.

The other young monks accompanied them across the courtyard. At the gates they all bowed to each other. Only Tenzin spoke.

"We will never forget you." His voice was low, near breaking. Summoning the last vestiges of his willpower, he ripped himself away from the life he loved and hurried into the enveloping darkness. Walking quickly so Nawang could not see him, he broke into tears, feeling smaller and more scared than he had since arriving at the monastery gates with his father more than ten years earlier. At that time he had had a home and a family nearby who loved him. Now he had no sense of what he was losing or where he was going. In a moment, his life had gone from predictable to unknowable; he was setting out on a journey with no timetable and only a vague destination. Neither success nor failure were certain. He held his life in his own hands now. No one else could help him. He and Nawang walked alone in the darkness. A biting wind seared their cheeks.

Three months later, Tenzin and Nawang stumbled into Delhi. They had worn through their shoes, exhausted their food stores, and nearly frozen to death. Nawang's feet were nearly black with frostbite, his back ached, and he could hardly breath because of his racking cough. The only good thing in their adventure was that they had no time to worry about what was occurring at the monastery. They had been too busy surviving.

One night, while walking in the moonlight, Nawang had slipped and nearly fallen into a deep crevasse. Fortunately, Tenzin had been practicing his Rinpoche's teachings about staying centered. He felt Nawang starting to fall a few seconds before he slipped. He reacted immediately, reaching out for Nawang so that when his legs buckled, Tenzin already had his arms around Nawang's chest. Panting, Tenzin dragged him the few feet between death and safety.

"Tenzin, how did you know?" Nawang asked, when the shock left him and he could breathe normally again.

"I almost fell once," he said. "Just like you did now. Rinpoche taught me to stay centered when crossing the field of stones one night when there was no light. I learned a painful lesson that night. This time I was prepared."

"You saved my life. Maybe someday I will save yours."

Tenzin only nodded. "We had better keep going."

They continued down the mountain along the edge of the crevasse under a dark sky laden with stars and the thin sliver of a silver moon. At the edge of their hearing, the wind whistled as it wound through the rocks. The only steady sound was the muffled whisper of their feet plodding slowly through the snow.

When the moon's light grew faint, they pitched the tent Ishan had packed for them and crawled inside for a few hours of desperately needed sleep. Sometime later, as the moon slunk beneath the peaks of the Himalayas, Tenzin drifted out of a restful sleep and into a disturbing dream.

He was in a small cave, deep inside the inner earth. How he got there was a mystery to him; there seemed to be no way in or out. Then a hidden door opened in the wall to his left and a terrifying figure stepped through it. Panic swept through Tenzin, leaving him nauseous and dizzy. The creature was taller than any human he had ever seen, a large, white lizard with wings, a tail, and two hands, each with three elongated fingers. Its eyes were snake yellow; its mouth cruel and ferocious. It reeked of decaying flesh. Slimy spittle dripped from its tongue. The creature stared long and hard at Tenzin. When it finally spoke, its words poured out in a harsh, guttural voice.

"My work in Tibet is child's play compared to the misery I will visit on the rest of your world. I bring destruction and the end of freedom. I bring war - endless war, and the complete enslavement of the human race." The creature paused, and then hissed contemptuously. "The most spiritually evolved country in the world was no match for me. My forces overran it like it was an ant colony. Your 'light' has no power. It is nothing more than a dream of goodness and love that doesn't exist and never did. I am everywhere. I control the world. I control its governments. Its wealth. Its military. Its media. Its religions. I control communist countries and democratic ones. I control tyrants, oligarchs, dictators, kings and queens, presidents, prime ministers, and Popes. They are all MY vassals. Humanity has been entranced, its mind controlled, its spirituality desecrated, its health compromised, its wealth stolen. YOU HAVE NO HOPE! There is no way out of the darkness that permeates your world. The only path to survival is complete submission to me. Now kneel and kiss my hand, fool. I am your only hope!"

Tenzin shuddered. "Who are you?" he somehow managed to ask. His knees shook and his body trembled. He dreaded the answer.

"Who am I?" hissed the creature. "You don't know? You are more the fool than I thought." The creature gathered itself, straightened its back and stood at its full height. A terrible darkness loomed behind its malevolent yellow eyes.

Tenzin stepped back, his eyes bulging.

"I am the Lord of Darkness," roared the creature. "And this is MY world. Renounce the Light or die. I am everywhere. I will appear in the eyes of people you love. I will turn them against you and laugh as they betray you. There is no escape. Kneel or die. This is your only chance."

With his heart pounding, Tenzin sat up and and shook his head. His temples throbbed with shooting pain. Waves of adrenaline surged through him. Cold sweat trickled down his spine. Was his dream real or was his subconscious symbolically releasing what he'd endured since the Chinese had overrun Tibet?

The question never really left him, not that day or in the days and years to come. It lingered in the back of his mind until, many years later, a young man he had never met arrived with the answer. For now, he could only try to fall back asleep and hope that the creature would not return to haunt him in his dreams.

The two young monks arrived at the American Embassy in Delhi on a Tuesday morning. Tenzin asked the guard at the gate for a Mr. Sean Wilson as his rinpoche had instructed him. Of course, he asked in Tibetan, and the officer had no idea what he said. Tenzin made several further attempts with the same results. Finally the soldier gave up and just said "No comprendo, Joe." He called in the embassy interpreter. The interpreter knew some Tibetan and Tenzin was able to tell him what he wanted. The interpreter took them to a waiting room and told them that Mr. Wilson would be along shortly. The room was warm and comfortable and furnished with two sofas and several chairs. Tenzin and Nawang collapsed on the sofas and fell immediately into a deep sleep, the first real rest they had had in weeks.

Finally, at 2:15 in the afternoon Sean Wilson appeared, rumpled and distracted. An unexpected emergency had kept him on the phone to Washington all day.

He wondered, what have we got here? More trouble? Tibetan monks. Not good. Not my day, that's for damn sure.

He cleared his throat loudly. That did no good. The young monks were too deeply asleep to notice. So much for being nice. He shook them until they opened their bleary eyes.

Tenzin and Nawang awoke to an impatient, angry stranger standing over them. They sat up quickly, eyes wide.

"Waiting long, gentlemen?" the stranger asked. He didn't wait for an answer. "It's been a long goddam day. And you two aren't going to make it any easier, are you? Well, follow me and we'll see what's to be done for you. I can't imagine it will be very much."

Tenzin and Nawang didn't move, but just continued to stare at the hostile man. Sean Wilson released a sigh of exasperation, pointed at them, and motioned for them to follow him.

Wilson ushered them into a cramped office. Folders, books, and dispatches cluttered every horizontal surface. Tenzin and Nawang were at a decided disadvantage except for the letter Tenzin had with him. Fortunately, the letter was in English. Tenzin pulled it out of his traveling bag and handed it to Wilson. As he read, his hostility disappeared.

"Damn. Emily Chase, well what do you know? It's your lucky day, fellas. She's very connected. Her husband was the ambassador here for many years. This letter says there's a ticket for L.A. waiting here for whichever one of you is

Tenzin. Says here that she's taking you in. Pretty amazing. Pretty damn amazing. Guess we'd better find out more. Just a moment."

Wilson flicked the switch on the office intercom. "Joan," he said "See if there is anything in our files from Emily Chase, would you."

A few minutes later, a slim, attractive woman wearing a blue suit and a big smile handed Wilson a crisp manila folder. The file contained a letter for Nawang, another for Wilson from Emily Chase, a visa for Tenzin, and an open plane ticket from Delhi to Los Angeles. Wilson read the instructions carefully. Tenzin was being granted special status from State as a representative of the Tibetan government. Wilson was no longer distracted.

"Which one of you is Tenzin?"

Tenzin nodded uncertainly.

"Well, fella," said a smiling Wilson."You've got some damn good karma. You're going to the States. Wish I were going with you."

Tenzin smiled back and nodded. He had no idea what Wilson had said. He only knew that the man wasn't being mean anymore.

Wilson shuffled through the remaining contents of the file and handed the other letter to Nawang. It had been written by one of the senior monks shortly after their departure. Nawang read it slowly, blinked, and then read it again. His mouth fell open. He could hardly comprehend his good luck and his sorrow.

> *Dear Nawang,*
>
> *Doezen Rinpoche believes that Tenzin's destiny is in America. His path calls him there. It is not so for you. You are to go to Darmasala where all the young monks from the monastery have been sent. See Tenzin off, then go there as quickly as you can. We have received word that your family escaped and is also at Darmasala. Unfortunately, we have had no word about the people in Tenzin's village or his family. No one can get through. The area is crawling with Chinese. Tell Tenzin that when all that remains is his connection to Supreme Truth to focus on that. It will see him through. Now is the time for courage. Stay centered, both of you, and all will be well.*

Nawang handed the letter to his friend. Tenzin felt a sense of dread as he took it.

He didn't want to read it but knew that he must. As he read the letter the color left his cheeks. He tried to stiffen up and hide his hopelessness. The trek through the Himalayas and across India had taken everything he and Nawang had, brought them beyond the endurable, and in the process bound them tighter than brothers. They had faced death, fear, hunger, bitter cold, and injury. They only had each other. Now that they had reached safety they were to be separated, wrenched apart by a relentless grace that had taken over their lives. At that moment Tenzin doubted that there was a Supreme Truth. Everything and everyone he loved had been ripped from his life. He wondered if any of them were still alive. My parents, my sisters, nephews and nieces, Doezen, Ishan, the others? Why must I leave here without knowing their fate and go half way around the world to a place I don't know? Life was evil and cruel. He was slipping down a dark well. It was as if someone had decided to manipulate the controls inside his body, diminish his power, and extinguish his light. He was powerless to stop it. He could do nothing but stiffen his back and stare at the wall.

Sean Wilson picked up the phone.

"Joan, call the airlines will you and find out when the next scheduled departures are for Los Angeles. We've got a young man here with powerful connections at State for whom we need to make a reservation. He doesn't speak English. He seems to be in a lot of shock. Then call Doc Otis and tell him I'm bringing him a customer. I want him to take a look at the other fellow's foot right away."

"Yes, sir. I'll get right on it."

Wilson hung up the phone and motioned for the monks to follow him. He lead them to the infirmary. Dr. Otis examined Nawang and gave him two packets of antibiotics, one for his feet, the other for his cough. "He doesn't have frostbite, Sean. He's got an infection under his nails that caused his toes to swell. The antibiotics should heal that as well as his walking pneumonia. How he ever made it over the Himalayas with all that beats me. He'll be all right soon enough."

"Thanks, Doc. I'll get Willie to translate."

When they returned to Wilson's office a list of flights to Los Angeles was on his desk. "Well, let's see. The first one's out tomorrow at 9 am. Think that one is going to be a little sudden for you. Looks like you two need a few days of rest and food. There's one leaving on Saturday at 8 a.m. You'll have one connection in Hong Kong, another in Honolulu. That gives you some time to rest. We'll put you on that one."

Wilson flicked on the intercom. "Great job, Joan. Get this fellow a seat on the 8 a.m. flight on Saturday morning."

Four days later Tenzin boarded the plane for Los Angeles. He had no way of knowing that he would never return to Tibet. While Tenzin was being driven to the airport by Sean Wilson, Nawang was on his way to Darmasala, accompanied by a reporter from the Times of London, there to do a story on the Tibetan holocaust. Wilson knew the journalist and had arranged for Nawang to travel with him.

Sean Wilson was not an unfeeling man, despite his initial negative reaction to the two young monks. After he calmed down and let go of his troubles he could see their pain and shock. He also saw Tenzin's decency and goodness. Within the context of his cool professional demeanor, he did what he could to help them. He was astute enough to recognize something special in Tenzin.

This one, he thought, has something pretty rare. I feel better just being around him. That's a magic not many people have.

When he left Tenzin at the boarding gate at the Delhi airport he did something uncharacteristic. He gave Tenzin a hug and wished him luck in America.

CHAPTER 6

The New World

LOS ANGELES 1951

NOTHING TENZIN HAD ever experienced could have prepared him for Los Angeles. He had grown up in a remote, technologically backward mountain village. He had lived in an isolated monastery for over a decade. Los Angeles was complete bewilderment. A huge, seemingly endless sprawl of people, buildings, roads, and automobiles. It was hot, noisy, crowded, and chaotic. Delhi was like that, too. But at least India and Tibet shared a border and a similar spiritual heritage. Here, people looked at him strangely. Wearing the red robe of a Tibetan monk guaranteed that he would stand apart and attract strange looks from the locals.

Emily Chase met him at the airport. She was in her early seventies, with snow white hair, well-coifed and carefully styled with a slight wave, her one remaining concession to vanity. Her clear blue eyes still sparkled. She wore little makeup, except for a touch of lipstick, and a dark blue dress with a single strand of pearls around her neck. She stood as near to the door to the tarmac as she could, but many other people had arrived ahead of her.

The passengers poured off the plane, eager to reach their destinations. Tenzin found himself caught in the middle of a throng, pushed and buffeted about like a leaf on a swollen river. Gradually, the crowd thinned, people drifting here and there to meet family and friends, leaving him to move forward at his own pace. He stopped for a moment and scanned the crowd wondering if his contact was among them. How would he recognize her? An older woman's face stood out from all the others. She watched him intently. Was this Emily? He didn't have long to wait. She waved her arm in greeting. Her warm, smile lifted his spirits immediately.

Emily Chase was a person of means, high intelligence, and integrity. Her bearing commanded respect wherever she went. She was a woman who told the truth, believed in the innate goodness of people, and treated everyone she met with equanimity and kindness, from household help to Presidents and Prime Ministers. Nothing about her presence suggested anything shallow or remotely superficial. If what she had to say made people uncomfortable, upset or angry, so be it. The truth was important and she would never compromise herself by speaking dishonestly. She was forthright and direct in her delivery. Her character simply left no room for pretension, duplicity, or condescension. Whatever course of action she decided upon was well-considered, not in terms of how people would react or what would secure her personal interest, but in the truth of the situation, and how it could best be stated. In this respect she thought like a monk.

On the surface, the elderly patrician woman and the young Tibetan monk were an unlikely pair. Despite overwhelming differences in age, ethnicity, culture, and social standing, they took to each other immediately. A strong and lasting connection resonated between them deep below the surface, as if two mutual powers had finally met. Each was aware and respectful of the other's sovereignty; each knew instinctively that they complemented rather than conflicted with each other.

Tenzin reminded her of Doezen whom she had met some forty years earlier when her husband had been posted to India. He felt the same to her, as if he were shaped by the same mold of compassion, vision, and power, only younger and less developed. From the moment she saw him at the airport, looking tired, lonely, and forlorn, Emily could feel the ancient wisdom of his land rooted deeply in him. He exuded a combination of majesty and purity that was rare in this world. An indefinable strength lived deep within him.

The spiritual power emanating from him reminded her of the hunger she had felt when she had gone to Tibet that first time. She had been spiritually starved then, and in need of deep emotional healing. While her pain had been addressed and healed long ago, the hunger in her soul existed even now. On her return to America years ago, she had deliberately set it aside to live a normal life. That hunger now walked up to her and looked her in the eye. The re-awakening of her spirituality jarred and surprised her. She hadn't expected it, hadn't expected much of anything at all, in fact. She had thought she'd take care of this young man as a favor to Doezen until he could find his own way in the world. She would give him shelter and help for a year; that should be enough.

Doezen had warned her about Tenzin in a letter to her some months ago. "I am sending you someone of great power," he had said, "although he doesn't yet truly know it. This young man is exceptional. He's the best of our lineage, the fruit of an ancient tree. He will go far, though he will likely encounter great difficulty in the beginning. I would appreciate doing what you can to help him." Then came the lines that caught her attention and that she had ignored as quickly as possible. "A deep inner connection exists between you and him; I believe you will find that you love him with all your soul. Do not be afraid of that love. It has been given to help you grow. This relationship is about a destiny that is bigger than either of you. You will not grasp it for a long time. You may never fully understand it or see it in its entirety. But you will feel it. Follow your intuition and all will unfold as it should."

She knew, of course, that Doezen always told the truth. He had written it simply and clearly, but still she didn't fully believe it. Her life was comfortable and orderly; she did not need it unsettled just now. She longed only to live out her days in peace, not have her life made complicated and difficult again. She had done enough for others, for her husband and children, and for anyone else who had come into her life. She had always been helpful and in great demand by charities and good causes. Now, after a long life, rich in experience and service to others, she wanted time to do as she pleased. So she folded the letter and put it away. And with it, any thoughts of more spiritual awakening.

Over time, she dismissed much of what Doezen had written. She focused instead on the particulars of the matter: getting Tenzin a visa and a plane ticket and making arrangements with the embassy personnel in Delhi to look after him when and if he got there. She was well aware that getting out of Tibet during the Chinese occupation was difficult and was surprised when everything fell into place as easily as it had. Getting a visa to come to the States from Tibet was not a routine matter. Only Emily's ingenuity and the use of well-placed connections in the State Department allowed her to accomplish it. Rather than waste time ,she had gone directly to the top, calling an old colleague of her husband's, Clark Whitman. They had not spoken since her husband's funeral eight years ago, but when she told him about her problem and what she needed, he had smiled and said, "Emily, consider it done. It will be my pleasure."

A week later she received a call from his secretary. Tenzin's visa was waiting at the embassy in Delhi in the office of one Sean Wilson. Of course, it helped that Tenzin was being sponsored by the wife of a former ambassador to India and would be staying at her house in Santa Monica when he reached America.

As Tenzin approached her in the waiting area, she could sense his pain, despite his attempt to appear inscrutable. At that moment, the mother in her took over and, against her better judgment, her heart opened to let him in. She was powerless to stop it. All her reservations and determination not to get personally involved disappeared.

How could I have imagined that I would be able to keep my heart closed to him, she thought. Doezen was right again. For that matter, I can't remember him ever being wrong about anything.

Tenzin was less than three feet away now. There was no more time for self-recriminations. It was time to say hello.

Emily lived close to the ocean in the most affluent section of Santa Monica, north of Montana Ave. They didn't speak much on the drive. Her Tibetan was worse than rusty; Tenzin's English was nonexistent. But the silence between them was not uncomfortable.

If anything, it was an easy and nourishing time and neither one felt self-conscious.

She slowed the car and turned into the driveway of a large, Spanish style house with yellow stucco walls and a red tiled roof. The house had three floors. Spacious gardens of beautiful flowers and plants embraced the front and sides. Orange, lemon, pomegranate, and peach trees stood in the back yard. The thick, green lawn was well manicured and highlighted by several flower beds that were changed often so that the flowers in them were always in bloom. A yellow stucco wall surrounded the property, and a wrought iron electric gate opened onto the circular drive.

Tenzin had never seen anything like it, except perhaps the embassy in Delhi.

Compared to the monastery and the homes in Tibet, Emily's home was a great palace. While very beautiful, the house was another shock in a steady series of shocks, each made more difficult to assimilate because he had no one of a similar perspective with which to share it.

Emily showed Tenzin to a corner bedroom on the third floor. Two large sets of French doors opened to the west and the north, each with a magnificent view of the Santa Monica Bay. The doors led out to a balcony at the back of the house furnished with several easy chairs, a table, and many pots of flowers. The room and the balcony were awash with afternoon light. A wisteria vine twined along the railing, mingling the fragrance of blooming flowers with the salty smell of the sea. A soft sea breeze wove the various scents into a pungent bouquet. A few butterflies perched lazily on the flowers, waving their wings from time to time, drinking in their nectar.

This room was Emily's favorite in the large house. She didn't visit it much anymore, but when she needed solitude or wished to meditate, she always came here.

Her housekeeper, Maria, brought food, and they ate a light lunch on the balcony, speaking in Tibetan. She still remembered a few words, but spoke poorly. Then she left him to sleep. It was obvious he was both exhausted and underfed. She made a mental note to tell Maria to feed him well and to fatten him up. This young man needed more flesh on his bones.

Once he was finally alone, without the crush of other passengers around him, or even the presence of this kind and bright woman, Tenzin faded quickly.

He removed his clothes and climbed into the clean, large bed. The steady breeze blew in from the ocean; the distant crashing of waves comforted him. He fell into a deep and dreamless sleep. He slept for twenty hours, the first really satisfying sleep he had had in many months.

Knowing that her Tibetan was inadequate and his English non-existent, Emily had found a professor at UCLA fluent in Tibetan. She met Professor Thomas Kerr for lunch a few days later. She expected to have a boring business meeting in which they would make the necessary financial arrangements, establish a tutoring schedule, then go home.

The professor was already seated when she arrived. He rose to greet her. Thomas Kerr was a tall, thin man with a premature balding pate, light hair, wire rimmed glasses, and sparkling blue eyes similar to her's.

"Mrs. Chase."

"Professor Kerr."

He extended his hand. "Call me Thomas."

"If you insist."

"I do. Otherwise I would feel compelled to call you Madam Ambassador."

"I see you've done your homework. But I've never been an Ambassador. My husband was."

"A small detail, easily overlooked."

Emily laughed and they sat down to lunch.

"I know you're a cultural anthropologist, Thomas, and that you speak Tibetan."

"And Russian," he said. "And Chinese. And Spanish."

"That's an impressive list of languages."

"And alphabets I'm afraid. It's enough to make you mad. You said this young man was a monk?"

"That's correct."

"Do you think he'd let me meditate with him?"

"I have no idea. You'll have to ask him."

"What's he like?"

"He's quiet, but he has great presence. You feel it immediately. Now let's work out the financial arrangements."

"There's no need for that. I'll get more from him than he'll ever get from me. We'll meet weekday mornings from ten to eleven."

"That is unacceptable."

"Why?" The professor's jaw dropped.

"I don't accept charity. This is a financial arrangement. I insist on paying for your expertise."

"But what of his expertise? I should pay you back for that."

"Very well," Emily said. She smiled. "Consider it deducted from your fee. I will pay you forty dollars an hour rather than sixty."

"That's too much."

"It's either that or no deal."

"Not fair," he said. "But I accept."

"I thought you might."

They laughed heartily and enjoyed dessert.

Emily let Tenzin have a few days to adjust to his new surroundings. Then she drove him to UCLA and introduced him to Prof. Kerr. She was well aware of the state Tenzin was in, knew what he had already lost and what more he stood to lose. Because of all that remained unknown, she decided to go into action immediately. She knew firsthand what idleness can do to the mind. She was not about to let him feel sorry for himself. Better to do something, almost anything, than to be idle and to let fear and panic take you down. Beside, the sooner he acclimated himself to America, the better. She was certain that being with Thomas Kerr would be good for him in many ways.

Emily had learned all about death and grief and tragedy from her life experience. While she and Randall were posted in Delhi, their youngest child, their only son, had died at the age of two. She had sunk into a deep depression. For months afterward she had stayed in her room, crying for hours at a time. Robbie had held a special place in her heart. He had blue eyes like hers and he had loved her in such a deep and open manner. He had been a happy child, buoying her when her spirits flagged. The two of them were inseparable. Then one night Robbie simply died while he slept. Because he hadn't known what else to do, Randall tolerated Emily's depression for several months. He had finally had to push her out of the bedroom and back to her painting and charity work.

At first she was angry at Randall, but after a few weeks she was glad that he had forced her back into life. She began volunteering at the American school near the embassy. Being with children made her feel closer to Robbie. Soon she began to feel useful again.

She also volunteered at a nearby Indian school, and worked with the children as part of the embassy's outreach program. Often, she would invite several of them over to the embassy for dinner. Then they would play in the back garden before they returned home with bags of homemade cookies.

It was during that time that Emily first heard about the monastery in Tibet. An American professor from Berkeley had stopped at the embassy to have his visa processed. He had just returned from Tibet, and he was full of excitement and incredible tales. The embassy staff could not get enough of his stories. Randall and Emily invited him to dinner that evening, where he related more of his adventures. He described how the monks could control their heart rates and other functions of their autonomic nervous system at will. Some advanced lamas could even be buried underground for days at a time with no air and emerge alive. They could sit outside in freezing weather on a slab of ice wearing nothing but a loin cloth, remain warm, and melt the ice. They had great powers of telepathy, communicating by thought over long distances. They could leave their bodies at will and travel anywhere, bringing back accurate reports about what they had observed.

The professor kept mentioning one lama, a rinpoche, or senior teacher in particular, who had made a very deep impression on him. The rinpoche's name was Doezen. According to the professor, Doezen was a small man, unassuming in physical appearance, but with astounding gifts. He possessed tremendous healing power and could know everything about you with one glance. The longer you were with him the better you felt. This monk, the professor said, was wiser and more perceptive than anyone he had ever met.

Emily Chase was as charmed by the erudite, intelligent professor as the rest of the embassy staff had been. She felt he was speaking directly to her. By the time the dinner was over she knew she had to meet this Rinpoche as soon as possible.

Two months later she was on her way to Tibet. Her hopes and expectations were high. She was impatient and on edge to meet Doezen.

When she arrived at the monastery Emily was taken to his room. Doezen was immersed in his work, reading and answering correspondence. He nodded to her, acknowledging her presence, but kept on working for nearly two hours. She sat there in the hard chair, tired, cold and hungry. She kept waiting for him to talk to her but he said nothing, nor did he even glance at her. She thought him rude, insensitive, and self-centered. Certainly not a great man or even an impressive one. Then, when she was fully exasperated and on the verge of leaving, he laid aside his pen with great care and looked at her.

"You had a young son who died in his sleep recently."

She was shocked. Speechless. He had stabbed her in her most vulnerable place while she was weak and agitated.

"You have experience much grieving," he said, "But it is not finished. There is more."

Emily's eyes opened wider. Her tight lips twisted into a grimace, baring her teeth. "Now you listen here," she said. "You have no right...."

But Doezen was not listening. Instead he walked directly to her and tapped her on the chest three times. With each tap, a strange electrical charge shot through her. Her head swam and she teetered on the edge of the chair. Before she knew it, grief flooded from her, more than she ever imagined her body could hold. Uncontrollable sobs wrenched her back in the chair. She was lost in a world of unfathomable anguish. Doezen stood nearby, his face full of compassion and tenderness, and let her cry. After a time, the wave of grief subsided, and she returned to her senses and opened her eyes. The kindest, most beautiful face she had ever seen gazed back at her. His dark eyes were suffused with the soft light of compassion. She never wanted to stop looking into them. They promised complete safety and peace.

"Grief will be your visitor for another three days," he said. "Then it will depart. Please go to your room and rest. You need to sleep. You will release more of your pain in your dreams. I will look in on you later."

Emily slept late the next morning, feeling lighter and freer than she had since Robbie's death. She was sure she had wrung all the grief out of her system. She washed and ate a light breakfast. Doezen came to her room. He said little, but observed her with the great gentleness that was his trademark. This time he tapped her twice on the back of her lungs. That same electricity rushed through her, the same lightheadedness came over her, and she collapsed to the floor in tears.

She cried all day. Doezen never left her side. When the first wave of grief had subsided, she saw that a bright golden light pervaded the room. Much later that day, when she glanced again in Doezen's direction, she couldn't see him at all, only a brighter intensity of the same golden light. She wasn't sure if she was still in her room or had been transported to some other realm; she didn't know if she was imagining the golden light or really seeing it. By the end of the day she was so depleted of tears that she was sure there wasn't another drop of water inside her.

By then it was early evening and dark outside. Doezen came up to her and touched her forehead. This time he kept his hand there. Her head filled with the same golden light she had seen earlier. The light slid through her body without resistance, flooding every organ, muscle, bone, and cell. She was deeply at peace. Her body seemed weightless, as if she were floating in space. She opened her eyes. She was looking down at her physical body lying on the bed with Doezen's hand on her forehead. He looked up at her and smiled. She heard his voice in her head, "Come back to your body, little sister. Your soul is nearly healed. You will be fine. There is no need to be anywhere else but where you belong. Your home is your body. Come to it now."

A second later she opened her eyes. Doezen looked at her intently.

"It has been a good day," he said. "Rest now, little sister. You have done well."

She fell into a dreamless sleep. When she awoke, light streamed into her room through cracks in the door and the window high above her bed. It was late the next morning. She stretched, feeling very light but exhausted. She lingered in her bed a while then went to the dining hall where she ate ravenously.

Doezen didn't come to her until the middle of the afternoon, so she had time to rest and think. But she couldn't think. Her mind kept wandering. She could not hold a single thought. When he finally came, he sat with her and said very little. Again, golden light filled the room. She began to feel stronger and more focused. Then he tapped her three times on the stomach. She doubled over in pain and started screaming and raging and thrashing about. Words that had never before passed her lips burst from deep inside her. She railed at God, her husband, the United States government and anyone else that came to mind. She found herself back in her childhood, a lost little girl screaming at her father for being so distant and unavailable, and at her mother for being so fearful and smothering. She screamed until she felt her vocal chords giving out, and then she shouted, "Damn it!" and screamed some more. When she had nothing left, she collapsed on her bed, soaked with sweat, and curled her body into the fetal position.

Doezen let her rest until her breathing normalized, then he came to the foot of the bed and placed his hands on the soles of her feet. A pleasant stream of energy flowed up her legs and settled in her lower belly, filling her womb with a deep sense of peace. Until that moment, she had had no idea how much anger and rage she had stored in her reproductive system.

"Good," he said at last. Doezen released her feet after several minutes of silent concentration. "It is done." His warm smile relaxed her. " If you hadn't released that anger you would have developed cancer later in life. Now the negative emotion in your system has been cleared. You are whole. You and your soul are one again."

As he spoke to her, love and compassion again suffused his face and touched her in a place that no one had ever reached before. Not parents. Not lovers. Not her husband. Not even her children. Until Doezen, she hadn't known that place inside her. It had become cold and barren from lack of contact. Now it was bursting with life. Doezen shook his head slightly and said, "I am only the vehicle for you to find the Supreme Truth inside yourself. Everyone has that place inside them, but few ever find it." He smiled at her. "You have good karma."

Perhaps, she thought. But you are so much more than just a vehicle. This is the greatest miracle I have ever experienced. You didn't give me riches. You gave me wholeness and freedom. What compares with that? And all you had to do was look at me and touch me. Where does such power come from?

Then he said something that cut her to the core and brought her back from her reflections. "Did you ever think your son might have died so you could be whole and free?"

"What?" she replied, shocked again. He seemed to throw her continually off balance. "God wouldn't do such a thing."

"The Supreme Truth had little to do with it," he said. "You and your son made an agreement on the soul level before he came to this birth that he would die early. His death was to propel you, through the deep wounding it would cause, to seek your wholeness. Your son only needed two years to complete his learning here. His death was the vehicle for both you and him to evolve to another level of consciousness."

Emily stared at Doezen. "That's not possible," she said. "You're saying that my soul set all this up for my growth? I killed my son? How dare you? That's crazy!"

Doezen remained calm. "Ah, little sister, it's not. The soul lays its path where the mind cannot follow. This world is here for growth. On the soul level we all know that. But we forget it once we get here. Instead we think the world is here to fulfill our desires. We substitute self-aggrandizement for Self-realization and cause ourselves needless delay and suffering. The soul can use any experience to promote our growth. We come to our senses when the time is right. Tragedy and loss often open the door to consciousness. But each of us must choose to walk through." Doezen smiled. "Or to remain asleep. If you grow, nothing is lost, only transformed. Your son died young. He chose that death to help you grow. Maybe he owed you a debt from another lifetime. Maybe you saved his life, and this is how he chose to repay you, sacrificing himself for your growth."

"That's a terrible thought. If he truly did that, I will feel awful and guilty forever."

"If you choose to," he said. "But to do so would be foolish. And wasteful of his gift to you. It was his choice and part of his growth. You had little to do with it. Because he accomplished his growth, his soul knows more joy. His choice led him into a more luminous state. He is free."

Doezen's voice grew gentle and compassionate, less the stern teacher, more the kind mentor. "It is time for you to move on as well, little sister. Remember, nothing is lost. You have not lost your son. He led you here and saved you. Someday you will be with him again. Ties of real love endure beyond the body, beyond death, forever. No purer love exists than that between a parent and a child. When you love your child unconditionally, you experience a glimmer of how much the Supreme Truth loves you. What is true and real here is also true and real there. When you meet again as souls, you may each decide to take on another body and play different roles in each other's development. The love will be even deeper, the tie even stronger next time. You have each served the other.

How could it be any different? You must learn to see with your soul, little sister. Put the limits and doubts of the mind aside. The soul is bound to the Supreme Truth. The conscious mind is only tied to the body."

"Do you really think I can get over Robbie's death?"

"You are doing so right now. Your past no longer owns you. Your karma has been cleared. Guilt, pain, and grief are gone. We wouldn't be having this conversation unless you were ready to look at the situation with new eyes instead of being stuck in old emotions."

"I'm still feeling very emotional."

"You still heard what I said. Your resistance was weak. My words reached inside you and struck a deep chord. They are now seeds that will flower in your soul when you are ready to take the next steps in your evolution. All will happen in the right time. That is what occurs when you find your center. Some day, your life will be about devotion and you will know a joy you can't imagine now. But that will come later when your hair is no longer rich and dark but thin and white."

"Thanks a lot. I'm not looking forward to being a little old lady."

"How would you know? You haven't gotten there yet. When you do, you will discover that while your body has aged, your soul has gotten younger and brighter. You won't feel old."

He turned his gaze full on her and looked in her eyes with the compassion and certainty that is the signature of a realized soul. Whatever tension and fight remaining in her drained away. She could not dispute his wisdom any longer and surrendered to the truth.

Emily returned to the monastery to study with Doezen two or three times a year for the next several years, until Randall was transferred back to the States. During that period she wrote Doezen at least once a month to tell him of her progress and ask him questions. He responded promptly, often sending her books.

Once she returned to the States, their contact gradually diminished. Emily had grown a great deal. She had become more centered and needed Doezen less. She returned to the life she had always known, living within the values of her class and culture. She painted, volunteered at the hospital, gave of her time to underprivileged children, and finished raising her two girls, who matriculated to prestigious universities on the east coast. After her husband's retirement, they hiked and painted together in the Santa Monica mountains, and toured ancient ruins in France, Italy, Greece and Turkey. In the last years of Randall's life they collaborated on his memoirs, which brought them closer together in a sweeter and gentler way than ever before.

When Randall died, Emily missed him dearly, but not despairingly. Their relationship had been whole and complete in itself. She had no regrets about things she might have said or done. She found that she could simultaneously miss him, love him, and go on. Something inside her was growing brighter after he died, and she was puzzled by it. She couldn't quite put her finger on it, or shake it off, and no one in her circle would understand it. So she put the feeling aside and continued to live the comfortable existence that she loved.

That was more than five years ago. Occasionally, when she slowed down a bit, the same feeling would come back. During those times she would climb the stairs to the third floor bedroom where Tenzin was now sleeping. She would sit among the books Doezen had sent her, reread his letters, and feel the brightness inside her growing. Sometimes her joy was so strong that she would cry. Other times, a feeling would come over her that her life was about to change drastically, so she would grow afraid. In those moments, Doezen's words would ring gently in her mind. "Little sister, everything will happen in its own time. Someday your life will be about service and devotion. But that comes later when your hair is thin and white."

Well, that part of it was certainly true, she thought ruefully. Then Doezen's letter had arrived. She had been worried about him ever since the Chinese invasion and had written him several times offering to get him out of Tibet. He had written back thanking her, insisting that his path was there. Whatever happened would be for the best. She was not to worry about him. However, he was sending her a special young man for her to assist on his path. Now Tenzin was here and the change she had felt coming had arrived. The love she was feeling for the young monk had amplified the brightness inside her. The two were intimately connected. Whatever was coming had a sense of inevitability to it. She decided not to fight the change, whatever it might entail, but cooperate with it, instead. The old life was over. It had been a wonderful life, rich in many things that mattered. A loving family, diverse experiences, world travel, excitement, pain, happiness and learning. She wouldn't change a moment of it. Now it was time to close that book and move forward. Something vastly different was being born inside her.

Very well, she thought. She let go of the final strands to the past. Everything happens in its own time. The moment had come for the next stage in her life.

CHAPTER 7

The Turning Point

THE NEXT DAY, Emily took Tenzin shopping. His robe was tattered. He had no other clothes to wear. She thought he'd protest wearing western style clothing and insist on keeping his robe. After all, it was all he had left of his life in Tibet. Tenzin, however, had already experienced people staring at him and whispering about him at the airport. He knew that adjusting to being in America would be easier for him if he blended in as much as possible. Beside, he was curious about western clothing. He wanted to see how it felt to wear jeans, t-shirts, shoes, socks and underwear. When they got home, Tenzin took off his worn robe and put on a pair of jeans, a yellow t-shirt, socks, and sneakers. Emily had his robe laundered and put away for safe keeping. It would hang unworn in the back of the closet for many years.

After lunch, Emily took Tenzin to the beach for a walk along the water. Tenzin had never been to the ocean. It totally captivated him. He loved the waves, the sea breeze caressing his skin, the feel of the wet sand as his feet sunk into it, the glistening dance of sunlight on the water, the play of light and shadow on the windows of the buildings behind him. Hope filled him and for the moment he forgot his sadness. He felt genuinely happy for the first time since leaving the monastery.

Emily saw how striking he looked in his yellow t-shirt, with his lean muscular body, bronze skin, and high cheekbones. His eyes shone with intelligence and gentleness. She was aware, too, of how the girls looked at him as they walked along the shore. He was exotic and strikingly handsome. Now rested, he projected a powerful charisma. She chuckled to herself. It's going to be very interesting to see just how deep this young man dives into Western culture. He's taken off his robe. Will he want a girlfriend? Young women certainly will be chasing him.

For his part, Tenzin was oblivious to the attention he was generating. He focused on the ocean, the light, and the sand; his senses drank in each new experience. He kept speaking to Emily in Tibetan, telling her how incredible the ocean was, and that he had to come here often because the energy radiating from the sea gave him the same feeling of peace as the mountains at home. She had no idea what he was trying to tell her. She only knew what her eyes and heart told her: he was happy, and he loved the sea. It warmed her to see him in this light and get a glimpse of whom and what he really was. He didn't seem to need as much time to regain his energy and balance as most people in his situation might.

There's no sense in waiting, she thought. He's ready.

That evening Emily called Professor Kerr and arranged for Tenzin to start English lessons the following Monday. At 10 a.m. on Monday, she appeared at Professor Kerr's office at UCLA with Tenzin. Professor Kerr greeted them warmly, saying hello to Emily and asking her how Tenzin was adjusting to life in America. Then he turned to Tenzin and spoke to him in Tibetan. He told Tenzin an old Tibetan joke a lama had once told him. They both laughed. Seeing the rapport between them she knew it was time for her to leave.

That day the two of them spoke in Tibetan, and Tenzin gave Thomas some simple instructions in meditation. That's how they came to decide on their schedule. Every day at ten a.m., Monday through Friday, they would begin their sessions with a meditation then move on to the work at hand, mastering the English language.

After the first week Tenzin insisted in speaking only English with Emily. In that way, his time with Emily became part of his daily discipline for learning the language. Every evening after dinner they would speak English about all sorts of things. His capacity to understand and speak the language grew quickly. He had an obvious gift for language and could probably learn any tongue as quickly as he was learning English. Two weeks into the tutoring schedule, Professor Kerr told Emily that Tenzin was moving so fast that he would be proficient in English in half the time allotted, three months instead of six. She was not surprised.

During the third week of Tenzin's English lessons, Professor Kerr called Emily one afternoon and wondered if he might stop by that evening.

"Of course you can come by. We'd love to have you visit," she responded. "Why not come for dinner?"

After dinner, Thomas asked if they could meditate together. Emily nodded approvingly. The sense of brightness inside her had grown stronger since Tenzin's arrival and she was eager to meditate with him. Secretly, she hoped the energy would be the same as it had been when she meditated with Doezen thirty years earlier. In those sessions her body had filled with light and her mind had become remarkably still. A peace had come over her that had left her feeling complete and at one with all that is. She was eager to recreate that experience with Tenzin.

They sat together in the downstairs study. Emily focused on her breath, inhaling deeply through her nose and exhaling slowly through her mouth. Soon she became peaceful; her body breathing itself. She observed the process without conflicting emotions or intrusive thoughts, only calm concentration on the breath. An intense sensation of heat built up at the base of her spine. At first, the heat was soothing and comfortable, confined to her hips. Before long, it began rising up her spine with increasing velocity, gathering at her neck like a pool filling with water. It soon surged into her head in a swift blast of brilliant light. The shock of so much energy exploding in her head made her mind go blank. She shook and trembled. The fire continued to flow like molten lava up her spine. A moment later she heard a sharp pop in her forehead and the reservoir of energy rushed out of her skull. A sequence of brilliant colors, white, silver, gold, green, blue, repeated itself until all the energy in her head had been released. Emily leaned back in her chair, exhausted and pale.

Tenzin was watching her carefully, observing everything. A moment later, she opened her eyes. Bright, golden light suffused the entire room. The light was brightest where Tenzin was sitting. Emily remembered the golden light she had seen around Doezen during their first encounter. No wonder she had thought of Tenzin as a younger version of Doezen when she met him at the airport. They had the same energy. Doezen's words flooded back to her. "Everything happens in its own time, little sister. Someday, when your hair is thin and white, you will enter the next stage of your path."

She had reached that point. The reality couldn't be more clear. A vast love for Doezen swelled in her heart. She understood then, perhaps for the first time, that everything he had done to her, he had done for her. His actions had sprung from a conscious, loving place in him. His gifts to her, however, had resided in an unconscious and unloving place through all these years. In healing her, he had redeemed and transformed her. That fact was becoming more and more apparent as she awoke to her destiny. The spiritual seeds he had planted decades ago were now bearing fruit.

Doezen's gifts, she thought, were the sacrifice that love makes to heal an unloving world. Love gives of itself to make others conscious, often suffering rebuke, misunderstanding, even hatred in return. Even now, Doezen continued to give. "I'm sending you someone special," he had written. "The best of our line." It was true.

Tenzin looked into Emily's eyes. "Now you see," he said. He laughed so deeply his belly shook. His laughter proved infectious. Before they knew it they were all laughing.

When the laughter subsided, Tenzin continued. "Before I left the monastery, Doezen told me that your karmic blocks had been burned and that it was time for your kundalini to awaken because you weren't as involved in worldly concerns anymore. He said I would do that for you. I said to him, "Rinpoche, how will I do that?" He answered, "Just by being you.'"

"It's true, Tenzin," she said. "I am the proof."

"Doezen also said that I had many tools to help free people in the west. I'm not sure what he meant by that."

The professor had said nothing since the meditation ended. He was having an experience as well, but his was markedly different from Emily's. A wave of nausea had engulfed him midway through the meditation. Sweat still dripped down his face. Tenzin had noticed his discomfort earlier but had decided to let it build. He now reached over and tapped Thomas twice in the stomach. A bolt of electricity surged through him. He stared at Tenzin, his eyes wide and face frozen with shock. Unable to contain himself, he burst into tears.

"This is about your father," said Tenzin.

"He was a cruel son of a bitch," said Thomas. "He never loved me."

"You've carried that hurt your entire life. Time to release it. Feel your pain. Let it rise up from where it's buried in your body and then express it. There's no other way."

A wail rose from Thomas. He collapsed into the fetal position and sobbed for several minutes. When the tears had finally passed, he wiped his face.

"I've made an ass of myself and monopolized your time," he said hoarsely, his voice no more than a whisper. "I'm sorry."

"A moment of beauty requires no apology," said Tenzin. "There is no shame in releasing your pain, only grace. I am honored to be part of it. Tonight you freed yourself from the demons of your past and opened a door to a better future. Was that not your wish?"

"It was."

"When you face yourself and release what has bound you, you create space for a better future. You will be tired for a few days, then you will feel reborn."

CHAPTER 8

The Unexpected Guest

IN THE FOLLOWING weeks students and colleagues alike commented on the change in Thomas. He had more fun teaching, and his enthusiasm and humor were infectious. For several weeks he had been sharing with his classes the progress of the Tibetan monk he was tutoring. He had even told them about his mystical abilities. His students were enchanted by these tales and were begging to meet him. Tenzin was a living mystery to them, a keeper of ancient wisdom and holder of hidden power. He represented an unknown reality, not just dry words on an impersonal page or a story about the spiritual powers of some lama or yogi who had been dead for hundreds of years. He was here now in the flesh, and like them, he was young.

The demand had begun when an attractive young woman in his seminar, Alice Perry, asked what at the time seemed an innocent question, a thought shared by several other students.

"Professor Kerr," she said. "You seem different, like a weight has been taken off you. Class dragged before, but it's been great lately. We've had a blast. Every time I leave here, I have more energy than I know what to do with. It's probably none of my business but, I mean, if you're doing something that's helped you, could you tell us because I think many of us might like to try it, too. Has that monk given you some secret power or something?"

"Yeah Professor, tell us," the rest of the class chimed in.

Thomas pondered the question. How much could he safely tell them? Should he tell them anything at all? The question, innocent and forthright as it was, would not settle in his mind and sort itself out. So he looked out at the eager, honest faces in front of him and followed his heart. He told them everything.

Instead of the academic discussion about Brahma, Vishnu, and Shiva he had planned for that day, Thomas recounted the transformational healing he had undergone with Tenzin and Emily. At the end of his confession the classroom became so still that you could hear the slight breeze whispering through the windows.

Their lack of reaction made Thomas nervous. He didn't know what to think. College students were not normally quiet. A few telltale beads of sweat formed on his forehead. He was worried about losing his standing with them, maybe even losing his job. Had he gone too far into the personal? Revealed too much? Alice finally broke the silence.

"Professor," she said. "We've got to meet this guy. You've got to bring him to class soon, like next week."

"Yeah! The sooner the better!" said someone else. The rest of the class eagerly embraced the idea.

Thomas' anxiety disappeared. He had done the right thing. Their excitement was contagious. He decided to ask Tenzin to come soon.

That night Thomas returned to Emily's for the first time since his healing. Now that he had come out of the dark side, he was eager to see them again. Emily greeted him at the door.

"Well, Professor," she said, happy to see him. "You look quite on top of things. I was getting worried and wanted to call you, but Tenzin wouldn't let me. He said you had to do this on your own, and you would get back to us when you were ready. I don't have much experience in these things, so I thought I'd better not meddle."

"You know, Emily," Thomas said. "Now that I think about it, Tenzin was correct. I had to go through it on my own. Now I understand the process. It will be easier the next time. I feel much better now."

"It's good to hear you say that, Thomas. It makes me feel better too. Not calling you went against my nature. But sometimes when you think you're doing good for someone you might be doing harm. I'm not used to taking anyone's orders, particularly in my own house, but this is an area where I don't possess much expertise."

"Don't apologize, Emily. I entirely understand. May I ask you a personal question?"

"As long as it's not about my love life," she said. "There's nothing much to report there anyway. When you get to be my age all the available men are in nursing homes."

Thomas laughed. "Not that kind of question."

"Then ask."

"When you went through your healing experience with Doezen, did you feel that you'd be exhausted and depressed forever? Because I sure did."

"That was such a long time ago. But yes, come to think of it, I did. I was drained, alone, terrified. Doezen was all I had and I hardly knew him. It was a scary time. But you know, when my energy came back, it came back stronger than ever. I felt filled with light. My life was really never the same again, although I did struggle for a long time to keep it as it had been. I did succeed in keeping the facade intact, but underneath I was changed, more whole and happy, and interested in different things. Since Randall died and Tenzin's arrival that inner person has re-surfaced. I feel that I need to make up for lost time. I have no interest in resuming my old life."

"My experience was a lot like yours. Where's Tenzin hiding? I need to ask him something."

"He's not hiding. We'll join him."

Tenzin was in the study sitting among the shadows in deep meditation. A dim pole lamp in the corner cast a scant glow over the room. The scent of frankincense floated in the air.

Tenzin's breathing was barely detectable. His spine was erect, feet and legs in the lotus posture, legs crossed, each foot resting on the inner thigh of the opposite leg. He was far way. Emily and Thomas felt it immediately. They sat down as quietly as they could, not wanting to disturb his meditation.

Their caution was hardly necessary. Tenzin was unaware of their presence. His soul was in Tibet, wandering through the pain of its people. He couldn't find his family, but he did feel their absence. Danger and death were everywhere, in every corner of the country. He did not feel hopeful about his family, Doezen, or the others. He wanted desperately to enfold them in his arms and bring them to where it was safe, here in this house, with his friend Emily. But that was a wish no one could grant. The sense of oppression was crushing. He sighed and with a heavy sadness returned to his body, shuddering as he re-entered it.

TIBET 1950

Tenzin did not know then how correct his intuition had been. Two days before he and Nawang left the monastery, the Chinese had stormed into his parent's village before dawn. They dragged the men and boys out of their beds. They ordered the village men to lace their fingers behind their heads, then marched them single file to the village center. An officer barked orders in a shrill voice. The soldiers forced the men and boys to their knees on the cold ground. Two soldiers walked down the line and ripped their shirts open down their backs. Boys cried out for their mothers. Men shivered. Some sobbed. Naljor maintained his dignity and remained still. He nodded to his young grandson kneeling beside him. The boy was shaking uncontrollably. He touched his grandchild's shoulder and smiled. The boy gained confidence from his grandfather's calm demeanor. He wiped his face on his sleeve and stopped crying. He did not want to lose face in front of his grandfather.

Each minute that passed seemed an eternity. Many of the men prostrated themselves on the ground and begged for their lives. The soldiers stood over them, laughing at their desperation to save their pathetic, worthless lives. A few of the villagers reached out and grasped the feet of the soldiers standing in front of them. The soldiers crushed their fingers under their boots. The men shrieked in pain. The commanding officer smirked at their stupidity and barked out his next order. The soldiers thrust their rifle butts into the backs of the prostate men. The men twisted in their torment and screamed louder.

Another group of soldiers herded the women and girls to the village center to witness what was about to happen. The women huddled together, sobbing and screaming hysterically. Soldiers stood between them and their men, with bayonets pointed at their stomachs. The sun emerged from behind the mountains and slowly climbed above the horizon. Light gleamed on hard steel. The soldier's faces were cruel masks, their eyes devoid of all feeling. A woman tried to push her way through the soldiers. A rifle butt struck her in the mouth. She crumbled to the ground, blood spurting from a split lip and broken teeth. The rest of the women froze. The only sound heard in the village square was the panting of the men and the barking of the dogs.

The soldiers nodded at each other. They knew how to control this Tibetan scum. The women were nothing but stinking whores. Not a pretty one among them either. Raping them would be more work than pleasure. Not much of a reward for their troubles. Their only satisfaction would come from making them pay for their ugliness.

The lead officer shouted the execution order in rapid staccato. Two lieutenants came forward with drawn pistols. Tenzin's father whispered to his grandson to be brave; there would be another life and it would be better than this one. He saw his wife in the huddled mass of women. He smiled at her. She touched her heart, wiped away her tears, and smiled back.

Two soldiers walked down the line from opposite directions and fired a bullet into the back of each man's and boy's head. One by one they slumped over under the first light of the sun, eyes vacant, bodies heavy and inert, laying like stones on the hard earth. Their blood seeped silently into the parched ground beneath them.

A piercing lament rose from the women. The commander glared at them and snarled out another order. The soldiers set themselves on the women and girls.

They hit them in the face, battered them bloody, then ripped off their clothes and threw them on the ground. They held them down and raped them over and over again. The more the women fought the more the soldiers laughed. When they were done with their sport they pulled out their pistols and put bullets in their foreheads. Then they left.

When the sun was directly overhead, a little boy crawled out of his hiding place in the underground cellar under the sleeping mat where Tenzin's sister had hidden him. He waddled into the village center, found the battered body of his dead mother and sat down in the pool of blood seeping into the earth beside her. He tried to awaken her, pleaded with her to come back to him, first with his screams and then with his tears. He stroked her hair, held her hand with his short, stubby fingers and felt the warm, sticky blood on her back and neck. He was too young to know why she wouldn't answer him.

A grim finality hung over the village, a dense cloud of smoke and agony that all who journeyed there in the ensuing months would feel. The child's sobs rose among the dead and the silent, the final testament to the cold and ruthless murder of his clan.

Two days later, the Chinese marched across the field of stones and took possession of the monastery. The few senior monks who remained offered no opposition. The others had been sent away shortly after Tenzin and Nawang had departed. The Chinese wasted little time. The commanding officer barked out his orders once more. Soldiers rounded up the old monks, shoved them against the courtyard wall and spit in their faces. The monks remained calm and unafraid in the face of their executioners. A firing squad was formed. The soldiers raised their rifles. The captain gave the command. A volley rang out in the courtyard where shots had never been heard before. The monks fell where they stood, bullets through their hearts, the sacred stones beneath them running red. An acrid cloud of gun smoke filled the air above them. Buzzards circled high above the walls, waiting for the soldiers to finish their business and leave them to their feast.

The soldiers stood at attention, their faces cold and emotionless, rifles by their sides. Killing the innocent and the unarmed meant nothing to them. They had been trained not to think, but to follow orders. The captain walked up and down the line observing them with a hardened eye. He was pleased to see their programming was intact. His men were tools, robots, and nothing more. He felt as little for them as he did the people he had them murder. They would survive as long as they performed their function. Otherwise, they were expendable.

When he reached the end of the line, he shouted out his next order. The soldiers broke the formation and ransacked the monastery, looking for treasures. They found none. They took what little food remained, then piled the monk's bodies in the center of the courtyard, doused them with holy oil, and set them on fire. High above, the buzzards screamed indignantly. They would not have their feast this day. The soldiers poured more holy oil over the monastery and set it ablaze. Then they retreated to watch the flames destroy the ancient and sacred institution.

They raised their rifles above their heads and sang a song of triumph. Religion could never threaten Communism. Prayer was impotent in the face of force. Where was the stupid Tibetans' Almighty now? The idea of a Supreme Truth made them laugh. That night they camped nearby. When they left the next morning all that remained of the monastery were piles of charred brick and stone.

SANTA MONICA 1951

Tenzin opened his eyes slowly as he emerged from meditation. He took a moment to adjust to the dim light. Emily and Thomas were sitting with him, both in deep meditation. His new friends brought him joy. In the near darkness he could see their energy fields clearly. He smiled when he saw that Thomas's aura had expanded and become brighter since their last session. The blue was strong and clear, and the white beyond was pure. No more areas of darkness clouded his field. Thomas had transformed the energy that had clogged his stomach and throat since his childhood. The increase in his power was obvious. Almost anyone coming in contact with his electromagnetic field would experience an increase of energy in his own field.

Perhaps I can help more people in the way I helped Thomas, he thought. Maybe that's why I'm here. If I can do that, I will be doing what Doezen said I would do. Nothing would make me feel better, except knowing that my family is safe, Doezen and the others at the monastery are alive, and the Chinese have left Tibet.

Tenzin's thoughts arrived with a sadness and sense of finality that belied the hope he wanted desperately to feel.

Thomas and Emily emerged from their meditations moments later.

"Well, Thomas. Let me guess," said Tenzin. "You feel great and wherever you go people tell you they feel better."

"How did you know that?" asked Thomas.

"Your field has changed. Your light is much stronger now."

"That's good to know."

"There are those who think you can't change, that the way you are is the way you will always be," said Tenzin. "But emotional wounds can be healed. When they are, you reconnect with your soul and your true light shines through."

"Emotional wounds are a universal problem," said Thomas. "Not many people overcome them."

"That doesn't mean they can't. You did."

"Only because I had you. How many people can do what you do?"

"When you heal your wounds, your energy heals people who have similar wounds. Now those people will have you."

"That's already begun to happen," said Thomas.

"You see? Healing is contagious."

"But I certainly was tired before I felt better."

"That's to be expected," said Tenzin. "When you release negative emotion you go through a cleansing period. During that period you're often exhausted and depressed. But after that you experience an upswing of energy that is higher than what you felt before. Your highs become higher." He smiled. "Your lows also become higher. This new energy becomes your new base level because you no longer have the weight of the past to drag you down."

"Won't meditation do the same thing?" asked Thomas.

"You've meditated before. Did you get the same result?"

"No. It felt great for a while but it didn't last. The healing changed everything."

"Meditation alleviates stress, quiets the mind and emotions, and opens the intuition," said Tenzin. "But unless we clear our emotional blocks, the results of meditation are not as powerful or long lasting as they could be."

"In the early years of the twentieth century," Thomas said, "physicists bombarded an atom with energy. Three things happened. First, the electrons absorbed the excess energy. Then they went into a higher orbit and orbited at much greater speeds. Finally, when the electrons had spent the energy, they fell back into their normal orbits at their usual speed. Maybe meditation is like that. It takes you into a more centered space until you expend the energy you gained from the meditation, then you revert to the way you were."

"Good analogy, Thomas. When you combine emotional healing with meditation, you have a proven way to quicken your evolution. Each process strengthens the other."

"I've told my students about my healing experience with you. They're anxious to meet you. They've been reading about lamas and yogis but you're a living example and you're their age. Would you come and talk to my classes?"

"I'm just a poor farm boy from a small village in Tibet. Your students are rich and educated. I have nothing to offer them."

"I'm their teacher and I'm more educated than they are and look what you did for me. Presidents, politicians, millionaires , Ph.D.'s and movie stars can't do what you do. I'm telling you, these kids are clamoring to meet you."

Tenzin grew quiet and thoughtful. "Exactly what did you tell them, Thomas?"

"I, uh, well. . . I sort of promised them that you would come," he confessed.

"You sort of promised them?"

"I'm sorry," stammered Thomas. "I should have asked you first. I'll tell them your schedule won't permit it."

Tenzin leaned back and smiled broadly. "Don't worry. I'll come."

When the day of Tenzin's talk arrived Thomas had a big problem. Word had spread quickly through the campus, especially among the co-ed population. There wasn't nearly enough seating to meet the demand. He was forced to move Tenzin's talk to a nearby auditorium. Even so, the auditorium was overflowing with students and faculty ahead of time. When Emily and Tenzin arrived the place was buzzing.

This is far too many people, thought Emily. He's not ready for this.

All the seats were taken. People were crowded along the back of the auditorium and along the side aisles. Tenzin had never been in front of a crowd before, let alone one of this size. Emily's first impulse was to grab him by the arm and drag him out of there. But she needn't have been concerned.

Tenzin wasn't worried. He seemed to be focused and happy. He was joking with Thomas and another professor. Well, if he's all right with all this, then I guess I'd better be, too. There were a few seats in the front row reserved for faculty members and her. She sat down in her seat and attempted to relax. She smiled and chatted with the professor seated next to her, but her stomach was tied in knots.

A few minutes later Thomas took the podium. He made a few introductory remarks about Tenzin and his experiences. Then he motioned for Tenzin to join him. Tenzin was beaming as he walked on stage and faced the audience. He scanned the audience for a moment before he spoke.

Emily felt a powerful current sweep through her. She looked up to see successive waves of golden light pouring out of Tenzin's hands. The auditorium glowed with light. The restive audience grew calm. All eyes were on Tenzin.

"At the heart of the universe there is only love," he began. "In the core of each person's soul there is only love. When we find that place inside us, we are whole and one with all that is. The discovery of that place of love inside us is the purpose of our life on earth. We are all here to transform and redeem ourselves. None of us has fully mastered love. Love is the language of Infinity. When we finally learn to speak it, The Supreme Truth becomes alive in this world. People everywhere will be at peace. Whether the Supreme Truth lives in this world or is shut out of it, is up to us. One thing is certain. The Supreme Truth won't enter our lives until we love without judgment and without conditions. That's the law. The more we grow in love, the greater presence and power the Supreme Truth has in our lives and in this world. Don't blame the Supreme Truth when bad things happen. Become more loving. Bad things occur when people turn away from love."

He spoke about his parents and his village in the mountains of Tibet. He told them how his father had placed his hands on his mother's belly and prayed for a son who would one day become a lama. He spoke of his early longing for more consciousness. He spoke at length about the monastery and about Doezen. He shared several stories of Doezen's greatness, his spiritual gifts, and his courage. He revealed that he had no idea if Doezen or his parents were still alive. He didn't know if the monastery still stood or if his village still existed. But he had come to America because the man he revered above all others had told him his destiny was here.

Tenzin's words flowed like a clear spring from his heart. He spoke for nearly two hours. He concluded by saying that the choice confronting the modern world was either love or war, freedom or tyranny. The most important thing an individual could do for both his own well being and the future of the world was to heal his emotional wounds. To do so opened the door to the soul. A healed person was a window through which the infinite could enter the world. "Imagine," he concluded, "what the world would be if we were all consciously connected to the infinite?"

When he finished there was hardly a dry eye in the place. Some cried quietly, others sobbed.

He observed their emotional responses and said, "You are not crying for me. What I have shared with you has opened a place of universal compassion within you. From that place, you are crying for yourself and for the pain each of us must feel when tragedy and evil strikes some part of the human family. In that place, we are all one and we feel for each other. To be in that place is a healthy situation. To shed tears from that place is a gift. For some of you, your tears will release negative emotion and buried pain you didn't even know you had. Do not be afraid of it. It is a necessary and important step in your evolution. I am honored that so many of you have come. If anyone would like a private word, I will remain a while longer."

Tenzin was unprepared for what happened next. He thought most of the people would leave. He had spoken longer than expected. It was late. Yet no one left. Instead, they formed a line and came to him one by one. They hugged and thanked him. Many put their heads on his shoulder and cried. Some asked how they could work with him. Some kissed him on the cheek and said how much his words meant to them. Almost everybody said they would pray for his family, for Doezen, and for the monastery.

Emily sat quietly taking it all in. The tension in her body had melted away shortly after Tenzin started to speak. Tenzin's talk had moved her as much as everyone else. She watched how the young women were drawn as if by a magnet to the love he emanated. Their eyes were wide with a combination of awe and need.

How many of these young women, she thought, are already in love with him? They see great strength combined with gentleness and sensitivity. Who else has that kind of balance? The only other person she had met like that was Doezen. What Doezen had been to her, Tenzin might be to them. They feel his power and want to absorb as much of it as possible. He has awakened needs in many of these young women that they didn't even know they had, and wouldn't have ever known, unless they had met someone with his consciousness. I remember when I was younger and Doezen woke up that part of me.

Good thing he was much older, she chuckled quietly to herself. Good thing I was older too. I was happily married and I had a family to ground me. I wanted to explore my spirituality, not to have a romance with the person who opened the door and showed me in. In that I was lucky. These young women are in a different place. They think it's Tenzin they want, but it's the power that flows through him that they really seek. They don't know it yet, but what they are looking for is an experience of their deeper nature. They want to feel their soul and to find God. To these girls though, Tenzin is God. Lord knows, if I were young I'd probably feel as they do. He's irresistible. I wonder if he'll want to have a relationship? One thing for sure, he is totally unaware of all the fuss he's stirring up inside these girls. He'll have his choice among them all, if he wants it.

Tenzin was talking with the last few people remaining. Thomas was on stage with other faculty members. The Professor was thrilled with their feedback. Both students and faculty alike had urged him to bring Tenzin back on a regular basis.

After everyone had gone, the three of them left the hall together, each lost in their own thoughts. Emily was bursting with pride over his success. Thomas was elated because he had risked his reputation and his gamble had paid off.

Tenzin was the least exuberant of the three. More spiritual power had flowed through him that evening than he could ever remember. His voice had done the talking and his body had channelled the energy, but he knew it had all come from a source higher than himself. In his mind, it was his rinpoche speaking through him, and his teacher's light that had flowed into the audience.

Two weeks later, Emily awoke from a deep sleep to a dark and silent room. She pulled the comforter over her shoulders, determined to go back to sleep, but a voice called her name. She knew that voice, though she couldn't immediately place it. Again the voice called her name, and she felt a slight touch on her right shoulder. She turned to see Doezen, his ageless presence all light and energy rather than flesh and bone. A brilliant field of golden and white light extended around him. She felt herself immersed in his light. She was no longer grumpy and tired.

"Hello, Emily," Doezen said. His voice spoke in her mind, not in her ears. "Thank you for caring for Tenzin."

"It's wonderful to see you."

"I must tell you why I have come."

A knot of fear formed in her stomach.

"The Chinese executed the senior monks and burned the monastery. We sent everyone else into exile before they arrived. Everyone from Tenzin's village was killed."

"Oh no," she said. "Oh, Doezen. Our worst fears have come true!" The enormity of the tragedy hit her like a hard blow to the midsection. She instinctively drew her knees to her stomach and collapsed in tears.

"The world will be a bitter place without you, Doezen. It needs your light. But what of that poor young man? He has lost everything and everyone he ever loved. He has lost an entire life. What will become of him?"

"That is the reason I have come, Emily. You must grieve privately. No one is to know. Collect yourself. Soon a letter will come to inform Tenzin of what has happened. Pass through the shadows of your own grief before it arrives."

"I'll try," she said, her voice cracking.

"Tenzin will need you, Emily. You are all he has now. From here, the path gets steeper, the road more difficult. Meditate when you feel overwhelmed, find your center, and let your soul nourish you. Whenever someone is prepared to advance in the Light the dark side tests him to see if he is ready. That time has come. For Tenzin. And for you."

"Will you come back, Doezen?" she pleaded.

"I am with you more than you realize. Stay centered, little sister. See him through. There will be a brighter day at the end of this dark night."

"But what of you, Doezen? Did you suffer?"

"I left my body before the Chinese shot us. My life was complete, my work finished. It was time. For now, I can do far more from this side than I could in the physical body."

"Oh, Doezen, I am so sad and angry."

"Don't be. Those emotions serve no purpose. What's done is done."

"This is horrible beyond words. I am so worried for Tenzin."

"You must find the strength to be the strength for others, Emily. Don't drown in your own grief. Too much depends on you."

She raised her arm to protest, but before she could answer he was gone, dissolving without a trace, leaving her alone in the darkness. The weight of her unspent grief hung in her throat like stale air in a stone tomb.

CHAPTER 9

The Letter

TENZIN'S NEXT TALK was to occur in two weeks. When he wasn't fine tuning his English with Thomas, he studied at the UCLA library. Each day, he would learn twenty to thirty new words and read the newspaper from cover to cover. Then he would find an interesting book and read for a few hours. Usually he kept to himself, but after his talk his anonymity completely disappeared. Before long, students, especially young women, started dropping by his table in the library to talk to him.

One of the first to do so was Alice, the same student who had first asked Thomas to bring Tenzin to class. She approached him shyly, blushing, and asked if she could join him.

"Yes," he said. "Of course." He felt somewhat foolish about her request. He was a foreigner, not enrolled in the university like she was. "But if you would prefer to have this table to yourself I can find another. I don't wish to inconvenience you. I'm not a student here. I'm using the library to improve my English. I'm being tutored by one of the professors."

She smiled, trying to hide her awkwardness. It had taken courage to approach him. Was he trying to get rid of her or just being honest and humble? Maybe he just doesn't like me, she thought. Since he's a monk, he's probably not into women.

But instead of running away, she steadied herself and looked straight into his dark eyes. She saw no dislike there at all, only kindness.

She decided to take a big gamble. "Well," she said, "I really wanted to sit here and talk to you. So if you go to another table, I wouldn't be able to do that."

He smiled at her and she felt herself fluttering inside. "Then please join me," he said. "But you must bear with my English. It's far from perfect."

"You speak better English than most of us who have been speaking it all of our lives. We just don't have your accent. It's really cool."

"Cool? What do you mean by cool? Do you think my accent is chilly?"

She laughed, charmed by his vulnerability and confusion. "No, nothing like that. Cool means that you really appreciate someone or something. I like your accent. That's why I said that it's cool."

"Oh. Well, thank you. It makes me feel very different to have such an accent. I don't feel at home here yet. I have only been in America a few months."

"I know. I was at your lecture a couple of weeks ago. You were really great. My name is Alice."

"Thank you. I am glad you liked it. My name is Tenzin."

"I know."

"Yes, I guess you would if you were there. I'm sorry. I should have known that. Are you a student in Professor Kerr's seminar?"

"Yeah."

"He's a good teacher. If it wasn't for him I wouldn't be able to speak English. We have become good friends."

"You've made a big impression on campus."

"Is that good?"

"Sure. Everybody likes you."

He frowned. She worried that she had said something terribly wrong. The luster briefly faded from his eyes. He looked away before replying in a voice slightly above a whisper. "Sometimes popularity is not an advantage."

"Oh? Why?"

"In my country, the Chinese kill people that are popular."

"I'm really sorry about all that's happened in Tibet and everything that's happened to you," she said, the words racing out of her. "I hope your friends and family are okay. I've put them in my prayers. I hope that's all right."

"Yes, of course," he said, looking at her again. "Thank you for your concern. What is happening in Tibet is always on my mind. It is very difficult not to know what has happened to the people you love and worse not to be able to do anything for them. It is a very helpless feeling. That is one of the reasons I have worked so hard on my English. It keeps me focused and provides an important goal. Otherwise, I would be wound up with worry and unable to function."

She grew quiet as he spoke. He paused, thinking she wanted to say something, but she didn't speak, so he went on. "But you wanted to sit down at the table here and I have kept you standing. Please forgive me. I would be very honored if you would join me."

Her face broke into a wide smile. Tenzin suddenly realized how pretty she was. She had high cheek bones, accentuating her emerald eyes. Her face was framed by long, chestnut hair that sparkled in the sunlight pouring through the large windows of the reading room. Her silken skin was slightly tawny. She was clean, neat, and well composed. For a moment, Tenzin thought he was looking into the sun. Her smile warmed him to his core, stirring something inside him that he had never felt before. His reaction startled him, though he managed to keep it hidden. It is difficult enough, he thought, to discover the Self. The mystery of a woman is a whole other matter. Would loving one draw him away from liberation or bring him closer to it? It had never been an issue for him before. He had been around women very little since becoming a monk, but now he was beginning to feel an increased interest in them. Women had become central to his new life in America. Where would he be without Emily's help?

"Thanks," she said and sat down across from him. "I don't know where you get your strength. You're an ocean and a continent away from home in a strange place where you know few people. You have no idea what's become of your family and friends. It would crush me. I could never cope. I think a lot about what you must be going through."

"Thank you for your concern. I take each day and fill it with things to learn. If I just focus on the day at hand I can stay centered."

"I wish I had that ability. Your discipline is amazing." She leaned in a little closer. "You know," she said, "every girl in the seminar has a crush on you."

"What does crush mean?"

"It means they think you're cute and want to be with you."

"Be with me?"

"You know, be your girlfriend."

"Oh, my," he said. "I have never had a girlfriend. I know nothing about that."

"That's part of your attraction. They all want to be the first."

"I see," he replied, not seeing at all.

"Are you allowed to have a relationship with a girl?"

"I don't know," he said. "I haven't thought much about it. I'm in America by myself. Doezen gave me no instructions concerning women. I will have to find my way. Why do you ask?" His eyes sparkled with mischief. "Do you want to be my girlfriend, too?"

The deep blush on Alice's face answered for her. She changed the subject again, hoping he wouldn't notice. But Tenzin noticed everything. "I can't believe how different Professor Kerr is since meeting you. That's part of the reason I wanted to speak to you. Do you think you could help me as you helped him? I'd love to have the same thing happen to me."

"Not in the library," he said. "But I would be happy to do what I can. Let me ask Emily and Thomas if it would be acceptable if you joined our meditations. I will be here tomorrow afternoon and can give you an answer then. Is that okay?"

"That would be great," she said. "Oh my God, it's late. I've got to get to my next class. I'll see you tomorrow. Thanks." She rose quickly. He invited me back, she thought. He invited me back. Now if I can only keep the other girls away from him.

Tenzin lingered in the library until five, but, try as he might, he couldn't concentrate on his reading. That evening he told Thomas and Emily of his conversation with Alice.

"I think very highly of Alice," Thomas said. "She's conscientious, always prepared, and very bright. She has a big heart. She's spiritually inclined. I like the idea."

"What do you think Emily?" Tenzin said.

"I'm at a disadvantage. I don't know the girl like Thomas does. But if you both want her here, it's fine with me. It would balance the energy."

She kept the rest to herself. Her antennae had been fully extended the moment Tenzin had mentioned the girl. Emily had also heard what hadn't been said. She sensed a connection had already been formed between Tenzin and Alice and was certain that sexual energy was moving between them. So the dance has started, she thought. Well, that was quick. She had sensed it when he arrived that afternoon. He seemed more alive and happier than she could recall. At least she'd be able to observe the girl without anyone knowing what she suspected.

If she felt the relationship was not in his best interest, she would try to divert it before anything happened. On the other hand, if the girl would be good for Tenzin, she could nurture them both and help their relationship along. A relationship with a woman was probably inevitable. She had known that since the first time she had taken him to the beach. Tenzin was going to need all the love and support he could get soon enough. Better to have someone else nearby who cared about him. What better way to find out what she's made of and if she would be a suitable partner for him?

It's strange, she thought, about this grief. It only comes at night when I'm alone in bed. Then the tears take over. During the day I'm fine. I hardly think about it. But as soon as I put my head on the pillow the pain pours out of me. I cry for Doezen and Tibet and all the good that has been destroyed. But mostly I cry for Tenzin and all that he has lost and all the grief he must soon endure. I don't know how anyone could go through this without being crippled for life. I worry so for his future. He is such an extraordinary young man. What has happened is so horrible and unfair. It's too much for anyone to bear.

Then she heard him addressing her. "Emily, you seem very preoccupied. We should meditate now. It's time."

"Thank you, Tenzin," she said smiling her best smile. "I was just going over the shopping list for tomorrow. You have rescued me from the trivial and the boring."

The next afternoon, Tenzin was at the same table when Alice arrived. He pretended to be very focused on his task but inwardly he was worried that she might not come. As soon as she appeared his anxiety faded.

"Well," she said, smiling. "Here you are, sitting by yourself at the same table. I figured that there would be tons of girls around you today. I thought yesterday was a mistake because I had you all to myself. "

"Then you have been lucky two days in a row. But no one is lucky three days in a row."

She laughed.

"Would you like to sit down?"

"I'd love to, but I can't. I've got a big midterm tomorrow. But I really wanted to see you. Did you find out about meditation?"

"Yes. Thomas and Emily said it would be fine. We meet again tomorrow evening at 7:30. Can you come?"

"I wouldn't miss it for the world." Her smile conveyed her delight.

"It will be at Emily's house. Do you need directions?"

"I'm pretty sure I know where she lives. The big yellow house on Eleventh with the incredible garden?"

"How did you know?"

"It was on the garden tour last spring. She has a fabulous home. My apartment isn't far away so it will be easy to get there. I've got to go now. I'm really sorry. But I'm looking forward to tomorrow. Bye."

"Bye." The anxiety had left him. She had come like she had said she would and he would see her tomorrow. He went back to reading the paper, able to concentrate for the first time that day.

The next evening she arrived promptly at 7:30 p.m. Emily greeted her at the door. The day before, she had arranged for Thomas to come a bit early "to discuss the subject matter of Tenzin's next lecture." The two men were so wrapped up in their conversation that they didn't hear the bell ring. That's the way Emily had planned it, of course. She wanted her initial inspection of the girl to be on her terms.

"You must be Alice," she said. "I'm glad you could come." Her polished tone came from years of hosting dinners for heads of state and other dignitaries. In the State Department she had learned the art of being personable and outgoing without being personally involved. It was a skill that had multiple uses. Primarily, it gave her the emotional distance necessary to see beyond her guests personas and into their real natures. Emily Chase was an astute woman and an excellent judge of character.

"Thank you for letting me join you, Mrs. Chase. I'm so excited to be here."

With those first words Alice flashed her smile, warm, bright, and genuine. The tone of her voice and the quality of her smile were the door to who she was. Emily observed how easily that door swung open and knew there was nothing devious in her nature.

What you see with this one, she surmised, is what's really there. She reminds me a lot of the way I was when I was her age. She's bright and attractive. She's got a heart of gold, and she's crazy about Tenzin. I can't help but think that this whole situation has been set up by a force far wiser than any of us. Tenzin may soon have to face the unendurable, but at least he's got the beginnings of a first class support system around him.

"Well, my dear. I'm very happy to have you here," Emily said. "You are lovely. The two men are in the study waiting for us. They both think highly of you, you know. Now I see why. Shall we go join them? "

"Really? I was a little nervous about meeting you. I was here last spring during the garden tour and I thought then that your home was amazing. I remember thinking at the time I'd love to spend time here someday." Alice took a deep breath and let out a happy sigh. "And now I get to meditate with you. Never in my wildest dreams did I think anything like this would happen. Thank you again for letting me come."

"Alice," Emily said, smiling now in a very personal way. "You are most welcome and I am very pleased that you have come."

Tenzin and Thomas were deep in conversation when they entered. "Tenzin, Thomas, Alice is here. And right on time, too."

The men rose together, smiling. They were both glad she was here, although for different reasons. Alice was one of Prof. Kerr star pupils and he wanted to show her off. He knew she'd make a strong impression on Tenzin and Emily. The girl was good with people. She was forthright, caring and warm. Alice was destined for success in whatever field she chose. He wished she'd go into Eastern religions and Asian culture as he had, get a Ph.D. and someday teach at the university level. He hoped that if she started meditating with them she'd get more involved in following the path he had projected for her. Of course, he was thoroughly ignorant of how involved she already was.

They sat in the chairs that faced the garden. Tenzin sat on the floor. Thomas lit a stick of frankincense, struck the meditation bell and dimmed the light. When the soft tone of the bell faded into silence Tenzin began to chant in Tibetan.

After a time, the chant, like the bell, disappeared into the silence of the study. "Tonight we will focus on the breath," said Tenzin. "Place your attention on your navel. Breathe into it. When you exhale, breathe out of it. Focus your mind there during the meditation. Your mind will wander. When you realize it is wandering, bring your focus back to your navel. Begin now."

At first, Alice had a great deal of trouble with the exercise. She didn't become as peaceful or as energized as she thought she would. Instead, an endless parade of thoughts wound out of control in her mind. Her discomfort was obvious. Tenzin watched her carefully. After letting her flail for a while he came to her aid.

"Deepen your breath, Alice. Find the power point four inches beneath your navel. Focus there. Breathe in and out from that point. Count your exhalations. The first exhalation is one. The next exhalation is two. Count until you reach ten. Then start the cycle over at one. Repeat it until the exercise is over."

God, thought Alice, even more agitated now. I thought this was going to be fun but it's worse than calculus. I'm no good at it at all. What am I doing here? I can't wait to leave.

On and on her mind spun, distracting and annoying her. She tried to follow Tenzin's instructions. After several minutes of what seemed like failure, a shift occurred in her nervous system. She became peaceful and relaxed. Her breath was breathing her now; she was merely observing it. She felt empty and weightless. Her mind was incredibly clear. She no longer desired to leave. Instead, her only thought was to remain in this state and deepen her tranquility. Her mind was at rest, no longer working against her. Her system seemed to be in perfect harmony. She had never felt this kind of peace before.

A moment later she became aware of a golden flame at the base of her spine. It warmed her hips and thighs and relaxed her even more. The flame soon gathered force, leaping up her spine and flowing into her skull. She heard a crashing sound like surf breaking on the shore. Then she was standing in front of a man in a red robe. He was bald; his deeply lined face seemed ageless. A soft golden light emanated from the center of his chest and a noticeable gentleness shone in his eyes. Much to her surprise, Alice realized that she wasn't at all afraid. Then she heard his voice in her mind.

"So, this time you have come with both your soul and your mind. Always before, your mind was sleeping and unaware of your soul's journey. This time you will remember your experience. Your friends have given you the energy you need to stay conscious at this level. Nothing happens by accident, little sister. Your path is about to unfold. Follow your inner voice. It will lead you in the right direction. To hear it, you must be still and peaceful, as you are now. You will know that voice because it will feel right and true in your body. Be deliberate and centered in what you do. Do not act on impulse or in haste. Remember that I am always with you, never more so than in the days to come."

He bowed and, without warning, vanished from her mind. His disappearance dropped her soul back into her body. The impact of her re-entry into her body was a shock. She opened her eyes, feeling dizzy and disoriented, her mind spinning. Part of her felt as if she were still in that higher realm with him. Tenzin saw that her soul was expanded and more luminous than before. What he didn't know was what she had experienced to produce that result.

"So Alice," he said as she adjusted to being back in her body. "How are you?"

"Okay, I guess. What just happened? I mean I don't know if I made that up or if it was real."

"Alice," Thomas said. "You look as if you've seen a ghost."

"You know, I really might have."

"What did you experience?" Tenzin asked.

"When we started, I was really restless and wanted to leave. But then, after you told me what to do, I became really peaceful. I'd never felt like that before. The next thing I knew I was in a place I'd never been with a bald guy in a red robe. I wasn't scared or anything. In fact, I felt as if I'd always known him. He told me to follow my inner voice; that my path was about to unfold."

"Anything else?" said Tenzin.

"He said he'd always be with me," Alice answered.

Tenzin looked at her quizzically. "I'll be right back."

When he returned he carried his robe and a worn, wrinkled photograph. "Was the robe the man wore anything like this one?" he said.

"It was identical. Only it wasn't torn."

"Do you recognize the man in this picture?" he asked, showing her the picture.

"That's him! Who is that?"

"Doezen."

"That's Doezen? Oh, my God, why did he come to me?"

"I don't know," said Tenzin. "But I'm sure we'll know soon enough."

So far, Emily had watched but remained silent. Her face showed no emotion but inside she was very relieved. She was more right about this girl than she had imagined. Doezen himself was orchestrating the whole thing.

Tenzin and Alice are already connected, she thought. Do they have a link from a past lifetime? They must. Old souls are drawn to old souls they have known before. The magnetic energy between them on the soul plane draws them to each other. Since the connection already exists, it doesn't have to be created. They only have to get to know each other again. That must be what's happening. And to think I was worried that Tenzin was going to get involved with women who would take advantage of his naiveté, hurt him terribly, and take him from his path. Instead, whoever is protecting him sent him what he needed when he needed it most. Too much energy is flowing between them to think otherwise. They are deeply connected. I would guess it's going to take them a little while to figure it all out.

She allowed herself a faint smile, relaxed a bit and let her tension dissipate. If they make it through the trials ahead, she reflected, they'll probably be together for a long time. Tenzin has such power to draw good things and people to him, but I don't think he's particularly conscious of it. People seem to appear when they're needed. He will face a hard, hard time but he won't face it alone, thank God. Her relief was tempered, however, by the knowledge of the pain ahead and the tears she was fighting to hold back.

"Emily," Tenzin asked. "Do you think Doezen would come to Alice without a purpose?"

Emily pushed back her tears. Tenzin never noticed. His concern was elsewhere.

"I don't think Doezen would ever do anything without a purpose," she said.

"Why do you think he came to Alice?"

"He came into my life when I was ready to find my path. Maybe he's here to help Alice find hers."

"Perhaps. None of us would be here without Doezen. Doezen healed you, Emily, and he sent me to you. You brought me to Thomas and Thomas invited me to speak to his seminar where I met Alice. Now Doezen appeared to Alice in meditation. He is the glue that binds us together."

"Where is this all going?" Alice asked. "It's all so new. I never experienced anything like it before. It's scary. My mind is whirring trying to figure it all out."

"The mind," said Tenzin, "is the last part of you to know. It will make trouble before it takes you to the truth. I learned that the hard way the night Doezen and I crossed the field of stones on the way back to the monastery from an outlying village. It was dark and there was no moon to guide us. As long as my mind was quiet and I listened to my intuition, I was safe. But as soon as I admitted a fearful thought, I slipped. There were deep fissures and crevasses all around us. To fall into one would have been fatal." He paused for a moment, reflecting on his adventure with Doezen, the rash impetuousness that had led him into trouble, and the lack of self-discipline that had almost gotten him killed. "I do not know what is being planned for us from the other side of life. That is veiled. But I feel certain that whatever comes has been put in place to help us go forward. These coincidences are neither random nor meaningless. They are links, pieces of a puzzle, that when put together will help us fulfill our destinies. One of those links was formed over forty years ago when Emily met Doezen. Another occurred more than ten years ago when I came to the monastery to study. Still another was put in place when Doezen sent me to America. Another link was created when Emily arranged for Thomas to tutor me. Another link manifested when I healed Thomas. Another link occurred when you asked Thomas to bring me to the seminar. The final link occurred when you asked me to teach you to meditate and I invited you to join us. Take any link out of that process and we never make it here. Each experience in itself seems complete and separate, but is part of a sequence of events leading somewhere. Life is a series of events woven together into an exquisite tapestry by a master designer. As we live our lives, we are often blind to our destination. I know no more about where we are going than you do."

Six days later, on a gray Wednesday morning, a letter arrived in the mail for Tenzin. Emily picked up the post that day in the mailbox at the front gate of the property as she always did. She had wondered each morning since Dozen's visitation if today would be the day.

She sorted through the mail order catalogs as she entered the foyer until she came to the personal correspondence. "Nothing dangerous so far," she thought, relieved. There were letters that day from one of her daughters, two of her friends, and a former colleague from her government days. There was also a letter from her alma mater, no doubt looking for money. She threw it out, along with all the mail order catalogs. As she did, a smaller envelope, hidden among the rest, fell to the floor. It was light yellow with the Indian words for Air Mail printed in red. It was addressed to Tenzin. She gasped as she picked it up. The color drained from her face; her legs turned to rubber. This day was not going to go as planned. She wasn't sure if she could make it out of the kitchen, let alone out of the house.

That day the Mercedes stayed in the garage. Her errands would have to wait. She retreated to her study, collapsed in her favorite chair, and tried to calm herself. The more she tried to regain her self-control the more upset she became. Finally, she stopped fighting her feelings and gave them free rein.

She screamed, damned God, and cursed the Chinese. When her screams stopped, her tears began. Her grief threw her into a bloated stream of endless suffering. She descended into a prison world that groaned with unending agony, a place shorn of all hope or any possibility of escape. Every minute in this cold hell seemed to last forever. She was sure her agony was eternal.

The dark prison was awash with the echoes of those who had perished there long ago, alone and in torment. It was a forsaken place, full of bitterness and rage. Forgiveness had never entered the hearts of those trapped here. Mercy had never found them. Grace had never redeemed them. Her own grief and rage had sentenced her to the prison of the unredeemed. She was surrounded on all sides with the undying screams of the dead, sentenced to remain here by their own stubborn failure to forgive. She was terrified that like them, she would never leave; that she would never find the way out. Darkness clamped itself around her heart.

Was she really doomed to lie down in darkness with those who had never found the light? This fate was too terrible to contemplate. A new series of screams rose out of the bitterness clogging her heart, a turgid river of sludge choking off the light inside her. She lost all semblance of control, writhed on the floor, screamed and flailed as the dark weight inside her refused to let her go. Sweat poured down her face, ran in rivulets down her back, and oozed out of her abdomen. She was soaking wet and exhausted by both her efforts and her fear.

Then inexplicably, it was over. She had found the way out. She didn't know how or why and didn't care. Escape was all that mattered.

At first, she didn't quite believe it. She felt her fingers and toes, looked out at the dying afternoon light. She was really back. She looked around, afraid of what she might see, thinking it would be the same darkness she had just climbed out of. But it was her room as she remembered it. Everything was in order. The only sound was the rhythmic ticking of the clock. She looked over to see what time it was. Four-thirty. She had been in hell for five hours.

Tenzin will be home in an hour, she thought. I've got to be ready. She forced herself to rise, went to her room and drew a hot bath, letting the water wash her clean. She put on her favorite red dress with a yellow belt around her waist. She wanted Tenzin to be reminded of the colors of his order when he learned what had happened. She wanted to remind him that even though the night may come, colder and harsher than anyone might think possible, light and warmth inevitably followed. She wanted to hold him and shield him from the pain, from going into that place she had just come from, knowing there was a chance that if he went there he might not get out, or might be a long time in doing so. She wanted to protect him from all of that but was powerless to do so. A red dress was all she had.

At five-thirty Tenzin returned from the library where as usual he had been reading. Alice had found him there after her last class and they had continued their conversation about the previous evening's events. He felt happy in her company and invited her home for supper. He was sure Emily would not object.

"You know, Tenzin," Emily had said that morning. "Alice is a very nice girl. I would like to see more of her. Bring her home any time."

And so he had. Emily was surprised to see Alice with him when they came through the front door, but she didn't show it. With all the upheaval, she had forgotten her remarks of the morning. Now she remembered. No accident, she thought, that both of us are here for him. The time has come for all of us to find out what we're made of. May God be with us.

"Hi, Emily. I brought Alice home for dinner. Hope that's O.K. I'm sorry I didn't call ahead to ask. We just got so caught up in our discussion that I forgot everything else."

He's already in love and doesn't even know it, she thought. I hope this is part of the plan. "Of course it's alright. Didn't I tell you this morning to bring Alice home anytime? Alice, I'm very pleased to see you and glad you can be with us for dinner."

"Thank you Emily. I'm very happy to be here." She didn't have to speak. It was in her eyes. She stayed very close to Tenzin, her hands touching him whenever possible.

Well, thought Emily, is now the moment of truth or do I put it off until later? Putting it off solves nothing. Better face it now while spirits are high and love is in the air. But at least, I'll wait until dinner is over. That gives them a little more time to enjoy the first sweet moments of love.

"Dinner will be ready at six-thirty. Why don't the two of you use the third floor study? I've got some correspondence to take care of. I'll have Maria call you when it's time."

When dinner was over and they were getting ready to leave the table, Emily decided the moment had come.

"Tenzin," she said. "A letter came for you today from India. It's in the study. I'll get it for you."

She tried to downplay it, make it a casual, mundane event of no great importance. She fooled no one. Tenzin tensed visibly the moment she mentioned a letter. His face became an inscrutable mask. Alice felt the energy in the room shift, as if someone had just slammed on the brakes. She was acutely aware of Tenzin's anxiety, even though he had done his best to hide it. She grew frightened for him.

Tenzin rose silently, betraying nothing. He maintained his dignity as best he could, and followed Emily into the study. Silently, she handed him the letter. He recognized the handwriting as Nawang's. He opened the letter and moved near a lamp across the room to read it by himself. Emily and Alice stood across the room by the big oak desk watching him. The two women said nothing, but their clenched hands and strained faces conveyed their terror.

Tenzin finished reading and looked up. His face was a cipher. He looked out into the darkness. He could feel nothing. He couldn't think. His mind was blank. His legs trembled slightly. He thought he might collapse but willed himself to remain rigid and show nothing of his inner state. He was determined not to lose his dignity in front of the women. His dignity was all he had left.

A few minutes passed. The atmosphere in the room grew heavier and more oppressive. Once again, the only sound was the ticking of the grandfather clock. Finally, Emily summoned her courage. "What did the letter say, Tenzin?"

He didn't respond, or even hear her question. His energy was consumed by his need to retain his pride and not betray his weakness. Emily spoke again, this time with more force. "Tenzin, tell us what the letter said."

The strength in her voice caught him off guard and brought him back to the room. "It was from Nawang," he said. He found speaking difficult. He stammered slightly. "H-horrible things have happened. The Chinese executed Doezen and the other senior lamas. The rest of the monks were sent to India just before the Chinese arrived, shortly after Nawang and I left. The Chinese executed everyone in my village. There were no survivors. My parents, sisters, nephews and nieces are dead."

In spite of being prepared, Emily felt the dark space in her abdomen opening again. She tried to close it but could not. Her strength had fled. She collapsed in a nearby chair. Alice could feel Tenzin's pain even though he was in shock and could not feel it himself. The more he tried to separate himself from his feelings, the more Alice felt the agony he was avoiding. She hurried across the room, put her arms around his chest, laid her head on his neck and sobbed, her cries rising from deep in the pit of her stomach. Tenzin was dimly aware that his arms held her. If circumstances were different, he would have long remembered the first touch of her skin, the softness of her breast as it rose and fell against him, the smell of her hair. But he remembered none of this. He hovered in some frozen place, unable to feel. He had crossed a line. Between him and the rest of the world, a wall stood thick and impenetrable. Nothing could reach across that invisible barrier and touch him now. They held fast together, but he wasn't there.

CHAPTER 10

Limbo

SANTA MONICA 1951

WEEKS WENT BY. Tenzin remained in shock, numb and silent, sitting in his room or on the porch staring blankly at the city and the sea. He did little, said even less. Thomas came in the late afternoons to talk with him, but Tenzin rarely responded. He barely noticed that he had a visitor. Thomas was not dismayed by Tenzin's lack of civility, at least in the beginning. He understood his friend's anguish and remained steadfast in his resolve to help him. He came when he could, as often as he could. He believed that if he spent enough time reading to him and conveying his love, Tenzin would return to the land of the living. Thomas was convinced the cure would be quick and the outcome certain. The Professor came of strong Scottish stock, and was as stubborn and determined as any of his kinsman. But he was out of his depth in dealing with the despair that had overwhelmed Tenzin.

Emily was lucid, but given to long spells of grief that came on without warning. Due to the unpredictable nature of her grief, she was unable to provide consistent comfort to Tenzin. Whenever she tried to do so, she inevitably broke down. In the end, she thought the best she could do was to let him be.

One day, Thomas approached her after another fruitless visit with Tenzin. He wasn't getting any better. "You know Emily," Thomas said. "This has been going on for a long time. I'm beginning to think that if we let it go on much longer Tenzin might never pull out of this. I'm afraid for him. Maybe we should have him admitted to a psychiatric hospital and placed under professional care."

Emily fixed her glare on him. Over the years, that look had withered many recipients. Thomas felt its cold intensity boring into him and wished that he could recant his words. Telltale beads of sweat formed on his brow.

"Where is your conviction, Thomas? You were the one who said that reading and love would bring him back. Why should we take him to a hospital? So they can fill him with drugs, subject him to electric shock, and house him in a ward for the disturbed? Do you want him stripped of his dignity? What chance would he have then?"

"But Emily, they might cure him. We haven't."

"Thomas, remember your roots. The Scottish have no quit in them. And remember about whom you're talking? Tenzin is a Tibetan monk. He will resolve his grief in his own way. Drugs and doctors would destroy him."

"But what can we do? I feel so helpless."

"Stop whining! You're feelings are counter productive. Sit with him. Talk to him. Pray for him. Be patient with him. Have faith in who he is. You have helped him, even though you can't see any visible improvement. The time you spend with him is an anchor that keeps him from slipping into darker waters. Your helplessness helps no one. If you really love him, be strong in his behalf. Healing happens in its own time, not in ours. Only you can decide to follow it through or to give it up. But there will be no hospital for Tenzin. Do you understand that, Thomas?"

"Yes, Emily, I do," sighed Thomas. "But is being with him really enough?"

"It is all we have. Give that young man some credit. He's been dealt a cruel, cruel blow. He's reeling. We all are. But his core is sound and strong. I have great faith in him. One day, something will happen that we can't foresee. The tide will turn and he'll come back to himself. Until then, we wait."

While Emily couldn't help Tenzin directly, she watched over and protected him as well as she could. Alice spent more time with him than anyone. When she wasn't in class, she sat with him in his room or on the porch, telling him about events in school and asking him questions about meditation, prayer, chanting, or anything she could think of. The questions he heard, he answered with a grunt. Those that he didn't were met with silence.

Sometimes, when it became too tough for her and the thoughts came that she had lost him for good and he would never come back, Alice would withdraw for a while and go to a movie with a friend or take a walk on the beach. Tears often dripped down her cheeks while she strode through the surf. But when the despairing mood lifted, she'd come back, determined to see it through, feeling in her heart that here was where she must be. She was certain that one day he'd come back, this beautiful man who had walked like a young god into her heart. The vision of his return fed her hope and sustained her through the long, dark time.

During this time Emily and Alice grew very close. Alice would sit with Emily in her study nearly every day before going up to see Tenzin. She'd bring her the afternoon paper and coffee. They would talk about the past and their hopes for the future. Emily told Alice stories of life abroad and the many ups and downs of her husband's career. Those stories were a barrier, however frail, against the gathering tide of grief inside her. Alice proved to be a good listener. Emily always felt better whenever Alice was there. Soon, both of them began to count on their time together. One afternoon, as Alice was preparing to leave, Emily made her an interesting proposition.

"You know, dear," she said, "You're here whenever you're not in school. You have been a very great help to me. I know for certain I would not be feeling better if it weren't for you. Your presence is very soothing. This is a big, old house. I've got more rooms than I can use. Why don't you live with us? The big bedroom on the second floor would be ideal for you. You could set up a study in the next room for schoolwork. UCLA is only minutes away and you wouldn't have to pay rent."

"Do you mean it? I could give up my part time job and be here more often."

"Of course, I mean it. How soon can you come?"

"Let's see. How about the weekend after next? That's the end of the month."

"That would be ideal. It gives me time to have the room repainted and the bathroom freshened up for you. You love him a great deal, don't you, dear?"

Alice's face turned a bright red. She hadn't anticipated the question or the direct manner in which Emily had asked it.

"I do," she answered quietly.

"He's very lucky to have you. I dread to think where any of us would be without you. When he first asked permission to bring you to meditation I knew that energy was flowing between you. And when I met you, I was also sure of you. None of this is an accident, Alice. It has all been planned. He needs you more than he will ever know. Because you're here, he can't fail. You're strong medicine. Stick to him as closely as you can, as long as you can. Remember who he is. He's too strong not to come back. There is so much light inside him. I don't think anything in life can really break him. Hurt him deeply? Yes. Cut him to the quick? Yes. But break him? No."

"Thank you for saying that. It makes me feel much better. I just want him back."

"Don't worry. He'll be back one day when we least expect it."

The time passed quickly. Alice was living at Emily's but little else had changed. A full three months had passed since Tenzin had received the letter from Nawang. May had arrived. The days were increasingly warm and bright. Flowers bloomed in the garden and on the balcony. The yard was awash in color. A gentle breeze blew in daily from the ocean and faint wisps of clouds trailed in the sky. The end of the semester was approaching. Alice prepared for finals, studying long hours and writing a term paper for Thomas's seminar. Except for going back and forth to class, she hadn't spent much time outdoors for weeks. She was pale and tired. The pressures of her life were taking a toll.

Emily watched from the distance, observing but not interfering, growing more concerned daily about the strain on Alice.

"You know, Alice," she finally said one afternoon. "You have gone way beyond what anyone should do. Enough is enough. You need time off. You're young. You need a life. You don't have much of one now. Get away for a while. Go out and have some fun. Go to the beach. Go hiking. Be with your friends. Go dancing. Get some fun in your life. I'm better now. I'll spell you."

"Are you sure? Are you really ready to handle it, Emily?"

"Until you appeared I was a mess. Now my grief is gone. I'm fine. Go have fun. That's an order. If you don't, I'll have to ask you to leave this house. I won't be responsible for another nervous breakdown."

"Then, I accept. Thanks, Emily."

"Young lady, you can't keep giving when you've got nothing left. When you feel ready to come back and sit with Tenzin, stay away for another week. Then come back. Now off with you."

For the next few weeks, Emily sat with Tenzin in the afternoon while Alice went out in the sunshine, visited with friends, and lived the life of the college student she was. During that time, Tenzin sat silently on the porch, often in meditation for hours. Emily would sit with him, knitting or crocheting until he emerged from meditation. Then she'd read aloud from the newspaper, hoping he would show some interest in the world and the people who loved him.

With the pressure of finals, it took Alice more than a month to recharge. She saw Tenzin infrequently, staying away intentionally. She knew that if she went to him, the pull on her heart would be too strong to ignore. But after several weeks, with her energy restored, she started to miss him mightily. Late one afternoon she made her way to the third floor. He was alone on the porch, looking at a newspaper Emily had left for him in the hope he might read it. Bored and restless, he had picked it up and flipped through the pages. He was shocked when he saw the date. He had no idea it was June. Where had the time gone? And where had he been? Everything about the last few months seemed so vague.

Alice walked out to the veranda. Tenzin looked up and nodded, the first sign of recognition he had given her since he had received the letter from Nawang. The nod was slight, barely there, but her heart soared.

He's coming back, she thought. He's coming back. I can't wait to tell Emily. She sat down beside him and told him about finals and how much she had missed him during that time.

"Really?" he said. "You missed me?"

She could hardly believe that he had spoken, but she answered without hesitation."Yes," she said. "I missed you a lot. How do you feel? You haven't said anything in months."

"It's been that long?"

"Yes. Do you remember what happened?" The question had to be asked some time. Might as well get it out of the way now. She held her breath and braced herself for his response.

A dark cloud passed over his face. "Yes," he whispered.

"Tenzin, you can't sit here forever. You have to get back to life and let people in. We've all been worried about you."

"You're right. I must get back to life. I just don't know how."

"Look, it's a beautiful day. It's June. The ocean is warm. Let's go to the beach. Being near the water will help. It's a start."

"All right."

Alice couldn't contain herself any longer. He was on his way back. She felt as if she would burst, so she ran over and gave him a big hug. Tenzin was caught by surprise. He blushed, but he did not push her away. Her warm body pressed against him comforted the raw hole in his heart. Tears formed in his eyes and a knot rose in his throat. If this continued he would fall apart. He still wasn't ready to do that in front of anyone.

"Come, Alice. Let's go to the beach," he managed to say.

She sensed his fragility and stepped back. "Your wish is my command, master," she said.

They went down the stairs to the first floor study. Emily was on the phone with her back to the door. Alice walked in with Tenzin behind her.

"Hi Emily. Sorry for interrupting, but I thought you'd want to know that *we're* going to the beach."

The "we're" rang in Emily's head like a bell. She turned to see an ecstatic Alice with Tenzin standing behind her. She felt the electricity surge through her too, but she did not betray her excitement. She simply nodded and said, "Have fun." She went back to her conversation as if nothing had happened. When she was sure the two of them were out of hearing she spoke quietly to her friend, her hand cupped around the handset as a precaution.

"Carol. You won't believe what just happened. Tenzin just came down the stairs with Alice. She's taking him to the beach. He's coming round. My God, I can't believe it. I knew he'd make it back. I knew it!"

Tenzin and Alice went down to the beach, making their way to the water's edge. They looked out toward the horizon where the sea joined the sky. The late afternoon sun made them squint. A few yards from where they stood, seagulls hunted for fish. Sunlight danced on the peaks of the waves as they rushed toward the shore and crashed on the sand. They took off their shoes and waded in the surf, the cool sand under their feet, the warm sea caressing their legs. Alice took Tenzin's hand, her heart beating rapidly. She had to fight hard to keep her excitement from getting the best of her. She told him about her finals and that everyone in the seminar had asked about him. He asked her what questions Thomas had given them about Tibetan Buddhism. She started to answer when the crying of a young child caught their attention.

A little boy of Chinese descent was sitting in the water sobbing, his chest heaving. A wave had knocked him down and frightened him. The child's father ran over and swept him up in his arms. He held the boy close to chase the fear away. A wave of remembrance rushed through Tenzin.

His own father had soothed his fears like that when Tenzin was a young boy. Loss and longing overwhelmed him. He tried to dismiss his grief but he could not. The wall he had constructed to shield him from his agony had been permanently shattered. He let out a low moan. His body shook. His legs trembled. He felt heavy and weak. The tears that had been dammed up for so long rushed out of him. Alice led him out of the surf to a deserted area on the beach. She sat him down, put his head against her breast, and wrapped an arm around his shoulder. She stroked his brow with her other hand. His tears didn't stop until the sun sank into the ocean.

When they returned to the house Tenzin went straight to bed. He wasn't hungry. His grief had completely exhausted him. Alice made sure he was comfortable, then went downstairs to eat with Emily.

"Well, my dear, you must tell me all of it. How is he?"

"He's coming back, Emily. His outpouring of grief has started."

"That's good. That's very good. The more he grieves the better. Grief cures grief, dear. Doezen taught me that. Such a strange thing to say isn't it, but so true. Who among us wants to face ultimate pain? But only in facing that pain do we grow strong. Do you think God gives us the unbearable for just such a purpose? I have often thought so."

"I don't know, Emily. I haven't had enough experience with grief to have an opinion."

"Of course not. How foolish of me even to ask that question. If we're fortunate, grief comes later in life, not while we're young. Can I share something with you that age has taught me?"

"Sure."

"Experience is the only true teacher. Real learning doesn't come from books, but from life. Books can instruct, inform, and inspire, but unless you have the consciousness to grasp what they are saying the words are meaningless. We earn what we learn from life. What you are doing, dear, is phenomenal given your youth. You have a maturity beyond your years."

"Thanks for the kind words, Emily," said Alice. "But I'm not so sure. I don't feel mature. I feel sort of lost really. I'm just feeling my way with Tenzin. I worry about screwing it up all the time. I'm way out of my depth. It scares me."

"We're all a little lost here, young lady, and we're all worried about "screwing it up". But you are not out of your depth. Not at all. Trust your instincts. They're impeccable."

"Do you know what I've been thinking lately?"

"What's that, Alice?"

"Do you think there is something important for Tenzin to learn from all this?"

"Undoubtedly. He lost his whole world. Everything and everyone he ever loved is gone. I expect his grief to be long and immense. The important point is that he has started the journey. Whatever he has to learn from this experience will unfold slowly and change him in ways we cannot anticipate now. Of that I am sure."

"Do you think those changes will take him away from us?"

"Oh, dear," said Emily, unable to stifle a laugh. "Whatever changes occur in Tenzin will only bring him closer to you."

"You think?"

"I certainly do. That young man is in love with you."

Alice sighed deeply. "Oh, Emily, I sure hope you're right. I keep hoping. What else can we do for him?"

"Just be there when he needs us. But don't smother him. He's a proud man. We can't make him feel as though he's losing his dignity or that we're emasculating him."

"At least he's here now. That helps."

"You've had a lot to do with it. Real love takes the jobs no one wants. When God sends us grief, he often sends his angels to help us through it. That's my belief, anyway. He sent us you."

"Oh, I'm no angel."

"Oh, dear, but you are." Emily gave Alice a hug. "I'm tired. It's been a long day. I'll see you in the morning."

That night the hard dreams started for Tenzin. He was back in his childhood with his parents and friends. He was with them but he knew it was a dream even while he dreamt it. He knew he would have to leave them when it was over. The dream resurrected his longing to go back to when things were innocent, when his parents were alive, when he still felt safe in the world. Knowing that he would never again be loved so thoroughly and unconditionally brought the tears, even though he was sleeping. He woke as the first light of day stole silently into his room. He hovered between then and now, between Tibet and Los Angeles. He wanted to climb back into the past, but his consciousness interceded and he was forced to realize that he was stuck in the present. Sweat soaked his pajamas. He felt as tired upon waking as he had upon lying down. He threw off the covers and stared at the ceiling, trying not to think about the past.

CHAPTER 11

The Sole Survivor

TIBET 1950

THE YOUNG BOY, recently turned four, wiped his face. His hands were covered in his mother's blood. It blended with the remnants of his tears and sent random red lines of grief running down his cheeks. He waddled over to where his grandfather lay motionless on the stained ground. He tapped his grandfather's shoulder but he did not respond. He called out for him but he did not move. He cried out to the villagers lying next to him but they did not stir. Abandoned, alone, and terrified by the horror that surrounded him, he collapsed in a new wave of tears. He climbed onto his grandfather's back, wrapped his little arms around the old man's neck and cried himself to sleep.

In the late afternoon, with the sun hovering near the horizon and the temperature dropping fast, a man and his teenage son crept warily into the village. Yesterday, they had been working in their fields a few miles to the north of their village when the Chinese attacked. The farmer and his son heard the distant sound of gunfire, dropped their hoes and rushed home. They were too late. Their family and friends lay lifeless, their blood slipping silently into the soil. In the distance, the long column of Chinese infantry snaked its way through the valley below.

They checked everyone in the village for signs of life: wives, children, neighbors, friends. No pulse. No breath. No sound. No movement. Nothing. They went into every house. Prone and lifeless bodies lay everywhere, dead eyes staring at nothing, faces frozen in terror. There were no survivors.

"Why did they do this to us, Father? We aren't soldiers. No one had a gun. We weren't a threat to them." The son sobbed violently. He doubled over and threw up. His name was Kalden. He was thirteen years old.

His father, Norbu, wrapped his arms around him. He had no words for this unspeakable horror, no answers. They stood in each other's arms, gripped by the first spasms of a terrible grief.

"We must go to the next village," said Norbu. He ran his fingers through his long gray hair. "We have to try to get there before the Chinese. Maybe we can save them. The Chinese went through the valley. We'll go through the mountains. If we're fast enough we might get there first. It's a big if, but we have to try."

"I can't go, Father," said Kalden. "I have no strength. I can't move. Beside, we can't leave our people like this."

"We can do nothing for them now, Kalden. We have a chance to save the living." He squeezed his son's arms and shook him. "Now is the time for courage, my son."

Norbu had many friends in the village some thirty miles away, including Naljor, Tenzin's father, and his family.

"Yes, Father," sighed the boy. "But can't we at least do something for mother?"

Kalden looked out over the corpses littering the village square. Norbu's eyes followed his son's. "Close her eyes, Kalden. The buzzards will do the rest. We must leave immediately."

Kalden gently closed his mother's eyes, then kneeled on the ground and kissed her cheek. His fresh, warm tears splashed on her cold face.

Norbu put food and a few blankets into woven bags. He returned to the square and handed one to Kalden. They tossed their only remaining possessions over their shoulders and left the village for the last time. For the rest of that day they walked through the mountains as fast as their tired legs could carry them. When the light was gone, they lay down on the cold stones and slept. They rose before dawn and resumed their journey to outrun the Chinese.

They entered Naljor's village late that afternoon. Their eyes darted into every shadow, their ears strained to hear every stray sound, wary of a Chinese ambush. The place was eerily still. Dead bodies lay in grotesque positions in the center of the village. They were too late. Norbu wiped his brow, covered his face with his hands and sank to his knees. An endless stream of tears oozed down his cheeks.

These people, like those in his village, had never harmed anyone. Now they were dead. Slaughtered without remorse. Tibet was a poor country. It had a scantily equipped army consisting of ten thousand men, mostly farmers, two hundred fifty machine guns, and a cavalry who fought with swords. They were no threat to a modern army. Tibet's only treasures were the mountains and an ancient spiritual tradition. Why were the Chinese doing this? Norbu sagged to the ground and struck his face repeatedly on the soil. In the midst of his agony he failed to see the obvious. The Chinese had invaded Tibet because they could.

His sobs woke the little boy. The child looked up from where he lay on his grandfather's back. His small body shivered with the cold and shock. Kalden heard the movement.

"Father!"

Norbu raised his head and saw the little boy staring at him. Kalden ran over and picked him up.

"He's freezing!"

"Bring him here, Kalden." Norbu wiped the tears off his face.

The young man brought the boy to his father. Norbu wrapped the child in his woolen cloak.

"I know this child," said Norbu. "This is Dorjee, Naljor's grandson. Get him some water, Kalden. Go into the houses. Find him some food. He probably hasn't eaten all day."

Dorjee ate like a hungry wolf while Norbu held him. When he had finished eating, Norbu washed the blood off his face.

"Check that house over there, Kalden," Norbu said. "I think that's his. Get him some warm clothes. Then we must leave. It isn't safe to stay here."

"And the dead?"

"If the Chinese return and find that anything has changed they'll send search parties after us. Leave them where they lay."

"Should I close their eyes?"

"No."

"And the baby?"

"He comes with us."

"But it'll be easier for the Chinese to find us."

"Would you leave him here alone to die in the cold?"

Kalden bowed his head. "No. Of course not. I wasn't thinking."

"It's all right, Kalden," said Norbu, patting his son's shoulder. "It's hard to think straight right now. We'd better get going."

They clothed Dorjee in a sweater and cap that his mother had knit for him, warm leggings, boots, and a heavy cloak. Norbu put him on his back. They loaded their supplies on the backs of two mules they took from a nearby pen and then hurried into the woods.

CHAPTER 12

The Discovery

SANTA MONICA, SUMMER 1951

GRIEF CAME TO be Tenzin's occupation. He never knew whether it would surface during the light of day or deep in the night. Grief kept to its own timetable, with no concern for Tenzin's wishes. When he was exhausted from the outpouring of tears that his grief frequently necessitated, he would seek out Alice or Emily to talk. The two women anchored his emotions, becoming an indispensable part of his healing process.

Sometimes, instead of grieving, Tenzin found himself raging at the Chinese. He'd go to his room then, close the doors and windows, lie down and scream his rage into his pillow. More often than not, he would thrash about, kicking and punching the bed. The rage he felt was overwhelming and he'd continue to express it until it was gone. The process might take a long time or be done quickly. He never knew what to expect when it came. But he was wise enough to give in to it, so it could leave him.

Tenzin realized that his healing process had three stages. First came the rage, then the sorrow, then the need to talk. This cycle was consistent throughout the period of his recovery. Without Alice and Emily, his healing would have been incomplete. He needed the nurturing and love that these two women provided in abundance.

One afternoon, Tenzin found himself slipping into an even darker and unexplored region of his soul. He felt himself in grave danger, although he was safe in his bed. His heart beat rapidly; his breath became shallow; his legs twitched. He wanted nothing more than to flee from his body. At that moment the vision came.

He was a Mongol warrior, dressed in light armor and armed with a sword, riding on horseback across the Asian steppes, part of a large army. Everywhere they went, they killed, pillaged, and raped. He led his men in a bloodthirsty frenzy. He hacked off heads and arms, killing wherever and whomever he could. He wore the splattered blood of his victims as a badge of his prowess.

What the Chinese had done to him and his country was what he himself had done in the distant past. Was his karma responsible for the deaths of his family, Doezen, and the destruction of the monastery?

He screamed and stumbled to his feet, trying to outrun his vision. He took a few wobbly steps and fell to the floor. Alice was downstairs and heard the thud. She found him sobbing on the floor in the fetal position, oblivious to the world around him. She sat down beside him, stroked his head, and waited for the storm to pass.

Eventually he became still. And then an unexpected realization flashed through his mind. The idea was so startling that it brought him to a sitting position. He had always wondered what Doezen had hinted at but never revealed about his identity. Now he knew. He was the incarnation of Doezen's older brother Trungpa. That explained the deep bond that had existed between them since the moment they met.

He gripped the mala around his neck, seeing its importance in a whole new light.

As Trungpa, he had given the mala to Doezen before he died. When he left Tibet, Doezen had given it back to him before he died. He was the mala's original owner. In losing Doezen, he had lost more than a revered mentor. He had lost his brother. He shivered with the knowledge of the unexpected truth. Alice slid her arms around him from behind and held him, her breasts pressed against his back. Her warmth comforted him. That night he slept deeply without troubling dreams for the first time in many weeks.

Alice was deeply shaken by what Tenzin had told her of his vision. It affected her viscerally, evoking a deep, palpable fear that, try as she might, she could not comprehend. She could almost see the battles and hear the screams. Only the thinnest of veils kept her from entering that dark world.

She had a hard time falling asleep that night. It was after two when she finally fell into a light sleep and dreamed a strange dream. She was in a poor, unremarkable farming village in the Asian steppes. The villagers eked out a meager living from the land. She was an attractive young woman who dreamed of getting away from her tyrannical father who treated her like a slave. Her dream was to have a husband and a family far away from here.

One day the Mongols appeared out of the steppes like a terrible storm. They burned the village and killed the old men and women, including her parents.

The soldiers bound the arms and legs of the young men who would be sold as slaves, then raped the young women. She was set upon by a group of soldiers.

Terror churned in her stomach as they held down her and spread her legs. The first soldier was mounting her when a commanding voice ordered him off. The soldiers grudgingly released her and stood to the side muttering amongst themselves. They had their earned their pleasure. Why was it being taken away from them? The young woman was attractive and they all wanted her, but they were also scared of their commanding officer. Not one of them had the temerity to challenge him. He pointed at her, motioning for her to come to him. He was a powerful man, not tall, but lean and muscular, with a stern, handsome face and eyes as hard and sharp as his sword. He was clearly someone to be reckoned with. The sight of him made her heart beat rapidly. He had killed her family, destroyed her village and would soon sell her friends and relatives into slavery. Nevertheless, she was strongly attracted to him and hated herself for it. When she reached him, he turned and walked toward the horses. She followed as if entranced.

He pointed at one of the horses for her to mount. She had never ridden a horse before and felt herself panicking. At that moment she woke, her heart pounding, her face and neck soaked in sweat. She glanced at the clock beside her bed. Ten after four. She tossed and turned, trying to calm herself, but the adrenaline coursing through her body made that impossible. She finally fell asleep just before the sun rose in the east.

When she woke in mid morning she felt calmer. She was certain Tenzin was the soldier that had saved her in her dream. The eyes were the same, only now they were kind and caring.

I was there, she thought. I knew him. She couldn't prove it objectively of course, but inside herself she knew it to be true, as certainly as she knew what time and day it was. Whatever had been between them then was still there now. Tenzin had saved her from rape and slavery, even though he had lead the attack on her village. Now here she was, helping him heal and deeply in love with him. "Was I as devoted to him in that lifetime as I am now?" she wondered. The answer to that question would have to wait.

CHAPTER 13

Out of Tibet

TIBET 1950

DAYLIGHT HAD NEARLY disappeared when Norbu and Kalden made camp by a swollen stream in a mountain gorge. Steep cliffs rose from both sides of the stream bed. The only way in was a narrow, obscure goat path known solely to the local villagers.

"Can we build a fire, father? It will be cold tonight."

"Too dangerous," said Norbu, shaking his head.

"But we'll freeze," said Kalden. "Surely, the Chinese won't find us here. They don't know this place exists. Beside, it's dark."

"We never thought they'd come to our village either, but they did. We have enough blankets. Dorjee can sleep with you. You'll keep each other warm."

They woke in the morning to a leaden sky and a biting wind. A thick fog had settled into the gorge. Dorjee woke as soon as Kalden stirred and instinctively cried out for his mother. Kalden tried to quiet him, wrapping a sheepskin over his head to block the wind, but Dorjee was inconsolable. The crows huddling in the branches above them added their chorus of shrieks to Dorjee's cries. Kalden, worried that Dorjee's sobs might alert the Chinese, lost his temper.

"Be quiet Dorjee! The soldiers will hear you and come after us! I lost my mother, too. We'll all be killed because of you! Now shut up!"

Kalden's threats scared the little boy, and his cries grew louder. The crows's lament turned to screeching taunts directed at Kalden, or so it seemed to him. Kalden grew more unraveled and screamed back at them. The tumult woke Norbu from a deep sleep. He threw off his blanket, ran over to the boys and picked up Dorjee, rocking him gently against his chest.

"You must be kinder, Kalden. Think of how your mother would treat him. Would she have screamed at him? Can you imagine what he's been through?"

Kalden lowered his head in shame. He couldn't do anything right. The strain of the last twenty four hours had taken its toll on him, too. He sank to his knees, lowered his head and sobbed.

Norbu gazed at his son with a tenderness that was tempered by an incurable sadness. He sighed, knowing he would never overcome his loss, but that his son must conquer his. Kalden was young and vital. His life was ahead of him. It was different for him. Without his wife, family and country what did the future hold? The only thing that kept him clinging to life were the two boys whose futures depended on him. He had to be strong for them.

"Don't be ashamed, Kalden. Crying for your mother and your family doesn't make you less of a man. You'll be stronger for it later."

Kalden's sobs deepened. Norbu rubbed his son's head lovingly, then turned his attention back to Dorjee.

"There, there, little one," he said softly, patting the boy on his back. "I know how much you hurt. You lost your whole world. We're the same. We've lost ours, too."

He rocked Dorjee in his arms and sang a lullaby, mostly off key. Dorjee wrapped his chubby arms around Norbu's neck and fell back asleep.

"What are we going to do now, Father?"

"We're going to eat. Get some food from the mules. Then, gather wood and build a fire. We'll brew some tea for warmth. Then we'll make a plan."

"But you said it wasn't safe to light a fire."

Norbu looked at the sky. "The clouds are low and heavy today. The fog is thick. No one will see the smoke. Beside, we are only going to keep it going until the water boils."

They ate a quiet breakfast. Dorjee again was ravenous. He even drank a full cup of hot tea.

"We must get him some goat's milk, Father."

Norbu smiled. "Now you're thinking like your mother."

He reached over and rubbed Kalden's head again. Kalden smiled, happy to be back in his father's good graces.

"Dorjee's your brother now, Kalden. We're all the family he has. Don't forget he's just a little boy who's lost everything. It's our duty to care for and protect him."

"Yes, Father."

"We must reach India before the snows come."

"Leave Tibet?" asked Kalden, crestfallen.

"It isn't safe to stay here any longer, Kalden."

"When can we come back?"

Norbu looked wistfully off into the mist. He took a moment before answering. "I don't think we'll be coming back."

They travelled slowly, staying to the network of goat paths that crisscrossed the area where there was less chance of running into Chinese patrols. They travelled in the early morning and late in the day when there was less light and less risk of exposure. During the heart of the day, they rested amongst the rocks or in the woods, if any were nearby.

Two weeks later, they came to a large expanse of high grass that stretched as far as the eye could see. In the far distance beyond the flat, exposed plain rose the mighty Himalaya. The only way to reach the safety of the mountains was to cross the plain.

"We'll stop here," said Norbu. "Tomorrow we'll start across the plain before sunup. We should be in the mountains by the end of the day. We'll be exposed, but we have no choice. Let's hope our luck holds."

They rose in the darkness. Dorjee was used to the daily routine now and didn't cry. They gathered their bags and put them on one of the mules. Kalden climbed up on the other mule. Norbu lifted Dorjee and sat him in front of Kalden. He reached into the food sack and handed them each a barley cake and a portion of dried meat. They ate as they travelled. A few hours later, the sun rose in the cloudless sky. The mountains beckoned in the distance. Safety was just a few hours away.

"Do you see that notch in the mountains, Kalden?"

"Yes, Father."

"That is where we are going. That is where Nathu La, the Old Silk Road begins. It will take us to Sikkim. We should be on it tomorrow. Let's hope the Chinese aren't watching it."

"It's high, father. Do you think we'll be able to climb it?"

"We'll climb it, alright." He laughed. "We're Tibetans. That's what we do."

By mid-afternoon they were close to reaching the end of the plain. Norbu stopped and gave them each a small cup of water which they drank greedily. The foothills were no more than a mile away. A large stand of trees lay directly ahead.

"We've been lucky," said Norbu, relieved the end was near. "We'll sleep well tonight."

He had just wiped his brow when they heard a faint buzzing in the sky. An airplane banked and turned in the far distance. They stood frozen as the plane bore down on them. They saw the Chinese markings on its wings.

"Run Kalden. Run for the trees!" screamed Norbu, He slapped the mule's rump as hard as he could. The mule raised its head, brayed loudly and ran. Kalden turned his head to look back at his father.

"Father! Father!"

"Hold Dorjee! Go into the trees!"

Norbu was a few hundred yards behind them when the plane dove, coming in low with its machine guns blazing. The first bullet hit Norbu in the thigh. He screamed but kept moving, dragging his wounded leg. The plane passed over him, pulled up sharply and banked into a tight turn to take another pass. It set in low and close. Several bullets ripped into Norbu's back. Blood seeped onto his robe and spurted out of his mouth. He was dead before he hit the ground. He fell face down in the tall grass, eyes glassy, body motionless, his life force spilling out of him.

The mule, as scared as the boys on his back, carried them deep into the safety of the woods where the plane couldn't find them. The plane made several passes overhead, then pulled up and disappeared in the distant sky. The boys jumped off the mule and huddled behind some large boulders, shivering with fright. They crouched there for some time after the plane had gone, making sure it was gone.

When the shock had subsided and they felt safe, Kalden stood up and looked around. "Where's Father?"

The boys called him repeatedly but there was no response.

"Wait here, Dorjee. I'm going to find Father."

Kalden ran, his heart pounding in his chest. Dorjee ran after him, but Kalden was much bigger and faster, and soon disappeared in the trees. Dorjee knew where they had come from and kept running, his little legs churning as fast as they could. When he reached the edge of the woods, he saw Kalden standing head bowed in the distance, his hands covering his face. Even though he was winded and scared, Dorjee pushed on.

When he reached Kalden he saw Norbu's body lying on the ground, his clothing soaked in blood. The image of his dead grandfather filled his mind. He fell to the ground beside Norbu and sobbed. Kalden stood devastated beside his father, feeling nothing but disbelief. If only we hadn't stopped for water. If only we hadn't stopped, father would be alive. It was the only thought in his head before he collapsed in his own spasms of grief. The sun was nearly extinguished when Kalden finally collected himself. He wiped the tears from his face, straightened out his father's body and closed his eyes.

"Come Dorjee, it will be dark soon. We must find our mule and make camp in the woods."

The mule with the supplies on its back grazed nearby, swishing its tail.

"But what about Father?" Dorjee asked.

"He's gone," said Kalden, expending his remaining energy to stay composed. "There is nothing more we can do for him. His soul is free now to join mother.

The buzzards will dispose of his body. That's what he'd want."

"What are we going to do now, Kalden?"

"We're going to take Nathu La to Sikkim like he wanted us to."

Dorjee reached for Kalden's hand. Kalden took it and held it tightly as they walked back into the woods. The mule followed placidly behind them. When they had made camp for the night, Kalden gave Dorjee a barley cake and some dried meat to eat.

Dorjee made a face and shook his head. "I'm not hungry."

"You must eat. We need our strength for the journey ahead."

Dorjee reluctantly picked up his barley cake and took a bite. "Are you going to eat?" he asked Kalden.

"Soon," Kalden lied.

Dorjee fell asleep as soon as he finished eating. Kalden covered him with his sheepskin. He sat in the cold night on the cold ground, looking into the darkness for a long time, numb with grief. Unbearable pain rose in his heart. He groaned, sure his heart was about to break into a thousand pieces. It was too much. He let out a deep sigh, hoping it would diminish the throbbing in his heart. Instead, it opened the door to his grief. He sobbed into his sheepskin all night with nothing to comfort him but the silence of the night and the occasional braying of the mules. Dorjee slept deeply nearby, not waking till dawn.

CHAPTER 14

Union

SANTA MONICA 1951

When Tenzin emerged from the dark phase of his grief, he passed through a slow, turgid period. The heartbreak was largely gone, but his life had become a fog of confusion and doubt. He no longer felt that he belonged in America, but returning to Tibet wasn't possible. India did not interest him. Nothing made sense; nothing he attempted worked. So he stopped trying to push forward and settled into a silent apathy, doing as little as possible beyond the necessary routines of daily life. He didn't know it, but the apathy he felt was the primary symptom of a deeper exhaustion. He would not have clarity or be able to move forward again until he had regenerated his energies.

Apathy was at least better than the dark, endless stream of pain and grief from which he had recently emerged. He kept waiting for a spark to ignite him and propel his life forward. But nothing happened. He existed in a torpor, with no will or direction. The little strength he had was just enough to hold him where he was. Then out of nowhere, while he lay in the paralyzing certainty that this was what his life would always be like, a light flashed inside him. A series of jolts brought a fresh wind to his back that propelled him onto a whole new path.

The first thing he realized when the fog lifted was that the Supreme Truth had given him a new family who loved him. They had proven it repeatedly when it had mattered most. The depth of their love overwhelmed him and he was lifted by a wave of profound gratitude.

One morning, soon after his energy had returned, he sat with Alice on the porch outside his bedroom. Tenzin watched as she spread soft butter over her toast and coated it with thick blackberry jam, and he suddenly realized how deeply he loved her. The truth swept into him like a tornado and almost knocked him out of his chair. He gasped involuntarily. Alice glanced up, a look of concern crossing her face.

"It's all right," he said. "Just a piece of toast caught in my throat."

The bright summer sun danced in Alice's long, chestnut hair. The gentle breeze caressed his skin, while the warm, mischievous light in Alice's green eyes intoxicated him. He had loved her before this, of course, but that love had been tempered by a detached, monk-like attitude. Today was different. The young monk had grown into a man who realized that he deeply loved a woman and wanted her to be his. She was his complement. Life would be far richer with her than without her.

As he ate his breakfast, he saw how well the Supreme Truth had provided for him. One world had been taken from him. Nothing could bring it back. In its stead, the Supreme Truth had given him a new country, a new family, and a new path. The difference between this new world and the one that had passed away was that in the new world he was the one everyone would look to for guidance. There would be no Doezen to go to when things got difficult or when he had questions no one else could answer. The burden would be all his.

Alice had been a rock to cling to in the most vulnerable and dangerous time of his life. She was bright and trustworthy. She had a deep, warm, and loving nature. And she was beautiful, incredibly beautiful. She bit into her rich toast and her face glowed with an inner light that only heightened her loveliness.

Tenzin knew from experience that Grace could be hard and merciless. She requires you to travel down a long dark tunnel before she allows you to emerge into the light. If you fail to overcome the obstacles she sets in your path, you will never receive her blessings. But if you face your fears, brave the darkness, and run her gauntlet successfully, she will return what you lost in a more luminous form.

They sat on the porch, kissed by the breeze and bathed in the light of the morning sun. In a moment that he had not rehearsed or even imagined, Tenzin placed his hand on hers and looked directly into her green eyes. "You are where I begin and where I end, Alice," he said. "There will never be anyone for me but you. One day this life will be over, but my love for you will never end. Will you marry me?"

Alice thought for a moment that she was dreaming. If only he had known how she had longed for this moment. She felt the presence of his warm, strong hand on hers. She had thought marriage was out of the question, so she had kept the flame of her love tamped down, hidden deeply in her heart. Only Emily had seen its flicker. Tenzin was, after all, a Tibetan monk. He had taken a vow of celibacy. Alice could never imagine loving anyone else so deeply. She thought she was doomed to go through life alone.

Her eyes were as large as saucers. Her mouth fell open. She couldn't speak. When she finally collected herself, she could hardly think. "Really? Really? Well, yes. Yes, of course." It was all she could manage to say. But as soon as she said yes, a cloud passed over her face and the luster left her eyes. She turned from him and looked out over the bay, collecting her thoughts.

"Tenzin," she asked. "You are a monk. You took a vow of celibacy. How can you marry me? Won't you feel terrible guilt and conflict if you do? Won't marrying me mean the end of the spiritual journey you've lived your whole life for? I don't want to destroy that. You'd resent me forever."

Tenzin smiled and took a moment before answering, all the while marveling at her goodness.

"The old life is over. Tibet is no longer free. My family is gone. The monastery and Doezen are gone. Everything is different. I am certainly different. I have wandered in the dark, consumed with grief for a long time. That is no longer the case. My grief is over. How long have you been waiting for me to find you?"

"Since the first day I saw you at UCLA," she said. Her laughter filled the air like chiming bells.

"That's a long time!"

"That's for sure. I knew that if I didn't marry you, I'd never marry. And since you were a monk, I figured I was going to end up as a lonely old lady. I just can't believe this, though. I'm in shock. Are you really, really sure you want to marry me? You won't end up regretting it? That part really scares me."

"I would only regret your refusal to marry me," he said.

"I see," she said teasing him.

"So will you marry me?"

"Well, of course I will, silly."

"I would like to have a family, too."

"You want children?" Alice's mouth dropped open again. This man was full of surprises.

"Don't you?"

Alice burst out of her chair and threw her arms around him. Tears streamed down her cheeks. "More than you can imagine."

"It won't be easy. Many people will have claims to my time in the future. Can you live with that?"

"I can, if I live with you."

He laughed and embraced her in return.

"Tenzin, when do you want to get married?"

"I don't know. I hadn't planned that far ahead. First you had to say yes. When do you want to get married?"

"Right now! But I want my parents and a few close friends to be here. It will take some planning. I'll have to call them in Palo Alto and find out when they can all come. Is that all right with you?"

"Of course. We'll get married whenever you want."

Later that day Alice was again assailed by doubts. She was worried, despite his protestations, that Tenzin would eventually come to hate her for taking him from his intended path. She kept her doubts to herself, not even telling Emily, but over the next two days they threw her into terrible confusion and anxiety. She couldn't eat or sleep. On the second night, she fell into a restless sleep only to find herself in a dark and unfamiliar world. The rocky terrain was inhospitable, difficult to navigate. A harsh wind swirled around her. A hostile presence shadowed her every step. Danger lay in every direction. Then, out of nowhere, when all seemed lost, a young woman with golden curls and blue eyes appeared out of the gloom and took her by the hand.

"Close your eyes," she said. "Don't open them until I tell you to."

Alice did as she was told. She had no other options anyway. A moment later the woman released her hand.

"You can open your eyes now."

Alice opened her eyes to a lush green meadow under a blue sky. Flowers that she had never seen before painted the landscape with brilliant color. They emitted scents that she had never encountered. A deep serenity pervaded the place.

"What you seek," said her guide, "Lies at the end of that path." She pointed to a space between two large bushes.

Am I seeking something, Alice wondered. "What's down there?" she asked.

"You can't know everything beforehand. That's not how things work. Be brave. Now go forward."

Alice took a deep breath, summoned her courage, and walked to the open space between the bushes. She looked back, but her guide had disappeared. Alice was alone in the shimmering grass, surrounded by the steady drone of cicadas in the nearby trees. It seemed safe enough. Besides, there was no way back, only a way forward. Her curiosity pushed her down the path. The trail took her through a dense birch forest, then up a steep hill. At the top of the hill, a circular temple of white marble stood in the center of a large clearing. Love filled her heart and banished all remnants of fear. At the end of the great hall, a man with a bald head and copper skin sat waiting on a dais. His dark eyes shone with wisdom.

"So, little sister," he said. "You have come." His smile warmed her through and through.

"Do I know you?" she asked.

He chuckled. "Could you have gotten here if you did not?"

"I have no idea. Who are you?" she said.

"I'm Doezen," he said.

"Oh my God! Please forgive me," said Alice. "I have seen you before. When I first meditated with Tenzin. I'm dreaming. This can't be real."

"You're in a higher world. It's as real as your physical world, just different from what you're used to. Everything here is made of light, not matter. What's worrying you?"

"You're going to think this is silly. But I'm afraid that if I marry Tenzin he will lose his life path and come to hate me for it. I couldn't bear that. It's been bothering me for days."

Doezen laughed. "Your marriage will not take Tenzin from his path. Your marriage to Tenzin is his path. It completes a relationship for both of you that ended abruptly when he was killed in battle many lifetimes ago."

"Oh, my God. I've seen some of that life."

"It will be different this time. You both have long, rich lives ahead of you."

"That makes me feel so much better," said Alice.

"The dark side was playing with you. Entities from the lower astral world played with your mind until you couldn't think straight. When you are about to step into more light, the negative comes against you. It happened to the Buddha. And to Christ. Why would it not happen to you? They're templates for humanity. Your marriage to Tenzin unites two bright souls to share a work that will help many people. The dark side wants to block it. They used your fear against you and brought you to a dark place where you were alone and exposed. But your angel came to your aid and brought you here. You see? You're protected. Put your fear aside. You have my blessing."

"Oh, thank you. Will I see you again?"

He smiled coyly. "Next time," he said, "I will come to you."

"Really?"

"Oh yes," He said. His smile grew broader. "But you won't recognize me."

"Oh, yes I will."

Doezen's eyes sparkled. "We'll see."

Alice and Tenzin were married two weeks later. Emily's minister performed the simple ceremony in the garden behind her home. Alice's parents were there, as were Emily, Thomas, and several of Alice's close friends.

Two years later Alice gave birth to Matthew, the first of their two sons. He had his father's golden skin and dark hair and his mother's green eyes. Matthew was a kind, sweet child. Early on, dogs would seek him out when he walked in the park with his parents and nuzzle their heads against his hand. He would pet them and let them lick his face until his parents shooed them away. Tenzin observed a pink energy field around his son's hands whenever he touched the animals. He knew they had come to Matthew for healing. He had seen the same light coming from his father when he was a young boy. The light reminded him of something Doezen had told him long ago, when Tenzin was still a youth.

"All souls return to the physical plane to find completion," Doezen had said. "If they do not find completion, they will return again and again until they do. Until people resolve their negative emotions, they approach the Light like donkeys."

Tenzin giggled. "Like Donkeys?"

"Slowly," said the Rinpoche, scrunching up his face. "And stubbornly. Most people are very resistant to growth."

One of the first things Tenzin had learned from Doezen was that unless you confront your inner darkness real spiritual growth is virtually impossible. But once you overcome your shadow, the Supreme Truth moves in harmony with you. Growth becomes fast and sure because you are moving toward the light rather than away from it.

"Those who overcome the dark side of their nature," Doezen had said, "are far better protected from the machinations of evil than those who have not. Because they are whole and consciously connected to their soul, there is no door for evil to enter, although it will try, and may be disruptive for a time. Those who have not overcome their dark sides are not so fortunate. Their lack of wholeness is an open invitation to evil. Evil wears many masks. It often appears to be supportive and caring. Those who are deluded by its false fronts are particularly vulnerable to its schemes. An honest self-appraisal is absolutely essential if the path is to be trod successfully."

Isn't it strange, thought Tenzin, that whenever I think about Matthew, I remember Doezen's teachings. My love for one extends to love for the other. Could they be one and the same?

Matthew had a magnet inside him for his father and hovered around him whenever he could. The two of them were exceptionally close. Until he was five, Matthew would never go to sleep until his father had kissed him good night. As soon as he started to speak, he would give Tenzin advice. "Eat more, Daddy. You're tired. You need to go to sleep now, Daddy."

One night as they were preparing for bed, Tenzin mentioned to Alice that he thought Matthew might be the incarnation of Doezen.

"Really?" Alice replied. "I don't think so."

"What do you mean?" he asked.

Alice smiled cryptically. "It's late," she said. Then she kissed him good night and fell asleep, leaving Tenzin to wonder anew how incredible his wife was. She was either right with him as Emily Chase had always been, or a step ahead. He never knew for certain which, but he suspected that it was more often the latter.

A year later, Alice and Tenzin's other son, Daniel, was born. Daniel was very different from his brother: feisty, athletic, and loud, but also big hearted. He had the same copper-hued skin and green eyes as Matthew, but his thick, wavy hair was rich chestnut, not black like his brother's. When he was just a little boy he displayed a remarkable concern for the elderly. He worried if they were alone and had no one to care for them. He wanted everyone to have a family and live in a nice big house like he did, with a grandmother like Emily Chase and an uncle like Thomas Kerr.

These were the years of normalcy and happiness for Tenzin and Alice. They had time to be a family and experience the joys and challenges of raising children. While Alice was a natural mother, Tenzin had to work at developing his parenting skills. Changing diapers and soothing crying babies in the middle of the night were substantial challenges for him. Nothing in his training had prepared him for raising children. But once he set his mind to it, as he had with learning English, he quickly became proficient. To his delight, he found that having children grounded him and made it easier for his students to relate to him as a normal person with everyday concerns.

After his marriage, Tenzin had resumed his commitment to Prof. Kerr's seminar, speaking monthly to at UCLA. His talks led to a burgeoning slate of classes, seminars, counseling sessions and speaking engagements. The work created a platform for the future and gave him an income for the first time in his life.

With Tenzin's work expanding in leaps and bounds, Emily decided to convert her house into a spiritual center. She created a non-profit educational corporation to support Tenzin's work and named it The Santa Monica Tibetan Center. The first floor was used for classes, counseling sessions, and administration. The second and third floors provided living quarters for Emily and Thomas Kerr. Tenzin, Alice and the boys lived on the third floor.

CHAPTER 15

The Old Silk Road

TIBET 1950

KALDEN WOKE DORJEE at dawn. Dorjee yawned, rubbed the sleep from his eyelids, wrapped his arms around Kalden's neck, and buried his chin in Kalden's shoulder. The boys held onto each other silently. Kalden's jaw quivered. I can't afford to be weak, he told himself. Father is gone. I must be a man now. There is no time for grief. I must be strong. Our survival depends on it.

He handed Dorjee a barley cake and a strip of meat. Dorjee frowned, and ate his breakfast without enthusiasm.

Despite his immense grief or perhaps because of it, Kalden had no intention of failing. He had vowed that his father's death would not be in vain. Kalden would go on because that is what his father wanted him to do. He would live for his father, his mother, his family, his village and his country. He would live for them and succeed for them, and one day he would bear testimony to the evil that had been visited on them. He would hold them in his heart forever. As long as he did, a part of them lived on in him. He wasn't going to let the Chinese win. They could wound him, break his heart, cut him to the core, hound him, and force him out of his native country. But they would never defeat him. They would never destroy his hope or undermine his resolve. He set his jaw and faced the rising sun.

"Let's go, Dorjee. It's time."

"I miss father."

"Me too. But we must go on. Keep him in your heart where you keep your family. As long as we remember them, they're alive. Do you feel them in your heart?"

Dorjee nodded.

"Let me help you up."

Kalden put Dorjee on the mule's back, then climbed behind him.

"Today we'll reach Nathan Lu, the Old Silk Road. Up there." Kalden pointed to the notch between the mountains. "It will take us into Sikkim. And safety."

"It's high," said Dorjee.

Kalden smiled a little for the first time since the Chinese had come. "We're Tibetans," he said. "We've been walking over mountains for thousands of years. If those Chinese dogs come after us their legs will turn to jelly. We'll see how brave they are when they can't breathe and they're spitting blood. They'll tuck their tails and run home to Mao."

Dorjee laughed. Kalden's smile widened at his own boldness. A wave of courage rippled through him.

Three nights later, they camped within a large outcropping of rocks half a mile off the main trail. Several scrawny bushes had managed to thrive in the harsh conditions. Kalden gathered the scattered, dead branches and lit a fire. They were sound asleep when the sharp sound of snapping twigs awoke Kalden. He sat up, fully alert, his heart pounding. He pressed his hand over Dorjee's mouth. "Shh!" he whispered. "Get up and follow me."

He grabbed a thick branch as they slipped away from the fire, taking cover behind a large boulder nearby. A man, a woman, and two girls emerged from the darkness.

"Watch where you're walking, Jamyang," the man whispered. "We don't know who's camping here. If it's bandits, they'll kill us."

The women shivered and crept toward the fire. The mules brayed when they caught the intruders's scent. The man motioned with his hands for the girls to inspect the animals.

"There's food on this one, Father," the older one whispered.

Kalden jumped atop the boulder and brandished his stick. "Touch it and you die," he screamed.

The man raised his arm, peering vainly into the darkness. "Please," he begged. "We are unarmed. We mean you no harm. We're fleeing the Chinese. Are you Tibetan?"

"Are you?" said Kalden.

"Yes," said the man.

"So what. You can't have our food," said Kalden.

"We have our own food," said the man. "And several sweets we can share with you." He pointed to a large pack on their horse as it ambled into the light. "Please. Can we make our camp with you for the night?"

Kalden wasn't sure. Were these people what they said they were? Or were they bandits who would steal their food and mules in the middle of the night? Or worse, would they kill him and Dorjee while they slept?

The man motioned to his wife and daughters. They joined him in the firelight. Kalden could now see them clearly.

"I am Choden," he said. "This is my wife, Llamo, and my daughters, Jamyang and Jinpa."

The women bowed and smiled nervously.

They don't seem like bandits, thought Kalden. And the older daughter is very pretty.

The girl blushed, as if she could read his mind.

Probably farmers like us, he thought. A bandit wouldn't be traveling with his wife and daughters.

"Are you going to Sikkim?" said Choden.

"Maybe," answered Kalden.

"You're so young," Choden said. "Where's your family?"

"Dead."

Choden shook his head. "So many of our people have died," he said. "I am sorry for you. Do you have family in Sikkim?"

"No."

Choden's face brightened and he nodded. "We do," he said. "They'll take you in."

Kalden put down his branch. "You can stay."

"Thank you," Choden said.

The womens' shoulders softened. Jamyang gave him an especially warm smile. Now Kalden blushed. He filled his arms with wood and threw it on the dying fire. The flames soon roared back to life.

"You can come out now, Dorjee," he said.

Dorjee slipped out from behind the boulder and approached the warmth of the fire. "He's so cute," squealed Jinpa, the younger daughter. Her mother and older sister smiled.

Several days later they began their descent into Sikkim. Kalden walked beside Jamyang as he had every day since they'd met. Jinpa rode on the mule with Dorjee, her arms wrapped around him. Jinpa was only ten but her mothering instinct was already strong. Dorjee was happier in the safety of her arms than he had been since the Chinese had destroyed his village. Choden and Llamo walked ahead with the horse.

Llamo was certain that Jamyang had met her future husband. The boy was solid. He wasn't mean, and he treated her daughter with respect. The chemistry between them was apparent. One day he would be good provider and husband. She would ask her brother, Goba, to teach him to farm and help him grow into a man. Maybe some good will emerge from this nightmare, she thought. But she didn't share her thoughts with Choden. He was attached to his girls and would not be happy to know that he had been replaced in his eldest daughter's affections.

The terraced hills outside of the rural villages in Sikkim overflowed with crops. The inhabitants were kind, and replenished their food and provided them with shelter.

Two weeks later, they reached the summit of a large hill in the southern part of Sikkim. Goba's village, Sebu La, lay partially obscured by haze in the distance. Ripe clouds hung heavily in the sky. Thunder clapped in the distance. They gazed at the lush valley; a few rain drops spattered on their heads. They hardly noticed. A strong wind whipped the high grass around them. They stared out at their new home, thankful that their journey was over and that they had reached safety unharmed. Several villagers were hard at work in the fields outside the village.

"I can't wait to see my brother," said Llamo.

"What's he like, mama?" asked Jinpa. The girls had never met him.

"He's got a big heart. You'll like him."

The rain began to fall harder. They made their descent as quickly as they could. When they got closer, the people working in the nearest rice paddy stopped and watched them approach. A teenage girl dropped her rake and ran to them.

"Who are you? Where are you from?" she asked. "We don't get many strangers here."

"I'm Goba's sister, Llamo. Do you know him?"

The girl's smile said everything. "I'll get him."

She raced back toward the village, announcing to the others who these strangers were. The workers dropped their hoes and surrounded them.

"You're Goba's sister?" asked an old woman.

"Yes."

"From Tibet?" her husband asked.

"Yes."

"We heard the Chinese invaded your country," said a young man. He wiped the rain from his face. "Is it true?"

"Yes," answered Choden.

"Did they kill many people?"

"Yes."

The realization rendered everyone silent. The only sounds were the steady beat of the rain as it hit the ground and the occasional braying of the animals. No one knew what to say.

All turned to see what was causing the sudden commotion behind them. A large man with wild, gray hair and an unshaven face ran toward them. The rest of the village followed fast on his heels.

A big smile lit up Llamo's face. "That's your uncle, girls."

The whole village crowded around them. The horse whinnied and rose on its rear legs. Choden rubbed its chest and calmed it. The mules brayed nervously. Goba rushed up to Llamo and nearly crushed her in his massive arms.

"You're alive!" he said. "We heard the Chinese had killed everyone in Tibet."

"They killed everyone in our village," said Choden. "And theirs." He pointed to the boys.

"How did you escape?"

"We were away visiting friends. We came home the next day. We were the only survivors."

"You've had a difficult trip. You must be tired. Let's get you a bath and food."

Later, when they were alone, Llamo asked her brother, "Where's your wife?"

The sparkle went out of Goba's eyes. "She died," he said. "Two years ago."

"I'm sorry," said Llamo. She touched her brothers arm to comfort him.

He shrugged. "It happens. At least you are all alive."

"And your children?" asked Choden.

"Married. With children of their own now. They don't need me anymore."

"Do you see them?"

Goba shrugged again. "They're very busy with their lives."

"No other woman?" asked Llamo.

"No."

"It must be lonely for you."

"I keep busy."

"You're the head man?" asked Choden.

"Yes."

"The boys need a home. They have nothing. Do you think someone here could take them in?" Llamo asked.

"I will."

Llamo let out a deep sigh. "I was hoping you would." She hugged her brother. Tears pooled at the corners of her eyes. "No one could raise them better."

Llamo leaned in. "Jamyang likes Kalden," she whispered. "I'm sure they'll marry one day."

Goba smiled. "Don't worry. I'll make a man out of him."

"And teach him how to provide for a family," said Llamo.

"Of course," said Goba, chuckling.

CHAPTER 16

The End of Normalcy

Things do not happen. Things are made to happen.
John F. Kennedy

SANTA MONICA 1963

Tenzin became a citizen of the United States on December 2, 1958. It was a special moment for him as he stood with the others who became citizens that day and swore his oath of allegiance to America. He had always been impressed by the vitality and ambition of the American people and touched by their openness and generosity. Now he was one of them and proud to be so. Alice, Emily, Thomas and the boys were in the audience that day to see him officially become an American just like them. Afterward, they celebrated by going to the most expensive restaurant in Santa Monica for lunch.

On the first Tuesday in November 1959, Tenzin participated in his first Presidential election, casting his vote for John F. Kennedy. He admired the young politician a great deal. He loved Democracy and enjoyed the animated political discussions that Thomas and Emily frequently shared. He kept himself informed by reading the Los Angeles Times and the New York Times as frequently as he could.

Then, on Friday morning November 22, 1963, slightly less than three years into Kennedy's Presidency, the years of normalcy and innocence for Tenzin and Alice came to an abrupt end. No one in the entire country would be left unscathed by the events in Dallas that day.

In the morning, Tenzin took the boys to school. When he returned, he went to the kitchen as usual to have a cup of coffee before his first appointment. Emily, Thomas and Alice were gathered around the TV, their faces drawn and somber. They didn't greet him when he entered as they normally did or even noticed that he was there.

Most unusual, he thought.

Alice's cheeks were bloodless, paler than the milk Tenzin had just poured into his coffee. Her brow was furrowed. She was so focused on the television that she didn't notice that he was standing beside her. He touched her shoulder and she jumped. Sorrow filled her eyes. She clutched at his arm.

"What is it? What's happened?" Tenzin whispered, not wanting to disturb Emily and Thomas.

"The President's been shot."

"The President of what?" asked Tenzin.

"The United States," said Thomas.

"Kennedy?" said Tenzin. Alice wrapped her arms around his waist and sobbed against his chest. He stroked her hair, then kissed her forehead. How could what happened to his family and to Doezen happen to the most powerful man in the world? How could their fate be his fate? How could anyone ever be safe in this world again? And who would be audacious enough do such a thing in broad daylight with a large crowd to bear witness?

"Is he dead?" he heard himself ask.

"He was pronounced dead as you walked in," said Emily, her voice near breaking.

"Do they know who did it?"

"They just arrested some guy named Oswald. Got him an hour and twenty minutes after he shot the President. Amazing detective work. At least the government got something right," said Thomas.

"That was fast," said Tenzin.

"Too fast," said Emily.

"What do you mean?" asked Alice. She pressed the heels of her hands to her cheeks, pushing the tears from her face.

"Oswald's a patsy," Emily replied. Her voice bristled with anger. "It's a setup."

"A setup?" said Thomas. "No way."

Emily shook her head. "It was a setup, alright. Look at the facts, Thomas. This was a professional assassination. Whoever was really behind it set Oswald up. Killing a President takes an enormous amount of planning. Many people would have to be involved." She scanned their faces, ending by staring into Thomas' eyes. "Even factions within our own government. One lone gun man acting on his own without detailed access to Kennedy's plans could never pull this off."

"You don't know that," said Thomas.

Emily frowned. "You're too old to be so naïve, Thomas. Mark my words. The real killers will never be brought to justice. The whole thing will be covered up. Many false theories will be floated to the public to sow confusion and doubt. That's how these things work."

"But why?" said Alice. "Why do such a thing?"

"I was on the inside. I know how the government works. The President takes orders. He does as he's told. The real rulers of this country are never seen by the public. They are never known and they certainly are never exposed. The public doesn't even know that they exist. Benjamin Disraeli, Queen Victoria's Prime Minister, said as much a century ago: *The world is governed by far different personages from what is imagined by those who are not behind the scene.* It was true then and it's true now. The President is only the front man. He has no real authority at all. Kennedy wouldn't play along and do what he was told, so they killed him." Emily sighed and shook her head. "He was the last real President of America. Whoever follows will be too afraid to act in the best interests of the American people. Kennedy's murder was a message to all future Presidents."

"Wouldn't play along?" Thomas asked. "What are you talking about? Wouldn't play along with whom?"

"Who did he fire recently?"

"Allan Dulles."

"Exactly," said Emily. "The CIA Director and a 33rd degree Freemason. Don't think for a minute that's not important."

Tenzin frowned, remembering a speech from early in Kennedy's Presidency. When he spoke, his voice was barely more than a whisper. "Kennedy said he was going to blow the CIA into a thousand pieces." He pulled Alice closer to his side.

"And what did he say about Vietnam?" Emily said.

"That he was going to end it," Tenzin said. "And bring the troops home."

"That's right," said Emily. "But here's the real crux of it. What was he planning to do about the Federal Reserve?"

"That I don't know," Tenzin said. Thomas and Alice both shook their heads. They didn't know either.

"Last June, Kennedy issued Executive Order 11110, stripping the Fed of its power to loan money to the government at interest. Executive Order 11110 returned to the government the power to issue its own currency backed by silver. Since Kennedy signed that order, four point three billion dollars of debt-free money has been issued by the Treasury."

"I didn't know that," said Thomas.

"Not many do. The real rulers of this country want a debt-based currency and they want this war. They make a fortune on the interest they charge us to print our money and they'll make another huge fortune on profits from the cost of this war. They control the CIA and use it to destabilize governments around the world, and put in place the puppets and policies they want. These people are absolutely ruthless. Do you think that they were going to let one man undermine their power and interfere with their agenda for world domination, even if he is the President of the United States. They killed him less than six months after he issued that order. Six months. These people are serious."

Thomas shook his head. "That's just crazy, Emily. The entire United States government? Controlled by a secret cabal? I don't believe it. I *can't* believe it."

"Nobody does, Thomas. Don't you see? That's precisely why they can get away with it. Everyone believes the lies the media and the government tell them. The people are asleep. If they ever wake up, this whole system of deception will come tumbling down. That's why the secret government will do whatever it takes to keep the people mind-controlled and locked into their agenda. Today proved that. Look up Kennedy's 1961 speech on secret societies. It's brief, but powerful. It might open your eyes. In fact, I've got a quotation from that speech in my desk in the study. Hold on. I'll get it."

Emily rose from her chair and strode purposefully from the room. She returned a moment later with a small notebook in her hand. She flipped through the pages till she found what she wanted. "Here it is." Emily cleared her throat and read aloud the few lines she had copied from Kennedy's speech. "*For we are opposed around the world by a monolithic and ruthless conspiracy...It is a system which has conscripted vast human and material resources into the building of a tightly knit, highly efficient machine that combines military, diplomatic, intelligence, economic, scientific and political operations.*"

"And you think that a conspiracy of that magnitude was behind Kennedy's assassination?" said Thomas.

"Most important government officials are Freemasons of high degree like Allen Dulles at the CIA. The Freemasons are an international secret society. While it's not commonly known, Lyndon Johnson, our new President, is a 33rd degree Freemason. That's not a coincidence, by the way. I'm sure he'll get the agenda back on track and undo everything Kennedy tried to do for the American people. You're recently retired. Here's something important for you to research. You'll be shocked by what you find. When you understand the connection between the high levels of the Masonic order and their role in our government, you'll have a better understanding of the way things really work. Nothing is what it seems, Thomas. Nothing."

CHAPTER 17

Ashes on the Water

THE LIFE SEEMED to have drained out of Emily after Kennedy was assassinated. She spent much of her time in her room, working on her memoir and putting her affairs in order.

One afternoon Matthew knocked on the door to his father's study. "Daddy, can I come in?"

"Of course, Matthew." Tenzin laid his pen aside and closed his notebook.

"I've got another headache, Daddy."

"Sit down," Tenzin said. "Let's see what we can do about it."

Tenzin rubbed the back of Matthew's neck, then put his hands on his son's temples.

"Your hands are hot, Daddy."

A moment later his pain was gone.

"Why do I keep getting these headaches, Daddy?"

"One day you'll see why. Then they'll disappear for good."

"Can't you do that for me now, Daddy?"

"There are certain things you must do for yourself, Matthew. Be patient, the time will come."

"But when?"

"I don't know. Some things are meant to be a mystery."

"But it hurts."

"I know."

"I'm worried about Grandma, Daddy."

"Why?"

"The colors around her have changed."

"What do you mean?"

"They're not as bright anymore."

"Maybe she's tired."

"It's more than that, Daddy."

"Why don't you spend some time with her after school? She'd like that."

After Matthew left, Tenzin found it impossible to concentrate on his work and decided to check up on Emily. He found her in her favorite easy chair by the large window in her bedroom, an open book in her lap. She had dozed off, her mouth open, her head resting against the side of the chair. Matthew was right. Her life force was significantly weaker. He placed his fingers lightly on the pulse on the inside of her wrist. Emily stirred.

"I'm sorry Emily. I didn't mean to wake you."

"That's alright. I didn't know I was sleeping. I must have drifted off."

"How are you feeling?"

"Fine. Just fine. Why?"

"Oh, just asking."

"Sometimes I don't sleep too well, that's all. The curse of old age."

Tenzin leaned close and kissed her cheek. "I'll see you at dinner. Call me if you need anything."

"Now, don't go troubling yourself about me. You've got enough to worry about."

"You're always at the top of my list."

"I shouldn't be. I'm not going anywhere."

Tenzin squeezed her hand. "Good."

Every day after school, Matthew went to his grandmother's room and held her hand, focusing on sending her energy as he had observed his father do. After a few visits, the luster returned to Emily's eyes and her exhaustion disappeared. She didn't stay in her room as much or need the same amount of rest as she had before.

That year, they had a wonderful Christmas despite the terrible trauma dealt to the country. Emily gave the boys new bikes, which they immediately rushed outside to ride. After dinner, Alice took a picture of Emily standing between Matthew and Daniel as they sat on their new red Schwinns. Emily's face glowed with happiness, her arms wrapped around the boys's shoulders.

Two days later Emily went to bed early but did not come down for breakfast the following morning as she always had. Alice was acutely aware of her absence. After feeding the boys and getting them ready for school, she went upstairs to Emily's room to check on her. She had a bad feeling as she climbed the stairs. She knocked on her door. There was no answer. She knocked again. Still no answer. Alice opened the door slowly. She hesitated to invade Emily's privacy but felt that she had little choice. When she looked in, Emily seemed to be fast asleep, laying on her right side, facing away from the door.

Alice called out softly. "Em? Em? Are you awake? Are you O.K.?"

Alice approached the bed, walking carefully to avoid waking her. Emily's body was still, her hand cold. Alice checked her pulse. There was none. Emily was gone. A scream rose from deep in Alice's heart. She collapsed in the old leather chair by the large window, covered her face in her hands, and sobbed.

Tenzin heard her scream and rushed upstairs. When he entered Emily's bedroom, his worst fears were confirmed. He stood silent for a time, then bent down and kissed Emily's forehead.

"First the President. Now Emily," cried Alice. "It's not fair. It's too much."

Tenzin wrapped his arms around his wife. Alice's grief poured out in huge spasms. Her body trembled with agony.

"I want Emily back," Alice said.

"So do I," said Tenzin softly. "But we both know that won't happen. We must use her passing to make ourselves stronger. That's what she'd want."

"The hell with that. I need to cry."

"That's part of becoming stronger. Remember what Emily taught us. Grief cures grief."

Emily was cremated, in accordance with her wishes. Shortly after the New Year, they took her ashes to the Pacific Ocean. Tenzin wore the tattered monk's robe he had last worn on his arrival in America. They shut down the engine and drifted on the current. Tenzin rose, stoic and composed, and recited a Tibetan prayer for the dead. Inside, he was anything but calm. He felt the same swirling emptiness as he had when he had lost Doezen and his own family, but he was determined not to break down in front of his sons and his wife.

Daniel, who loved Emily deeply, stood and said a few words, "Grandma, you were the best. You made me feel good about myself when I was troubled. You helped me to understand my mother and father, when I couldn't understand why they wouldn't come to my soccer games. I could tell you anything. I'll keep you in my heart forever. I miss you, Grandma!"

Matthew stood and embraced his younger brother. The two boys stood with their arms clasped around each other, their stomachs's heaving with grief, their tears flowing freely down their cheeks.

Alice had been sobbing for three days and nights and thought she could cry no more. But when Daniel spoke, an unexpected deluge of tears covered her face. Tenzin clenched his jaw, and with great willpower, forced back his grief.

With Thomas' help, Tenzin lifted the vase that held Emily's ashes. He handed the cover to Thomas and raised the open vessel to the sky and the wind and the sun. The wind didn't hesitate. It scooped out the top layer of ash and spiraled it into the air. Tenzin turned the mouth of the vase to the ocean. Emily's ashes poured out in a stream, settling on the surface of the sea where the tide and current swept them away.

As her ashes were lifted into the air and pulled under the waves, Tenzin remembered Emily's wishes about her death. "When I die, see that I am cremated and my ashes scattered on the sea. I am going to a place of peace and light and do not need to be called back by the weight of a decaying body stuck in a box in the ground. Scatter me so that no one can find me and grieve over me. Indeed, there will be nothing for which to grieve. I will be free as a bird. Promise me you will not mourn. Life is so short. You've had enough grief, more than most people could ever bear. You don't need more. My life has been full and rich and blessed by having Doezen, then you, Alice, and the children in it. Do you promise me that, Tenzin?"

Of course, he had promised. Tenzin had not shown his sorrow to anyone, not to his boys, or Thomas, or even Alice. When he was alone in his study, silent tears would pour down his cheeks as he wrote to his students or meditated. He cried often and over a long period of time, but no one ever knew it. He wondered if Emily could sense it from where she was now. He often felt her presence at the center and knew that wherever she had gone, she came back to visit often.

After Emily's passing, Matthew made a habit of meditating with his father in his study on Sunday mornings. He would sit cross-legged directly across from his father, his eyes focused on Tenzin's head.

"Daddy, when you sit down, I see gold around you. When you meditate the gold gets bigger. There's a lot of white, too. The energy in the room shifts when you meditate."

"How do you feel when that happens, Matthew?"

"Very peaceful."

"That's good. You need inner peace to experience your true self."

"I want to go to Tibet some day."

"That's not possible. The Chinese won't let anyone in."

"Why did the Chinese steal Tibet? It didn't belong to them."

"That's why they took it."

"I still want to go."

"Maybe it'll be different when you're older."

"Grandma would have taken me. She was an ambassador. They wouldn't dare hurt her."

"Grandma's not here anymore," said Tenzin.

"I miss her, Daddy."

Matthew burst into tears and threw himself onto his father's lap, wrapping his arms around his neck.

CHAPTER 18

The Walk Home

SIKKIM 1953

"YOU'RE A HARD worker, Kalden," said Goba as they walked home from the fields in the slanted, afternoon sunlight. "Your father would be proud of you."

"He taught me to work hard. Not to cut corners."

"Your father must have been a very good man."

Kalden sighed "The best I ever knew," he said.

"You miss him a great deal still, don't you?"

"Do you think I will ever get over what happened, Goba?"

"You must. Life goes on. Your parents would want you to be happy. You are safe now. But only you can make yourself happy."

"How?" said Kalden. His face was engraved with hopelessness. "My whole life is gone."

"But you're not, are you?"

"No."

"Time will help. Working with the earth, being outdoors will help, too. Peace will come. You'll see."

"I'm going to sneak back into Tibet and kill as many Chinese as I can."

"You'll only get yourself killed doing that. Is that what your father would want?"

Kalden bowed his head. "No."

"Killing will not heal your heart, or bring back your family. Do not think of such foolishness again."

"At night I cry myself to sleep. How can I be a man when I am so weak?"

Goba put his arm around Kalden. "Grieving is not weakness. It empties the poison from your heart. Weakness comes when you let your heart turn to stone.

You can't be a man with a woman if you have a stone for a heart. When my wife died, I cried for a year."

"You did? Did you think the pain would ever stop?"

"No. But it did."

"When will mine end?"

"When the poison is gone."

"When will that be?"

Goba shrugged. "No one knows. The heart is deep and mysterious. Have faith. In time, all will be well."

Kalden was silent. Goba squeezed his shoulder. "What do you think of Jimyang? You like her?"

Kalden blushed.

Goba smiled. "Don't worry. She likes you, too. Now, no more talk of killing Chinese. Happiness is the best revenge. If they could, the Chinese would kill all Tibetans. So give them what they don't want, - more Tibetans."

The thought pleased Kalden greatly.

CHAPTER 19

The Edge of Darkness

How fortunate for the leaders that men do not think.
Adolf Hitler

SANTA MONICA 1965

As Emily had predicted, Lyndon Johnson reversed Kennedy's policies and expanded the Vietnam War. The country erupted in protest marches, civil disobedience, racial tension, and generational conflict. Detroit, Chicago, and Los Angeles burst into flames from the racial friction. America would never be the same.

While the country became more polarized and the voices on either side grew shriller, Tenzin thought often about what Emily had said about the Kennedy assassination. In the immediate aftermath of the shooting, his own disbelief and shock had led him to dismiss her statements, ascribing them to the cognitive decline that often accompanies advancing age. He wasn't yet ready to accept that something as heinous as the murder of a sitting President could happen in America. Not in broad daylight. Not by powerful interests within our own government. He had hoped Johnson would prove Emily wrong and implement executive order 11110, end the Vietnam War, and shut down the CIA as Kennedy had intended.

Now he was ready to admit that Emily had been right all along. Johnson was a 33rd degree Freemason, placed in office to enact the elite's agenda, not Kennedy's. The war would continue. Great profits would be made by Wall Street and the international bankers. Thousands of innocent young men would die to satisfy their greed. The purpose of the war was not to save the "democratic" government of South Vietnam. That was just a cover story to placate the masses. The war was about profits, the control of natural resources, and the domination of the drug trade. Ideology was the rationale, not the reality.

The bankers had won. Kennedy had lost his life and America had lost its way. It was all too much. Tenzin pressed his fingers hard against his temples. His head was throbbing. He thought about all the fine young men who had fallen in a foreign land and all those who would follow; about the damage the war had already done to the social fabric of the country, and would continue to do to its moral character and economic strength. In that moment of despair, he vowed that never again would he dismiss a hard truth or bury his mind in a comforting lie. He was finished with political delusion; with believing without question whatever the government told the country. The time of blind faith was over. He would never again trust what the "authorities" said without doing due diligence first. Recent events had proven to him that a hidden agenda controlled the country and that agenda was something far different from, and much more sinister than, what was in the best interests of the American people.

Tenzin's next step was to research the Warren Commission. Johnson had convened The Commission only a few days after the assassination, to discover who had killed Kennedy. The seven members were Chief Justice Earl Warren; Senators Richard B. Russell and John Sherman Cooper; House Majority Leader Hale Boggs; Representative Gerald Ford; former CIA Director Allen Dulles; and former President of the World Bank John J. McCloy.

He was shocked to discover that, of the seven members of the Warren Commission, six were high ranking Freemasons. The lone exception was Hale Boggs. Why was Dulles even there? Kennedy had fired him in 1961 for his role in the Bay of Pigs fiasco. His appointment to the commission constituted a conflict of interest. Why was a man fired from an important government post investigating the death of the man who had fired him? Were the conspirators giving Dulles a chance to spit figuratively on the grave of the martyred President? Who's laughing now, you dead Irish prick, Dulles must have said in the company of his fellow elitists. I won. You lost. And don't forget, you lousy Catholic s.o.b, that I get to write history the way I want and say that Oswald killed you. The laughter in that room must have been thunderous as his peers raised their glasses and washed down their Dom Perignon.

Tenzin wasn't smiling. These men were colder than ice. Everyone outside their circle was expendable.

Oswald was conveniently murdered two days after the assassination on November 24, 1963 by Jack Ruby, a nightclub owner with mafia connections, in the basement of the Dallas Police Headquarters. Oswald never had a chance to stand trial and tell his story. Was that why he was killed? How did Jack Ruby get into Police Headquarters with a gun? And why was he allowed anywhere near Oswald? There was only one answer that made sense. Powerful people wanted him eliminated before the truth came out.

When the Warren Commission's report was released, Tenzin was not surprised by its finding. He was certain that the conclusion had been decided before the Commission was even formed. It was the sort of thing that lent itself to secure rooms, with conversations held in hushed tones and heads nodding in solemn concurrence. It was something a secret society like the Freemasons would be especially adept at.

Reasoning from the particular to the general, Tenzin went one step farther. If there were a secret political agenda decided by Freemasons in both parties, then there were no substantial differences between Democrats and Republicans, only nominal ones. What disparities and disputes they had must be staged events to placate the public and lull it into believing the country's political system was a thriving democracy; that the people determined the country's direction. Meanwhile, the corporate and banking elites tightened their grasps on political and economic power, concentrating an ever greater share of the country's wealth and resources in their hands. Which held precedence for the Freemasons in government, he wondered, their constitutional oath or their Masonic one?

Tenzin recalled what Thomas had said to him in an earlier conversation. "Franklin Roosevelt once said, *there are no accidents in politics. If it happened, it was meant to happen.* Roosevelt was a 33rd degree Freemason. Many Freemasons of the 33rd degree have held high political office. Chief Justice Earl Warren was a 33rd degree Freemason. So were Gerald Ford, Lyndon Johnson and Allen Dulles. I don't think that's a coincidence. I'll never again be able to think of a 33rd degree Mason in government without suspicion."

Now that Thomas was retired, he had the time to dig deeper into the world of shadows where the truth had been encrypted, camouflaged, and buried. That search became his calling. After his initial forays into this labyrinthine world, he was certain that what Emily had told them was merely the tip of the iceberg.

Among the first things he uncovered was a speech given by Major General Smedley Butler, United States Marine Corps, on Interventionism in 1933. When he read the speech his lips narrowed, his eyes turned hard and his blood ran cold. When he finished, he went to the Xerox machine in the UCLA library, made a copy, folded it into his shirt pocket, and went home.

Tenzin was preparing for his next client when his office door flew open.

"Thomas? What are you doing here?"

Thomas's face was a portrait in cold fury, something Tenzin had never seen before. He pulled the speech out of his pocket and dropped it on the desk.

"What's this?"

"Read it."

"My next client will be here in a minute."

"It's short."

Thomas stood glowering above Tenzin. His intensity said more than words ever could. Tenzin sighed and reluctantly unfolded Butler's speech.

> *War is just a racket. A racket is best described, I believe, as something that is not what it seems to the majority of people. Only a small inside group knows what it is about. It is conducted for the benefit of the very few at the expense of the masses.*
>
> *I believe in adequate defense at the coastline and nothing else. If a nation comes over here to fight, then we'll fight. The trouble with America is that when the dollar only earns 6 percent over here, then it gets restless and goes overseas to get 100 percent. Then the flag follows the dollar and the soldiers follow the flag.*
>
> *I wouldn't go to war again as I have done to protect some lousy investment of the bankers. There are only two things we should fight for. One is the defense of our homes and the other is the Bill of Rights. War for any other reason is simply a racket.*
>
> *There isn't a trick in the racketeering bag that the military gang is blind to. It has its "finger men" to point out enemies, its "muscle men" to destroy enemies, its "brain men" to plan war preparations, and a "Big Boss" Super-Nationalistic-Capitalism. It may seem odd for me, a military man to adopt such a comparison. Truthfulness compels me to. I spent thirty- three years and four months in active military service as a member of this country's most agile military force, the Marine Corps. I served in all commissioned ranks from Second Lieutenant to Major-General. And during that period, I spent most of my time being a high class muscle-man for Big Business, for Wall Street and for the Bankers. In short, I was a racketeer, a gangster for capitalism.*
>
> *I suspected I was just part of a racket at the time. Now I am sure of it. Like all the members of the military profession, I never had a thought of my own until I left the service. My mental faculties remained in suspended animation while I obeyed the orders of higher-ups. This is typical with everyone in the military service.*

I helped make Mexico, especially Tampico, safe for American oil interests in 1914. I helped make Haiti and Cuba a decent place for the National City Bank boys to collect revenues in. I helped in the raping of half a dozen Central American republics for the benefits of Wall Street. The record of racketeering is long. I helped purify Nicaragua for the international banking house of Brown Brothers in 1909-1912 (where have I heard that name before?). I brought light to the Dominican Republic for American sugar interests in 1916. In China I helped to see to it that Standard Oil went its way unmolested.

During those years, I had, as the boys in the back room would say, a swell racket. Looking back on it, I feel that I could have given Al Capone a few hints. The best he could do was to operate his racket in three districts. I operated on three continents.

Tenzin folded the paper and handed it back to Thomas. "Who wrote this?"

"Major General Smedley Butler, Unites States Marine Corp. The only man in history to win two Congressional Medals of Honor and a Marine Corp Brevet. What do you think of it?"

"What do I think?" Tenzin put down the speech and looked at Thomas. "I'm thinking about all the young men who have lost their lives in Vietnam. And for what?"

"I don't know the particulars," Thomas said. "Only a small inside group knows for sure. But I do know there's a big drug trade in the Golden Triangle and that since the war began, America has been steadily overrun with drugs. That's not a coincidence. The drug trade produces obscene profits. I think one goal of the war is to wrest control of the drug trade from whoever the hell runs it now. There's your money motive. To say nothing of population control which, from what I can tell, is a goal of any war. Kill off the young men so they can't impregnate the young women."

Tenzin sighed. The truth was becoming increasingly dark and disturbing. Who knew how far and deeply it went?

"The kids have been sold a bill of goods by guys like Timothy Leary," he said. "They don't know what they're doing. They think drugs will liberate them. They don't realize that drugs punch openings through their energy fields, making them easy prey for the demonic entities that inhabit the lower astral worlds. These entities are always looking for host bodies in the physical world. Possession is real. It doesn't just happen in movies. And it's happening much more now."

"There's the irony," said Thomas. "Kids think God comes in a pill. Instead, they're falling into the trap the dark side set for them."

"All too true," said Tenzin. "Drugs lead to addiction. They destroy lives and lower moral standards until they disappear. They raise the crime rate, break families apart and destabilize the society. Drugs create a culture of depravity and a society of lost souls. That's what the dark side wants. It looks like they'll get it."

"Try telling the kids that."

"I have."

"And?"

"Those that listen aren't taking drugs."

"And the others?"

"I hope they'll come back when they're ready to change."

"It might be too late, if it happens at all," said Thomas.

"I know. But we can't choose for them," Tenzin replied. "We can only educate those willing to listen. Give the conspirators their due. They're brilliant strategists. They ensnare the kids in drugs and promiscuity and call it spirituality and love. They make a fortune turning the younger generation onto drugs and they destabilize the country at the same time. They kill two birds with one stone."

"So what are we going to do about it?"

"We? We're a tiny boat on a huge ocean," said Tenzin. "We will do what we've always done. We'll help make those who come to us whole and strong. We'll teach them how to center themselves in their souls so that they can't be caught in the traps the dark side has set for them. We'll build a community of like-minded people to support each other. The stakes are higher now, that's all. If enough people learn to stand in their true power, the planetary reality will shift to accommodate the influx of higher energy that shift will generate. Light will supersede darkness. This is a spiritual war. The world is a reflection of our inner states. We win by turning away from polarization and conflict to find unity within and peace among us. They win by instilling more fear, hatred, and prejudice in our minds. If we allow ourselves to be consumed by hatred, endless wars are the inevitable outcome. We will always be divided and easy to conquer. Fear and hatred are only choices. We must learn to make better choices."

"That's asking a lot."

"But it's not impossible. This war will be won by love, not hatred. Love self, love others, love our enemies. Love increases our power. When love is present, fear is absent. We might not like them or what they do, but we will love them. Loving them makes us stronger. Hating them makes them stronger. Hatred is their ally, not ours."

"I'm not sure I see that," said Thomas. "How can you fight what you love? Sounds like a contradiction in terms."

"Not really. When you love, there is no fear. Loving your enemies makes your opposition more effective because you don't fear them. The dark side instills fear to control us. Take that fear away and they lose their power. Other solutions will appear when the time is right. If we are centered in our souls we are linked with the Infinite. There is no shortage of solutions. This is where we start."

"I hope you're right, but frankly I'm not as optimistic as you are."

"You're Scottish," said Tenzin, smiling for the first time since their conversation began. "You're not supposed to be."

"Well, you got me there," said Thomas. "By the way, I've found a number of interesting coincidences between the Kennedy and Lincoln assassinations. You want to hear?"

"Of course."

"Lincoln was elected in 1860, Kennedy in 1960. There are seven letters in each name. Both Presidents were killed on a Friday in the presence of their wives. Both had the legality of their elections contested. Kennedy's secretary was named Lincoln. He warned Kennedy not to go to Dallas. Lincoln's secretary was named Kennedy. He warned Lincoln not to go the theater. Both of their Vice Presidents served in the Senate and were Southern Democrats. Lyndon Johnson was born in 1908. Andrew Johnson was born in 1808. Both names contain thirteen letters. Both were Freemasons. Lincoln and Kennedy were carried on the same caisson during their funeral processions."

"That's quite a lot of coincidences," said Tenzin.

"Too many."

"What do you think they mean?"

"I'm not sure, but I know the dark side loves symbolism. And there's a lot of it here."

"What do you think their ultimate goal is?"

"You sure you want to know?" said Thomas.

"Yeah."

"Complete planetary control by a one world government. The end of freedom and liberty as we know it. Worldwide enslavement. A severe reduction in living standards. They were sending a message to future Presidents when they killed Kennedy."

"What message?"

"That no President has the freedom and power to do things to help the American people; that any President who dared to depart from their agenda would meet a similar fate; that they could eliminate anyone, anywhere, at any time. They were demonstrating their reach. They were telling the world to be very afraid."

"Psychological warfare?"

"I believe so. Now here's another interesting coincidence I found in Lincoln's assassination. John Wilkes Booth, Lincoln's killer, was also a 33rd degree Freemason. When I found that out, it raised my suspicions that he didn't act alone; that there was a much bigger conspiracy behind Lincoln's murder."

"As there was with Kennedy," said Tenzin. "It's interesting that both Oswald and Booth were killed so quickly after the assassinations."

"It would be. Except that it's highly probable Booth wasn't killed."

"But he was tracked down and killed in a barn. His body was burned beyond recognition. It was identified by Edwin Stanton, Lincoln's Secretary of War. I read that in one of the history books I used when you taught me English."

"And if it's in the history books it's legitimate, right?"

I see where you're headed," said Tenzin.

"Do you? Back then there was a lot of dispute about the identification of that burned body. Many people were sure it wasn't the body of John Wilkes Booth. And don't forget that Stanton, like Booth, was a Freemason of high degree."

"You think that Stanton was involved in the plot?"

"The evidence points heavily in that direction. Booth escaped from Washington over the only bridge that wasn't heavily guarded. He used a Masonic gesture that the guard recognized and let him pass. How did he know to use that bridge? Or, to give that gesture?"

"You suspect Stanton of providing Booth with that information?" asked Tenzin.

"He was in a perfect position to do it. And they were both Masons. Masons help Masons. Their Masonic oath supersedes their oath to defend the Constitution of the United States."

"Can you prove beyond a reasonable doubt that Stanton was involved?"

"No. It's circumstantial. But when we put everything we know together it makes sense, doesn't it?"

"I suppose," said Tenzin. "While the evidence is compelling, it's not conclusive."

"Perhaps. But it gets more interesting," said Thomas.

"How?" said Tenzin.

"On January 13, 1903 a man named David E. George died in Enid, Oklahoma. Before he died, he confessed to the woman who owned the boarding house where he lived that he was John Wilkes Booth. George had fractured his right leg decades earlier in the same place that Booth had broken his leg when he jumped to the stage after shooting Lincoln. George was sixty three when he died. John Wilkes Booth would have been sixty three at the time of George's death."

"Again, an interesting coincidence," Tenzin said. "But still no definitive proof."

"And there probably will never be. Just as in Kennedy's murder. Do you see the pattern?"

Tenzin nodded. "Use controversy to obscure the truth."

"Exactly. That's how the dark side operates. In 1937 a relative of Booth's named Izola Forrester wrote a book titled *This One Mad Act.* In it, she claimed that members of her family had been in contact with Booth for over a generation after 1865. Why would she write that if it weren't true?"

"I have no idea. What do you think?" said Tenzin.

"This is what I believe: These killings were planned at the highest levels of power, not by an individual or by the leader of a deranged group of ne'er do wells and psychopaths. The authorities want us to believe in a tale full of holes. They can't stop the questions. So their only option is to muddy the answers."

Tenzin looked shrewdly at Thomas. "You've found more, haven't you?"

"A lot more. In 1866 Albert Pike, a former Confederate General, 33rd degree Freemason, and head of the Freemasons in North America, met at the White House with President Andrew Johnson, a 32nd degree Freemason and the titular head of Freemasonry in Tennessee. Pike brought along his entire Supreme Masonic Council to the meeting, dressed up in their Masonic regalia. During that meeting, Johnson pardoned Pike for his role in the conspiracy to kill Lincoln. Booth, Johnson, and Pike, were all Freemasons of the highest degrees. Johnson, a 32nd degree Freemason, considered Pike, a 33rd degree Freemason, his superior even though Johnson was the President of the United States. Some sources even claim that while he was President, Johnson took his orders from Pike. After Johnson pardoned Pike there was an uproar in the country. Pike was forced to flee to Canada. The pardon was a significant factor in Andrew Johnson's impeachment."

Tenzin shook his head. He was speechless.

"Lovely, isn't it?" said Thomas.

"Lovely?" answered Tenzin. "A country run by criminals? None of this is in the history books."

"Of course not. Now brace yourself. It gets even stranger. There's a statue of Pike in Washington. Right across from the Department of Labor. He's holding *Morals and Dogma,* the Masonic book of initiation rites that he wrote. Now what is the statue of a suspected conspirator in the murder of an American President doing in Washington?"

Tenzin tapped his fingers on the desk. "Is there any political murder that you know of that doesn't involve the Freemasons or another secret society?"

"I'm beginning to think not," said Thomas. "There's another piece to Pike's story. An important one."

Tenzin shook his head, then nodded. "Go on."

"Pike was recruited into the highest degrees of Freemasonry by one Giuseppe Manzini. Manzini had been commissioned in the mid nineteenth century by his European brethren to overthrow the established governments of Europe. The goal was to unify Europe into one political entity as the basis of a New World Order. Manzini failed. But failure never stops these guys. They always come back to their goal. The European Common Market is the latest attempt to fold Europe into one entity. It started as an economic union in 1958."

"I'm aware of that," said Tenzin.

"Everyone is. My bet is that the European Common Market will end up as a political union someday. Do you know anything about the Mafia?"

"Not much. Just that they're criminals," said Tenzin. "Why?"

"Manzini founded the Mafia. It was part of his plan to destabilize Europe. In fact, the M in mafia stands for Manzini. The press touted Manzini as the Great Liberator when in fact he was the great criminal. A lot of the correspondence between Pike and Manzini has survived. I have copies of some of it."

"Like what?" said Tenzin.

"In 1870, Manzini wrote a letter to Pike about using the Freemasons to serve their agenda. Listen to this:

> *We must allow all the federations to continue just as they are, with their systems, their central authorities and their diverse modes of correspondence between high grades of the same rite, organized as they are at the present, but we must create a super rite, which will remain unknown, to which we will call those Masons of high degree whom we shall select. With regard to our brothers in Masonry, these men must be pledged to the strictest secrecy. Through this supreme rite, we will govern all Freemasonry, which will become the one international center, the more powerful because its direction will be unknown.*

Thomas peered at Tenzin over the bifocals perched halfway down the bridge of his nose. "How do you like that?"

"Not much."

"Didn't think you would. Now get this. There's a bust of Manzini in Central Park. He was a Freemason and a criminal. He was not a citizen of the United States. So why is there a bust of him in Central Park?"

"Because he was a Mason?" said Tenzin. "That seems to take precedence over everything else. The traitors get statues. The heroes get graves. They've demonstrated again and again that they won't allow anything to interfere with their hold on power. A hundred years of history speaks to that point. I wonder how far back it really goes."

"A long way, I'm afraid. We've just touched the edge of darkness." Thomas thumbed quickly through his notebook. "This one will send a chill through your heart. It's a letter Pike purportedly wrote to Manzini in August 1871. In 1925 a Cardinal Caro Rodriguez from Chile told a researcher about this letter. At the time, the letter was on display in the British Museum. It was right out in the open. The researcher claims he went there and read it. After he published it, the letter disappeared from view. The British Museum later denied that the letter was ever in its possession." Thomas put down his notebook and stared at Tenzin. "Now you tell me. Why would a Cardinal of the Catholic Church lie about something like that?"

Tenzin stared back. "He wouldn't."

"Here. Read it," said Thomas, handing a copy of the letter to Tenzin. Tenzin took the letter and read it slowly.

> *The First World War must be brought about in order to permit the Illuminati to overthrow the power of the Czars in Russia and of making that country a fortress of atheistic Communism. The divergences caused by the "agentur" (agents) of the Illuminati between the British and Germanic Empires will be used to foment this war. At the end of the war, Communism will be built and used in order to destroy the other governments and in order to weaken the religions.*
>
> *The Second World War must be fomented by taking advantage of the differences between the Fascists and the political Zionists. This war must be brought about so that Nazism is destroyed and that the political Zionism be strong enough to institute a sovereign state of Israel in Palestine. During the Second World War, International Communism must become strong enough in order to balance Christendom, which would be then restrained and held in check until the time when we would need it for the final social cataclysm.*
>
> *The Third World War must be fomented by taking advantage of the differences caused by the "agentur" of the "Illuminati" between the political Zionists and the leaders of Islamic World. The war must be conducted in such a way that Islam (the Moslem Arabic World) and political Zionism (the State of Israel) mutually destroy each other. Meanwhile the other nations, once more divided on this issue will be constrained to fight to the point of complete physical, moral, spiritual and economical exhaustion... We shall unleash the Nihilists and the atheists, and we shall provoke a formidable social cataclysm which in all its horror will show clearly to the nations the effect of absolute atheism, origin of savagery and of the most bloody turmoil. Then everywhere, the citizens, obliged to defend themselves against the world minority of revolutionaries, will exterminate*

> *those destroyers of civilization, and the multitude, disillusioned with Christianity, whose deistic spirits will from that moment be without compass or direction, anxious for an ideal, but without knowing where to render its adoration, will receive the true light through the universal manifestation of the pure doctrine of Lucifer, brought finally out in the public view. This manifestation will result from the general reactionary movement which will follow the destruction of Christianity and atheism, both conquered and exterminated at the same time.*

Tenzin put down the letter. The color had drained from his cheeks. "The first two have happened," he said.

"Let's hope the third never does," said Thomas.

"The history they teach the kids is a tale of lies," said Tenzin.

"And guess who writes it?" said Thomas. "The winners and the killers. What the kids are taught in school is an indoctrination into a belief system. It's a form of mind control." Thomas flipped through more notes. "While we're at it, here's something else you'll be interested in. This is a toast made by John Swinton, Chief of Staff of the New York Times, at the New York Press Club in 1953. It's quite illuminating. Here."

Tenzin took Thomas's notebook and read the speech.

> *There is no such thing, at this date of the world's history, as an independent press. You know it and I know it. There is not one of you who dares to write your honest opinions, and if you did, you know beforehand that it would never appear in print. I am paid weekly for keeping my honest opinions out of the paper I am connected with. Others of you are paid similar salaries for similar things, and any of you who would be so foolish as to write honest opinions would be out on the streets looking for another job.*
>
> *If I allowed my honest opinions to appear in one issue of my paper, before twenty-four hours my occupation would be gone. The business of the journalist is to destroy the truth; to lie outright; to pervert; to vilify; to fawn at the feet of mammon, and to sell the country for his daily bread. You know it and I know it and what folly is this toasting an independent press. We are the tools and vassals of the rich men behind the scenes. We are the jumping jacks, they pull the strings and we dance. Our talents, our possibilities and our lives are all the property of other men. We are intellectual prostitutes.*

Tenzin put down the speech. "Emily was right," he said at last.

"About everything," said Thomas.

CHAPTER 20

After the Lecture

SANTA MONICA 1965

WITH THE STORM of war engulfing the country, a dramatic shift occurred in the type of people attracted to Tenzin's teachings. Besides the professionals, professors, and college students who were the backbone of Tenzin's constituency, college dropouts, long-haired hippies, and the parents of young men fighting in Vietnam flocked to see him.

The new wave of young people found the materialism of the west empty and meaningless. They had "turned on, tuned in, and dropped out" as Timothy Leary had urged them to. Sadly, their experimentation with drugs had left them as empty and confused as the materialistic culture that they had renounced. They hungered to go where drugs had failed to take them: to a direct experience of their true self.

One balmy evening, shortly after Tenzin and Thomas's discussion, Tenzin was scheduled to speak at UCLA. Royce Auditorium was packed. After his talk, a large crowd gathered around Tenzin in the lobby, each hoping to share a private word with him. A young man with a scruffy beard and uncombed, shoulder-length blond hair elbowed his way to the front of the crowd, generating hostile stares from those he had pushed aside. He hardly noticed. When the woman talking to Tenzin turned to go he seized his opportunity.

"I'm next!" he screamed.

All eyes turned on him.

"No you're not!" said a woman standing near him.

"Wait your turn, asshole!" said a young man on the other side of him. "You're not next. You're last."

The crowd murmured its assent. Who did this belligerent young fool think he was?

Tenzin watched the drama unfolding in front of him. His face was a mask. He showed no emotion. He said nothing. The crowd listened and grew silent. His eyes bore into the young man. Terror and fear widened his blue eyes; a wave of uncertainty rippled through his torso.

At first, the young man clenched his jaw and stared back defiantly. But under Tenzin's steady gaze his resolve withered. Soon he looked down. His legs shook slightly. When Tenzin concluded his examination and had seen what he needed, he smiled.

The young man felt the shift in Tenzin's demeanor. He gathered his courage and looked up again, shorn of his defiance. He felt the love and acceptance in Tenzin's eyes and broke into tears.

"Come to my office tomorrow," said Tenzin.

"But I need to talk to you now," he said.

"Eleven o'clock," said Tenzin. His eyes left the man and scanned the crowd. "There are people here whose needs are more pressing than yours. You are not the only one in a difficult situation."

He motioned to a middle aged woman standing nearby. She came forward, her face clenched in suffering, her eyes clouded with sorrow. Her lips trembled as she spoke. "My only son was killed two weeks ago in Vietnam." She paused, summoning the last ounce of her self control. "I can't deal with it," she said. "Please help me."

Tenzin gathered her into his arms.

"Give me your pain," he whispered in her ear.

The woman sagged into him, her body racked with deep spasms of grief. A hush fell over the audience. Tears ran down nearly every cheek, young and old, men and women. No one was untouched by her agony. The young man bowed his head, his face flushed, ashamed of himself.

After a time, the woman stopped shaking, although she continued to hold onto Tenzin, taking as much strength as she could from him. Thomas handed her a tissue. She blew her nose and wiped her eyes.

"Thank you," she said.

Thomas nodded and touched her gently on the shoulder.

"I know something of what you're feeling," said Tenzin. "Years ago I lost my family, many brother monks, and my country. When I came here I was alone. I knew no one and did not speak the language. But many people came forward to help me. America is a great country because its people are caring and compassionate."

Tenzin pointed to Alice, who was standing near him. "This is my wife, Alice. She stood by me when I was lost, as you are now. She, and Thomas, who gave you the tissue, and Emily, who passed on a while ago, were my healers. I would never have made it without their help. We all need each other. We are stronger together than we are apart. When we stand together and are centered in our souls we are the most powerful force in the universe. Nothing can stop us. We are all family. And family helps each other."

Several people in the audience applauded. The rest nodded.

"As Emily used to say, grief cures grief. Don't be afraid of your pain. Face it, feel it, express it. Do that and one day it will depart, leaving in its wake only pure love for your son."

The woman wiped away her tears. "Your wife is beautiful."

"She loves me no matter what I do," he said. "So I know she has a large heart."

The audience laughed. The woman surprised herself and laughed with them.

"Thank you,"she said. "I don't know what else to say. Words are so inadequate."

"When you feel lost and alone you need to remember that you are never alone. The Supreme Truth is always with you. The living and the dead are separated by a thin veil. Those who have passed on are all around us. Love unites all planes of existence. Grieve. One day your heart will open again, in an even larger way. I know, because mine did."

The woman turned to leave, a fresh stream of tears flowing down her cheeks. As she wiped them away, the young man with the scraggly beard and wild hair approached her. He took her hand gently in his own, raised it to his lips, and kissed it.

"Please forgive me," he whispered.

"For what?" replied the woman, stunned.

"For putting myself first."

The fragility in his face reminded her of her own son. They were so similar. She reached out and pulled him to her. He laid his head on her shoulder, his tears joining hers.

CHAPTER 21

The Journey

SIKKIM 1958

When Dorjee entered puberty, Goba gave him a plot of rich land to farm.

"Someday, your family will depend on you for their survival. It's time for you to grow your own crops. We will go the fields together every day, but you will farm your land from now on."

"Do you think I'll have two sons like Kalden and Jamyang?" Dorjee said.

Goba laughed. "First, you have to find a wife. You're twelve. Kalden's twenty."

Dorjee bristled at the perceived rebuke. "One of my sons will be the incarnation of my grandfather."

Goba stopped laughing and put his arm around Dorjee's shoulders.

"Who better for him to return to?" he said.

Dorjee nodded, placated by Goba's tenderness.

Goba had loved the child since the day he first saw him, a forlorn little boy sitting on a mule, vulnerable and scared, clinging to Jinpa. The shock and pain in Dorjee's eyes had touched him deeply. With time, the shock had left, but the pain remained, a wound of such magnitude that even Goba's love and the passage of time might never heal it.

In the years since Dorjee had come to him, Goba had done his best to heal the boy's heart, but there was no way to undo what had been done, and Goba knew it. Dorjee would have to make his peace with what had happened in his own way and in his own time.

For his part, Dorjee knew that Goba loved him, but the unbearable sadness of losing everyone he loved had hung over him like a life sentence for a crime he did not commit. He had been a dutiful child, not a joyous one, and had grown into a serious, observant adolescent who did not talk much.

"Can Jinpa help me?"

Goba shook his head. "No. You can't run to your mother. It's time to stand on your own."

"Jinpa's not my mother!"

"She's not your birth mother, but she's your mother, alright. She did not give you life, but she gave you a mother's love. Jinpa needs her own life now, Dorjee," he said gently." It's time she married and had children of her own. She's eighteen. Her devotion to you has held her back. Let her go."

"No!"

Goba handed Dorjee a rake. "You're not a little boy anymore, Dorjee. It's time you thought about others more and yourself less. The sun's getting high. It's time we got to work."

One hot afternoon later in that year, in the time of the harvest, a solitary monk entered the village. His robe was dusty from his long trek. His throat was parched, his tongue swollen, his lips cracked. He stopped at the village well to quench his thirst and wash the dust from his face. While he drank from his cup, an old woman arrived with a herd of goats. The monk put down his water and bowed to her.

"Do you know where I might find Goba," he said.

The old woman cupped her hand to her right ear. "What's that you say? Speak up now. Stop your whispering."

The monk smiled inwardly and asked again, this time much louder.

"Goba? Well, why didn't you say so?" said the old woman. "Come, I'll take you to him myself. It'll be a relief to get away from these stinking goats for a while. They smell like shit."

The old woman limped across the village, the monk walking slowly by her side. They turned down an alley and approached a small stone house on the left side of a narrow lane. "Here," she yelled. She pounded on the door. "Goba! Have you got your pants on? There's an important monk here to see you!"

The door opened a moment later. A perturbed Goba stood in the doorway, pulling his pants over his protruding belly. His hair was white now, but still long and wild. His sunburned face was deeply lined.

"What are you screaming about now, old woman?"

Bolormaa was the village gossip, poking her head into everyone's business, and stirring up trouble wherever she went. Goba couldn't stand her.

The woman pointed at the monk standing in the street behind her. Goba looked beyond her and broke into a smile.

"Please sir, come in. Join me for some tea."

The monk nodded. Goba stood aside as the monk entered his home.

"Thank you, Bolormaa. You can go now."

"Hey, I'd like some tea, too."

"The monk is here to see me, not you."

"Nobody important ever comes to see you," said Bolormaa. "Everybody knows you're an idiot."

"Goodbye, Bolormaa." He slammed the heavy wooden door in her face.

Bolormaa strode off in a huff. "That Goba is too damn big for his britches," she muttered. "What a fatso. He'll get his soon enough, and I'll laugh my ass off."

An hour later the two men emerged from the house. Goba looked stunned and disoriented. They walked in silence to the fields. Goba swatted at the swarm of flies that tormented him. Several times he missed the flies, slapping his own face instead. "Goddam flies," he swore aloud. The monk wasn't bothered. The flies left him alone.

Since Goba had given Dorjee his own plot to cultivate, the boy had proven himself to be an excellent farmer. He spent most of his day with his crops, loving them and chanting over them as he had seen his grandfather do. His crops responded by growing prolifically. So had he. From the time Goba had given him his own plot, he had grown three inches and added several pounds of muscle to his lean frame. Today, like every other day in the hot summer, he was dressed in loose cotton pants and a wide-brimmed straw hat. Sweat poured down his bare back in the hot mid afternoon sun. His bronze skin glistened in the light. He was bent over, focused on harvesting his beans when the two men reached him.

"Dorjee," Goba called.

Dorjee was surprised to see a monk with Goba. What did he want? Couldn't they see he had work to do? He was proud of what he had accomplished. His crops had thrived and he had flourished with them. He already had more food than he would need for the winter ahead. He had divided some of his excess among Goba, Jinpa, and Kalden, who had a wife and two hungry boys to feed. At first, Kalden had refused to take the food, but Dorjee would not be rebuffed.

"You saved my life, Kalden. I would not be here but for you and your father. I have a debt to you that I can never repay. Please take these crops. I have more than enough. Who knows what the winter will bring? This way, you'll be sure to have plenty of food for your children. If you have more than you need you can always give it to someone whose need is greater."

Kalden shook his head. He was just as stubborn as Dorjee. "I can't take it."

"This is for your family. Think of them," said Dorjee. "You wouldn't want them to go hungry."

Kalden was silent for a moment. "I don't know," he said. "It's not right."

Dorjee persisted. "Take the food, Kalden. I took yours when we left Tibet."

"O.K.," said Kalden, relenting at last.

Relief flooded Dorjee's face. He had never been happier.

Today he was harvesting beans for Kalden and Jinpa. For some reason, the monk's presence annoyed him. He did not look up as he ripped the beans from their stalks and threw them in his basket.

"Dorjee," Goba said. "This monk has come a long way to see you."

Dorjee ignored him. The monk could wait. He had more important things to do than waste his time in idle conversation.

"Dorjee," said Goba again, losing his patience. The boy was making him lose face in front of the monk. "This is important."

"So is harvesting my beans."

The monk had been watching Dorjee carefully the whole time, a faint smile on his lips.

"I knew Naljor," he said.

Dorjee dropped his hoe. He hadn't heard that name in years. A powerful shockwave pummeled his nervous system.

"My grandfather?"

"Yes."

"Why should I believe you?"

"Tenzin is my best friend and my brother monk."

"My uncle's dead. He was killed at the monastery."

The monk shook his head. "Your uncle and I were sent to India a few hours before the Chinese attacked the monastery. Your uncle is very much alive. He is in America."

Dorjee's mouth fell open. He was too aghast to speak.

"He has a wife and two sons. You're a few years older than his boys. You have blood family you've never met, Dorjee. An uncle. An aunt. Cousins. You're not alone anymore."

Dorjee's eyes darted from the monk to Goba and back again. How could this be?

"It's been decided, Dorjee," said Goba. His eyes were heavy with sorrow. "You're going to Rumtek Monastery with this monk. "

"No, I'm not! This is my home. Now leave me alone. I've got work to do."

Goba wiped his eyes.

"When your uncle was close to your age," said the monk, "Naljor brought him to the monastery to follow his path. I was the first person he met there. Now the time has come for you to follow in his footsteps. There is much of your uncle in you. This is what your grandfather would have wanted for you."

"You don't know that," said Dorjee.

"He wanted it for Tenzin. Why would he not want the same for you?"

"I'm a farmer."

"We need farmers at Rumtek with your gift for growing things. Unfortunately, we have none."

"Anyone can grow things," said Dorjee.

"Not like that," countered the monk. "Beside, it's time you picked up where you left off in your last life. It would be a shame to waste your potential."

Dorjee grew quiet. Something in what the monk said had resonated in his soul. "When would we leave?"

"Tomorrow."

Dorjee shook his head. "Too soon."

"You must go, Dorjee," said Goba. "This is your path. I feel it, too."

"If it doesn't suit you, you can leave whenever you want and come back here," said the monk. "We would never keep you against your will. The path concerns liberation, not unhappiness. Try it. Then choose for yourself. You come from a distinguished blood line. The Karmapa himself is eager to meet you."

The next morning at first light, two figures walked out of the remote village of Sebu La, their silhouettes outlined against the horizon. Languid clouds drifted across the azure sky. They hadn't gone far when the anguished cries of a young woman tore open the silence of the waking fields.

"Dorjee! Dorjee!" screamed Jinpa. "Why are you leaving me?" She ran after them trying to catch up. The monk and the boy stopped and looked back. Dorjee looked at the monk. The monk nodded. Dorjee turned and ran back to Jinpa.

"I'm sorry, Jinpa," he said as he tried to catch his breath. "There wasn't time to tell you."

"You were going to leave without seeing me?"

Dorjee hung his head. "It happened so suddenly. I had no choice."

"When are you coming back?" she asked, wiping her eyes.

Dorjee shrugged.

"Will I see you again?"

"I hope so."

"You had better come back."

"I'll try."

"What am I going to do when you're gone?"

"If you don't have me to worry about, you'll find a husband."

Jinpa looked down and was silent.,

"I'm leaving all my crops to you and Kalden. You'll have to harvest them, though."

"Thank you," she said wiping more tears.

Dorjee looked toward the monk. "I've got to go."

Jinpa grabbed Dorjee and hugged him. "I'll miss you."

"Me too," he whispered.

Dorjee turned to leave. His body suddenly felt heavy. His eyes were filled with tears. He walked a few steps, then turned back and waved, a sad smile on his face. Jinpa waved back, her tears trailing down her face. She did not try to stop them. Dorjee nodded a final time, and then ran toward the monk. Jinpa watched them go until the two figures disappeared in the distance.

CHAPTER 22

A Necessary Confrontation

SANTA MONICA 1965

The young man arrived on time for his appointment with Tenzin the next morning at eleven. Alice sat at the reception desk taking calls from people desperate to see Tenzin. Unfortunately, there were no openings for several weeks. She scheduled as many appointments as she could, and put others on a waiting list. There were always cancellations. Despite her best efforts to be accommodating, many callers weren't happy, and they let her know it.

Alice was feeling aggravated and highly stressed from taking the brunt of their anger when she looked up to see a beautiful young man walking down the corridor toward her. He was well groomed and clean shaven with intense blue eyes. Who was he, she wondered. She was quite sure she had never seen him before.

"I'll call you back shortly, Mrs. Rose," she said. "There's a matter here I must adress." There was a brief pause. "Yes, Mrs. Rose. I know you're upset. Please know I'm doing everything I can, but Tenzin is only one man and it seems that everyone in L.A. is demanding to see him today." She placed the phone back in its cradle.

"What can I do for you?" she said brusquely.

The young man smiled. "I have an appointment to see Tenzin at eleven."

"I'm sorry. You're mistaken," said Alice. This was really too much. People had so much nerve.

"He said eleven. I'm sure of it."

"What's your name?" Alice said.

"Charlie."

Alice checked and rechecked the appointment book. "I'm sorry, but there's no one named Charlie here."

"But last night Tenzin told me to come today at eleven."

"You're the young man from last night?" Alice's jaw went slack. "But you had a beard."

The young man flashed a dazzling smile. "That was last night."

"Yes, I suppose it was," said Alice. "Well, Charlie, it seems you're right. You do have an appointment with Tenzin at eleven. With all the commotion last night we forgot to get your name. Have you put last night in the past?"

"Not really."

"Think of it as a learning experience. Then let it go. We all start fresh every day."

"Then I wouldn't have learned anything."

"Don't be so hard on yourself. It's easy to forgive mistakes when you love yourself, impossible when you don't. Self-love is crucial to leading a successful life. Last night you started badly, but you ended beautifully. That's quite an arc to follow in a few minutes." She looked over at the clock on the mantle above the fireplace. "Tenzin will see you now. Down that corridor to your right. Third door on the left."

Tenzin heard the knock on the door and put down his pen. "Come in," he said. The young man entered tentatively. He had steeled himself for a stern rebuke. That's what he'd get from his father if he was there.

"Please," said Tenzin, pointing to the chair in front of his desk.

"Thank you," said Charlie. He sank into the comfortable, old leather chair and thought for the first time that he might not be reprimanded after all. More relaxed now, he looked around the office. A profound peace pervaded the room. The walls were light taupe, the dark wood floor freshly polished. A subtle, yet elegant oriental rug had been perfectly placed in the middle of the room. Several of Emily's impressionist landscapes hung on the walls. A small fountain gurgled in the far corner. Behind Tenzin, sunlight streamed through the French doors that opened on the flower garden behind the house.

"I'm glad you've come," said Tenzin. "Forgive me for asking, but I never got your name."

"It's Charlie."

"What do you want to speak to me about, Charlie?"

"First, I want to apologize for my behavior last night and thank you for seeing me today."

"Don't worry about last night. We can't change what happened yesterday, but we can change what happens today. That way, our mistakes are productive and contribute to our growth. There's no learning without making mistakes. Never be afraid to fail. Now, what did you want to speak to me about?"

"I've gotten myself into a terrible mess and can't find the way out. I don't think one exists."

"Go on."

"I've been drafted. I have to report in two weeks."

"You're not in school?"

"I dropped out," said Charlie frowning and hanging his head.

"Why?"

"I don't want to be a doctor."

"You were pre-med?"

"Yeah."

"Why didn't you just change your major?"

"My dad's a doctor. He wants me to be one."

"So you dropped out in a fit of rebellion?"

"I never wanted to be a doctor. That was my dad's idea. My dad wants me to be just like him. That's the last damn thing I want to be."

Tenzin noted the anger in Charlie's voice. There's a history that needs to be untangled here, he thought. "Maybe he wants you to help people and earn a good living."

"Money's all he thinks about."

"What would you like to study?"

"I don't know."

"You didn't think it through or consider the consequences of your actions when you left school. You acted impulsively," said Tenzin.

Charlie looked down. An overwhelming wave of shame washed over him.

"Who have your actions hurt most?"

"Me," said Charlie.

"Your emotionalism has put you in harm's way and robbed you of your ability to think clearly. This is not your father's fault, Charlie. It's yours. Blaming someone else for the situation you're in changes nothing. You're not a victim. So stop thinking like one. Change comes when you are willing to take responsibility for your actions, not before."

Charlie clenched his jaw while his self-loathing increased exponentially. He didn't enjoy facing the truth.

Tenzin continued. "Who put you in harm's way?"

"I did. I did! Oh God," moaned Charlie, bursting into tears. "I've made a mess of everything." He covered his head with his hands.

Tenzin pressed on. "Why do you think your Dad's upset with you?"

"Because he's a jerk."

"No," said Tenzin. "Because he loves you."

Charlie's eyes whirled with shock. The truth had finally hit home. "Oh God, what do I do now?"

"You report to the induction center or you leave the country."

"My grandfather and his brothers fought in World War One. My Dad and my uncles fought in World War Two. There's a long tradition of military service in my family. I come from a long line of patriots. I can't leave."

"That's one path," said Tenzin.

"Is there another?" said Charlie, hoping against hope there was a way out.

"You need to remember who you are. That's why you're here."

"What do you mean?" said Charlie, completely confused.

"Look in my eyes."

"What?"

Charlie lifted his head and looked at Tenzin. A focussed beam of white light burst out of Tenzin's eyes and into Charlie's. The energy shot through Charlie's nervous system like a lightning storm, engulfing him in a tempest of light. His body twitched and shook; every cell vibrating with more energy than he had ever experienced. He passed out seconds later.

When he came to, the room glowed in a soft golden light. He was sure he was hallucinating. Was he finally having the psychotic break he had always feared? His mother was a paranoid schizophrenic. She had been hospitalized repeatedly while he was a boy. He could not remember a time in his childhood when he had felt loved. She was a brooding, dark presence in his life, prone to fits of explosive rage. She threw things, beat him, and screamed streams of obscenities in her shrill, piercing voice. His father had dealt with it by spending long hours at work, hoping she would be asleep or heavily medicated by the time he returned home.

Over time, Charlie had learned to maintain his distance. It was safer that way. He stayed at his friends's homes or locked himself in his bedroom. The certainty that his mother didn't love him left a gaping hole in his heart that made him feel broken and unfixable. He was convinced that his life was a colossal mistake that could never be redeemed. He was doomed to flounder and fail until he took his final breath. Death was the only way out.

Maybe that's why I got myself in this mess, he thought. I'll go to Vietnam and die with honor. That's the best I can hope for. My dad would like that.

Tenzin had been watching Charlie carefully. He reached across the desk and tapped Charlie on his heart. All the energy in Charlie's body rushed to that point. He grew light-headed, bent over, and clutched his chest. He tried to scream, but only a strange gurgling sound emerged. He leaned back in the chair and lost consciousness again. Tenzin was standing over him when he came to.

"What happened?" he asked.

"You took the first step," said Tenzin.

"What step?" asked Charlie. " I passed out."

"Remembering."

"Remembering sucks. It hurt like hell."

"You have a deep wound in your heart from childhood. Remembering your pain caused you to pass out. The healing has started. Come back in three days."

"I don't want to go through anything like that again."

"Every time is different," said Tenzin. "When your wound heals you'll have more peace and clarity."

"How long will that take?"

"That depends on you."

"I'm not going through this again."

Tenzin shrugged. "You choose to grow or you choose not to grow. A spiritual warrior chooses to face himself."

"And if I don't?"

"You will have more of what you have now. Failure. Confusion. Pain."

"Then I'm damned if I do and damned if I don't. I don't have a choice, do I?"

"You're not damned, Charlie. That's just what you decided when you were a child and what your subconscious mind still believes. The subconscious mind does not have a filter for wrong conclusions. It believes whatever you tell it and creates your reality based on those beliefs. Your instruction set is flawed and self-destructive, but that can be corrected. You always have a choice. You can choose to change your imprinting or do nothing and let it be the cause of your undoing. Most people spend their lives controlled by bad internal programming. They blame their parents, their spouses, their children or their bosses for their problems. They never realize that they have the power to change everything in their lives. Change the inside and the outside changes. Blame the outside and nothing changes. Where is your power, Charlie? In taking responsibility or in assigning blame?"

Charlie sighed. "In taking responsibility."

"That's right. What you don't resolve in this lifetime you will have to resolve in a future lifetime. Death is just an interlude between lives. It's always better to learn your lessons now. It's harder to do in the future. Your life is in your hands, Charlie. What are you going to do with it? I'll see you in three days. Same time."

CHAPTER 23

Facing the Truth

When the people fear their government, there is tyranny; when the government fears the people, there is liberty.
Thomas Jefferson

SANTA MONICA 1965

Thomas came home from the UCLA Library later than usual that evening. The boys had finished eating and rushed out to play. Tenzin and Alice were enjoying a rare moment of peace and privacy at the kitchen table, sharing a warm slice of apple pie.

"We should take a vacation," said Alice.

"How?" said Tenzin. "There's no break in my schedule for several months."

"I know. Just dreaming."

"Maybe you can rework the schedule and find time for us to go away."

Alice shook her head. "Your clients would be beside themselves. I can't keep up with the demand as it is. There's a long waiting list and many unhappy people."

The door swung open and crashed into the wall. Thomas entered the kitchen looking drained and upset.

"Have you eaten?" asked Alice.

"Not since breakfast," he said wearily.

"I didn't think so. Your dinner's in the oven. I'll get it for you."

Thomas mumbled his thanks and sat down. He toyed with his food rather than attacking it with his usual gusto. Tenzin and Alice watched quietly. The vivacious, outgoing, erudite, happy professor had undergone a disturbing transformation. In his place was a morose imposter. Alice nudged Tenzin, nodding toward Thomas. Tenzin frowned, but knew that resisting her was pointless. He sighed and surrendered to her will.

"What is it, Thomas?" Tenzin asked.

"What's what?" said Thomas. He continued to stare down at his food.

"You haven't been your normal cheery self lately."

"Neither would you, if you knew what I know."

"And what's that?"

"You're sure you want to know?"

"Of course."

"Okay then, but you won't believe what I tell you."

"Maybe so. But let's hear it."

"In March of 1933 Franklin Delano Roosevelt declared that the United States was a bankrupt corporation and handed the paper of the corporation we call the United States of America over to the international bankers in the City of London. You know what that means?"

"No," said Tenzin.

"It means America hasn't been a sovereign nation since 1933."

"That's insane," Alice said. "America is a constitutional republic. No one owns America. Certainly not a foreign power or a cabal of international bankers."

"I told you, you wouldn't believe it. Your response is exactly what these guys bank on. No pun intended. The truth is so monstrous and inconceivable that no one will believe it. Unfortunately, there's a lot more to it."

"If there is, I don't want to know," said Alice.

"I do," said Tenzin.

Alice frowned and gave Tenzin an unhappy look. "So much for apple pie."

Tenzin wasn't listening.

Thomas continued. "This rabbit hole reaches all the way back to the thirteenth century. England was bankrupt, and deeply in debt to the Catholic Church. So, on October 3, 1213 King John assigned the sovereign rights of England to the Pope, in perpetuity. In return, the Pope granted executive control to the English monarchy over all of its present and future dominions. This includes the Virginia Company that was founded in 1604 to explore and settle America. To this day the Virginia Company owns all the land in America, but no one knows that, either. According to the treaty of 1213 the British Crown is the chief executive of the United States and the Vatican is the owner."

"How can that be?" asked Alice, her mind reeling. "That can't be true. No way."

"These guys are masters of deceit and duplicity," said Thomas. "That's standard operating procedure for the dark side. They've been at it for millennia.

Remember this dictum: nothing is what it seems. They intermarry within their own bloodline. That way they keep their DNA pure and their agenda secret. They're psychopaths. They have no feeling for any of us. They care only about their power, wealth, and control. They control all of the branches of government. The present administration, like those that preceded it —Kennedy's excluded— does not function in the best interests of the American people but rather in the best interests of the corporate elite. Meanwhile, the charade of democracy continues while the corporations continue to consolidate their power. Real democracy is too unpredictable. They want order and predictability. Their loyalty is to the New World Order agenda, not to the American people. Their long-term goal is to dismantle our industrial base, destroy our economy, bankrupt the country, and revoke our freedoms. They masquerade as Republicans and Democrats, but make no mistake, they're fascists and communists. Do you remember the speech by Smedley Butler on Interventionism?"

"Of course," said Tenzin.

"There's more to that story. In 1933 Prescott Bush approached Butler on behalf of Wall Street and the international bankers. The bankers wanted Butler to assemble a 500,000 man army, lead a coup to topple the Roosevelt administration and to replace it with a Fascist one."

"That could never happen in America," said Alice. "We have the Constitution. And the Bill of Rights."

"The only reason it failed, Alice, is that Smedley Butler was a patriot and a very brave man. I'm surprised that a movie has never been made about him and the Bush conspiracy, but I shouldn't be. Prescott Bush went on to be a Senator from Connecticut while Butler was thrown into the cellar of history and conveniently forgotten."

"Again, the traitors get the glory and the patriots get the grave," said Tenzin.

"It's a recurrent theme," said Thomas. "This was only thirty years ago. But nobody remembers Smedley Butler. Hardly anyone today has ever heard of him. But we know who controls the newspapers, TV, and the movies, don't we? Controlling the mass mind is child's play to these people. Humanity is very malleable. They exploit our weaknesses brilliantly."

"Americans love freedom," countered Alice. "We're not stupid. No one I know would ever stand for this. I think you overestimate the power and influence of these people."

"I wish that were true. Let's take another example. The constitution specifies that the government of the United States has the sole power to issue coinage and provide money. No one else was granted that power in the Constitution. Yet the government hasn't issued our money since 1914 when the Federal Reserve

System was created. The Federal Reserve is not Federal and it has no reserves. It is a private corporation mainly owned by foreign interests. Woodrow Wilson was the President when the Federal Reserve Bill was passed into law." Thomas reached into his briefcase and pulled out a black binder. "Shortly before he died, Wilson wrote this:

> *I am a most unhappy man. I have unwittingly ruined my country. A great industrial nation is controlled by its system of credit. Our system of credit is concentrated. The growth of the nation, therefore, and all our activities are in the hands of a few men. We have come to be one of the worst ruled, one of the most completely controlled and dominated governments in the civilized world. No longer a government by free opinion, no longer a government by conviction and the vote of the majority, but a government by the opinion and duress of a small group of dominant men.*

"Wilson said that?" said Alice.

"He most certainly did. And by the way, here's the list of the ten member banks of the Federal Reserve System."

Thomas handed the list to Alice. She took it and read it aloud.

"Rothschild Bank of London, Warburg Bank of Hamburg, Rothschild Bank of Berlin, Lehman Brothers of New York, Lazard Brothers of Paris, Kuhn Loeb Bank of New York, Israel Moses Seif Banks of Italy, Goldman Sachs of New York, Warburg Bank of Amsterdam, Chase Manhattan Bank of New York."

Alice frowned. "Only four of those banks are American. Why do foreign banks have that much control over our money supply?"

"From what I can see," said Thomas, "all ten banks are part of the Rothschild banking cartel. If that's true, it means that they're all controlled by foreign interests, even if four are American 'owned'. The international bankers stole the most important power of government, the power to mint and regulate its currency. That power is granted to Congress in Article 1 Section 8 of the Constitution. The international bankers replaced a monetary system that was debt-free with one that is entirely based on debt. In essence, they create money out of thin air, then charge the American people interest on it. That's why we have an income tax and the IRS to collect it. Like the Federal Reserve, the IRS is a private corporation. And like the Federal Reserve, it is not part of the Federal government. We are forced to pay interest on a debt that is completely unnecessary. The income tax that we pay does not fund our government but is paid to the owners of the Federal Reserve as interest on the money that they create from thin air. It's the greatest scam ever perpetrated on the American people. The Fed has been stealing the wealth of America since 1913. Given what they've accomplished already, revoking our remaing freedoms would not be terribly difficult for them."

"Do you really think they could do that?" Alice said.

"I'm going to let Thomas Jefferson answer that one," said Thomas. He flipped through his binder until he found the quotation he was looking for.

> *The central bank is an institution of the most deadly hostility existing against the principles and form of our Constitution. I am an enemy to all banks discounting bills or notes for anything but coin. If the American people allow private banks to control the issuance of their currency, first by inflation and then by deflation, the banks and corporations that will grow up around them will deprive the people of all their property until their children will wake up homeless on the continent their fathers conquered.*

Alice's mouth was a grim line. "My God," she said.

"All they would need do is create a large enough incident on American soil so they could invoke martial law to ensure our "safety and security," said Thomas. "The strategy is called PRS: problem, reaction, solution. Create a problem, wait for the predictable outcry from the public to do something, then unveil the solution they had intended to impose all along. A frightened and unthinking public would be relieved to give up their freedoms in exchange for security, however false that security might be. The loss of common sense and good judgment are the first casualties of fear. The dark side knows that, and uses it against us. I'm sure that something like that will happen one day."

"My God," said Alice. "This is so hard to believe."

Thomas continued. "I know. That's what they count on. So even if the truth is revealed, only a few people will find the courage to believe it. They killed Kennedy because he intended to take the power to print our money away from the Federal Reserve and give it back to the government where it legally belongs. Andrew Jackson terminated an earlier attempt at creating a central bank when he closed down Nicholas Biddle and the Bank of America in 1836. The major difference between Jackson and Kennedy was that they killed Kennedy before he could terminate the Federal Reserve, while all their attempts to assassinate Jackson failed. Kennedy had four billion dollars in debt-free money printed by the Treasury. One of the first things Lyndon Johnson did after Kennedy's assassination was to recall those Treasury notes and permit the Fed to continue as if nothing had happened. So if you want to find the truth, follow the bankers's trail. Johnson is a 33rd degree Freemason and the bankers's boy, pure and simple. You know, the best kind of prison is one where you don't think you're a prisoner. Thanks to the war we have an exploding national debt, rising levels of inflation, soaring interest rates and increasing levels of personal debt. The banksters have made us economic slaves, and we still think we're free. You have to hand it to them. They're good at what they do."

"But what about the Peace Movement, the protests against the war, the editorials, the Civil Rights Movement? Those things wouldn't be possible in a country that isn't free," Alice said.

Thomas stared at the table and shook his head. "All part of the plan. Protests only create the illusion of freedom. Meanwhile, they generate more conflict among the people. This is one of the dark side's favorite games, divide and conquer. We demonize each other while the real demons spin unseen webs around us. They laugh at our stupidity. If we don't wake up and unite, their agenda will continue. God knows where it will end. The destruction of America? The de-population of the world? All of us poor and enslaved, living in terror and doing their will?"

"This is truly awful. You need to put it aside, Thomas. It's eating you up."

"Not now. At the risk of boring you, let me quote Jefferson one more time: *Eternal vigilance is the price of freedom.* If they're not discovered; if their deeds are not revealed; if their treason goes unnoticed they'll enslave this country and the whole world. The conspiracy is not theory. It's time we stood up for the truth and restored this country to its greatness before it's too late."

"I understand how you feel. But look at you. You're tired and angry. The light has left your eyes. Is it worth it? " asked Alice.

"I'll get back to myself soon enough. I'd rather know the truth than not know it."

"Do you remember the quotation from Nietzsche that you were fond of sharing with us in your seminars?" said Alice.

"There were many. Which one are you referring to?"

"Beware that when you are fighting monsters, you yourself do not become a monster...For when you gaze long into the abyss, the abyss gazes also into you. I've never forgotten that quote, Thomas. And I'm worried that's what happened to you."

"I appreciate your concern, Alice," said Thomas, smiling for the first time that evening. "And I'm grateful that you remembered something I once said in class. That was a long time ago."

"I remember much of what you said. You were the best teacher I ever had."

"I'll have a piece of that pie now, " said Thomas, smiling.

"Of course," said Alice. She rose to get it, smiling for the first time since Thomas had joined them.

"Thomas," Tenzin said, anxious to get the discussion back on topic. "How does the Federal Reserve create our money? You said it was based on debt."

"It works like this. Congress appropriates money to fund its programs. It then issues government bonds to the Federal Reserve so that it will print the money. For example, if the Congress appropriates a hundred billion dollars to fund a program, it issues bonds to the Fed for that amount. The Fed takes the bonds and prints the money. This creates another hundred billion in debt that the people have to repay to the Fed with interest. This all because the Fed holds our bonds. So, every time the Fed prints money the American people go into more debt. And that's not all. As more and more dollars go into circulation, each dollar is worth less. Inflating the money supply reduces the purchasing power of our dollars, destroying our wealth. If the government had retained the power to print its own money as specified by Article 1 Section 8 of the Constitution, rather than allowing the Fed to steal it, none of this would happen. We wouldn't have much debt or need an income tax to service that debt. The IRS is a private corporation, just like the Fed. Both are incorporated in Puerto Rico. The Fed is the only for profit corporation in America that is exempt from both paying federal and state taxes. The more than one trillion dollars we pay each year in income tax does not go to run our government. It goes into the pockets of the owners of the Federal Reserve."

"Look at the endorsement on back of the check you write to pay your taxes when you get it back. It says, "Pay Any FRB Branch or Gen. Depository for Credit U.S. Treas. This is in payment of U.S. Oblig." If there were no Federal Reserve, our government wouldn't be controlled by foreign interests. The Fed's never been audited and the names of its shareholders have never been revealed. The Fed is secretive, just like every other element of the conspiracy."

"I appreciate what you've uncovered, Thomas," said Tenzin, "and understand what that learning has cost you. But Alice has a point. You cannot lose your center and your capacity to love over this. The less love in the world, the more they control it. They are parasites who feed off humanity's negative emotions. Our negativity makes them strong. Don't give them additional fuel. The day will come when humanity will reclaim its spiritual power. On that day the dark side will enter its death throes."

"A lovely idea, but a pipe dream I'm afraid. This is the real world," Thomas said. A dark shadow was suddenly visible behind his eyes. His eyes, normally a sparkling blue had a strange yellow tint to them. There was a malice and hatred in their gaze that Tenzin had never seen before in Thomas.

Tenzin recoiled involuntarily. He had seen that shadow and those yellow eyes before but couldn't remember where or when. All he remembered was how lethal it had seemed at the time. He breathed deeply and collected himself. "It may seem impossible now, but it will be real later," he said.

"How much later?" said Thomas.

"In the next century."

"That won't do us any good."

"We can only do what we can. Our task is to open people to the true power inside them. The world will change through the power of silence, not through the constant proliferation of noise. When we meditate in silence and connect with the Oneness we attract the energies that will change the world. That is the way to bring about a real and lasting change. Running around, protesting this and that, giving speeches and holding rallies are not lasting solutions. They are just more noise and emotion. The conspiracy operates unseen and unknown from deep in the shadows. Secrecy is its key. Silence is ours. In silence we feel the Oneness and become clear and peaceful. We are true agents of change, then. That is the real change the world needs."

"I guess we'll see. I hope you're right and I'm wrong. That's damn good pie, Alice." said Thomas, relishing the last bit of it on his plate. "Could I have another piece?" His eyes had returned to their normal sparkling blue.

CHAPTER 24

In the Woods

SANTA MONICA 1965

CHARLIE STRODE CONFIDENTLY into the Santa Monica Tibetan Center three days later. There was a spring in his step that had been lacking before.

Alice was at the reception desk sorting through the mail when he arrived. She smiled as he approached her. "Feeling better, are we?" she said.

"Yeah."

"Good luck today."

"Luck's got nothing to do with it."

Alice paused and looked into his eyes. "You're learning," she said. "The outer world mirrors your inner one. Change your mind patterns and life gets better. The future is in your hands, Charlie."

"You would have to remind me."

Alice laughed. "You brought it up," she said. "Go ahead. Tenzin's waiting for you."

"How are you feeling?" asked Tenzin when Charlie had settled into the old leather chair in front of the desk.

"Fine. Say, what is it about this chair? I feel better whenever I sit in it."

"It belonged to Emily. She meditated in it daily. You're feeling her energy."

The tinge of sadness in Tenzin's voice at the mention of Emily's name didn't escape Charlie's notice. Until then, Charlie had thought of Tenzin as serene and strong no matter what he had to face. The fleeting crack in Tenzin's exterior evoked the latent empathy in Charlie's nature, curtailing his chronic self-involvement.

"I'm sorry about her passing," he said.

"Don't be. Being in the body is never easy for the soul. Death liberates it from the harshness of earth. Emily is free now. She saved me when I most needed saving. But I will always miss her."

"If life is so harsh, why bother incarnating at all?"

"Oh, there are reasons," said Tenzin.

"Like what?"

"To heal ourselves, resolve our karma, advance our growth," said Tenzin, fixing him with that piercing gaze. "And to increase our light."

"Even you?"

Tenzin laughed. "Even me. If you're in the body, you have things to learn. We're all alike in that. There are no exceptions. No one is superior to anyone else. We're just at different stages in our development, that's all. We're all part of the Oneness. Separation is an illusion. The ego believes in the illusion. The soul knows better."

"Have you ever experienced the sort of thing I went through the other day?"

Tenzin bowed his head for a moment before he answered. "I spent many months in agony," he said. "I had an ocean of heartbreak and hatred to overcome. It was overwhelming at the time, but my grief finally ended. It taught me an invaluable lesson."

"What was that?"

"That we always have a choice. We can use our pain to become better or to let it make us bitter. Most people do little when life breaks them. They slide into bitterness and stay there. While doing nothing is the path of least resistance, it creates great internal resistance to our happiness and fulfillment. Bitter people's lives get worse. Those who have the courage to confront their suffering get better. They rise in the Light. Their capacity for compassion expands."

"So why is facing yourself so difficult if it's so important?"

Tenzin swiveled in his chair to look through the French doors into the garden. Charlie had reached a pivotal point in his healing. Tenzin wanted to frame his answer in a way that would encourage Charlie to go forward.

Tenzin knew that he could help people become whole, aid them in defeating their egos, and in aligning their personalities with their souls. But he could not enlighten them or wave a wand that would allow them to merge into the Oneness. No one could.

Enlightenment was a matter between the individual and his soul. Tenzin's job was to prepare his students for that moment of union between soul and self. In the service of that goal, he never tolerated pretension of any sort. Delusion was cheap and easy to come by, but no substitute for real growth. He saw it as a great danger, particularly for those who believed that they had arrived at the end of a journey they had never really begun. He didn't want Charlie to become discouraged and lose heart for the work ahead. He knew despondency was a weakness of his. If he was to move forward, Charlie needed to develop persistence in the face of difficulty and learn to endure until he attained his goal. Defeating the ego was no easy matter.

Over time, Tenzin had developed the Nine Maxims of Transformation to explain the healing process to his clients when they reached this particular crossroads. These maxims countered the mistaken notion that spirituality would make them feel better right away. They thought all they had to do was meditate, repeat a mantra, do some yoga, think positively and they would find inner peace.

"Perhaps you will feel better right away," Tenzin would tell them. "It's possible. But it won't last."

Most students were crestfallen by this news. "Why?" they would ask. "I need to feel good. My life has been painful for far too long."

Charlie was growing more agitated. Why was Tenzin taking so long? It was a simple question, for chrissakes. He didn't have to sugarcoat it. What did he see out there, anyway? The Buddha? Charlie looked out the French doors. There was no Buddha and no answers he could see, just orderly rows of flowers sparkling in the sunshine. The ticking of the grandfather clock grated on his nerves. He had half a mind to open the clock's glass door and stop the pendulum before it drove him to madness. He was about to get up when Tenzin turned back to face him.

"Do you know the Nine Maxims of Transformation, Charlie?"

"Never heard of them," said Charlie.

"Let me share them with you then."

"Fine," said Charlie. What the hell did a bunch of maxims have to do with his question, he wondered. If he wanted maxims he could read the Bible, the Gita, or Ralph Waldo Emerson. Maxims were not why he was here.

"To go up into the light, you must go down into your darkness. To overcome your pain, you must first embrace it. To experience your power, you must feel your powerlessness. To realize your destiny, you must face your hopelessness. To arrive at the point of freedom, you must acknowledge the power of that which binds you. There is no resurrection without a crucifixion. You will not find freedom until you release the past. All healing is emotional. If you cannot find your pain, face it, feel it, and forgive it, you won't overcome it."

"Isn't that why I'm here?" said Charlie.

"You seek the easy way, Charlie. I see it in your eyes. The easy way is an attempt to escape from your pain without feeling it. This leads to delusion, the belief you have freed yourself from your pain when you haven't. Delusion is a form of avoidance. Anything that masks your pain is dangerous because it can easily become an addiction. There will be no lasting change, only an increase in your sense of powerlessness. What I am offering you is the chance to confront the hidden pain that has limited you for many lifetimes and clear it from your soul, once and for all. Are you ready to proceed on that level?"

Am I, Charlie wondered? He had hoped today would be easier, that Tenzin would see how changed he was, and praise him for his courage and growth, not push him further into hell.

"I guess so," he mumbled. Today sure wasn't going the way he had scripted it.

"Despair is a weakness in your nature, Charlie. If you give into it, it will defeat you before you take your first steps to freedom. Your true power, like everyone else's, is blocked by the negative side of your nature. When you release the negative, your fear turns into love and acceptance, the door to your soul opens, and your inner light shines through."

"I see what you're saying. It's the getting there that scares me."

"Fear is the ego's ally, Charlie. The ego is the part of you that has no light and feels completely separate from other people. Fear enhances the ego's sense of separation and increases its dominance in your life. You have come into this life to earn your freedom. Negative emotions like fear, anger, and resentment make you reactive. When you're reactive, you blame others for your shortcomings and try to hurt them. Reactive behavior is vindictive and destructive. It widens the gap between your mind and your soul, and strengthens the ego's grip over your life. Negative emotions and reactive behavior block your ability to love, accept others, and create positive momentum in your life. They represent a kind of self-imposed tyranny. You can't transform yourself when you are reactive and ego bound. You can only be a victim who creates more negative karma that he must contend with at some point in the future. All victims feel powerless. The irony is that the more power the ego has in your life, the more powerless and impotent you will feel. Fear generates reactive behavior that strengthens the ego and weaves more karmic webs around you. There's no freedom in this form of debased behavior, only a deepening sense of self-enslavement. This applies to most people in the world.

You transform yourself when you take responsibility for everything that happens in your life. Instead of blaming others, you use the emotions their behavior evokes in you to change yourself. Love and self-acceptance dissolve the ego's reactive nature and reunite you with your soul. Love more. That's the key to real freedom. Self-love is how you increase your light and dispel your fear."

"I'll try," said Charlie. "But who knows how deep the pit inside me is? I feel like Sisyphus."

"Is that a friend of yours?" Tenzin said.

Charlie laughed, his mood lifting slightly.

"No," he said. "It's a story from Greek mythology. Zeus sentenced Sisyphus to push a huge boulder up a hill only to see it fall back down as soon as he reached the top. Then he had to go down and push it back up, again and again, forever."

Tenzin nodded. "Sisyphus' boulder is the ego," he said. "That's the life you will lead until you face yourself. But the only thing that's truly endless is Divine love. Your ego stands between your personality and your soul. Its goal is to prevent you from experiencing unconditional love. Its purpose is to separate you from the oneness of life. When you clear the negative emotions buried in the subconscious the gap between the personality and the soul closes. As it does, the ego dissolves and the struggles of Sisyphus, with which you identify, will come to an end."

"Who knows if I'll ever get through it," said Charlie.

"If you don't confront the darkness inside you, Charlie, the distance between your personality and soul will grow. You'll become a slave to the negative within you. The ego will win. The ego doesn't want you to evolve. It does not seek the Light. It does not want union with the soul. For the ego, evolution is death. The ego is a creature of darkness that does not want to be exposed. The more fragmented we are, the more power and authority it has over us. The ego is not interested in integration, but seeks instead to increase our fear and fragmentation. Facing your pain is a small price to pay for freedom. It is not the hopeless journey you think it is. That's your ego talking, not your soul." Tenzin took a deep breath and looked at the sunlit flowers in the back yard. He turned back to Charlie. "Your journey will not take as long as you think."

Charlie remained silent. This was a vast amount of information to digest.

At least he is moving in the right direction, thought Tenzin. A little progress is still progress.

"The negative needs to be understood, Charlie. While it's a barrier to growth, it also holds the key to our evolution. It's a springboard to a better future, provided that we are willing to confront and transform it. Fear is the only enemy. Face it and the ego will dissolve in due course. Confronting the negative side of our nature is the basis of all growth. The ego generates constant resistance to the soul's purpose. That's its job. When the ego dies, resistance dies with it. The joy of the soul replaces the ego's frustrations, self-absorption, grievances, and general unhappiness. By healing the negative side of our nature, all that energy is finally liberated and lifts us higher in the light. Life becomes a far richer experience."

"Okay, okay," said Charlie, flinging up his hands. "Let's do it."

"Good," said Tenzin.

"You weren't going to stop until I agreed to do it, were you?"

"No."

"So what do we do now?"

"There's more transpiring in your life than you've told me, isn't there?"

Charlie looked away and shook his head. His jaw clenched tighter.

"You have to talk about it, Charlie. It's in your way," said Tenzin.

Charlie let his head fall back against the old leather chair and closed his eyes. When he finally spoke his words burst out rapidly as if he couldn't get it over with fast enough. "My girlfriend's pregnant. So go ahead, tell me I'm a selfish bastard. My father sure would." Charlie gripped the chair so hard the knuckles on both his hands were white.

Tenzin replied without the slightest touch of disapproval in his voice."What does she want you to do?"

Charlie let out a tortured sigh. "Leave the country. She'd go with me to Canada."

"So now your situation has an extra layer of complexity. On one side, the government has ordered you to report for induction and go to war. On top of that is the pressure you feel to uphold your family honor. Then, on the other side, your girlfriend wants you to leave the country and avoid being drafted. And then there's you. What do you want to do?"

"I may be many things, but I'm not a coward. The war sucks. Why can't all those American Legion patriots and rednecks with buzz cuts see that? Why all this my country right or wrong stuff? This isn't World War Two. We're not fighting to save the world from evil, this time. Look at what we're doing to the people of Vietnam. Raping and killing them to ensure their freedom? That's insane. Lots of guys my age have died and more are going to. Since when is coming home in a body bag patriotic? Those guys aren't the ones doing the fighting this time, are they? I'd rather go than run but I gotta tell you, the whole thing stinks."

"Wars are fought for profit," said Tenzin, "not patriotism or ideology. If the people on this planet were free of their egos they would never permit another war to take place. No one would be stupid enough to fight so that rich people could get richer."

"What should I do, Tenzin? I'm so confused."

"What do you think you should do?"

"I think I should go, even though I hate this war."

"Okay."

"You're in favor of my fighting?"

"I'm in favor of you making the decision you feel is right for you."

"But you were trained as a monk. Your'e a man of peace. How can you counsel me to go to war? You saw what the Chinese did to Tibet."

"I saw."

"So how you can tell me to go and do to the Vietnamese what the Chinese did to your people?"

"I haven't told you to do anything. You told me. I listened."

"But you approved it."

"I said okay. That's neither approval nor condemnation. It's an acknowledgment of your thinking, nothing more."

"But you would support my decision to go?"

"I'll support any decision that's right for you."

"But this war is wrong. It's immoral."

"Yes."

"And you'd still support me if I decided to go?"

"I'll support the decision that is best for you."

"You'd support me killing innocent Vietnamese?"

"It's not in you to do that."

"But if I go that's what I'd have to do."

"There's another way."

"What other way? War is about killing the enemy."

"Not if you're a medic. You'd be saving lives."

"I hadn't thought of that."

"If you go, your reason will be much different from what you think it is. Not to please your father. Not to maintain your family's honor. Not even to fulfill your girlfriend's wishes."

"What do you mean?" asked Charlie.

"This journey is about your soul's needs. In another lifetime you ran from your enemies. You have never forgiven yourself for that."

Tenzin's words hit a nerve inside him that Charlie hadn't known existed. His mind went numb. He stared out the French doors but registered nothing. A strange whirring sound spun inside his head. His chest throbbed. He tried to move his arms and legs, but they had become numb. A deep terror held him in a death grip.

Tenzin came quickly around the desk and tapped him three times on his back. Warm, viscous energy snaked up his spine and beat against the back of his head like a drum. A door in his mind opened. Charlie slipped down a dark tunnel to the distant past.

A thick forest of towering oaks blocked the sun. Less than a mile away from the edge of the forest, a Roman legion marched in battle formation across an open field, bearing down on his tribe. There was pandemonium in the woods. The men furiously sharpened their swords and axes, readying themselves to fight, their faces drawn and determined. Children were sobbing. The women were petrified with fear. They clung to their fathers and husbands as long as they could. Finally, the old chieftain ordered the women and children to flee immediately for the tribe's stronghold, a sacred oak grove hidden deep in the forest. The men released their families, urging them to make haste and save themselves.

The men knew that they would die. There were too many Romans for there to be any other outcome. The chieftain ordered the men to form a battle line. They turned for one last look at their fleeing families, then marched resolutely toward the oncoming legions, mouths and jaws set in grim resolve, eyes cold as stone. They were determined to take as many Romans into death with them as possible.

Charlie moved forward with the rest of the men but when he saw the Romans in disciplined formation with their shields up and swords drawn, he realized the folly of this fight. The tribesmen crouched in the heavy thicket of the forest waiting for the Romans to enter the killing zone. The sheer numbers of soldiers and the sound of their swords as they beat their shields sent a shiver through them all. They were outnumbered five to one. Soon they would all be dead.

For what, Charlie thought. Nothing was to be gained from this fight. They'll shred us and keep going. Better to hide deep in the forest and fight a guerrilla action, sweeping down from behind the trees to attack their rear. We could slow them down and keep them from our women and children. This fight meant the end of the tribe. Unfortunately, there was no time to convince the old chieftain to change his strategy.

Charlie looked around at his friends and fellow tribesmen. Without exception, they were committed to fight to the death. No one was thinking what he was. Their allegiance to the old chief had blinded them. They would follow him into disaster.

Charlie stepped off the line and slipped away into the forest. No one noticed. The battle had begun. He ran until he reached the crest of a nearby hill. The din of battle filled his ears. The screams of the wounded assailed him from every direction. But not for very long. A victory cry rose up from the Romans. They had suffered a few casualties, but the tribesmen were all dead.

The Romans threw the bodies of the dead into huge piles, doused them with oil and set them on fire. Thick, dark smoke billowed into the blue sky. The stench of burning flesh filled his lungs. He fell to his knees and vomited. He had been right, but what did that matter now? His people were dead, their flesh burned to ash while the Romans celebrated their kill and groused about the absence of spoils. They were determined to find the women and children. They would not be denied their sport.

Roman patrols spread out later in the day to search for survivors. Charlie huddled in the undergrowth as the Romans came close, but failed to discover him. When night came the patrols stopped. At dawn the Romans moved out. Charlie lingered behind briefly, hoping to find survivors. There weren't any. Grief stricken and shocked, he set out to find the women and children.

Shortly before dusk Charlie reached the grove where the women and children had gone. The place was eerily silent. He entered carefully, his senses on high alert, worried that Roman sentries might be lurking in the shadows. Blood covered the ground and speckled the trees. Bodies were strewn about the grove, their faces bloated and bloody. Many were children. He found his wife under a canopy of ferns. Her naked thighs were caked in blood. Her stomach had been slit open. He fell to his knees, gently wiped the matted hair off her face and cradled her in his arms. His tears fell on the dried blood on her cheeks and ran red down her neck.

Darkness had nearly fallen before he was able to stand. He kissed her a final time, then searched the rest of the grove for survivors. The Romans had been thorough. It was another fruitless search.

As the enormity of the tragedy sunk in, he sat against a towering oak and threw up blood. His tribe was extinct, his family murdered. Time fell away. The world disappeared. In his mind appeared the dragon of the abyss, a fearful creature with greedy jaws and sharp teeth dripping with blood, eager to swallow him into eternal darkness.

"No!" he screamed. He rose and stumbled away in the dying light, his mind incapable of coherent thought. Darkness settled over the forest; he came to a jagged cliff. A swollen river raged below. He looked over his shoulder at the last sliver of light on the horizon and felt the cold of the night beating against his cheek. He shivered. His breath hung like a ghost in the frigid air. They were all gone. The men turned to ash, the women and children left where they lay, to decay and be swallowed by the earth, or to be torn apart and devoured by buzzards and beasts. Only their bones would remain to testify that they had once lived. He was alone. He would be alone forever now. At least the men died not knowing what had happened to their families. His was the worse fate. He lived. He knew. The extinction of his tribe was his alone to endure. No one else could share his burden or know his agony. The shame, the horror, and the guilt would never leave him.

It was time to end the unbearable; time to escape the unendurable. The swollen river beckoned. No one would miss him. No one would grieve his passing. No one would care. No one would ever know. This way was best. His wife would be waiting for him in the land beyond death. He breathed deeply one last time, felt the cold air sear his lungs and jumped into the darkness.

Sitting in Emily's chair, the ancient shame and grief poured from him, a broken dam that once breached could not be stanched. Tenzin watched in silence, his face both solemn and grave. The shadows in the room deepened and grew longer, and still Charlie clung to his grief. Late in the afternoon his primal fury was finally spent. He returned from the distant past, wiped away his tears, and opened his eyes.

"I had no idea," Charlie said. "No idea at all."

"We never do, until it surfaces."

"I'm gonna go to Vietnam. I need to redeem myself. I need to prove that I'm not a coward."

"You're not a coward, Charlie. You weren't then, either."

"I ran."

"You saw the futility of what was about to happen. You had a better plan. But there wasn't time and no one would have listened anyway. Your thinking was superior."

"It doesn't matter. I still ran."

"Running was the only sane thing you could do. You wanted to save your tribe, but you could save only yourself."

"It didn't work out very well."

"It's time to stop blaming yourself."

"They all died."

"You didn't kill them. There was nothing you could do to prevent it."

"Yeah," said Charlie. His voice held the weight of regret.

"Can you connect what happened in that lifetime to your relationship with your mother in this one?"

"She was there?" said Charlie, shocked.

"No. But you died feeling unworthy of being loved."

"My mother never loved me."

"Exactly."

"I attracted that relationship to me?" Charlie was dumbfounded.

"The decision that you made about yourself before dying generated the circumstances of your childhood. You created the experience of not being loved in order to punish yourself."

"Oh, God."

"There's more."

"I can't handle any more."

"You have to. It's important. Your pregnant girlfriend..."

"What about her?"

"She was there."

"My wife," he whispered, burying his face in his hands, "was pregnant when the Romans killed her."

"Yes."

"I have nothing left," Charlie whispered. He covered his head in his hands. "Nothing."

Tenzin leaned forward and placed his hand on Charlie's shoulder. Charlie looked up. Their eyes locked.

"From nothing," said Tenzin, "everything is born."

CHAPTER 25

The Field of Light

SIKKIM 1959, RUMTEK MONASTERY

SHORTLY AFTER DORJEE and Nawang arrived at Rumtek Monastery, Nawang reported to the Karmapa, the titular head of the monastery and the leader of the Black Hat sect of Tibetan Buddhism. The Karmapa listened respectfully while Nawang told him about Dorjee's unique talent for growing things. The Karmapa, whose manners were as impeccable as his intelligence was impressive, did not respond until Nawang concluded his report.

"How many times has the boy produced an oversized harvest?"

"Once, Holiness."

"On how many acres?"

"It was a small plot, Holiness."

"Smaller than an acre?"

"Yes, Holiness."

"How much less?"

"Significantly less, Holiness."

"I see," said the Karmapa. He stared into Nawang's eyes for a long moment. "This is beginner's luck, Nawang, nothing more. The boy has no record of consistent accomplishment that would indicate otherwise. It is a worthy achievement for a young man, but not worthy enough for me to place the monastery's fate in his hands."

"If he did it once, Holiness, he will do it again."

"I must think for the entire monastery, Nawang. What you're asking is imprudent. The risk is too high."

"Holiness, the boy has a special gift for growing things. None of the others to whom you entrusted our food supply did. In the end, what good did their experience or their past success do for us? They all failed."

The Karmapa grunted, turned his back on Nawang and stared through the window at the ancient, snow-capped peaks in the distance. The wind shifted direction frequently. People arrived and departed. Only the mountains remained unchanged. He appreciated them most in moments like these when he had to make decisions that determined the monastery's future.

The only thing the boy had in his favor was the high regard in which Nawang held him. And the most important advantage Nawang had was the high regard in which he, the Karmapa, held him. Nawang was loyal and trustworthy, his judgment impeccable. Combined with his administrative skills and adroitness in handling people, those traits had made him indispensable. Nevertheless, the Karmapa was reluctant to assign a young, untested novice to such a critical mission as increasing the monastery's harvest.

Could the boy really do it again? Circumstances here were quite different from those in the small village he had recently left. There was more pressure and a great deal more land. There would also be skirmishes between cliques in the monastery that he would have to handle. Perhaps he could rise to the challenge of increasing the crop yield, but he would be undone by the treachery that would quickly surround him. Experienced infighters would be envious of him and insecure about their hold on power. They would want him to fail and would work to undermine him. It was far too much to ask of a boy. The Karmapa turned away from the mountains and back to Nawang.

"If I give him this task and he fails, it would reflect poorly on you, Nawang."

"I know, Holiness."

"A failed harvest would doom us. Are you really sure you want to put our future in a boy's hands? It's too much responsibility for a child, no matter how gifted he may be."

Nawang returned the Karmapa's stern gaze without flinching. "Yes, Holiness. I am sure."

The Karmapa's eyes flared. "If he fails I would be forced to dismiss you from your position. You would lose face and suffer great humiliation. His failure would be your failure."

"I am prepared to take that risk, Holiness."

"Why?"

"We have survived every failure of the experts we brought in. We still have food."

"Yes, but our reserves are nearly gone. This year's harvest will determine our fate. There is no margin for error like there was before."

"He won't fail, Holiness."

"He's a boy, Nawang," the Karmapa said. His exasperation slipped through the cracks of his otherwise calm exterior. "The infighting alone will destroy him and doom us. Why do you persist?"

"His bloodline, Holiness, is exceptional. Failure is not a part of his heritage. If it were, the murder of his family would have destroyed him. He succeeded beyond all expectations when he first had to grow his own food. He will do so again. He's heir to Naljor and Tenzin. I don't have to remind you about them."

"Of course not," said the Karmapa. He had reached the end of his patience. Nawang would not be deterred.

"The boy has greatness stamped all over him, Holiness. He will meet the challenge. Beside, it's not as if we have a better alternative. Do we really want to entrust the harvest to the head of the agricultural department again?"

"I see your point," said the Karmapa, not happy with the decision he was about to make. "We'll give the boy a chance."

"Thank you, Holiness," said Nawang, bowing his head.

"Do not thank me, Nawang. I am doing this despite my better judgment. Pray for his success. Your future depends on it. You may make the necessary arrangements."

"Yes, Holiness." Nawang bowed again and withdrew from the Karmapa's presence. A moment later he entered his office and slumped in his chair.

What have I just done? he thought. He stared out the window but barely saw the panoramic view. The burden of what he had won fastened itself to his shoulders, a yoke of iron poised to crush him. He had just placed the fate of the monastery's existence in the hands of an untested boy. If he was wrong, there would be no more monastery. The monks would be scattered throughout India and Nepal like the falling leaves of a dying tree.

In the midst of his dark mood, he recalled the long ago morning when he and Tenzin had left the monastery to make their way to India. Back then it had been the Chinese knocking at the gates; now it was the specter of famine. Once again, he stood at a crossroad of hope and peril. Tenzin would not be here to save him this time. What if his faith in Dorjee was misplaced? A deep shadow creased his cheek. His mouth was a tight, thin line. He was a young man walking once more in the high mountains on a black night with a harsh wind bruising his face, about to fall into a crevasse and a death that would slice him to ribbons.

The head of the agriculture department and his senior staff took one look at the new pup when he walked into their offices and laughed in his face. A boy who didn't shave was going to succeed where trained and accomplished men had failed? They turned their back on him and clamored around Nawang, reciting their litany of grievances and lobbying for more funds as always. Nawang listened to them as he had every other time, his countenance grave and attentive. He did not speak until they had exhausted their list of complaints.

"I am sorry, gentlemen. We all must make do with what we have. There is no extra money. The Karmapa has appointed Dorjee to increase the crop yield. See that he gets all the help he needs."

The words were like a slap across the face to the head of the agriculture department. He bristled like a vain woman at Nawang's lack of respect.

"Of course," he replied.

Nawang permitted himself a faint smile. The man was so obvious.

"Please, Nawang Rinpoche," begged the head of the agricultural department, "intercede with the Karmapa. He listens to you. It takes money to get anything done. We can't repeat the miracle of loaves and fishes. Why send a boy to do a man's work? It's disrespectful."

"We all have the same problem, honorable Department Head. There is no money for anything. Do the best you can as we all must." He fixed his eyes on the Department Head and lowered his voice. "You are to help Dorjee, Department Head. If he fails, you fail."

The head of the agriculture bowed his head. "Yes, Nawang Rinpoche."

Nawang bowed his head in return, and turned to leave. The Department Head folded his arms and smirked at Nawang's receding figure. Nawang was so damn superior in his attitude. Who was he to put on such airs? Nawang had never run a department as important as agriculture. Nawang was the Karmapa's tool, a mosquito buzzing around the monastery annoying everyone in sight. The Department Head made a mental note to put Nawang at the top of his revenge list. The list was long, even though many names had been accounted for over the years and crossed off.

With Nawang gone, the Department Head focused his frustration in Dorjee's direction. He'd show the little brat who ran things around here. And guess what? It wasn't Nawang. The pup was wet behind the ears. It would be a simple matter to run him off with his tail between his legs. The thought of humiliating Dorjee made the Department Head feel better. He would kill two birds with one stone. Destroy the boy and throw Nawang off his high horse. Maybe the Karmapa would even dismiss Nawang from his service. The Department Head chuckled at the thought. He would savor this particular victory for a long time.

In his haste to deal Nawang a mortal blow, however, he overlooked the cardinal rule of bureaucratic warfare: Know your enemy. Dorjee was young and inexperienced, but not the naïve fool the Department Head assumed him to be. The head of the department and his sycophants would ignore and ridicule him? Treat him with disrespect? Fine. He'd ignore them right back. They could flail away in the well-worn groove of their own frustration for all he cared. He didn't need them. He was a loner anyway.

Since the murder of his family, no one but Kalden, Jinpa, and to a lesser extent, Goba, had penetrated the fortress around his heart. He thought most people were idiots and fools. These monks in agriculture were that and more. No wonder they couldn't grow anything. They weren't worthy even of his contempt. He turned his back on their taunts and walked away.

His sole responsibility was to the Karmapa and the monastery. The challenge of producing a successful harvest where no one else had succeeded excited Dorjee, heightening his creativity. He had a task to fulfill, an important responsibility to complete. The Karmapa had treated him as a man and shown him respect. Dorjee wanted nothing more than to be worthy of that trust. In his mind he was already a man.

He didn't test the soil, try new fertilization methods, or tamper with the irrigation schedule as had those before him. He was not schooled in science. He could not read. His strength was in his mystic nature, his connection to the hidden world. Rather than adopting the latest scientific methods, he walked among the acres of barley, beans and vegetables. He chanted the names of the Buddha and sang the sacred growing songs his grandfather had taught him. When he reached a spot where the energy felt unbalanced he would sit and meditate, often for hours, bringing down from above a new and productive energy and anchoring it in the soil. Day after day, week after week he followed this procedure until he was certain the energy he had brought from above had taken root in the soil.

For Dorjee, growing things was an act of divine love. When he walked the land, he was a tuning fork that distributed the invisible harmonies of the infinite through the waving fields of grass. The plants were his children. They felt his love and thrived under his touch.

When he walked among them, a strong electrical current circulated through his body. The energy stimulated his pineal gland, opening his spiritual sight so that he could see the divine energy pouring through him blessing everything it touched.

He perceived this energy as an expanding field of white light, brighter than sunlight shimmering on white sand. The light infused every blade of glass and every plant, uniting everything, from the largest to the smallest, from the most significant to the least important, in an all-encompassing field of love and harmony. Unlike people, the light never discriminated. It had no bias. It did not play favorites. It embraced all things equally in love.

Occasionally, the light was so strong that the life in the fields became light itself. In those exalted moments, all forms disappeared, including Dorjee's. He was no longer a body with a separate ego struggling in a world of separate bodies and egos, but a soul in deep union with the infinite, a point of light in an unending field of light.

Nothing else existed. He was everywhere at once. There was no separation. He was ecstatic, drunk with divine love. The loneliness of the world, with its separation from the Supreme Truth and its attendant suffering, completely disappeared.

These experiences filled him with extraordinary peace. They taught him that the world of the invisible was the real, eternal, lasting reality and the visible world was what we mistook for reality. Anything that could be measured, quantified, or studied wasn't real. True reality had no form. It never changed. It never aged. It never died. It was a constant, unchanging field of energy, bliss, and consciousness. There was no separation in the world of the invisible and only one truth: eternal, endless, ecstatic love.

Intrigues, hidden agendas, and quests for power existed only in the material world of form and ego. He cared little for that world, preferring to spend as much time as possible alone in nature where he could enter the field of Light at will.

Nawang watched him from afar, tracking the expanding light in his energy field. The brilliance of that light and the manner in which it had flowed inward indicated to Nawang that Dorjee had experienced states of consciousness far beyond the ego's grasp.

Nawang had first seen Dorjee's spiritual potential when Goba took him to the village fields to meet the boy. Nawang had observed a large band of white light pulsing on the periphery of the youth's energy field. He knew then that the boy needed to be at Rumtek if he was to realize his spiritual potential. He wouldn't get that opportunity in a village of farmers and goatherds. He might never know he even had it.

Now, several months removed from the village, the white light filled most of Dorjee's energy field. Areas of constriction still circulated around his heart and lungs, layers of grief and heartbreak that would need to be addressed before he completed his inner journey.

Nawang was not the only one watching Dorjee from afar. Rangjung Rigpe Dorjee, the 16th Karmapa and third most important person in Tibetan Buddhism, also observed him. He was an austere man who was aware of everything that happened in the monastery. Like Nawang, the Karmapa saw the superconscious light around Dorjee. Since Dorjee had started working in the fields, the Karmapa noted that his monks were happier, worked harder, and complained less. The meals were more nutritious, the food more plentiful. For the first time in years, there was no need to ration the meals.

It is time, thought the Karmapa, to meet with the head of the agriculture department and thank him for his efforts.

One hot humid afternoon, when a rare break in his schedule permitted it, the Karmapa had Nawang send for the head of the agriculture department and his team. When they arrived, the Karmapa wasted no time on superficial chatter.

"Thank you for seeing us, Holiness," said the Department Head. He and his staff bowed to the Karmapa.

"I wish to congratulate you and your staff, Department Head. The food is better. There is more abundance. The monks are happier. What has changed?"

"Thank you, Holiness. But nothing has changed."

"Then why is the food more nutritious? And why is there more of it?"

The head of the agriculture department shrugged. "It was time for things to change, Holiness. Everything runs in cycles."

The Karmapa scrutinized the monks, his arms folded across his chest, his eyes probing them for sincerity. The agricultural staff shrank under his gaze.

"Perhaps the change is due to Dorjee's efforts, Department Head?"

"I don't think so, Holiness. The boy sits in the fields all day. It's not that easy. It takes knowledge and hard work."

"I see."

"Holiness," peeped up the youngest monk.

"I'm listening."

Belatedly, the young monk looked at his boss. The department head glared back at him, his withering stare warning the young monk to keep his mouth shut. But it was too late to turn back. The Karmapa was waiting.

"Dorjee's younger than me." The young man spoke rapidly. "But when it comes to farming, he's full grown. I've watched him in the fields. The plants respond to his touch, his meditations, and his chanting. You can almost see them grow. He has a gift, Holiness. The plants love him."

"That's ridiculous," countered the Department Head. "Plants can't give or receive love. They're not sentient beings. They grow because of the richness of the soil, the sun, water and fertilizer. Everyone knows that. Dorjee has done nothing about any of those things."

The Karmapa stood quietly, hands behind his back, lips pursed, staring at the Department Head. "Yet the plants grow. How do you explain that, Department Head?"

The department head was silent. The Karmapa turned his attention back to the young monk.

"Bring Dorjee to me."

"Now, Holiness?" asked the young monk. "He's out in the fields."

The Karmapa nodded.

"You may all go," he said.

The head of agriculture and his assistants bowed deeply and left. When they were out of hearing range the Department Head hissed at his young assistant. "You will pay dearly for your insolence. No one shows me up."

The assistant swallowed hard, his Adam's apple bobbing up and down.

"Starting today, you're transferred to the Sanitation department. You'll clean the latrines. Your new name is Stinky."

The other monks burst into laughter. The Department Head suddenly felt much better. Retribution was the best cure for insubordination. From years of experience, he knew it was important that the penalty imposed exceed the crime committed.

The young monk's face lost color. He struggled as hard as he could to maintain his appearance of indifference. A few beads of sweat popped out on his forehead. The older monk saw them and smiled. No one made him lose face in front of the Karmapa.

That evening, Nawang ushered Dorjee into the Karmapa's office. Dorjee stood nervously in front of the Karmapa's desk while he read and signed several documents. He did not acknowledge Dorjee until he had completed his work. Finally, he put down his pen and looked up at the young novice. His glance was penetrating, but not unkind.

Dorjee swallowed hard. The Karmapa held one of the most important positions in Tibetan Buddhism. What could he possibly want from him? Was he sending him back to Goba? What else could it be? He was crestfallen. He didn't want to go. He loved being in the fields with his plants. His legs shook under him.

"You've done well, Dorjee," said the Karmapa.

Dorjee's mouth dropped open. He couldn't hide his shock. "Thank you, Holiness," he managed to say.

"We share the same name you know."

"Yes, Holiness."

The Karmapa smiled. "Let's hope that that's a good omen for both of us. Tell me about your spiritual experiences in the fields."

"What do you mean, Holiness?" Dorjee was puzzled. His experiences couldn't be important to someone of the Karmapa's stature. He was just a novice monk.

"There are monks here who are envious of you. They want what you've achieved. They've been working years. Some for decades. Then a boy comes along and in a few months attains what they have devoted their lives to. And he's done it alone in the fields, not in the meditation hall with them."

"I'm just a beginner, Holiness. My experiences can't be that important."

"I'll be the judge of that. Now, tell me."

Dorjee gathered his thoughts. He wanted to give an accurate accounting of his experiences. "When I meditate in the fields everything disappears. The world disappears." Dorjee's eyes sought out the infinite as he tried to articulate his feelings. "I disappear, too. The only thing that remains is the Light. I believe there is only one reality, one existence, one being, and we're all part of it. Everything else is an illusion. No one is independent of the Oneness or separate from it. We are all equal in the Oneness."

"I see. What do you feel when that happens?"

"Bliss. I'm filled with bliss, Holiness."

The Karmapa looked out at the mountains and let their peace flow through him.

"From now on, I want you to watch over all of our fields. Go where you feel needed. Trust your intuition. Spread your light. Be thorough. Don't rush."

"Yes, Holiness," Dorjee bowed and turned to go.

"Dorjee, do you think the plants feel your love for them?"

Dorjee stopped and turned back to face the Karmapa. "I know they do, Holiness."

The Karmapa smiled. "I think so, too."

Nawang accompanied Dorjee into the hall. "Tell me Dorjee, do you have the same experience when you meditate in the hall with the other monks?"

"No."

Nawang nodded. "I see. You've done well."

A moment later the Karmapa interrupted their conversation, calling Nawang back to his office.

"Nawang, assign the young monk who spoke up earlier to work with Dorjee."

"The head of agriculture assigned him to latrine duty as soon as they left your office, Holiness."

The Karmapa shook his head. "I'm not surprised. How would you remedy the situation, Nawang?"

"It's not my decision to make, Holiness."

"I'm well aware of that," the Karmapa said. "Still, I would like your advice. Would you rescind the orders of a department head knowing that he would lose face with the other monks? Should I protect a senior monk who has given long service to the monastery or rescue a young monk from a fate he doesn't deserve? The boy risked his future to tell me the truth. He put the monastery first. Should I let him be destroyed for that?"

"I don't believe so, Holiness."

"Nor do I. Decisions should never be made to protect someone's ego or status. My job is to do what is right for the monastery. If I let the department head have his way, he'll never change. He'll be more insufferable tomorrow than he is today. Make the young monk the new head of the Agricultural Department. Tell him to give Dorjee all the support he needs. An infusion of youthful energy will be good for the monastery. You are to supervise them. I am transferring the head of the Agriculture Department to the Sanitation Department. He is the head man there now. Keeping the latrines clean is his responsibility."

"Yes, Holiness. I will do to it right away," said Nawang. He didn't have to add, and gladly.

CHAPTER 26

An Unexpected Encounter

SANTA MONICA, 1965

THAT WEEK, CHARLIE came to Tenzin's Thursday evening class. With him was an exotic young woman who was clearly with child. Every eye in the room followed them as they made their way to the empty seats in the rear of the room. Many of the regulars whispered among themselves, trying to guess who the attractive young couple might be. They looked like Hollywood stars, but no one could place them. Charlie was tall, tan and athletic, with long blond hair bleached by the sun and blue eyes as bright as the noon sky. Coupled with his good looks was a distinct vulnerability that never failed to bring out the tenderness in women. They swooned over his beauty and wanted to care for him. Few saw the turbulence hidden behind his handsome exterior.

The young woman was of mixed descent. She had high cheekbones, full lips, olive skin, green eyes with an Asian slant, and long black hair that glistened in the lamp light. She walked with a gentle sway that underscored her femininity. Something inexplicable hid in that walk and something unknowable danced behind those eyes. She radiated a sense of feminine mystery lacking in most modern American women. To see her was to want her. Every man's longing for her was made more acute by the realization that they would never possess her. She was unattainable, beyond their reach. Yet that knowledge didn't blunt the force of their desire, but only deepened it. Every man in the room wanted what Charlie had.

The young woman was acutely self-conscious and embarrassed by all the attention focused on her. She hated the sexual desire that was directed her way. It made her feel cheap and dirty. Sometimes, she even hated her beauty. Beauty wasn't always an advantage. More often than not, it was a curse. It brought out lust in men and jealousy in women. Why couldn't she be less beautiful and treated like everyone else?

She frowned, kept her eyes down and reached for Charlie's hand. Touching him was like a drug for her. It made her feel safe. When he wasn't beside her, to see and to touch and to talk with, her anxiety rose to intolerable levels. She never understood why that was, even though she had asked herself a thousand times. Without him, an abyss opened in her heart, an emptiness that made life unendurable. Charlie was everything to her, never more than now with the new life growing inside her.

Strange, she thought. Before Charlie, I never felt this way.

She had always been quite capable of taking care of herself, although she suffered from a nebulous loneliness that at times left her mildly depressed. She couldn't define it other than to say that when the depression came over her she felt lost and incomplete, as if she were missing an important part of herself. But she had no idea what caused it. Over the years she had learned to adapt to it. At least it wasn't as bad as missing a limb or blindness.

When she met Charlie, the vague sense of loneliness and its accompanying depression vanished, only to be replaced by an even greater fear of losing him. What's worse, she often wondered, the old loneliness or this new fear?

Why couldn't she ever enjoy what she had? Why was she so cursed? It must be karma for sins in another life. She squeezed Charlie's hand even harder. He leaned over and kissed her cheek. She blushed, but was glad for the visible sign of his love. It provided comfort and protection in what was otherwise an uncomfortable situation.

She didn't like being in a room full of strangers gawking at her. She couldn't wait to leave and be out in the open, and under the night stars where she could breathe freely and have Charlie all to herself with no other hungry eyes staring at her.

Charlie was unaware of her emotional distress or the reaction their presence had caused in the room. He was too intent on finding them seats. The pregnancy had subjected her to bouts of morning sickness, and low-back pain. He felt terrible about the situation he had put her in. And the decision he was about to make was going to make things worse, not better. He was wracked with guilt. He was too absorbed in his own troubles to be aware of anything else.

By now, the large room was completely full. Tenzin would enter at any moment. Charlie and his girlfriend sat down. She kept her hand in Charlie's while he scanned the audience for the first time. The woman who had lost her son in Vietnam was seated nearby. He nodded to her. The woman waved and made her way to them. He released his girl's hand and rose to meet her. The young woman felt a sharp thrust of rejection cut through her. She needed his attention right now. Surely, he knew that. Why was he talking to another woman?

"Hi Marie," he said. "How are you? I'd like you to meet my girlfriend, Clare."

"You look better, Charlie."

"Thanks. I am," he said. "Clare, this is Marie. She's the woman at the lecture I mentioned."

"Hi, Clare," said Marie.

"Hi," said Clare without much enthusiasm.

"Charlie reminds me of my son, Scottie."

"Is he the one who died in Vietnam?"

"Yes," said Marie, her lower lip trembling.

"Oh, my God. I shouldn't have said that. I'm so sorry. I didn't mean to hurt you."

"Why? It's true," Marie said, wiping the tears off her cheeks. "I've got to get over it sometime."

Clare looked down, touched her stomach, and frowned. "I don't know how you ever get used to something like that."

"What other choice is there? Life goes on no matter how we feel about it, doesn't it? I'll never love anyone again as I loved my boy."

Clare reached for Charlie's arm. "If we women had our way, there'd never be another war. We bring the boys into the world and raise them to be men and to lead good lives. No mother raises her son to die. I don't want Charlie to go to Vietnam. I'm afraid of what could happen to him if he does. My baby needs a father."

"I agree, honey. Keep him home if you can. Men can be such idiots. Johnson and McNamara are butchers. Their hands are drenched in blood. They're responsible for the deaths of thousands of young men like Scottie. They're criminals. Throw them in jail and let them rot."

"That's too nice," said Clare. "Put them in the jungle and let them be the ones who bleed and die. If they believe their bull about saving democracy then they can sacrifice their lives to keep South Vietnam "free", whatever that means. Not my Charlie."

"It'll never happen," sighed Marie.

"I know," said Clare.

"How far along are you?"

"Four months."

"Do you have family here?"

Clare shook her head.

"Is there anyone you can depend on?"

"Only Charlie."

"You need a mom to help you through your pregnancy. Let me help. It'd fill a void in my life."

The hum of other conversations came to a sudden halt. The room fell quiet. They looked up to see Tenzin making his way to the dais. Until that moment, Clare's impression of him had been second hand, shaped by what Charlie had told her. When she first listened to Charlie describe Tenzin she was certain that his depiction of the man was quite excessive. Charlie had a dramatic streak, and tended to exaggerate whatever enamored him at the moment. No one was that good, that wise, or that powerful. She knew how confused and pressured Charlie was lately, so she had kept her doubts to herself. He needed peace, not a moody pregnant woman to make his life more difficult than it already was.

While she watched Tenzin put on his microphone, something inside told her that Charlie's description of him had been on target. If anything, this man was greater than the portrait Charlie had painted. He exuded a majesty that she had never felt before in any human being. Just looking at him gave her hope. As long as this man was in the world, the madness was bound to end. In that moment, her fear fell away and hope rose in her heart.

Tenzin looked slowly around the room, seeing everyone who was there. When he saw Charlie, he nodded. When he noticed Clare, he smiled. His glance sent a shiver through her. A stranger had looked at her in passing and seen the real person, not just the beautiful exterior. She leaned forward and hid her face in her hands. The room was so quiet. Every person was meditating. She felt Tenzin's eyes on her again and blushed. She felt vulnerable, but not frightened. She summoned her courage and raised her head. There was nothing in Tenzin's gaze but kindness and acceptance. She knew he could see everything about her, but there was no judgment, only love. She wiped the hair off her face and returned his gaze. When she did, lightning shot from his eyes into hers. Her body shook, as if a thunder clap had passed through it. She clutched her stomach and leaned over. She felt more nauseous than she had at any other point in her pregnancy.

The room disappeared. The present faded away. She was in a primeval forest of towering oaks. Terror and pandemonium were all around her. Roman soldiers had found them. Women and children screamed in terrible agony. Her heart beat so fiercely that she was sure it would burst. She slithered under a thick canopy of ferns, silent and still, desperate to save her unborn child and to avoid the fate of the others.

Soon, the screams around her faded away. She breathed more deeply. She was safe. The soldiers were preparing to leave. A soldier relieving himself on a nearby tree saw caught a slight movement in the thicket. He pushed the tops of the ferns aside with the point of his sword. She looked at him with eyes wide with terror. He dragged her out into the open by her hair. This wench was better looking than the others. Since he had found her, he would have the first go.

"Hey boys, look what I've found," he called out.

Several soldiers swarmed around her, their eyes still crazed with lust, their tunics splattered with the blood of her loved ones. They reeked of sweat, sex, and death. She fought like a trapped animal, but they just laughed, goading her on, her fear heightening their lust. When their lust reached a peak of frenzy they ripped off her clothing, and each one raped her. Her insides were on fire; the pain in her womb unendurable. She prayed aloud for a quick death. A soldier slapped her hard across her mouth.

"Shut up, bitch," he screamed.

Blood spurted from her broken lip. She coughed, choking on the blood pooling in her throat. When they were finished with her, the soldier who had discovered her unsheathed his short sword, ripped open her belly and pulled out her unborn child. He held it up to his comrades then smashed it against a nearby tree.

She screamed hysterically. The soldiers laughed. The legionnaire who had cut out her unborn brought his face close to hers. His eyes glared with cruelty and hatred. With one quick cut he slit her throat. She gurgled on her blood as her final breath escaped, her eyes open and vacant.

The soldiers gathered their things and walked away, leaving the dead bodies as carrion for the buzzards to feast on.

When the vision ended, Clare was freezing and shaking all over. She reached for Charlie, her hands cold and clammy. He opened his eyes, saw the terror on her face, and pulled her to him. She closed her eyes and fell into a deep sleep against his chest. When she awoke, the room was empty, the class over. Tenzin stood over her. Charlie sat beside her, his arm still around her.

"Are you O.K.?" Charlie said.

"I don't know."

"What happened?"

"I was in a forest. Roman soldiers killed everybody. They raped me, tore the baby out of my belly and killed us both." Her tears started again.

Charlie's eyes grew larger. "Oh, God. I was hoping it was just a bad dream."

"What do you mean?" asked Clare.

"I saw the same thing in my session with Tenzin. I found you and all the other women and children murdered. I didn't want to tell you."

A look of panic flashed over Clare's face. "We've got to leave the country, Charlie. You'll get killed if you go to 'Nam."

Charlie looked at Tenzin.

Clare's eyes darted back and forth between the two men.

"Tell him he can't go. Tell him!"

"It's not my decision to make," said Tenzin.

"Please!" screamed Clare. "He'll be killed, just like Marie's son. What about my baby? My baby needs a father! What about me? I need Charlie!" She collapsed in sobs.

Tenzin put his hands on her shoulder. A comforting warmth flowed into her. "Center yourself. Fear solves nothing."

Clare reached forward, put her arms around Tenzin's waist and her head against his stomach.

"I'm so scared," she sobbed.

Tenzin put one hand on the back of her neck. His touch felt warm and safe. A stream of comforting energy flowed into her, releasing the knot of anxiety in her stomach. "Don't give your fear any energy. Go deeper. Breathe in slowly. Breathe out slowly. Put your mind in the Oneness. It changes everything."

"How can it do that? It's not stronger than the government."

"Countries rise and fall. Governments come and go. The Oneness remains. Place your consciousness in the Oneness. You are always safe there."

CHAPTER 27

The Midnight Conference

Our lives begin to end the day we become silent about things that matter.
Martin Luther King

SANTA MONICA 1965

At midnight, long after everyone had left, Tenzin and Thomas sat quietly in the kitchen, drinking tea, their thoughts elsewhere. Tenzin was thinking about Clare and Charlie's dilemma and what he could do to help them. Thomas was fuming over how the dark side had ripped the country apart. Because of what they had done, hostility and hatred had supplanted civility and reason in the nation's political discourse. The old game of divide and conquer had worked with great efficacy. He had to give them their due. They were masters of manipulation. Would honorable and reasonable men, men who weren't fronts and puppets for the New World Order, ever lead the country again?

While he sipped his tea, Tenzin formulated a plan. If Charlie went to Vietnam, Clare could move in with them. He would have to ask Alice, of course. The final determination would be hers. She ran the center and all decisions regarding its operations, including living arrangements, were in her purview.

Emily's bedroom on the second floor was available. No one had slept there since she had passed away. He was sure that Emily would approve of Clare living there. The girl had lots of potential and a new life growing in her womb. She was going to need their help. He would take it up with Alice in the morning.

Thomas had opened his research notes, and was thumbing through his files, underlining important findings.

"Anything new, Thomas?"

Thomas looked up at Tenzin, a blank expression on his face.

"What?"

"With your research."

"Well," said Thomas. "I found another Lincoln quotation. Funny how these things never make it into the textbooks."

"Would you read it to me?"

"Sure," said Thomas pulling out his notes.

> *The money power preys upon the nation in time of peace and conspires against it in times of adversity. It is more despotic than monarchy, more insolent than autocracy, more selfish than bureaucracy. I see in the near future a crisis approaching that unnerves me, and causes me to tremble for the safety of our country. Corporations have been enthroned, an era of corruption will follow, and the money power of the country will endeavor to prolong its reign by working upon the prejudices of the people, until the wealth is aggregated in a few hands, and the republic is destroyed.*

"It sounds as if he were speaking about the present," said Tenzin.

"Doesn't it, though? I also found a very illuminating excerpt from a speech given by Rep. Louis McFadden of Pennsylvania in 1932. McFadden had been the Chairman of the House Banking and Currency Committee for more than ten years when he made this speech to Congress.

Want to hear it?"

"Sure."

"It's long."

"I'm not going anywhere."

Thomas smiled grimly, adjusted the glasses on the bridge of his nose and began:

> *Mr. Chairman, we have in this country one of the most corrupt institutions the world has ever known. I refer to the Federal Reserve Board and the Federal Reserve Banks. The Federal Reserve Board, a Government board, has cheated the Government of the United States and the people of the United States out of enough money to pay the national debt. The depredations and iniquities of the Federal Reserve Board has cost this country enough money to pay the national debt several times over. This evil institution has impoverished and ruined the people of the United States, has bankrupted itself, and has practically bankrupted our Government. It has done this through the defects of the law under which it operates, through the maladministration of that law by the Federal Reserve Board, and through the corrupt practices of the moneyed vultures who control it.*

Some people think the Federal Reserve banks are United States Government institutions. They are not Government institutions. They are private credit monopolies which prey upon the people of the United States for the benefit of themselves and their foreign customers; foreign and domestic speculators and swindlers; and rich and predatory money lenders. In that dark crew of financial pirates there are those who would cut a man's throat to get a dollar out of his pocket; there are those who send money into States to buy votes to control our legislation; and there are those who maintain international propaganda for the purpose of deceiving us and of wheedling us into the granting of new concessions which will permit them to cover up their past misdeeds and set again in motion their gigantic train of crime.

These twelve private credit monopolies were deceitfully and disloyally foisted upon this country by the bankers who came here from Europe and repaid us for our hospitality by undermining our American institutions. Those bankers took money out of this country to finance Japan in a war against Russia. They created a reign of terror in Russia with our money in order to help that war along. They instigated the separate peace between Germany and Russia and thus drove a wedge between the Allies in the World War. They financed Trotsky's passage from New York to Russia so that he might assist in the destruction of the Russian Empire. They fomented and instigated the Russian revolution and they placed a large fund of American dollars at Trotsky's disposal in one of their branch banks in Sweden so that through him Russian homes might be thoroughly broken up and Russian children flung far and wide from their natural protectors. They have since begun the breaking up of American homes and the dispersal of American children.

Thomas paused and sipped his tea.

"The powers that be sanitize everything, don't they?" said Tenzin. "They twist the truth into a shape that serves their agenda. We don't get the truth. We get propaganda. McFadden was a very brave man."

"And most astute. There's more."

"Go ahead. I'm listening."

Thomas turned the page and continued reading the speech.

Mr. Chairman, when the Federal Reserve act was passed, the people of the United States did not perceive that a world system was being set up here which would make the savings of an American school-teacher available to a narcotic-drug vendor in Macao. They did not perceive that the United States were to be lowered to the position of a coolie country which has nothing but raw materials and heavy goods for export; that Russia and China was destined to supply the man power and that this country was to supply financial power to an international superstate — a superstate controlled by international bankers and international industrialists acting together to enslave the world for their own pleasure.

The people of the United States are being greatly wronged. If they are not, then I do not know what "wronging the people" means. They have been driven from their employments. They have been dispossessed of their homes. They have been evicted from their rented quarters. They have lost their children. They have been left to suffer and to die for lack of shelter, food, clothing, and medicine.

The wealth of the United States and the working capital of the United States has been taken away from them and has either been locked in the vaults of certain banks and the great corporations or exported to foreign countries for the benefit of the foreign customers of those banks and corporations. So far as the people of the United States are concerned, the cupboard is bare. It is true that the warehouses and coal yards and grain elevators are full, but the warehouses and coal yards and grain elevators are padlocked and the great banks and corporations hold the keys. The sack of the United States by the Federal Reserve Board and the Federal Reserve banks is the greatest crime in history.

Mr. Chairman, a serious situation confronts the House of Representatives to-day. We are trustees of the people and the rights of the people are being taken away from them.

Through the Federal Reserve Board and the Federal Reserve banks, the people are losing the rights guaranteed to them by the Constitution. Their property has been taken from them without due process of law. Mr. Chairman, common decency requires us to examine the public accounts of the Government and see what crimes against the public welfare have and are being committed.

What is needed here is a return to the Constitution of the United States. We need to have a complete divorce of Bank and State. The old struggle that was fought out here in Jackson's day must be fought over again. The independent United States Treasury should be re- established and the Government should keep its own money under lock and key in the building the people provided for that purpose. Asset currency, the device of the swindler, should be done away with. The Government should buy gold and issue United States currency on it. The business of the independent bankers should be restored to them. The State banking systems should be freed from coercion. The Federal Reserve districts should be abolished and the State boundaries should be respected. Bank reserves should be kept within the borders of the States whose people own them, and this reserve money of the people should be protected so that the international bankers and acceptance bankers and discount dealers can not draw it away from them. The exchanges should be closed while we are putting our financial affairs in order. The Federal Reserve Act should be repealed and the Federal Reserve banks, having violated their charters, should be liquidated immediately. Faithless Government officers who have violated their oaths of office should be impeached and brought to trial.

Unless this is done by us, I predict that the American people, outraged, robbed, pillaged, insulted, and betrayed as they are in their own land, will rise in their wrath and send a President here who will sweep the money changers out of the temple.

Thomas closed his notebook and laid it on the table.

"A great man," said Tenzin. "What happened to him?"

"He died suddenly of a heart attack in October 1936 after experiencing flu like symptoms. Before that, there were two unsuccessful attempts on his life. The first attempt was a shooting as he got out of a cab at the Capitol. Both shots missed. The second attempt was food poisoning at a political banquet. A friend had his stomach pumped. It saved his life."

"The third attempt succeeded," said Tenzin.

"It would seem so."

"These people never stop."

"That's their m.o."

"That makes two great American heroes from the 1930's, Butler and McFadden, who have been stricken from the pages of history and forgotten."

"Damn shame, isn't it? It's easy to do when you control the media and the publishing industry. I've got more vintage Lincoln material here, in case you're interested."

"I'm always interested."

"This one is from a speech Lincoln made to Congress in 1865," said Thomas, turning the pages in his notebook.

I have two great enemies. The Southern Army in front of me, and the financial institutions in the rear. Of the two, the one in my rear is my greatest foe.

"Does that mean that slavery was not the real reason for the Civil War?" said Tenzin.

"We'll get to that in a minute. When the war began, Lincoln went to the international bankers hoping to secure a loan to finance the war. The Rothschild's offered him terms at 24% and 36% interest. Knowing that this would bankrupt the country, Lincoln turned down the offer and with the help of Salmon Chase, his Treasury Secretary, directed the Treasury of the United States to print our currency. By April of 1862, 449 million dollars of debt-free money had been printed and distributed. This is what Lincoln had to say of his accomplishment:

We gave the people of this republic the greatest blessing they ever had, their own paper money to pay their own debts.

"He did what Kennedy wanted to do," commented Tenzin.

"Exactly," said Thomas. "In that same year, The Times of London published an editorial about Lincoln's monetary policy. Here's a quotation from that article."

If that mischievous financial policy, which had its origin in the North American Republic, should become indurated down to a fixture, then that government will furnish its own money without cost. It will pay off debts and be without a debt. It will have all the money necessary to carry on its commerce. It will become prosperous beyond precedent in the history of civilized governments of the world. The brains and the wealth of all countries will go to North America.

That government must be destroyed or it will destroy every monarchy on the globe.

"And upset the bankers' plans," said Tenzin.

"Since the bankers control the media I'm sure they ordered that editorial. Here's a quotation from Otto von Bismarck, Chancellor of Germany, that he made in 1876.

The division of the United States into two federations of equal force was decided long before the civil war by the high financial power of Europe. These bankers were afraid that the United States, if they remained in one block and as one nation, would attain economical and financial independence, which would upset their financial domination. The voice of the Rothschilds' predominated. They foresaw the tremendous booty if

> *they could substitute two feeble democracies, indebted to the financiers, to the vigorous Republic, confident and self-providing. Therefore they started their emissaries in order to exploit the question of slavery and thus dig an abyss between the two parts of the Republic.*

"So it wasn't about slavery," said Tenzin. "That was the rationale, just as preserving democracy in South Vietnam is the rationale for the Vietnam War. It's interesting that both are essentially civil wars."

"Isn't it?" said Thomas. "In 1849 Gutle Schnaper, the wife of Mayer Amschel Rothschild, died. Mayer Rothschild was the patriarch of the Rothschilds and the architect of their financial empire. Their five sons would eventually control the finances of many countries by establishing central banks and debt based currencies. Shortly before she died, Gutle Schnaper purportedly said, *If my sons did not want wars, there would be none.*

Thomas paused a moment. "You see how it works now?"

"How could I not?"

"Yesterday I found a speech given by Joseph Welch in 1958."

"Isn't he the right wing fanatic who founded the John Birch Society?"

"That's how he's portrayed. They discredit him, so that the people will shut their minds off to his message. If I've learned anything from all of this, it's that the truth, like the wind, can come from anywhere."

"So can disinformation."

"True. The elite want to keep our minds narrow and shut so that we'll dismiss the truth and accept their lies. They want us to think Welch is deranged and that what he has to say is crazy. That way, we'll keep our minds shut and throw out the truth before we can consider it. One of our most important tasks is to resist the media, the movies, the magazines, the nightly news shows, and the newspapers that program our minds. They only tell us what they want us to think. If we don't think critically, they can get away with it. Heck, how many important things go unreported? They hide the truth. Nothing is what it seems. So listen to this. Welch outlined the elite's agenda for the next fifty years."

"I'm listening."

"Their goal is to destabilize America. Welch listed ten steps to fulfill their objective. Expand government spending as masterfully as possible; raise taxes; unbalance the budget; create runaway inflation; institute wage controls; socialize every aspect of the economy; expand the bureaucracy; concentrate power in Washington; eliminate state lines; centralize control of public education in Washington."

"That sounds like Communism."

"It is Communism. It was either Lenin or Stalin, I think, who said that America would fall from within," said Thomas. "Those two were the bankers' boys. They had inside information."

"Emily said that the dream of a free America ended the day Kennedy was murdered. I don't think that she wanted to live after that," said Tenzin.

"We'll never be free as long as the Fed prints our money and runs up our debt," said Thomas. "Foreign banking interests control our money supply and therefore control our country. It's the greatest scam ever perpetrated on this nation. The fact that no one questions it is astounding. It just shows you that when you control the media, mind controlling the public is child's play."

The two grew silent. The seriousness of their discussion and its implications for the future weighed heavily on both of them. Tenzin rose and went to the stove.

"More tea, Thomas?"

"Sure."

Tenzin filled their cups to capacity and sat down. They sipped their tea in silence, the stillness in the room heavy with dark forebodings.

A few moments later, the door opened and Alice entered the kitchen. She felt the solemnity in the room's atmosphere immediately.

"You two have been discussing politics again, haven't you?" she asked frowning.

Tenzin nodded.

"Why? Nothing good ever comes of it. You both just get depressed."

"Not depressed," said Thomas. "but thoughtful. There's a lot to consider. Our freedom and way of life is under a slow, relentless attack. Few see it. The agenda that shapes seemingly random events has been cleverly hidden."

"You have a full day of clients tomorrow, hon. You need your rest. It's time to put all this aside, at least for tonight."

"I've been thinking, Alice. How would you feel if Clare came to live with us? She's pregnant and will be alone if Charlie goes to Vietnam. She could be your assistant. That would take a lot of pressure off you."

Alice was not pleased. "I don't even know her. If you had your way, you'd save every stray pup in the world."

"You'll like her."

"I'm sure I will. But we've both got more than we can handle right now. The center is booming. Your time is filled. The phone never stops ringing. The boys and I see little enough of you as it is. I don't have the energy to care for a pregnant woman on top of all that."

"She'd take some of the burden of running the center off you."

"Pregnant women need a lot of attention. I don't have any to spare."

"She'll get plenty of attention. All the single guys that come here will hover

over her. And Marie wants to help her. They can both assist you. If you delegate some of your work to them, you'll have more time for other things."

"Why don't I think it will happen that way?"

"I'll make sure that it does."

"You make promises and I clean up after you. Where would she stay?"

"In Emily's room."

"Emily's room? No one's stayed there since she died. You've made it a shrine."

"I think Emily would be happy if a pregnant woman lived there. You know how she loved children."

"You're not going to stop, are you?"

Tenzin smiled at her.

"I have one condition," said Alice.

"Name it."

"If it doesn't work out, you'll be the one to tell her to leave."

"Agreed."

"There's one other thing."

"What's that?"

"You're going to bed now."

"I'll be up soon."

"Now!"

Tenzin saw the fire flash in his wife's eyes. It wouldn't be wise to push her further. He summoned his dignity and rose from the table. "Goodnight, Thomas."

Thomas looked up through the bifocals perched halfway down the bridge of his nose, a wry smile on his face, his eyes sparkling with mirth. "Goodnight, Tenzin."

CHAPTER 28

The Center of Attraction

SANTA MONICA, 1965

CLARE FELT NAUSEOUS on the way home after class that night. She had a sick feeling in the pit of her stomach that Charlie had made up his mind about the draft. She tried to shake off her premonition, but the more she tried to free herself from its effects, the more nauseous she became. She clung to him like a wet shirt against his body while they walked home. Neither spoke in the uncomfortable silence. Physically united, they were worlds apart mentally, both consumed with their concerns. It wasn't until they got into bed that Clare broke the uneasy silence that hung like a shroud between them.

"You're going, aren't you?"

"What?" said Charlie.

"You're going to 'Nam, aren't you?"

Charlie turned away, wrapping the blanket over his shoulder. He didn't answer.

"Tell me the truth, Charlie," Clare said.

"Yes," he screamed. "I'm going. Are you happy now?"

Clare burst into tears. "You selfish bastard! You don't give a damn about me or your baby! I need you here! We can leave for Canada tomorrow. I'll pack now."

"No."

"Why not?"

"There's no guarantee we'd be safe in Canada, Clare. They could come after me at any time. And even if they didn't, there's no assurance we could ever come home."

"So what? We'd be together. You'd be safe. That's all that matters. It won't end as it did in that other lifetime. We'll build a new life in Canada."

"I can't do it."

"Why not?"

"I'm not going to go through life feeling like a coward. I couldn't live with the shame if I ran again."

"What you did in some other lifetime doesn't matter now."

"It does to me. It's in my soul. I couldn't live with myself if I ran. Can't you understand that? I'd be no good to either of us. Look what you went through tonight. You felt that life, too. Don't tell me that you didn't. I don't want to go, Clare, but I must."

Clare sat up and leaned the back of her head against the wall, her eyes swollen with tears.

"I'm not going to sit around and wait for a letter saying you've been killed in action, Charlie. My child needs a father. I need a husband."

"Now who's being selfish?"

"You're the one who's leaving."

"You're a bitch, you know that?"

"I'm a bitch? You're abandoning me, you bastard. I'd follow you to Canada. I'd go with you anywhere. I love you Charlie, but I don't want to be alone, not with a baby and no family here to help me. I'm terrified. Can't you understand that?"

"You used me. I'm a sperm donor, that's all I ever was. Things get tough and you walk away. You never loved me, Clare. I understand that!"

"How can you say that?" screamed Clare. She turned her back to him. Her muffled sobs were the only sounds in the apartment. Tortured, confused, and at a loss for what else to do, Charlie got out of bed and flopped on the sofa in the living room. All night, he heard her crying through the closed bedroom door. Neither of them slept.

In the morning, Charlie packed his bag. Clare busied herself in the kitchen, ignoring him.

So that's the way it's going to be, he thought. She's going to punish me for doing what I have to do. It was a great ride but it had to end sometime, I guess.

He grabbed his bag and slammed the door on the way out. Too late, Clare rushed into the living room, saw that he had left, and collapsed. She spent all that day crying, alone in her bed.

Charlie reported to the induction center later that morning, accompanied only by his bitterness.

A few days later Clare went back to the Center to find Tenzin. She had no one else to whom she could turn, nowhere else to go. Maybe he would have some kind words that would put her at ease and make her feel better. Alice was at the reception desk. Clare's eyes were still red and puffy from several days of crying. Alice wasn't sure at first who this lovely creature was, but her heart went out to her immediately.

"You okay, honey?"

"Not really. My boyfriend walked out on me. We had a big fight. I was so mean to him. He'll never come back. He's going to 'Nam. I'm so scared that he'll get killed. I'm carrying his child. I'm sorry to bother you, but Tenzin is so wise. He helped me a lot the other night. I was hoping to talk to him. I'm sorry for just showing up, but I didn't know what else to do."

"What's your name, honey?"

"Clare."

"Your Charlie's girl."

"How did you know?"

"Charlie talked about you a lot."

"Really?" Clare said. "What did he say?"

"That you were the sun and the moon and the stars and the most beautiful girl he'd ever seen."

Clare wiped her eyes. "Not anymore. He hates me now."

Alice smiled. "Oh, I doubt that. The anger will fade. The love is still there. He'll be back, don't you worry. How far along are you?"

"Four months."

"Well, I could use some help around here."

"I'd love to help," said Clare grasping at the opportunity to do something constructive with her time. Anything was better than being alone.

"Good. Help me put labels and stamps on these flyers."

The work was a tonic for Clare. Time sped by. The women talked non-stop. Alice liked the girl. Tenzin had been right about her. He was always right. Sometimes that irked her, but not often: Only when she was under a great deal of stress or he was working too hard and ignoring his own needs. She looked up at the clock.

"I'd say we've done enough for now. I bet you're starved."

"I am."

"When was the last time you ate?"

Clare had to think about it. "Day before yesterday."

Alice frowned. "Not good. You need to eat for two."

"I know. My stomach's been knotted up since Charlie left. I'm frightened that I won't be a good mother, and scared to death of being on my own. How will I survive?"

"You'll think better after you've got some food in you. Let's go fatten you up."

The two women busied themselves in the kitchen preparing a lunch of tuna sandwiches, green salad and iced tea. They had just sat down to enjoy their meal when Tenzin walked in. He smiled warmly when he saw Clare sitting with Alice, the two of them already fast friends.

"Hi, honey," said Alice. "You remember Clare."

"A beautiful woman is hard to forget."

Clare blushed.

"Charlie's reported to the army," said Alice.

Tenzin nodded. The lines in his face seemed deeper. Alice reached for his hand.

"I was just thinking," Alice said. "We have an extra bedroom that hasn't been used in a long time. Clare could live with us and help me. We'd be here for her when her baby is born. I'd love to have a baby underfoot again, wouldn't you?"

"I think we should ask Clare how she feels about it," said Tenzin.

They both looked at Clare. She was speechless, her mouth wide open.

"A change would be good for you," said Tenzin. "There are too many ghosts at your apartment."

Clare nodded and swallowed hard, her tears flowing without restraint. The phone rang at the reception desk, and Tenzin excused himself to answer it.

"I don't understand it," said Clare, wiping her eyes. "I've met Tenzin twice and both times I've fallen apart. He must think I'm just another highly neurotic female."

"Tenzin has a powerful effect on people. That's what his energy does. When you're around him everything that's been repressed rises to the surface. Don't fight it. It's a good thing. You've been through a lot in the last few days."

"Thanks for understanding," Clare replied.

"There's something I must tell you."

"What's that?"

"Tenzin asked me if you could live with us last night."

"He did?" Clare's eyes opened wide.

"He wants the best for you, Charlie, and your baby, and he figures the best place for you to be while Charlie's away is here."

"Why? He doesn't even know me."

"Oh, he knows you. And now that I've met you, I agree."

"Oh, thank you." Clare began sobbing again.

"I know Tenzin feels responsible for Charlie."

"I chased him away," said Clare lowering her head.

"No you didn't. It was his decision."

"I said horrible things to him," said Clare.

"We've all said things that we later regret. That's love. It's passionate. There'll be a child he's never seen when he returns. He'll be back."

"I'm so scared that he'll get killed."

"Tenzin will protect him."

"How? Charlie's going to be shooting at people and they're going to be shooting at him. Tenzin can't stop bullets."

"I've seen Tenzin do many things that defy explanation."

"But this is war. And it's an ocean away from here. It's beyond Tenzin's reach."

"The only things that limit us are our beliefs. Reality is much more fluid than we think. All things are possible."

"Science says that Tenzin's ability to protect Charlie in a war several thousand miles from here is impossible. To believe it's possible is irrational," Clare countered.

"Science quantifies the material universe, Clare. In our society, when someone exceeds the limitations of the material universe, he's seen as either a magician or a saint. Holy men throughout the ages have discarded limiting beliefs, attuned themselves to the Oneness, and performed miracles. Our potential is vast. There's a holy person inside each of us. It's up to us to unlock that power, and perform our own miracles. The first step is to let go of limiting beliefs. Charlie will come home. Focus on that."

"How do you open your mind to let go of fear?"

"By silencing it."

"My mind is never silent."

"Meditation and breathing techniques will cure that. I think that you'll be surprised by what will happen after you've been here for awhile."

After Clare moved in, she took over the reception desk for Alice in the afternoons. Word spread quickly through Tenzin's constituency about the beautiful new receptionist. It wasn't long before several young men began to show up regularly in the afternoon. Clare enjoyed the attention and developed a genuine fondness for several of them. They filled a vacuum in her life and made her feel attractive, despite her growing belly and thickening hips. But that was as far as it went. Her focus was elsewhere. No matter how hard she tried, she couldn't get Charlie out of her mind. The nearer these young men came, the closer she held Charlie to her.

The young men interpreted her laughter at their jokes and interest in their lives as a sign that she was as interested in them as they were in her. A few gathered their courage and asked her out. They were awkward in their attempts, as if expecting her to say no, but the power of her beauty was intoxicating and clouded their judgment.

"Look at me," she would say when they asked her out. "I'm fat and pregnant. You deserve a beautiful girl whose heart is available and not pregnant with another man's child. But thanks for asking. I'm very flattered."

With few exceptions, their faces would redden. They'd look down at the floor, shuffle their feet and mumble, "Ah, sure," or "okay" then retreat as fast as they could. Clare would smile after them, feeling badly that she had to hurt their feelings. They were sweet. All she could do when they asked her out was tell them the truth and turn them away as gently as she could.

Their pursuit of her turned her thoughts to Charlie. Why hadn't he written? Why was he being so cruel? She said a prayer of protection for him every night and prayed that her child would know its father and have a loving relationship with him. She missed him most then, when she was warm in her bed, but feeling vulnerable and scared without his strength to comfort her and make her feel secure.

One young man was different from the others. Tony wouldn't take no for an answer. He was tall, dark, and handsome and had fallen for Clare. He had never been rejected before. Girls had always pursued him, but not Clare. She was different from all of the others, mysterious and unknowable and not at all interested in him. He couldn't get her out of his mind.

After she initially rejected him, he came by daily and made a joke of it. "Changed your mind yet?" he'd ask, flashing his perfect smile.

Clare would wrap her arms around her belly and smile. "No," she would say, every time. She was not immune to his considerable appeal, and appeared happy whenever he was around. He had an infectious charm that never failed to buoy her. Unlike the other young men who were less experienced, he had taken no offense at her rejection. Instead, he had been clever, using it as an opportunity to get closer to her. For her part, Clare was relieved that he hadn't taken her rejection personally and decided to ignore her as did several of the young men. Tony was a welcome diversion. But that was it.

The other young men noticed the growing friendship between Clare and Tony, but they didn't see it through Clare's eyes or realize they could have had the same relationship with her. As spiritual as they strived to be, they suffered from inexperience and were also far from conquering their jealousy. One of these young men, Wayne, also happened to be a good friend of Charlie's.

Regardless of their friendship, he secretly coveted Clare. With Charlie away he was sure that his time had come. In his estimation, he was smarter than Charlie, had the superior personality, and was better looking. Of course, he was the only one who thought so. In his mind there was nothing to stop them from being together now. He was sure that Clare was secretly in love with him. If he felt so strongly about her, she must feel as strongly about him. All he had to do now was approach her. Why else would she have rejected all the others? She was obviously waiting for him.

He couldn't believe it when she turned him down. He nursed his rejection, brooded on it privately, and let it consume him. He built his bitterness into a holy war on behalf of his friend, Charlie. Clare was a cold bitch who played with men's hearts, while Charlie risked his life daily for his country. She was a slut who needed to be punished. Wayne watched and waited, nurturing his anger until it became a cold instrument of revenge.

One evening Clare relented and let Tony accompany her to class and sit beside her. She only did that because Marie, who always sat with her, had another matter to attend to that night. Tony was Marie's replacement. That was alright with Tony. All that mattered to him was that he got to sit next to Clare for a few hours. Maybe she'd hug him afterward or even better, give him a peck on the cheek. It wasn't much, but to Tony it was the next step in advancing his ambitions. He could afford to be patient. He had plenty of cute coeds from which to choose and usually dated two or three girls at a time. While they were pleasant amusements, he was fixated on Clare.

When Wayne saw them sitting together, his jealousy rose to the surface, ready to erupt at any moment.

She chose Tony over me, he thought. I can't believe it. This bitch is carrying Charlie's baby and now she's sleeping with Tony?

The time had come for the hammer to pound the nail and defend his friend's honor. That dude wasn't going to screw Clare while Charlie risked his life for his country.

The evening began with a meditation. Clare had come to love these meditations. With practice, she had learned to quiet her mind and had found a deep peace. During tonight's meditation however, she felt something she had never felt before. A sense of danger cloaked the room, an anger that might explode at any moment. Someone was extremely out of balance. She tried to put it aside, but she couldn't shake the feeling that this rage was directed at her.

My imagination is out of control, she thought. I'm probably feeling like this because Marie isn't here tonight. Everything is always peaceful when she's around.

When the meditation ended, Tenzin addressed the class. "No one wants to face his dark side. Most people think that it's normal to suffer and be unhappy. Just because something is common, however, doesn't make it normal. Facing yourself can hurt, but only temporarily. If you're unwilling to face yourself, you cannot grow. A commitment to revealing what is hidden within you and blocking your progress is absolutely essential if you want to heal your life, accelerate your growth, and experience inner-freedom."

Wayne stood up. "Nice talk, Rinpoche," he said. "Very cool." Every head turned to stare at him. "Since you're talking about commitment to the truth, how about we make it real? What about Clare's commitment to Charlie? He's in the jungle fighting for his country. His life's in danger every day. Clare's carrying his child, and she's sleeping with Tony while Charlie's away. That ain't right, know what I mean? Seems as if you should be looking out for Charlie's interests. Clare needs to face herself. That's for sure."

All eyes now turned to stare at Clare and Tony. Clare's cheeks turned crimson. She had never felt so small. She wanted to crawl under her chair. Tony glared at Wayne and stood up. Wayne glared back and tightened his hands into fists.

"You want a piece of me, pretty boy? Come on. You won't be so pretty when I'm done with you." Tony took a few steps toward Wayne, realized that he was in an impossible situation, and staring at Wayne, sat back down.

Wayne smirked. "I didn't think so."

Tenzin looked at Wayne. "Sit down, Wayne."

Wayne ignored Tenzin's command. "What about it, Rinpoche? We still haven't heard from you. We heard from Tony. Tony's a pussy. Are you saying promiscuity's acceptable? Charlie ain't here to defend himself, so I'm standing in for him." Tenzin's voice became harsher. "Sit down, Wayne."

Wayne folded his arms across his chest. "Not until you answer the question."

"Sit down or leave."

Wayne did a quick calculation. He was satisfied. He had accomplished his mission. Clare had been humiliated. He sat down, not bothering to hide the smirk of triumph apparent on his face.

"Who are you to judge?" asked Tenzin.

"Nothing to judge," he said. "Looks pretty obvious to me. Anyone can see it."

"Are you upset that you're not the one sitting next to her, Wayne?"

Wayne's face turned crimson. "She's a whore," he screamed.

"I see," said Tenzin. His voice was calm. A cold, hard darkness filled Wayne's eyes. Where, thought Tenzin, have I seen that look before. A sudden chill passed through him.

"You don't see nothin'. You're as blind as the rest of 'em."

"An angry denial is often an admittance of the truth," said Tenzin. "The ego judges and condemns. The spirit loves and accepts. Which is the better way, Wayne? Envy and hatred never healed anyone of anything. Your charges are nothing more than a vendetta. You are guilty of character assassination. You need to ask for Clare's forgiveness."

"No way! She's a slut!"

"And what are you?"

"I'm the only one here who gives a damn about Charlie!"

"How do you think Charlie would feel if he knew you had called the mother of his child a horrible name and made her feel terrible about herself? She has done nothing wrong. And she has certainly done nothing to you."

"Like you said, the truth hurts," Wayne said.

"There is no truth in either envy or self-righteousness, and you are full of both. Look to your delusions instead of projecting them elsewhere. Small people never face themselves. If you persist, your mind will close further. You will become even less of a man than you are right now. The choice is yours. Face yourself and grow. Refuse and whither. Now leave. When you can offer Clare a sincere apology for your actions you may return. Not before."

"I ain't apologizing for nothin'. Charlie's goin' to hear about this."

"You are correct about that. I will tell him myself when he comes home. Now leave."

"Up yours!"

Wayne stood up and strode defiantly out of the hall.

Clare had covered her face in her hands and was sobbing. Tony's face was flushed with anger. He rose to follow Wayne out of the hall.

"Sit down, Tony," Tenzin said. His voice held a stern edge that no one in the room had ever heard before. "Just because Wayne lost his mind doesn't mean you have to lose yours."

"He humiliated Clare. He insulted me. Nobody does that."

"Spilling blood solves nothing. The only reckoning you are going to have is with yourself. Sit down. Calm down. Center yourself. Don't get up until you can laugh about what happened. Revenge is never the way. Remember that. And forgive Wayne. When you forgive him, he loses all power over you. Negative experiences are tests of character. They provide an opportunity to expand the soul or see it shriveled. A person with an expanded soul has compassion for his enemies. A person with a shriveled soul is full of rage. An expanded person is happy. A shriveled person is miserable. Do you aspire to be like Wayne?"

"No," said Tony unclasping his fists.

"Then sit down."

"But I'll be here all night."

Tenzin let a slight smile creep onto his face. "You may stay as long as necessary."

One of the other young men who had asked Clare out spoke up. "What Wayne did pissed me off, too. Can I stay until I feel centered?"

"Yes. Does anyone else feel that way?"

Nearly everyone raised their hands.

"You may all stay, then. Don't leave until you have burned through your anger and forgiven Wayne."

"Will you stay with us?" someone asked.

"No. You need to resolve this on your own. I can't always hold your hand. When you regain your center, bless Wayne for providing you with this opportunity to grow. Pray that he conquers his delusions and finds the courage to apologize."

While Tenzin spoke, Alice went over and wrapped her arms around Clare. "Come on, honey," she whispered. "Let's leave."

They went to the kitchen, where Alice made them a cup of tea. Clare couldn't speak for a long time. She could barely sip her tea.

"I'm scared I'll lose the baby," she said at last.

"Are you having cramps and bleeding?"

Clare shook her head.

"Then you won't lose the baby."

"That was the worst thing that ever happened to me."

"He's a sick and jealous man."

"Do you think I'm being unfaithful to Charlie? I think about him all the time. I've never encouraged any of the guys. Tony's a friend, nothing more."

"I know. Wayne used Charlie as a pretext. Did he ask you out?"

Clare nodded.

"I thought so. He was mad you chose Tony over him."

"I didn't choose anyone. It's always been Charlie."

"I know. A beautiful woman does funny things to men. Particularly when she's not interested in them."

"Beauty's so overrated. It's made my life hell. Beside, I'm fat and pregnant. I'm not beautiful anymore."

"Those young men would disagree."

The kitchen door opened. Tenzin walked in.

"Quite an evening, honey," said Alice. "How are you feeling?"

"I'm fine," he replied, bending down to kiss his wife. "How are you, Clare?"

Clare wrapped her arms around Tenzin's waist and nuzzled her head against his stomach.

"How am I ever going to face anyone again? They all think I'm unfaithful and a cheater."

Tenzin stroked her head. "Have more faith in people. Wayne fooled no one. He made a fool of himself, not you."

"You really think so?" she said, clinging to any sliver of hope she could find.

"I know so. This will pass. You'll be stronger for it."

"I hope that you're right."

"Don't worry, honey," said Alice. "He's right."

CHAPTER 29

Birth

SANTA MONICA, 1965

WAYNE WASN'T THE only one who stopped coming to the Center after that night. Tony did, too. Clare didn't miss him. It was a relief not to have to be reminded of her night of humiliation.

Even several weeks after the incident, she still hadn't forgiven herself for letting him get close to her. If she hadn't, nothing would have happened that night. It was her fault and she was determined not to repeat the mistake. She had just put down the phone when she felt a sharp pain in her uterus and warm fluid running down her thigh. "Oh, my God," she said. "My water just broke!"

Marie was sitting nearby. "Be calm," she said. "I'll get the car."

Marie found Alice in the kitchen. A moment later the three women were on their way to the hospital. Charles Prescott the Third entered the world in the late afternoon. He had black hair, blue eyes, red cheeks, and a strong, throaty cry. He was perfect in every way.

"He's Charlie all over again," said Alice as the newborn lay sleeping on his mother's breast.

"He sure is," added Marie.

"See, honey," said Alice. "You never had anything to worry about. Your baby is beautiful and healthy."

"I wish Charlie were here," Clare said. Her voice quivered on the verge of breaking.

"He'll be back soon enough."

"I need him now."

"I know," said Alice, patting her arm.

"One day at a time, Clare," said Marie. "Take care of today and he'll be here sooner than you think."

CHAPTER 30

Night in the Jungle

VIETNAM, FEBRUARY 1966

Charlie hadn't shaved in weeks. His uniform was soaked in sweat. He stunk more than a skunk. He had stopped caring about his appearance after his first patrol. The only priority in the jungle was survival. Personal hygiene wouldn't stop a VC bullet, so why bother? There would be plenty of time to be clean when he got home, if he ever got home. He badly missed Clare. He wished that he had listened to her and gone to Canada. Hindsight was such a bitch. He reached up and splattered another fat mosquito full of someone else's blood against his cheek. Didn't the damn things ever get enough to eat? He lifted a dirty sleeve to his face and wiped the blood. According to his calculations, Clare had the baby in November of '65. Was it a boy or a girl? Was Clare still angry at him? Had she found someone else? Would he ever see his child? He ached for her more now than he ever had. How could he have been so goddam stupid as to walk out on her?

He had written to her many times but his letters had been returned. She had moved on and not left a forwarding address. Guess she didn't want to hear from him. It was clearly over.

She would never take him back now. He'd better get used to it, and move on himself. Except that he couldn't. The more that he tried to forget her, the more the thought of her possessed him.

He slogged through the deepening shadows with the rest of his company, the medic band with the red cross on his arm stained with blood, sweat, and dirt. They came to a hill higher than the others and made camp on the summit. The lieutenant established the perimeter and posted sentries. The men dug foxholes, then retrieved their C rations and ate another lousy meal.

"I'm sick of this shit," said Sam, the grunt in the next foxhole. "It's worse than Spam. You got any weed, Billy?"

"That depends."

"On what?"

"On sharing your girlfriend. She needs a real man to drill her."

"Up yours, asshole. I don't need your fucking dope."

Billy laughed and tossed the bag of weed across Charlie's foxhole. "Here you go, dickface. Tweakin' you is too fuckin' easy. You owe me."

"You want some, Charlie?" asked Billy.

"Nah."

A moment later the pungent scent of marijuana filled the air. The animosity was quickly forgotten.

"That's some good shit, Billy. Where'd you get it?"

"Bar girl at the Black Peacock."

"Sally?"

"Yeah."

"Great ass."

"That ain't the half..."

The pop pop pop of AK 47's erupted without warning in the shadows of the dying day. Blood and brains oozed out of a gaping hole in Billy's forehead. The joint lay beside him, a thin stream of smoke blending into the acrid cloud of gunpowder encircling the camp.

CHAPTER 31

Firefight

SANTA MONICA, FEBRUARY 1966

TENZIN MOANED IN the darkness. Perspiration drenched his body. In his dream, a battle raged around him. The rat tat tat of automatic weapons drowned out all other sounds, except for the screams of the dying. Charlie was crawling from foxhole to foxhole trying to save the wounded. The VC were everywhere. One stood silently over the foxhole where Charlie was trying to stanch the bleeding of one of his buddies, his back to the V.C. soldier.

"Goddamn it, Sam!" he screamed. "Hold on! Don't you die on me. I'll have you patched up in a minute."

The VC raised his pistol and shot the wounded soldier in the head. Blood and brain spurted onto Charlie's face and chest. Charlie spun to see the merciless face of his enemy, a pistol aimed at his head. He pointed frantically to the Medic's band on his arm. The VC smirked and squeezed the trigger. A shot rang out. It grazed Charlie's arm, shredding the sleeve of his uniform, but didn't seriously wound him. He grabbed Sam's rifle and fired back. The Vietcong crumpled into the foxhole. Another VC arrived and poured more shots into the foxhole. Charlie screamed. His left arm was on fire. Bone protruded from his forearm, and a warm, thick goo soaked the sleeve of his uniform. His arm hung limp and useless against his side. It was over. He was surrounded. There was no way out of this. He lay back in the foxhole and prayed that death would come quickly, then passed out from the loss of blood.

When Tenzin awoke from his nightmare, there were streaks of blood splattered across his chest. His hands held several pebble-like objects. He dropped them onto the bed, rose as quietly as he could, went into the bathroom, and turned on the light. His hands were covered in blood.

He washed away the blood in the sink, then took off his pajamas and climbed into the hot shower. He could not remember ever feeling so exhausted.

The sound of running water awoke Alice. She turned on the night light and found the pastel blue sheets stained with pools of blood. She threw off the blanket and ran into the bathroom.

Tenzin leaned against the shower wall. Blood was running down his arms. He looked as if he had just returned from war. But that was impossible. What had he done to himself?

"Are you okay?" she said. Her heart was pounding.

"Yes."

"What happened?"

"I had a nightmare."

"Nightmares don't make you bleed."

"This one did."

"What was it about?"

"I was in a jungle. There were guns. Lots of screams. Lots of killing. That's all I remember."

"Charlie?"

"Maybe."

"Is he okay?" Fear kept Alice's voice low.

Tenzin shook his head. "I wish I knew."

"Get under the shower and get that blood off you. You smell awful."

Satisfied that Tenzin was okay, Alice stripped the bed. She heard what she thought were several coins fall to the floor. She bent down to retrieve them. But they weren't coins. These objects were cylindrical. She picked a few of them up and held them to the light.

"Oh my God," she said. In her hand were several bullets. They had Chinese characters on them. She retrieved the rest of the bullets and placed them on the nightstand.

Alice's mind was spinning when Tenzin got back in bed. He fell immediately into a deep sleep. She thought about letting him get his rest. The man certainly needed it, but she had to know what had happened. He could return to sleep after she was better informed. She poked Tenzin in the side. He didn't respond, so she poked him again.

"How did you do that?"

"Huh? What?"

"How did you do that?"

"Do what?"

She jerked open the nightstand drawer and dumped a handful of bullets on his lap. "These bullets were in the bed, Tenzin!"

Tenzin sat up and shook his head. He examined one of the bullets, then gathered them and handed them back to her.

"I don't know," he said. He collapsed back onto his pillow. "I prayed for Charlie. Then I fell asleep. Next thing I knew I was in the jungle. That's it."

"That's it? You were in two places at once. There's got to be more to it than that."

"There isn't."

"Is Charlie alive?"

"I don't know."

"Was he wounded?"

Tenzin's brow furrowed. "He was bleeding, I think."

"God, he could be dead! You have to go back and save him. Clare needs him!"

"I can't control it."

"He's got a woman and a child to take care of!"

"I did everything I could."

"I'm sorry," Alice said, regaining some semblance of self-control. "Go back to sleep. I'm just so worried about Charlie and Clare."

Tenzin nodded. Seconds later he was sound asleep again. It was four-thirty in the morning. Alice went down to the kitchen and made herself a cup of coffee. She sipped it slowly, staring at the bullets in her hand.

CHAPTER 32

Dawn in the Jungle

VIETNAM, 1966

Dawn broke in the jungle. The first rays of the sun illuminated the hill and the bodies of the dead. The light woke Charlie from an uneasy sleep. His head throbbed. His arm ached. An awful goddam noise whirred in the sky above him. He opened his eyes. What the . .? Several Huey helicopters rose over the crest of the hill. When they touched down, troops jumped out and secured the area. A soldier soon found him and signaled for a medic. Minutes later he was on a stretcher being carried into one of the helicopters.

"How many others survived?" Charlie asked the medic attaching an IV to his good arm.

"You're the only one."

Charlie turned away, tears streaming down the corners of his eyes. The guys in the platoon had been tight. They had been through too much to have it end like this, killed in their foxholes on a meaningless hill in the jungle on another pointless patrol. He had lost a lot of blood. His eyelids fluttered. He lost consciousness a moment later.

CHAPTER 33

Thinking It Over

RUMTEK MONASTERY, SIKKIM 1966

Nawang stood in the Karmapa's office. The Karmapa sat behind his desk listening to Nawang's report.

"The harvest was larger than expected, Holiness. The storehouse is full. We even have a surplus. Dorjee and his assistants will plant a new crop soon. Shall we give some of the surplus to the exiles in need?"

"By all means."

"There is another matter, Holiness."

"Yes?"

"The Sangha holiday is in a few months. Tenzin has not been home since 1950."

"This is not home, Nawang. This is Sikkim. We are guests."

"Yes, Holiness. But it is the closest we are likely to be to home for some time."

The Karmapa sighed, revealing a rare glimpse into the sadness that burdened his heart. "True," he said.

"I would like to invite Tenzin to come for Sangha, Holiness. He has achieved great things in America. He triumphed against great odds. We should honor him. The monks would all benefit from meeting him. And you have never met him."

"Tenzin is married, Nawang. He's no longer a monk."

"He lost everything, Holiness. In going to America, he did something none of us have done."

"We lost everything too, Nawang."

"Yes, Holiness. But we still have each other and live in a culture where monks are revered. Tenzin is alone. There is no culture to support him."

"It doesn't matter. He should have been able to stand on his own."

"In his own way he has, Holiness. He adapted to a different culture with different values from ours."

"There are rules in our order that we all must follow, Nawang. Marrying is not one of them."

"Yes, Holiness. But we are no longer in Tibet. We have all had to adapt to conditions that we never expected to encounter. Being married and living a normal western life has made Tenzin more credible to people in the west, not less. He has never wavered from Doezen's directives. Isn't delivering the dharma more important than the language it is taught in, or the lifestyle of the teacher? Tenzin's way of life has changed, Holiness, not his commitment to the dharma."

"You've made your point," said the Karmapa. "You may go now."

"Yes, Holiness," said Nawang, bowing.

The Karmapa turned his back and gazed at his beloved Himalayas. Beyond those peaks lay his homeland and his heart, now overrun by Chinese Communists and repopulated with Chinese immigrants. They had destroyed his country, murdered his people, stolen their homes and property, and desecrated thousands of monasteries. He would do his duty. The monastery depended on him. The Tibetan people needed him. But no one would ever know how deeply the Karmapa suffered from the loss of his beloved country.

CHAPTER 34

Clare's Surprise

SANTA MONICA, SUMMER 1966

CLARE WAS NURSING Charles Prescott the Third at the reception desk. It was lunch-time and the center was deserted. Three, as everyone called him, was nine months old and growing rapidly. He was a happy baby with a hearty appetite. All he knew so far was love. Love came at him from everywhere. Alice and Marie took turns holding him. Matthew and Daniel crawled around the living room floor with him, picking up his pacifier when it fell out of his mouth. Tenzin and Thomas cooed at him and discussed politics while rocking his cradle in the evening.

With a baby to care for, and all of her attention focused on him, the young men who had gathered around Clare now faded away. In their stead, many of the young women came to visit her, fuss over Three, hold him, and talk about motherhood. It didn't hurt that they no longer had to worry about a more beautiful rival stealing their boyfriends. A nursing infant in her lap had lessened her sexual allure. Clare did not mourn the change or miss the male attention.

For the first time in her life, she experienced a sense of sisterhood with women her own age. They conversed about the joys and struggles of motherhood and their problems with their boyfriends. Clare was no longer on the outside, alien and alone, excluded from the community of women her own age. Only Charlie was missing from her life.

She had no idea of where he was. Did he ever think of her and his child? Why hadn't he written? Was he still alive? And if he was, did he still love her? Maybe he had found some hot Vietnamese girl to take her place. She tried not to worry and fret and become consumed with jealousy. Instead, she wiped a solitary tear from her cheek and focused all of her love and attention on Three.

Three sucked happily on his mother's breast, oblivious of her concerns. He was hungrier than normal. He sucked so hard that her nipples hurt. He burped suddenly and threw up all over her new blouse. She sighed and laid him down in his stroller. While she wiped her blouse with a baby towel she felt eyes watching her intently from the front door. Her cheeks burned. The hair on the nape of her neck stood up. She was afraid to look up.

Please God, let it not be Wayne, she thought.

She felt violated to have someone watching her at such a vulnerable and private moment. When at last she summoned the courage to see who was staring at her, her mouth dropped open and her eyes grew as large as stars. It couldn't be. It had to be a mirage. He was wearing his dress uniform. The sling holding his left arm partially covered the medals on his chest. He was so beautiful. His face was thin and pale; his cheeks were sunken and gaunt. But it was her Charlie, alright. She had dreamed of this moment every day of every month since he had gone to war. Now that he was here, she could only stare at the apparition in the foyer as he moved slowly toward her.

He smiled as he walked toward her. He was limping slightly. She could see by the stress on his face and the lack of color in his cheeks that he was in pain. The questions sped through her mind. What had happened to him? Was he badly wounded? Would he recover? What about the wounds you couldn't see? The ones in his mind. Did he have many of those? How deep were they? Was he haunted by what he had seen? Was he still the same Charlie? Did he love her? Did he?

Her eyes overflowed with him as he came closer. She reached out and grabbed his hand. It was warm and soft as it always had been. She sighed and kissed it and clutched it to her cheek. As soon as she felt his warmth on her face, the dam broke and the tears that had been stored behind it poured out. She had promised herself that this wouldn't happen; that she wouldn't be reduced to a slobbering fool on his return; that she would maintain her dignity. In spite of her resolve, she couldn't help herself. Her relief was too great. He was alive. He was back. He was here with her. That's all that mattered. Charlie leaned over, wiped away her tears, kissed her forehead, stroked her cheeks with his good hand, traced her lips, and kissed her deeply and long.

"Is it a boy?" he whispered in her ear.

Clare nodded.

"What's his name?"

"His name is your name."

"Charles Prescott?"

Clare nodded.

"He's beautiful," said Charlie.

Little Three looked up at his father, his solemn eyes wide open, seeing everything. He no longer cried or fussed or demanded his mother's milk. He was silent for the first time that day. Clare picked him up and put him in Charlie's right arm. Charlie held his son and softly kissed the top of his head.

"I've thought of this moment every day since I left," he said. "It's better in real life than it ever was in my mind. I missed you, baby. I missed you every minute of every day of every week of every month."

"Why didn't you write, Charlie? I've been so scared. I didn't know if you were alive or dead, or where you were, or if you still loved me or wanted to see your son. I thought you hated me."

"Oh, baby, I could never hate you. And I did write. I wrote a lot. But my letters came back, marked "return to sender", no forwarding address. I figured you didn't want me to know where you were, and didn't want to have anything more to do with me. I had no idea you'd be here. I didn't expect to see you today."

A light went on in Clare's head. "Oh, my God! It's all my fault. I forgot to file a change of address form with the Post Office."

"It's okay, baby. Forget it."

"You have no idea how much I've missed you, Charlie. Your son needs his father and I need you. I love you, Charlie, more than you'll ever know."

Now the tears poured down Charlie's face. He coughed several times and cleared his throat, fighting to regain his composure.

"I'll never leave you again, babe. Never."

Clare looked up at him. Her face was solemn. "You better not, Charles Prescott. You better not."

She drew close and kissed him. Little Three cried. It was the first sound he made since meeting his father.

Clare took the baby from Charlie's arms. "This is your Daddy, Three. This is the man whose proud name you carry. "

Just then the kitchen door opened. Alice stood in the doorway, mouth open, watching. The files in her arms fell to the floor. Tears ran down her cheeks.

"Welcome home, Charlie," she said.

Charlie grinned and limped over to hug her.

"Thanks, Alice. It's great to be back. I never thought I'd make it. Where's the boss?"

"With a client. He'll be finished soon. You two go upstairs and get reacquainted. I'll take care of Three."

"Are you sure?" asked Clare.

"Of course I'm sure. Now go. Oh, and Charlie?"

"Yeah?"

"You live here now. Your family's our family. I hope that's okay with you, because there's no way we're letting Clare and Three leave."

Charlie smiled. "That's good 'cause I've got nowhere else to go."

"It's settled then. Emily's room is yours."

"I don't know how I'll ever repay you. But I'll find a way."

"Don't be silly. You're back safe. That's all we ever wanted."

"Thanks," Charlie said, bowing his head. He was humbled by her generosity.

Alice turned serious. She cocked her head to the side and looked at him with new eyes. "You've changed, Charles Prescott," she said. "You're not a lost kid anymore."

"Nothing like a war to make you grow up quickly," he said. "When you lose all your brothers in battle, every life and every day becomes precious. When the VC killed everyone in my company all I thought about was getting back to Clare. Finding her was all that mattered."

Clare's arms were wrapped around Charlie's waist, her head resting against his chest. As he spoke, she drew as tightly to him as she could.

"You saw a lot out there," said Alice.

"I'd like to forget it, but I never will. It's etched too deeply in my mind. War turns men into animals. I wouldn't be here if it weren't for Tenzin. He saved me."

Alice looked at him strangely. "Clare needs time with you, Charlie. Now give me Three."

Alice was sitting at the reception desk with Three, when Tenzin emerged from his study an hour later. He looked around, clearly baffled.

"Isn't Clare supposed to be here?"

"I sent her upstairs to rest."

"I see."

"Do you?" Only the glint in Alice's eyes hinted at her secret.

"What do you mean?"

"Oh, nothing. Will Thomas be on time for dinner?"

"Who knows? You know how he is."

"I'm worried about him. He's lost too much weight."

"He'll be fine."

"Dinner's at 6:30 sharp. Don't forget to pick up the boys from soccer."

"Don't worry."

CHAPTER 35

The Invitation

RUMTEK MONASTERY, SIKKIM 1966

The Karmapa summoned Nawang to dine privately with him. "Tell me about your trip to Darmasala, Nawang." He nodded to the young monk serving them. The monk poured a cup of dark tea for Nawang. Nawang took the cup in both hands and blew on the rising steam.

"The Dalai Lama sends his regards, Holiness."

"Has any progress been made with the Chinese?"

Nawang frowned. "They have accelerated their program to resettle Tibet with Chinese immigrants, Holiness. Our people continue to suffer great indignities. The Chinese are determined to instill fear in the population and to eradicate Tibetan Buddhism. The Communists beat, jail, rape, or kill those who dare to oppose their policies."

The Karmapa lowered his head and frowned. "And Dorjee?"

"His work goes well, Holiness."

"That's not what I meant," said the Karmapa. "Does he meditate with the others?"

"No, Holiness."

"He's been here for several years. Has he made new friends?"

"A few. But he would rather be in the fields than sitting in the meditation hall with the other monks."

"I see," said the Karmapa, tapping table with his fingertips.

They sipped their tea silently. The Karmapa put down his cup. He had come to a decision.

"You may write Tenzin."

"Holiness?"

"Tell him to come."

CHAPTER 36

The Dinner Guest

SANTA MONICA, 1966

TENZIN HAD PICKED up the boys and returned to his study to complete some work before dinner. Danny burst in on him as he was writing the summation to a talk he was to give in a few days.

"Guess what, Dad?"

"What?" said Tenzin, only partially paying attention to his son.

"We have a guest for dinner!"

"Oh? Who?" said Tenzin absentmindedly. Having a guest for dinner was a common occurrence. It didn't take much to excite Danny, though, no matter how much Tenzin reminded him to keep an even keel. His advice bounced off Danny like a rubber ball. Alice had constantly to assure him that Danny would gain more self control as he got older. Tenzin sighed and hoped that she was right.

"I can't tell you," said Danny.

"Why not?"

"Hurry, Daddy."

Danny turned and scampered down the corridor. Tenzin extinguished his desk lamp. Work would come later. It was not like Danny to burst in and keep information from him. What was going on? Well, he would know soon enough. Maybe Thomas had brought a fellow scholar home. When he entered the kitchen, everyone was seated at the table. Alice stood at the stove with her back to him. Clare was nursing Three. Thomas wasn't home yet. Everything was normal. There was no secret guest. Only the conspiratorial smiles on the boys' faces seemed out of place.

"Danny said that we have a special guest."

"Did he?" said Alice. "You know how Danny tells tales. I'm surprised you believed him."

"Then, why are the boys smiling like Cheshire cats?"

Alice shrugged. "They're boys."

Clare put Three into his high chair and rummaged through her bag. "I have something for you."

Tenzin noticed the glow on Clare's face. "You're all acting strangely. Is anyone going to tell me what's going on?"

The boys laughed. Alice turned back to the stove. Clare put something small and metallic in his palm, closed his fingers over it and kissed his hand. "Thank you," she said.

"For what?" said Tenzin, mystified.

A voice behind him answered. "For saving my life."

Tenzin turned to see Charlie wearing his dress uniform. For once, Tenzin was speechless. Charlie wrapped his good arm around him and hugged him forcefully.

"Thanks, boss."

"What are you talking about?"

"The ambush in the jungle. You saved me from certain death. I don't know how you got there, but you did."

"Shh! Not so loud."

"It's too late. They all know. Open your hand."

Tenzin raised his hand and uncurled his fingers. In his palm was a Purple Heart.

CHAPTER 37

Gaining Wisdom

The great man is driven by neither ambition nor anxiety. He has no desire for recognition or fame. Instead, the great man has discovered his true nature and is guided by love. From this discovery, his greatness flows. For the great man, life is internally rich and peaceful. He is content. Neither struggle nor conflict stirs within him. Because of his contentment, clarity and compassion fill his activities. Such is the essence of his greatness. The great man does not desire to be different from his friends and neighbors. Instead, he wants them to be as fulfilled as he is. This is the secret of his greatness.

Alan Mesher

SANTA MONICA, 1966

CHARLIE MET WITH Tenzin in his office the next morning. Tenzin proudly wore the purple heart on his chest.

"Alice told me that you were wounded in the jungle," said Charlie. "You earned that medal."

"My wife talks too much."

"She said you were covered in blood."

"See what I mean?"

"Don't be so hard on her. No one loves you like she does."

"And no one loves you, Charlie, like Clare does."

"Thank God for that. I wouldn't want to think what my life would be like without her. Alice showed me the bullets she found in your bed," said Charlie. "You should be awarded the Medal of Honor. How did you do it, Tenzin? How did you get there?"

Tenzin turned his head to gaze out the window. The oleander was in full bloom. He loved the white flowers but knew how lethal they could be. "I was meditating and felt great danger around you. Then I was there. That's all I can tell you. These things happen."

"These things happen?"

"Apparently."

"Are you kidding me? It was a miracle of Christlike proportions."

Tenzin laughed. "Do I look like Christ to you?"

"No."

"Well, there you are. Our souls are infinite. We all have that potential inside us. The danger around you activated that potential in me, that's all. You're back, you're safe. That's all that matters. Let's forget the past and concentrate on what's next. How's your arm?"

"The bone was shattered. It'll never be the same. It brought me an honorable discharge and a ticket home, so I'm glad for that. Now I can go to med school on Uncle Sam's dime."

"Do you know what branch of medicine you want to practice?"

"I want to open a clinic for vets. They fought. They were wounded and maimed. They have psychological scars and they received nothing for their sacrifices. They come home and they're treated like lepers. Heck, they didn't start the war. They didn't want it, and they're not responsible for it. They were forced to fight it by the bastards who engineered it. I'm gonna help them."

Tenzin smiled. "That's how becoming a great man begins. Greatness comes from helping others."

"We're doing bad things over there."

"All wars are terrible," said Tenzin.

"This is different," said Charlie.

Tenzin raised his eyebrows. "What do you mean?"

"You know about Agent Orange?"

"Yes, of course."

"A lot of what you hear about it is disinformation."

"How so?"

"Much of the sickness among the troops and the defoliation of large areas of the jungle are from nuclear bombs."

"We're using nuclear weapons?" Tenzin hadn't thought there was much more that could shock him, but this revelation did.

"Yeah. They're called bunker busters. They burrow deep underground before detonating. The fallout reaches the surface and defoliates the forests. Many of our guys are suffering from radiation poisoning. A high percentage of them will die from leukemia and other cancers. My source told me that one of the main reasons for this war was to test weapons for future wars."

"I hope that your source is wrong."

"I don't think so. When I was over there, I met a CIA spotter with a real bad case of malaria. He thought he was dying and talked to me a lot, sort of like a confessional. His mission was to locate VC bunkers and report their coordinates. Then, the Air Force would launch airstrikes and drop bunker busters on 'em."

Tenzin shook his head. "So many lies."

"Yeah," said Charlie. "They call those lies patriotism and label anyone who speaks out against them a terrorist. The sad thing is that most people believe what they're told. They think that the government would never lie to them and is there to protect them. Did you know what else I learned?"

"What?" said Tenzin.

"In the fifties government psychiatrists gave massive doses of LSD to little kids on a daily basis to see what it would do to their minds. That's how they protect us. We're guinea pigs for their psychological experiments and cannon fodder for their wars."

"Thomas will be very interested in this."

"It seems that the government uses every opportunity it can to turn us against each other. Long hairs versus buzz cuts, patriots versus protestors, blacks versus whites, men versus women. On and on. Either I'm paranoid, or they truly want us at each other's throats."

"Why would they want that?" asked Tenzin. He wanted to see how far Charlie had gone in his analysis.

"It increases their power. If they can keep us divided it's easy to control us. As long as the people of this country believe the lies they're fed, the few will always be able to control the many."

Tenzin leaned back in his chair. "The war has awakened you."

"The price was awfully goddam high."

"It always is," said Tenzin.

"Too many good men I knew died over there for me to remain ignorant. I have a duty to make what happened count for something good. I don't want my boy to be cannon fodder for the next war. No more Prescott's as designated soldiers. I intend to be the last of that line. The s.o.b.'s have all the power, and that makes me feel insignificant and helpless."

"That's the way they want you to feel. That's how they steal your power. Begin with what you do have, your mind. Release your patterns of victimization and your fear. Do that, and your mind will be yours, not theirs. Release the negative and you will not attract harm."

"How do I do that?"

"Close your eyes. Inhale slowly. Exhale slowly. Focus your attention on your breath. When you begin to feel clear and peaceful, imagine a radiant sun a few inches above your head. See a beam of golden light from that sun pouring into you, filling every cell of your body. When your body is full of light, visualize that light expanding into your energy field. You are now sitting in a sphere of gold light that extends beyond your body for three feet in all directions. At the outer edge of the sphere, visualize a global mirror that has its reflective surface pointing away from you. Negative energy directed at you bounces off the mirror and returns to the sender. This is a powerful form of protection."

"Now, inhale golden light through your nostrils. As you exhale, release any negativity you feel, directing it up your spine and into the sun above your head. The sun represents your soul. It will purify the negative energy and return it to you when needed."

"This simple form of attunement raises your frequency and increases your light. If enough people were to practice this simple exercise, it would call down a great wave of spiritual light to the physical plane and change the world."

"I do feel better. But do you really think that this exercise could change the world?"

"If enough people did it."

"How many would it take?"

"Three percent of the world's population."

"Why don't you organize it then?"

"I'm not an organizer and the time is not yet right."

"Will it ever be?"

"Yes."

"When?"

"When technology is more advanced. When the time comes, people all over the world will organize it. There will be a network, not a hierarchy with a leader at the top, and the dark side will not be able to stop it."

"Speaking of the dark side, who are the people that really run the country?"

"Thomas is working on that right now."

"But do you really think spirituality can defeat them? They control the military, the clandestine services, the media, the major corporations, the banks, the educational system, the major religions, and organized crime. They determine the curriculum in the schools, what people read in the newspapers, what movies get made and what they see on TV. They control all the levers of power," said Charlie.

"But," Tenzin said, "the one thing they can't control is the human soul. The soul is indestructible and eternal. This is a psychic war, a battle to control minds.

If we let them control our minds, we will never be able to activate our spiritual power. They think that they can control us indefinitely, but they're truly afraid of the power inside us. They have their agenda of worldwide domination, but if we wake up, the future is ours, not theirs. Gandhi said that if you want to change the world, be the change you seek. We are all spiritually connected. All division based on race, gender, color, and economic status is artificial, designed by our controllers to isolate and divide us permanently. If they keep dividing us, they win. If we purify our minds, pull down the Light and stand together, we triumph. That's what it will take to change the world."

"I dunno," said Charlie, shaking his head. "I'm not that optimistic. Most of the time, man acts like a stupid beast. It's hard to believe humanity would ever unite like that."

"Man has been made that way by his controllers. His spiritual potential has been deliberately obscured. I see a future where there may be fewer people, but more light, a world where freedom, happiness and love thrive, a world at peace. There will be too much spiritual light for the dark side to remain. The earth will be free of them."

"When will this happen?"

"In your lifetime, perhaps. In your son's, certainly."

"What about in yours?"'

Tenzin laughed. "That depends on how long I live."

"Don't you want to be here for that?"

"Certain things are beyond my control. Life goes on whether we're here or not. It doesn't matter if I'm in the body or in the spirit. Wherever I am, I will work for humanity's freedom."

"Well, I hope you're here."

"There are more important things than life and death, Charlie. What truly matters is our journey into the eternal light. Extend your bad arm across the desk, please."

Charlie grimaced. His left arm was bent and rigid. Extending it even a small distance was very painful. Nevertheless, he laid his arm as best he could across the desk as Tenzin had instructed. Tenzin put one hand on Charlie's wrist, the other under his elbow. Heat and electricity surged through Charlie's arm, causing it to shake uncontrollably. Several minutes later, Tenzin removed his hands from Charlie's arm and examined it closely.

"The bones will heal correctly. I will treat it again in a few days."

Charlie raised his arm and lifted it above his shoulder.

"The pain's gone! I've got more range of motion than I've had since I was wounded. I'm speechless. But I guess I should know better by now."

"If you intend to open a clinic you will need both arms to treat your clients."

"How can I ever repay you for all you've done for me? You've saved me in every way possible."

"Pass it along. Do the best you can for others. Now, when are you planning to make an honest woman of Clare?"

"I just got back. I need time to adjust. Everything's happening so fast."

"Don't wait too long. Clare needs the sense of security that being married will give her. Things happened while you were gone."

"What do you mean?" said Charlie, alarmed.

"Many men tried to date Clare while you were away. Even Wayne."

"Wayne? That's impossible. He'd never do that."

"Clare's a beautiful woman. Wayne coveted her."

"You don't know that."

"Clare didn't tell you?"

"Tell me what?"

"One night Wayne stood up in front of the whole class and called Clare a whore because she was sitting next to someone else instead of him."

"Someone else? Who? I can't believe that Wayne would do that!"

"Don't worry. Clare wasn't doing anything improper. Another guy was sitting next to her, that's all. He had a crush on her, but so did every other guy there. She wasn't interested in any of them."

"I'll ask her, alright. I can't believe this."

"Wayne's envious of you, Charlie. I know you don't see it, but he wants what you have. In his mind, he's better than you and thinks Clare should be with him."

"Why didn't Clare tell me about it?"

"You've just come home. That's the last thing she wants to talk about. Maybe later. It was very traumatic for her. She almost lost the baby. And she's scared of what you might do if you knew. Would you go after Wayne? Would you think she'd been unfaithful and leave her? You left her once. She's terrified you'd do it again. She's well aware of how hot-headed the male ego can be when there's a beautiful woman involved."

"I'd never leave her."

"Then tell her."

"It was the first thing I said when I got back."

"That's before you knew about Wayne."

"That's true," Charlie admitted.

"So tell her again. Tell her that you know about Wayne and you're not going to go after him. Tell her that you love her and you're sorry it happened. Tell her that you're sorry you weren't there to protect her. Tell her that it's your fault for not seeing who he is."

"But it's not my fault."

"Does it matter? What's important is that you relieve her anxiety about what happened, and about what you might do, if you found out about it. Be smart. Use the negative to make your relationship stronger. Ignore your ego. Act from your soul. It's good practice. Think of what Clare needs from you and provide it. This will deepen the trust between you and strengthen your relationship. That's the power of understanding and forgiveness. It will bring closure and help Clare to release the trauma from her body."

"That's sound advice," said Charlie.

"A wise man acts from his soul, not from his ego. That's what makes him wise."

CHAPTER 38

The Wedding

SANTA MONICA, 1966

Clare and Charlie married later that year. Charlie's father, Charles Sr., and Clare's mother, Connie, came to the wedding. Connie flew from Hong Kong to meet her grandson and her daughter's husband. Connie arrived the day before Charlie's father. Charlie picked her up at the airport, carrying a sign in Chinese that Clare had made. When he asked Clare to translate it all she would say is that it was her mother's name in Chinese.

"That's a mighty long name, Clare. Did you put a few titles in there to bulk it up?" Clare shrugged and turned away to nurse Three. "I wrote her formal name. She'll like that. You want her to like you, don't you?"

A long line of people was waiting to go through customs when Connie's flight from Hong Kong arrived. This was her first trip to America. She arrived tired and irritable. The plane had flown through several patches of turbulence, and that had unsettled her stomach. The people in the line ahead of her were loud, pushy, and worse; they talked to strangers. Like most barbarians, they had no manners. Were all Americans like this? If so, she wanted to turn around and go right home. And where was Clare? She should be here. Did she bring the baby?

The thought of her new grandson brought a smile to her face. She stood in the back of the long line and scanned the crowd waiting beyond the customs desk. A sign with bright red Chinese characters caught her eyes. Underneath it stood a young man with blond hair and blue eyes. Her jaw dropped. He was so beautiful. He must be a movie star. She stared at him transfixed. He was better looking than either Clint Eastwood, Robert Redford or Paul Newman, her favorite American actors. Then she read the sign and laughed for the first time in America. The young man would soon be Clare's husband. Her grandson was going to be gorgeous! Wait until she got back to Hong Kong and told her friends about her beautiful American son-in-law. They would all be so envious. Imagine, a baby with those blue eyes and Clare's cheekbones and olive skin. Maybe Clare knew what she was doing after all. Half an hour later she finally cleared customs and made her way to Charlie.

"Clare didn't tell me you were so good looking," she said in Chinese.

Charlie stared at her with a blank expression on his face. He had no idea what she was saying, only that this must be his future mother-in-law. Well, she was small and didn't look at all formidable. Clare was guilty of exaggeration, again. He made a mental note to discount future warnings about her family.

Connie talked in Chinese all the way home. She asked how they had met, how the war had been, how her daughter was liking motherhood, how much he loved her, and would he always be faithful and kind to her. But most of all she asked about the baby.

How big was he? Did he have a big appetite? Was he happy and healthy? Was Clare breastfeeding? Did he get enough love? Could he speak Chinese? Did he like dumplings? Charlie was completely befuddled by the exhausting stream of incoherent noise. He could only nod and smile and pray that she would shut up soon.

Connie was not concerned at all with his feelings. She was going to see her daughter and grandson. That's all that mattered to her. She wanted to hold the baby in her arms and cover him with kisses.

Charlie, of course, had questions, but none of them escaped his lips. Why was it that women never seemed to know how exhausting it was for men to have to listen to them? Most women assumed that talking to a man was like talking to a woman. Well, it wasn't. Not at all. Most women he knew talked in repetitive circles. Why?

I'm not stupid, I understand it the first time. Please, please shut up, he silently implored her, but Connie kept chattering along. He sighed and admitted defeat. Clare had been right about her mother. She was more than formidable.

He was realizing how complicated marriage could be. Landmines were hidden everywhere. He would have to find a way to appease competing factions. But how? Never mind the language problem. He was already sick of his mother-in-law's voice. It grated on him like the sound of fingernails scratching a blackboard. And then there was the small matter of his father. How would he handle her? Would he withdraw as he did with his mother? Would he be condescending or utterly charming? Charlie's head was throbbing. What a nightmare.

Stupid Barbarian, thought Connie. He should know Chinese. It was Clare's tongue. He needed to honor her by learning it. After all, she spoke his miserable language. China was an ancient culture, far deeper, more subtle and mysterious than America would ever be. America was rich, she had to admit. There was so much wealth everywhere. Look at all the cars and shops and beautiful houses. Was Clare's home beautiful, too? Was Charlie rich? The thought tantalized her. She might make allowances for his crudeness if he were. After all, money excused a multiplicity of faults, especially if it was your son-in-law who had it. It was something else she could brag about to her friends. Her eyes swept over his jeans, t-shirt, bare feet and sandals. She shook her head with disgust. Is this the way the rich dress in America? Watch out, young man. One day China will be a world power again. We have a glorious future. You Americans are too self-absorbed to see what's going on in the world. Change is coming. Vietnam will bankrupt you. A frown crossed her face. She stopped her chatter temporarily.

Charlie relaxed, glad for the moment of peace, however fleeting it might be.

"Make sure my grandson speaks Chinese," she said a moment later, pointing her finger in his face. "It's the future."

Charlie's body tensed, his jaw bulged, but he nodded nevertheless. He had learned to follow orders in the Army. He hadn't known it would be invaluable training for dealing with his mother-in-law.

A moment later, they turned into the Center. It wasn't soon enough for Charlie. He parked in front of the entrance and beeped the horn. Clare appeared seconds later with young Three in her arms. The two women squealed with delight and ran into each other's arms. Clare handed Three to her mother. Connie cuddled him in her arms and cooed, her face all smiles. Three cried.

Connie was completely taken with her grandson. He was the most beautiful baby she had ever seen, even more beautiful than Clare had been. Charlie saw his opportunity to escape, and took Connie's bags to the second floor guest bedroom.

He stopped in the kitchen when he had finished his task. A plate of freshly baked oatmeal raisin cookies was cooling on the counter. He took one, walked down the hall to Tenzin's office, and knocked on the door.

"Do you have a moment?"

Tenzin put down his lecture notes. "Of course."

Charlie eased into the old chair and closed his eyes.

"How was your trip to the airport?" asked Tenzin.

"Did you always get along with your mother-in-law?"

"She died recently."

"But did you get along with her while she was alive?"

"We had an understanding."

"What sort of understanding?"

"As long as I let her run things when she was here we got along fine."

"You let her run things?"

"Why not? She was good at it. It made my life easier."

"I see."

"We're men, Charlie. Women run the house and family. We have our work. We each have our own spheres. Otherwise, there would be resentment, and resentment destroys relationships. My mother -in-law was great with the boys. They adored her. It worked well for everybody."

"That's comforting."

"Clare's blossomed since you came back. You and Three are the center of her life. You'll be very happy, just as I have been. Beginnings are always difficult. You'll make the necessary adjustments. I'm sure you'll learn to co-exist with your mother-in-law. Healthy female energy is necessary for a happy life. We all need female energy, support, and nurturing. It's the bedrock of the family and the foundation of a society. Without it, a culture will wither and die and the family unit will disintegrate. She will leave soon enough. Mine went back to San Francisco. Yours will go back to China. Treat her well, be respectful, and she will not be a problem in your marriage. She will sing your praises. You'll see."

"Does it bother you that Clare's family is Chinese?"

"Why should it?"

"You know. The Tibetan thing."

"Are Clare's family murderers?"

"Nah. Just regular people trying to live in peace."

"So why would I be upset with them? Love everyone without exception. Your mother-in-law is teaching you to extend your ability to love. Honor her."

Charlie sighed. "I wish it were that simple."

"When you get out of your own way it will be."

"How do I do that?"

"When you clear the hurt and anger you still have about your mother, loving your mother-in-law will be easy."

Charlie leaned back in the chair and groaned.

"There is so little love in the world because people indulge their dark side instead of healing it. They let their anger, resentment, and hatred possess them, brooding endlessly over perceived wrongs. By doing that, they cast themselves as victims and draw more unhappiness to them. Why postpone one's happiness? Don't get bitter, get better. Self-righteous people are unhappy people." Tenzin leaned back in his chair. "When does your father arrive?"

"Tomorrow."

"I look forward to meeting him," said Tenzin. He tapped the purple heart on his chest. "He and I have something in common. We're both decorated warriors," Tenzin laughed. "Only he has a Distinguished Service Cross. He's a true hero."

"C'mon."

"Your father has his flaws. Who doesn't? Someday you'll realize that he's a great man and the two of you will be close."

"I doubt it. We've never been close."

"Things change."

"It's too late for that."

"It's never too late to forgive, Charlie."

The next afternoon, Charlie met his father at the airport. They spoke the same language, but that was all they had in common. Charlie arrived early, parked outside the baggage terminal at American Airlines and waited. Moments later Charles Prescott Sr. walked through the glass doors into the bright light and honking horns of LAX. Charlie got out of the car and waved. "Over here, Dad!"

Charles Sr. was a tall, athletic, handsome man. His hair had turned gray years ago, but it was still full and thick. The sunlight made it shine as he made his way along the sidewalk, enhancing an already distinguished appearance. He walked with shoulders back and spine erect, a carryover from his years in the military. His eyes were piercing blue like his son's. His face was lined with suffering. Watching him, you had the feeling that he would be cool and calm in an emergency, in control, and decisive.

"Hi, Dad," said Charlie.

"How are you, son?"

"Good."

Charles Sr. tossed his suitcase in the rear seat and got in the car. Charlie started the engine and eased his way into the traffic.

"So, are you ready to be a husband and father and support a family?"

"I hope so."

"Me, too."

The conversation ended there. Charles Sr. looked out the window, re-familiarizing himself with Los Angeles. The last time he had been here was just before he shipped out to the Pacific in forty-two, some twenty-five years ago.

Christ, he thought, has it really been that long? Charlottesville is a long way from here in more ways than one. It has a different culture, a different climate, and a different kind of people. He was glad he lived there. Charles Sr. was an East-coast guy, always had been. He wished that his son would take his family back home. He longed for the chance to heal the rupture that existed with his boy. He rubbed his eyes, the underlying sadness etched in his face now clearly visible.

They drove in silence most of the way. Was his boy really ready for marriage and family?

He thought of his former wife and what his son had suffered at her hands. She was a paranoid schizophrenic who had terrorized him, hardly great preparation for his future. He thought for the ten thousandth time about his absence from Charlie's childhood and grimaced. He had been a coward. Strong in war, weak at home. Defeated and humiliated by insanity. He hadn't protected his son. He would always bear that stain. As the years passed, the knowledge of his inadequacy weighed ever more heavily on him. He coughed. Sometimes, the guilt was too much to bear.

"You O.K., Dad?"

"Sure. It was a long trip. I'm a little tired, that's all."

"We'll be there in a minute."

Charlie turned into the driveway and parked by the front door of an elegant yellow stucco home.

Nice place, thought Charles Sr.. Classy, well maintained, but not ostentatious. Great garden. Someone's got a gift for landscape design.

Clare had been waiting by the window. As the two men got out of the car, she scooped up Three and flew down the hall to meet her father-in-law. Charles Sr.'s jaw dropped when he saw her approaching them with the baby in her arms.

That's a fine, healthy woman, he thought. Incredibly beautiful. She's nothing like Charlie's mother. A wave of relief rippled through him for the first time since he had boarded the plane in Washington.

Clare handed Three to Charlie and embraced her new father-in-law without reservation. Charlie was speechless while he watched his father melt in her embrace.

"I'm Clare. Thank you so much for coming. I've been dying to meet you. Can I call you Dad?"

Charles Sr. grinned. "I'd like that."

"Dad it is," she said, and kissed his cheek.

Did his father have a heart, after all? If so, Clare had found in a moment what had eluded him all his life.

Clare took Three back from Charlie and held him up to Charles Sr.

"Would you like to hold Three? He's your namesake, you know."

"I certainly would."

Clare handed young Three to his grandfather. Charles Sr. took his grandson in his arms and looked into his happy blue eyes. Three gurgled, and laughed, and tapped his grandfather on the chin with a chubby finger.

"He's so beautiful," said Charles Sr.

"He looks like the pictures Charlie showed me of himself when he was that age," said Clare. "Except that his hair is black and his skin is olive."

"I was thinking the same thing," said Charles Sr. "The eyes are the same."

"They're your eyes," Clare said.

Charles Sr. nodded, tearing up. He flexed his jaw muscles, determined not to let his emotions betray him.

Just then, Connie joined them.

"This is my mother, Connie," Clare said.

"I'm glad to meet you, Dr. Prescott," said Connie. She bowed formally to Charles Sr.

"And I am glad to meet you, Connie," said Charles Sr. in perfect Mandarin. He bowed in return. "Aren't we lucky to have such a beautiful child to bind us together?"

It was Connie's turn to be speechless. He spoke her language. She hadn't expected that. The Barbarian was a cultured man, so handsome and dignified.

"Your daughter is beautiful," Charles Sr. continued in Mandarin. "She's the best thing that's ever happened to my boy. Thank you." He bowed again.

Connie's eyes widened. This barbarian was thoughtful and respectful. Her attitude toward her son-in-law underwent an immediate shift. Someday, he will be as good a man as his father. Clare will mold him into a great man.

But he must learn to speak Chinese! They were married the next day. Tenzin presided. Charlie wore his dress uniform. Tenzin wore his purple heart. Clare dressed in a simple white gown. She glowed with happiness. Her mother had brought with her a pearl necklace with matching pearl earrings that her own mother had worn on her wedding day and she had worn on hers. Now it was Clare's turn.

Three slept on his grandfather's chest. Connie sat next to him, patting the baby's back. They both sniffled throughout the ceremony. Connie handed Charles Sr. a handkerchief that he used several times.

Later, after a fine meal that Marie had spent days preparing, Tenzin invited Charles Sr. into his office.

"I would offer you a cigar, but I don't smoke," said Tenzin.

"That's alright. I don't either."

"Would you like some special Tibetan butter tea, perhaps?"

"Sure. You've really helped my son, Tenzin. He's a man now. I can't thank you enough." He looked out the back window for a moment, then returned his gaze to Tenzin. "I wasn't a very good father."

"It's never too late to change."

"It's nice to think that could be true," Dr. Prescott said.

"I didn't really do that much, you know. Charlie's experience in Vietnam played a big part in his growth. He saved many lives. He grew up over there."

"Being a medic takes a lot of guts. You have to navigate the battlefield without a weapon. Often, there's no cover and enemy fire all around you. I was terrified for him, but I'm really proud of how he handled himself."

"Does he know that?"

"We don't talk much. I love my boy with all of my heart. I don't know if he knows it."

"Tell him."

"There's a long and painful history. It's not that easy."

"Emotional distance is a bad habit. Habits can be broken. It's time to break yours, Dr. Prescott."

"I don't know how."

"What scares you the most?"

"Being seen as weak, I guess."

"Telling your son that you love him is not weakness. It's truth. Running from your true feelings and hiding your love? That's weakness."

"But what if he rejects me?"

"What if he does?"

"I'd be crushed."

"Your son loves you, Dr. Prescott, but feels you abandoned him when he was young. He's still angry about that. Let him express his anger if necessary. Don't react or feel rejected. Just listen. When he releases it, the love between the two of you will blossom. He needs your love and approval so that he can be successful and happy. Otherwise, he will always feel incomplete, no matter how much Clare loves him. This is an important moment for both of you. Provide what he needs."

"I'll do my best."

"You are a man of high intelligence and character. You'll see. It will work out."

The next morning after breakfast Charles Sr. and Charlie took a walk down to Palisades Park, overlooking the Santa Monica Bay. The morning sky was cloudless, a high blue canopy stretching over the ocean as far as the eye could see. Underneath, the sea sparkled. A soft breeze threaded through the palm trees and rustled the leaves on the rows of carefully manicured shrubs. They walked for a while, then sat down on a bench with a view of the Santa Monica Pier to the South and Point Dume in Malibu to the North.

"What are your plans, son?"

"I want to go to Med School and open a clinic for vets."

"Following in your old man's shoes?"

"Sort of."

Charles Sr. permitted himself a small smile. "You know Charlie, I'm really proud of you. You're a man now and you've got a great family of your own. I'm sorry I wasn't there for you when you were young and needed me." He choked back the tears that were forcing their way to the surface.

Charlie was silent for a moment. He looked out over the far horizon, grappling with his emotions. Tears welled in his eyes when he turned back to his father.

"Why Dad? Why didn't you protect me?"

Charles Sr. sighed deeply. The lines on his forehead seemed deeper, the torment in his eyes more pronounced. "God knows I should have. I was a damn coward. It was easier to pretend it wasn't happening. I didn't know what to do with your mother. I was afraid of her, I guess. I never could deal with anything irrational. I could never make sense of her behavior and if I can't make sense of something, I can't deal with it. So I stayed away. It's all on me, son. You didn't do anything wrong. I did."

Charlie couldn't fight the river anymore. He looked away, trying to contain himself and maintain his distance. Damn the man! He wasn't worth the pain. But his father's confession had torn through his defenses and forced him to confront his emotional wounds. He covered his face with his hands and burst into tears.

At first, Charles Sr. felt helpless in the presence of his son's tears, his face tortured by pain. He sat with his hands grasping his knees tightly, not knowing what to do, feeling even more inadequate. Finally, he reached out and put his arm tentatively around his son. Charlie collapsed against his father's side.

"Go ahead, son. Go ahead. It's O.K.," Charles Sr.'s response surprised even him. An unexpected feeling of peace rose inside him. "I've always loved you, son. More than you will ever know. More than anyone else in my life. I just never knew how to show it."

"I'm glad you finally did."

The pain that had been bottled up for decades in Charles Sr. poured out. The two men sat on the bench with the great blue sea before them and the great blue sky above them and sobbed together. Later, when the tears had stopped and Charles Sr. had collected himself, he reached into his pocket and handed his son an envelope. "This is for you," said Charles Sr.

"What is it?" asked Charlie, wiping away his tears.

"Open it."

Charlie tore the envelope open, pulled out the contents, then looked at his father in amazement. "It's a check for fifteen thousand dollars!"

"Along with what you get from the GI Bill, it should get you through medical school and pay your family's expenses. If you need more, just ask."

"That's a lot of money, Dad. Are you sure?"

"Son, I've never been surer of anything."

CHAPTER 39

A Letter from India

SANTA MONICA, 1966

On a warm and lazy Sunday afternoon, Alice and Clare cooked dinner while Three slept soundly in his stroller by the large bay window in the kitchen. Charlie had taken Emily's fine china out of the closet and was busy setting the antique oak table in the dining room. Charles Sr. and Connie had left the week before. Tenzin went out front to call the boys to dinner. As usual, the boys ignored him. They were playing football across the street with their friends and having too much fun to heed their father's summons to dinner. O.K., thought Tenzin, shifting his tactics to produce a more favorable outcome. Let's see you ignore this.

"Your mother baked an apple pie for dessert," he yelled through cupped hands. "Clare bought chocolate chip ice cream to go with it. But I guess you two would rather play than eat."

Tenzin turned to go.

"What?" screamed Danny.

Tenzin pretended he didn't hear him and kept walking up the drive.

"Be right there, Dad," shouted Matthew. He tossed the ball to one of his friends. The boys ran to catch up with their father. Tenzin chuckled. The dessert card never failed. He loved his boys. They were full of energy and high spirits, but wanted everything in life on their terms. Had he and Alice spoiled them? Parenting was a constant challenge. He wished his father were alive so that he could ask his advice. He wanted to give them as much as he could, more than he had had as a child, but not too much. He didn't want to spoil them and have them turn into self-centered adults, insensitive and indifferent to the well-being of others. The question was what was too much? It was a fine line and it kept shifting.

Tenzin rubbed his boys's heads as they caught up with him.

"Can I have seconds on the ice cream, Dad? I'm starving," asked Danny.

"You have to eat your dinner first."

"Ah, Dad," said Danny. "You always say that."

"Don't 'Ah Dad' me," warned Tenzin. "When I was your age I never had ice cream or chocolate chip cookies."

"Ah, you're always saying that too," said Matthew.

"Only because it's true."

"You're guilt tripping us, Dad," said Danny. "It's not fair."

"What's fair in life, Daniel?"

"I don't know. I never thought about it."

"Well, maybe it's time you did. Now go wash your hands. Dinner is ready. Everyone is waiting for you."

After dinner, Thomas and Charlie cleared the table while Alice cut the pie and Clare doled out the ice cream.

"Mom, may I have two scoops?" asked Danny. "I ate all my turkey and vegetables."

"No."

"Dad said I could have two scoops if I ate my meal."

"You probably misunderstood him."

"No I didn't!"

"Daniel, you mind your manners or you won't get any ice cream, period. Too much sugar is bad for you. You know that."

"I received a letter yesterday," Tenzin said.

"You get letters every day," said Alice. "How's Three doing, Clare?"

"He's really hungry today. He's already working on the other breast," Clare answered.

"A healthy appetite is a sign of a happy child," replied Alice.

"The letter was from Nawang," said Tenzin.

"Who?" asked Thomas, choking on a large bite of pie.

"Nawang?" said Alice. The tremor in her voice caused all eyes to turn her way. For a moment, she was standing in the study with Emily while Tenzin read the last letter Nawang had written, informing him that everyone he loved was dead. What new tragedy lurked inside this latest letter? In Alice's mind, Nawang was the bearer of dark tidings, the bringer of terrible suffering. That wasn't a fair characterization of the man, and she knew it. Nawang had been the messenger of tragic events, not their perpetrator, but that didn't matter to the emotional side of her nature. Alice had never been able to break the association, despite its absurdity. She frowned. Her stomach knotted with anxiety.

"What did he say?" she finally managed to ask. She tried to keep the fear out of her voice. She fooled no one, not even the boys. Everybody held their breath, waiting for Tenzin's answer.

"He was writing on behalf of the Karmapa," answered Tenzin.

"Who's that?" asked Charlie.

"The head of the Black Hat school of Tibetan Buddhism," said Thomas. "He's one of the three most important personages in Tibet. His lineage precedes the Dalai Lama's by two hundred years. Tenzin was Black Hat before he came to America and married Alice. The Karmapa is his spiritual leader."

"Black Hat?" said Charlie. "That's a weird name for a school of Buddhism."

Clare elbowed him.

"Ow!" he said. "What did I do?"

Tenzin laughed.

"According to legend," said Thomas, "the first Karmapa attained a very high level of enlightenment. He was rewarded with a hat woven from single strands of hair from ten thousand angels. That hat was the Black Hat. Supposedly, it still exists and the Karmapa wears it on special occasions."

"I want to see it," said Matthew, a sparkle in his eyes.

"What does the Karmapa want?" asked Alice.

"He's invited me to visit Rumtek monastery in Sikkim. They want to honor me for my work in the west."

"Do they still consider you a monk in their order?" said Alice.

"I don't know," said Tenzin. "Nawang didn't say."

"Where's Sikkim, Dad?" Matthew asked.

"It's in northeast India."

"Can I go?" A faraway light sparkled in Matthew's eyes.

Tenzin studied his son for a moment. "Yes," he said. "It will be a great adventure for you. It's time you learned more about your heritage. Danny, I want you to come, too."

"No way," said Danny.

"Why not?" asked Tenzin.

"I'm American, Dad. That's all the heritage I need. Beside, I don't want to miss any soccer games. I'm the captain. I have responsibilities. And a girlfriend."

"But half of your family is Tibetan, Daniel. Wouldn't you like to find out more about your roots?"

"Why? They're all dead."

"I see," said Tenzin, lowering his head, a frown on his face.

"Daniel, you are being rude and hurtful," Alice said.

"Sorry, Mom. But you taught me to tell the truth, remember?"

"And I also taught you to respect other people's feelings. You can express yourself in a gentler and more compassionate way. Your father invited you to go on a trip that is important to him and you insulted him. Would you want someone to do that to you?"

"No," said Danny, temporarily humbled. "Sorry, Dad."

"Apology accepted. Alice, would you like to come?"

"How long will you be gone?"

"Three weeks perhaps. Maybe more. I'm not sure."

Alice sighed. "Someone's got to run the center while you're gone. There's more to do than I can deal with as it is. It wouldn't be fair to dump it all on Clare. She's got the baby to think about. And someone's got to be here for Danny."

"I see," said Tenzin. He tried not to let his disappointment show. "Well, it looks like it's just you and me, Matthew."

"Great!" said Matthew. He was secretly pleased that Danny and his mother weren't going.

"You didn't ask me," said Thomas.

"I'm sorry, old friend. Of course you're invited."

"I'd like to go, too," said Charlie, a strange gleam in his eyes. "It's the chance of a lifetime."

Clare gave Charlie a hard look. "Charlie," she said. "You've got your entrance exams to prepare for. I thought you were serious about going to medical school."

Charlie sighed. "Another time, I guess."

Clare leaned over and kissed him on the cheek.

"Charlie," Tenzin said. "While I'm gone I want you to lead the Tuesday and Thursday night classes."

"Me?"

"Yes."

"But I have nothing to say," said Charlie. "I don't have your wisdom about life, your insight into people or your knowledge of Buddhism. I'm not qualified. I can't answer anyone's questions. I'd be a disaster. Alice should do it."

"Just tell your story."

"Oh, right. The one about my traumatic childhood, or the one about walking out on Clare? How about the one about nearly getting killed and watching all my buddies die? No one wants to hear my stories. They're too depressing."

"You're wrong. Your stories will help many people. You've learned more from your experiences than you realize. Share them. It will make you stronger."

"No one could ever take your place," said Charlie.

"Then don't try. Just be yourself. Talk about your journey. How your relationship with your father went from bad to good. Your war experience. The past life connection you and Clare share. What you've had to face and clear from your past. How it changed you. You have a lot of rich material to draw from, Charlie. Your stories will inspire people. A man begins to be great when he overcomes adversity and people identify with his journey. It's time for you to lead. You're ready."

"With all due respect Tenzin, you're nuts," said Charlie.

Tenzin smiled. "I've been called worse things."

"You're different Tenzin, that's for sure," said Thomas, rising to his friend's defense. "But nuts? No. Most people don't want to know who they are and what they could be. It's too much work. They're more focused on avoiding their potential than on developing it. That's the real insanity. That's not you now, is it Charlie?"

"Of course not."

"Then own your power, man. Be a leader," said Thomas. "If Tenzin says you're ready, you are."

"If I do it will you all get off my back?"

Thomas and Tenzin both smiled.

"You'll be great, Charlie," said Clare.

"I think so too," said Alice.

"No matter how you feel when you stand in front of people," said Tenzin, "project confidence. You survived the war. This is much easier than getting shot at in the jungle."

"It's different alright," said Charlie. "But I'm not sure it's any easier."

"Believe in yourself, Charlie. Without self-love we all feel inadequate. When we have it, our power is amplified and we become a door through which the Supreme Truth can enter this world. That is what being on the podium will do for you."

CHAPTER 40

A Visit to Rumtek

SIKKIM, 1966

Six weeks later, Tenzin, Matthew and Thomas arrived in Delhi after an exhausting flight from Los Angeles with stops in Honolulu and Hong Kong. The next morning, they boarded the train to Gangtok in Sikkim state. At the train station they were besieged by homeless children begging for food and money. Some were missing eyes, legs, or hands. Matthew had never seen such poverty and desperation.

"Dad," he said, "can I have some money? We've got to help them."

Tenzin handed Matthew a handful of coins. The child beggars were alert to every nuance and descended on Matthew like a swarm of locusts. They grabbed at his clothes, waved their hands in his face, screamed for his attention, and demanded his money. The coins were gone in seconds. Two older boys threatened and cursed him when they didn't receive any. Matthew looked at them blankly, stunned by their reaction. One of the boys raised his fist to hit him. A policeman standing nearby blew his whistle. The crowd of child beggars surrounding Matthew dispersed in all directions. The policeman rushed forward and grabbed one of the boys who had threatened Matthew. The boy unleashed a stream of obscenities at the officer and kicked him in the leg. The policeman pulled out his truncheon and hit the boy on the back of his legs several times. The boy's swears turned to screams as he fell to the ground. The policeman continued to rain blows on the boy's body, now curled into a fetal position with his hands covering his head.

"Come Matthew," said Tenzin. "It's time to board the train." He put his arm around the boy's shoulders and steered him away from the scene. It took a few minutes for them to reach their cabin. When they were safely inside, Matthew crumpled onto the bench, shaking and crying.

"Why did the cop beat him like that, Dad?"

"India is not the United States, Matthew. There is terrible poverty here. Desperation, poverty and violence are all that boy knows."

"But I was just trying to help. I didn't want that to happen. It's all my fault."

"It wasn't your fault that he threatened you. Not everybody will appreciate your help."

"Why?"

"There are many people who feel that no matter what you do for them it's never enough. They always want more than you can give. That is the nature of resentment. When you are older, you will recognize it more quickly. When you see it, walk away. It is a disease. You can do nothing for those who are infected with it. They will punish you for helping them. They can't be helped or trusted."

Matthew nodded and wiped his eyes. "Should I hate them, Dad?"

"No," said Tenzin. "Never hate. Hatred only hurts you. It cuts you off from your soul. When you hate, you lose your Light. Love them, and pray that they find their way. Then release them into the Light. Do not let them into your life. Give them instead to the Supreme Truth. Now sleep."

The train stopped in every village along the way. Matthew watched in fascination as villagers in loin cloths boarded with goats and chickens at every stop. Three days later, they arrived in Gangtok. From Gangtok it was a two hour car ride to Rumtek Monastery. They arrived tired and hungry, glad that their journey was finally over.

Two young monks met them at the main building and took them to their quarters. Hot baths had been drawn for them. They lay in the hot water and relaxed. Tenzin and Thomas fell asleep in their baths, but not Matthew. He changed into clean clothes, and sat by the window, gazing out at the Himalayas. They didn't seem new or imposing, more like an old, long lost friend. Why he felt that way, he didn't know. Tenzin found him still by the window when shadows had filled the room and darkness had swallowed the mountains. Matthew sat in deep meditation, his eyes closed, his legs folded in the lotus position. He had rarely meditated on his own back home. He was too busy being a normal kid and playing with his friends.

Interesting, observed Tenzin as he watched his son, how different places bring out different aspects of ourselves. His son's energy field was a bright gold. An auspicious beginning to an important trip. When he finished meditating several moments later, however, Matthew was shaking.

"What's the matter, Matthew?" asked Tenzin.

"I had a vision, Dad. I was in a small village in the mountains. It was dawn and really cold. Someone grabbed me and pushed me outside, hitting me in the back. People were screaming. Everyone was scared. What was that about, Dad?"

"You will find out soon enough, Matthew."

"Can't you tell me?"

"Some things you must find out for yourself. Are you hungry? We should get some dinner. It's getting late."

"Yeah."

They ate in the dining hall with the other monks. The dinner consisted of thick barley and vegetable soup, squash, beans, and rice. Matthew had never tasted food so naturally flavorful.

"Excuse me," Thomas said in Tibetan to the older monk seated next to him. "What's your chef's secret? Does he use sugar? This is amazing."

The old monk smiled. "No sugar," he said. "Everything we eat is infused with spiritual energy in the fields."

"How?"

"Some years ago a boy came here with a gift for growing things. He grows all our food."

"Where did this boy come from?" said Tenzin.

The monk shrugged his shoulders. "No one knows for sure. He's an orphan."

"The Chinese killed his family?"

The old monk nodded.

"They killed my family too," said Tenzin.

"Mine as well," said the monk.

One of the young monks who had greeted them earlier in the day came to their table and bowed to Tenzin.

"Excuse me, Tenzin," he said. "Nawang has asked me to invite your party to join the Karmapa for breakfast tomorrow morning."

"It will be our pleasure. Where shall we go?"

"To His Holiness's apartments. I will come for you at six."

"Where is Nawang? I was hoping to see him tonight."

"He sends his sincerest apologies, Rinpoche. He was looking forward to joining you. However, an unexpected matter has come up. Nawang Rinpoche is the head administrator of Rumtek Monastery. He rarely has free time."

"I am not surprised. Nawang was always extremely capable."

"He said you once saved his life, Rinpoche."

"That was a long time ago. We were both young then, as you are now."

The young monk bowed and left.

The new Head of the Sanitation Department stood rigidly before Nawang. His eyes betrayed the defiance and contempt he thought he had hidden. Nawang had had it in for him ever since Dorjee had forced him out of his job in Agriculture. So what was it now? Whatever it was, he wasn't going to quiver with fear, feign humility and pretend that Nawang was his superior. He was a better man than Nawang. What was the worst he could do? Relieve him of his post? He laughed at his own pun. I come from an aristocratic family. Nawang's a peasant from a remote village, a nobody from a long line of nobodies. Who's he to lord it over me?

"The latrines stink," said Nawang. "There have been many complaints."

The Head of the Sanitation Department shrugged his shoulders. "Shit and piss stink. Even monks' shit stinks. I can't help that."

"The latrines are unclean. You're not doing your job."

"It's not exactly a prestige position, is it, Nawang?" said the Head of Sanitation. "Why don't you find someone more suited to the job? Perhaps someone with a peasant background." The Head of the Sanitation department paused before delivering his blow. "Someone like yourself."

Nawang's expression did not change. He had expected nothing less from the Head of the Sanitation Department. "I'm sorry you feel that way. You are relieved of your position and demoted to latrine cleaner, effective immediately. You will now scrub the latrines yourself."

"I refuse."

"If you refuse, I will have no choice but to excommunicate you from the order and banish you from this monastery."

"You forget yourself, Nawang. Remember who you're speaking with. You're a peasant. I'm from a distinguished aristocratic family. You come from a mud hut. I come from a manor house. I have a long lineage and noble blood. My family gave a great deal of money to this order. I will go to His Holiness and have you disciplined."

"His Holiness is more tired of your antics than I am. He wanted me to dismiss you from the order when we relieved you of your position at agriculture."

"You're a liar."

"You have been a part of this order for thirty years. Because of your service I asked His Holiness to give you another chance."

"You call being in charge of the latrines another chance? I piss on this monastery. I piss on you. I resign."

"Your resignation is accepted. Gather your possessions and leave."

The former head of the Sanitation Department glowered at Nawang. "This isn't over, Nawang. You'll pay for your impudence."

"You're in no position to make threats."

The defrocked monk snorted. "Be wary of the dark, Nawang Rinpoche."

CHAPTER 41

A Surprise Meeting

THE NEXT MORNING, the young monk knocked on their door. Matthew had been up and ready to go for more than an hour. When he heard the knock, he ran to the door.

"I've got it," he shouted. Tenzin and Thomas smiled at each other.

"Good morning, young master," said the monk. "I see that you're ready."

"Oh, I'd say he's more than ready," said Thomas in Tibetan.

The young monk smiled. "We'd best not keep His Holiness waiting."

They descended the stairs and emerged into the cool morning air, walking briskly through the courtyard to the main building. The Karmapa's quarters were on the third floor. They entered the building and removed their shoes, leaving them by the door. A profound silence permeated the place; it reminded Tenzin of his monastery in Eastern Tibet. Years of group meditation by the monks had created a vortex of spiritual power in the building. As Tenzin absorbed the energy, an unexpected wave of melancholy rippled through him. He wished Doezen was waiting upstairs and not the Karmapa; he longed to be back in Tibet and not in Sikkim. Emotions that he thought he had left behind years ago stirred anew. His feet felt glued to the spot where he stood, his legs as unyielding as cement posts. The color drained from his face. A sudden, sharp pain pierced his heart like a sword. He grabbed at his chest and grimaced.

"Are you O.K.?" asked Thomas, alarmed.

Tenzin nodded. He clenched his jaw and pushed his feelings aside. He couldn't fall apart in front of his son and within hearing distance of the Karmapa. Now was not a convenient time to face what still lingered inside him, unconscious and hidden till now.

The young monk coughed discretely. It was his responsibility to see that his party arrived on time. He didn't want to risk the Karmapa's disapproval.

"Come, Tenzin," he said, touching Tenzin's arm gently. "The Karmapa's quarters are on the third floor. We must go."

"Yes, of course," he managed to say. Somehow, he got his feet to move forward again.

By the time they reached the third floor he was alright. The young monk wasted no time knocking on the door to the Karmapa's apartments.

"Please enter," said a voice behind the door.

Tenzin smiled. The voice was a bit deeper than he remembered, and had a ring of authority that had not been there before, but it certainly was Nawang's voice. The young monk opened the door and stood aside to let them enter. Nawang smiled and embraced his old friend. "It is good to see you, Tenzin. You haven't changed a bit."

Tenzin laughed. "Who are you kidding? We're not women. You don't have to flatter me. Look at us. Our hair is graying, although I do have more left than do you. Our faces have lines. We aren't pups anymore."

"Who cares?" laughed Nawang. "Everything changes. That's life. I would know you anywhere. Holiness, this is Tenzin."

"Holiness," said Tenzin bowing.

"You are a legend, Tenzin," said the Karmapa. "Thanks mostly to Nawang, who never tires of talking up your exploits. Our young monks will be disappointed to see that you're just a man and not a god who soars through the sky. It's a pleasure to meet you."

They all laughed, instantly dissolving the awkwardness of their first meeting.

"Thank you, Holiness," said Tenzin.

"What are Americans like?" said his Holiness. "Are they all rich? Do you know many movie stars?"

"They are like everyone else, Holiness. Some are good. Some are bad. But most are friendly and helpful. America is a prosperous country, but most Americans aren't rich, although by our living standards, we would think differently."

"And movie stars?"

"I have met many, Holiness. In person they are very different from the way they appear on screen. They are people, like everyone else, and they have problems of their own. Fame, good looks and money do not insulate one from life's challenges."

"Well said. Is this your son?"

"Yes, Holiness. This is Matthew."

"It is an honor to meet you, Matthew," said the Karmapa. He rubbed the top of Matthews head, making him blush.

The Karmapa turned to Thomas. "And you are Tenzin's tutor?"

"Tenzin has been more my teacher, Holiness," said Thomas, bowing, "than I have been his tutor."

"You taught him English?"

"Yes, Holiness."

"Perhaps you can help me learn more English while you're here."

"I would be honored, Holiness."

"Good. Now you must all be hungry. Please come to the table and enjoy our humble offerings." The breakfast table was laden with platters of food.

Nawang clapped his hands. A monk appeared with a steaming pot of butter tea and poured them each a cup of the thick purplish liquid. Matthew took one look at his cup and grimaced. It looked like dirty engine oil.

Nawang smiled. "It tastes better than it looks, Matthew. Blow on the froth on the surface, then sip the tea slowly, like this." Nawang raised his cup and showed Matthew how to drink the tea.

Matthew stared at his tea, unconvinced.

The Karmapa laughed. "Do as I do," he said, sipping his tea then putting down his cup.

"Now you try."

All eyes were now on Matthew. He was trapped. He couldn't lose face in front of the Karmapa or embarrass his father, so he picked up the cup, blew on the butter scum, and took a tiny sip. He was sure it would sicken him. The taste surprised him. It was both sweet and sour, different from anything he had ever tasted before. He took another sip, this one larger.

Everyone laughed.

"You are a brave young man," said the Karmapa.

"Is there salt in it?" asked Matthew.

The Karmapa nodded.

"My mom would like it."

"I will send the recipe home with you. Do you like to grow things, Matthew? I understand that California has an excellent climate."

"You mean like fruits and vegetables?"

"Yes."

"My mom's got a green thumb. Women like stuff like that. I like sports."

"Have you ever tried?"

Matthew shook his head.

"There's a young monk here who has an unusual gift for growing things. He grew everything on the table."

"It's really good. The food here is amazing."

"Would you like to meet him?"

"Sure," said Matthew. He was too busy enjoying the meal to think much about the young monk who had provided it.

The Karmapa nodded at Nawang.

"Excuse me," said Nawang, rising to leave.

"Tenzin," said the Karmapa. "We will honor you tomorrow night at a special ceremony. Will you address the sangha?"

"Of course, Holiness."

Nawang returned a few moments later. With him was a young monk.

Tenzin's jaw dropped when he saw the young man. The sharp pain in his heart returned. He was looking into his sister's face. It can't be, he thought. They're all dead.

Dorjee was equally shocked. He was staring into the face of his grandfather. His mouth was agape, his eyes wide open.

"Dorjee," said Nawang gently, putting his hand on the young man's shoulder to steady him. "This is your uncle Tenzin and your cousin Matthew. They are your family."

Years ago, when he was barely more than a toddler, Dorjee had erected an elaborate façade to protect himself from further trauma. People were dangerous. You never knew when they would hurt you or leave you. It was safer to keep them at a distance and feel nothing for them. And now he had family? His heart beat rapidly. His legs shook. His breath came in short bursts as the pain and loneliness locked in the hidden recesses of his heart slammed repeatedly against the door of his consciousness. He could not harbor his grief any longer, and the elaborate facade made of equal parts of disdain and contempt began to crumble. Tenzin saw the young man's shock. He rose to embrace him. Dorjee lay his head on his uncle's shoulder and sobbed. Both of their hearts were breaking.

Tears ran down Tenzin's face. Nawang watched quietly. He had waited many years for this moment.

"The last time I saw you, Dorjee, was shortly after you were born," said Tenzin. "It was the last time I was in the village and the last time I saw my family. I had no idea that anyone had survived the massacre."

"Neither did we," said Nawang. "Years later, rumors reached us about a young boy who had survived the massacre. I made inquiries. It took a long time. I finally located Kalden, the son of Norbu, the man who had saved him. Kalden told me that he had found Dorjee asleep on your father's body. He told me where to find Dorjee. When I saw him, I recognized the family resemblance right away. He has your father's gift for growing things."

"Why didn't you write to me earlier?"

"We wanted to be sure that Dorjee was ready to meet you. He keeps to himself and trusts no one. But his heart has been opening slowly. The time was finally right to bring you together."

"Come, Dorjee," said Tenzin. "Sit down with us. Have some tea. It will do you good."

Dorjee slumped down between Matthew and Tenzin. He was still shaky. Matthew put his hand on Dorjee's shoulder. He couldn't explain the overwhelming love that he felt for this cousin he had never known existed. In many ways, his shock was as great as Dorjee's. His head was throbbing. Would he never be rid of these headaches?

"Matthew," said the Karmapa. "Do you believe in past lives?"

"My dad does."

"Did he ever tell you about yours?"

"No."

"Would you like to know about one?"

"Sure," said Matthew. His fingers massaged the back of his neck, trying to rub the pain away.

"Did you have nightmares when you were a little boy?"

"I used to dream about soldiers with lots of guns. I'd always wake up with bad headaches. I've got one now."

"You were Dorjee's grandfather in your last life."

Matthew stared at the Karmapa, his eyes wide with shock.

"Dorjee inherited his gift for growing things from you."

"I was my father's father?"

"Yes."

Matthew's eyes sparkled with mischief. "Can I tell my Dad what to do from now on?"

The Karmapa smiled. "Your roles are reversed in this lifetime. It would be most inappropriate."

"It hasn't stopped him, Holiness," said Tenzin. "He gives me unsolicited advice all the time."

Everyone laughed.

"I'm the youngest now," said Matthew. "But before, I was the oldest."

"What's true in one life," said the Karmapa, "may not be true in another. But the feelings of love you have with each other remain. That's the important thing."

CHAPTER 42

The One

THAT AFTERNOON, DORJEE took Tenzin, Thomas, and Matthew on a tour of the acreage under cultivation. The fields were bursting with life. Matthew was sure that he heard the plants singing. Tenzin looked over the waving acres of grass and noted that a golden light suffused the entire area. He smiled knowingly to himself. Dorjee had absorbed a lot in the short time he had spent with his grandfather.

"How do you produce such abundance, Dorjee?" Tenzin said.

"I meditate and chant with the plants from the time they are seeds to the moment we harvest them. I feed them with love."

"And what happens to you when you do this?"

"I often leave my body and enter an infinite field of light. Nothing exists in the field but light, including me. I have no body there, only consciousness."

"How is that possible?"

Dorjee shrugged his shoulders. "I have no idea. All I know is that the field is everywhere. We just don't see it with our physical eyes."

"How do you feel when you become part of the field?"

"Ecstatic."

"That energy is here in these fields, Dorjee. I can feel it. You have drawn down the infinite and anchored it in the soil. What you have done is miraculous."

"Thank you, Uncle," said Dorjee, bowing his head.

Tenzin put his arm around his nephew. "Do you feel the same sense of ecstasy around people that do you do in the fields?"

Dorjee shook his head.

Just then a loud rustling in the distance broke their peace, and drew their attention to the tall grass swaying in the fields. They turned in time to see the former head of the Sanitation Department brandishing a sword and charging toward them, his face apoplectic, his eyes bulging with rage. Tenzin noted a familiar dark shadow that appeared briefly in his malevolent eyes.

They turned and fled from the oncoming madman. All except Tenzin. He stood his ground, unconcerned for his own safety, his eyes boring into the defrocked monk charging at him.

"Run, Dorjee, you piss head!" screamed the monk. "You won't escape from me, you pathetic little shit!"

Tenzin's eyes narrowed and grew hard. Streams of light surged from them, striking the former head of the Sanitation Department in the chest. The man stumbled forward clutching his heart. His eyelids fluttered. His face turned ashen. Spittle laced with blood seeped from the corners of his mouth. He took a few more halting steps then collapsed in a heap at Tenzin's feet.

"Is he dead?" said Matthew, his eyes wide with disbelief.

"No," said Tenzin. His eyes were focused on the prostrate form laying at his feet. "He's unconscious. Dorjee, go get Nawang. He will need to shackle him. The man is insane. There are several demonic entities attached to him. Take Matthew. Thomas and I will wait here."

Nawang arrived a short time later with several assistants. He looked at the former monk lying unconscious on the ground, his sword still clasped in his hand, and had his assistants shackle him.

"Your power has grown," said Nawang.

"A pity to have to use it in such a way," said Tenzin.

"That's why you have it," said Nawang. "The great ones only use it when there is no other way."

"Doezen was great. I do not compare."

Nawang smiled. "Oh, but you do, dear friend. You have mastered every challenge that life has hit you with. I have never forgotten how you saved my life that night in the mountains."

"I remember. It's a good thing I had my wits about me that night," said Tenzin. "Where would Rumtek be if something had happened to you?"

"It would be fine. I'm replaceable. You're not."

"Nonsense," said Tenzin.

"You're the bridge between east and west, Tenzin. Between heaven and earth, too," said Nawang. He glanced down at the still unconscious former monk, then up at the cloudless blue sky above them.

"You exaggerate my influence, Nawang. Come see America. You'd like it."

Nawang shook his head. "America was always your destiny, not mine. That is why Doezen sent you there and had me stay here."

That night, the entire sangha gathered in the meditation hall to honor

Tenzin. Three chairs stood on the dais, each on a different level. The chair on the highest level belonged to the Karmapa because he was the head of the order. Tenzin was seated in the chair on the next level, a foot lower than the Karmapa's chair. The chair on the lowest level remained empty.

"Tenzin has come to visit us from America," said the Karmapa. "Confronted with challenges none of us has ever had to face, he has proven himself the worthy successor of Doezen Rinpoche. In Tenzin the great tradition of the Black Hat lineage continues, but with one major difference. Tenzin Rinpoche reached his greatness in America, away from the support of the sangha, his country, and his tradition. He did it alone, with a different people, a different culture, and a different language. For this singular accomplishment, we honor him tonight."

The Karmapa looked out at the sea of faces. Those of the young monks were open and earnest, those of the older ones more inscrutable, their feelings carefully guarded. How many of them are jealous of Tenzin, he wondered. How many feel that life hasn't granted them the one thing they desired? More than a few, no doubt. Bitterness, he reflected, is self-defeating, jealousy self-destructive.

"The challenges Tenzin had to face alone would have defeated a lesser man. Which of you will do likewise? Which of you will carry the great Black Hat lineage forward? Whoever succeeds in attaining the heights will do so because of merit, not favoritism. Set your goals high. The highest attainment is already inside you. The Oneness cares nothing for your age or your status, only for the purity of your heart. The Oneness lives everywhere and in everyone, waiting to be liberated and then, to liberate you. Strive always to be more conscious, compassionate, and forgiving. The greatest power in the universe is cloaked in gentleness, not aggression. The Oneness is merciful, not self-righteous. It is an uplifting force, not a destructive one. It is my hope, as I look out at you tonight, that greatness sits where you sit. May you all realize the highest truth in this life. May you all attain Buddahood. Matthew, please come forward and join us on the dais."

Matthew was stunned. Had he heard correctly? Why would the Karmapa want him on the podium? It was his father's night. Thomas saw his hesitation and whispered in his ear. "Go."

Matthew rose and made his way to the dais. When he climbed onto the platform the Karmapa put his arm around him, then nodded to Nawang. Nawang came forward. He carried a monk's red robe in his arms. He put the robe on Matthew with great care, and tied the sash around his waist.

Horns sounded, the monks bowed their heads and chanted.

Matthew stood as the chant rose and fell, overwhelmed by the honor given him. When the chant ended the Karmapa continued.

"Welcome to our Sangha, Matthew. You are now one of us."

Matthew was sure that he was dreaming. Wait until he showed his mom his robe and told her about his cousin, Dorjee. Boy, was Danny ever going to be pissed.

"Matthew, please take the remaining chair on the dais," said the Karmapa.

The ceremony concluded shortly thereafter. The monks filed silently out of the hall. Tenzin, Thomas and Matthew made their way back to their quarters. Tomorrow would be their last day at the monastery. "How do you feel Matthew?" asked Tenzin, noting how proudly Matthew wore his robe.

"Good. But I feel bad for Danny."

"Why?" asked Tenzin. His son's answer surprised him.

"He'll feel left out. He didn't get to meet Dorjee or get a robe of his own."

"Don't worry," said Tenzin. He put his arm around his son. "Danny won't be jealous. I got him something he'll like even more."

"What?"

"You'll see."

When they got back to their rooms, Tenzin took a silver bracelet with bright turquoise and coral stones from his suitcase.

"Wow! That's beautiful, Dad."

"Do you still think Danny will be jealous of your robe when I give him that?"

"No way."

"He'll think his gift is better than yours."

"You're right, Dad. Danny loves flashy things."

"Which gift would you rather have?"

"The robe."

"Exactly. Danny will wear his bracelet to school and be the center of attention. Would the girls flock around him if he showed up in a red robe?"

"No. They'd laugh at him."

"That's what I thought."

"I want to come back here, Dad."

"You will."

Matthew nodded, suddenly subdued. Tenzin noted the shift in his son's mood.

"What is it, Matthew?"

"Do you really think I'm the incarnation of your father?"

"How did you feel about Dorjee when you first saw him?"

"Weird."

"Why?"

"I never knew it until I met him, but it was like I've been looking for him my whole life. As if there was something missing and I never knew what it was. Now I know. Crazy, huh?"

"Not really."

"No, Dad. It's really, really weird. I'm your son, but I'm also your father? How can that be?"

"Relationships between souls change from one life to another. Father in one life, son in the next. What does it matter? That's just how it goes. The truth operates in the background. It orchestrates everything, bringing souls together at the right moment to facilitate their growth. Reality is so much bigger than what we see with our eyes. The only thing that matters is that we grow, Matthew. One day, we will all return to the Oneness. Relationships are teaching devices that help us learn what we need to advance."

"I'm glad you're my father this time. You're the best Dad in the world."

Tenzin rubbed his son's head. "That's the nicest thing anyone has ever said to me."

"Can I invite Dorjee to California?"

"You can," said Tenzin. "But he won't come."

"Why not? We're his real family."

"It's Dorjee's decision."

"He'll want to come, Dad. Everybody wants to live in California."

"Not everyone."

"What do you mean?"

"What you think is appropriate for someone else, may not be."

"Dorjee'll love living with us. Charlie, Clare, Three and Thomas do."

"They're not Dorjee."

"Thomas can teach him English, Charlie can teach him about western medicine, Clare can find him a wife, and I'll teach him how to play football and soccer. He'll love Mom's cooking. And he can grow a garden in the backyard."

Tenzin laughed heartily. "Somehow, I don't see Dorjee playing football."

"Dad!"

"It's late. Time to go to bed, Matthew. Take off your robe or it will get wrinkled."

"Do I have to?"

"Yes. A monk must be disciplined. Particularly a novice monk."

The next morning Tenzin, Matthew and Thomas joined Dorjee in the fields for the last time. When they got there, Dorjee was wading through the acres of plants, whispering them encouragement.

"How are you today, Dorjee?" shouted Tenzin to his nephew.

"Fine, Uncle," Dorjee shouted back. "My heart is happy for the first time since I was a little boy."

"Dorjee," asked Matthew loudly. "Why don't you come back to America with us? Thomas will teach you English and Clare will find you a girlfriend.

My mom's a great cook and you can work with my Dad." Thomas translated Matthew's words into Tibetan.

Dorjee shook his head. "My place is here. These are my fields. I can't leave them."

Matthew was visibly dejected. "Can't someone else do it?"

"No. But one day you must come back and help me. We can work together. I'll teach you my secrets."

The smile returned to Matthew's face. He now had something for which to plan.

"Do you remember what we spoke about last night, Matthew?" Tenzin asked.

"Huh?" said Matthew. "Oh. You told me not to wear my robe to bed."

"What else?"

Matthew's face was blank. He did not answer.

"I told you about the danger of thinking that you know what is best for someone else."

"Oh yeah," he said. "That."

"Today, your assumptions of what would be best for Dorjee made you unhappy."

"But it would be great if Dorjee came to California."

"For whom?"

"Oh," said Matthew. "I see what you mean, Dad."

"Dorjee belongs here. You must accept that."

"Okay. But I'm coming back here as soon as I can."

"First, you will complete your education."

"But, Dad."

"Would you like to meditate?" asked Dorjee. "It would be interesting to see how our energies affect the plants."

The four of them sat in a square to meditate. The light flowing through them was electric. Dorjee and Tenzin left their bodies, their souls merging in the field of light. The energy had a different effect on Matthew. He became undone and broke into sobs. His pain brought Tenzin back to his body.

"What is it, Matthew?" he asked quietly.

"I saw what happened to me in the village, Dad."

"Tell me."

"The Chinese shot me in the back of the head. They killed everyone."

Matthew collapsed in a spasm of grief. Tenzin folded his son into his arms. Dorjee came back to his body and also burst into tears.

"What do you see, Dorjee?" asked Tenzin.

"The earth was soaked with blood. I begged my mother to wake up, but she wouldn't. I climbed on top of my grandfather and begged him to wake up. He couldn't. I didn't understand what was happening. I didn't know what death was. I cried myself to sleep." While Dorjee recounted what had happened, a new cry rose from his heart, this one sadder than the one that had preceded it.

Tenzin wrapped his free arm around his nephew.

"Hold nothing back, either of you. Grief cures grief. The time has come for both of you to be free of this nightmare."

Tears poured down their faces until there was nothing left in either of them.

"Today the plants helped you to heal," said Tenzin.

"Thank you, Uncle," said Dorjee, his voice cracking, "for everything."

"No, Dorjee. The honor is mine. Your heart is open now. You'll find it easier to trust people again."

"Not everyone is good," said Dorjee.

"No. But you'll have a better feeling about whom you can trust and whom you can't. There are many people that love you. Don't forget that."

"Yes, Uncle."

That night Nawang came to their quarters to say goodbye.

"What you did for Dorjee exceeded my expectations," said Nawang.

"I'm glad I could help my nephew. What a tremendous surprise to find out that he survived. Thank you for making it possible, Nawang."

"Do you ever wish that we could go back to Tibet?" asked Nawang.

"Of course. But Tibet is also a state of mind. The Communists stole our country, but they can never steal our minds, unless we hate them. I will not do that. I will not be a victim. I choose to love the Self in everyone, including my enemies. Hatred never freed anyone. One liberated individual can change the world. It has happened before. We all need to be that person now. We will use love to fight those who would enslave us. If we love, the Light remains in this world. If enough of us love, the Light will protect this world from those who wish to steal our freedom and enslave us. When we love, we are not victims. And if we aren't victims, we won't attract oppressors. It is up to us, Nawang, and others like us. No one is coming to save us. Not in Tibet. Not in America or anywhere else. We must save ourselves."

Nawang brought his palms together in front of his chest and bowed to his old friend. "I have never heard it said better. Doezen would be proud. The student has exceeded the master."

Tenzin shook his head. "I'm not in Doezen's class. Every day I struggle with things that he mastered."

"You have come a long way since you left Tibet, my friend."

"Yes. I now have a wife, two sons, a center to run, a large overhead and several mouths to feed."

Nawang laughed. "You sound just like me - with the exception of a wife and children."

They left at dawn the next morning. The car bounced through the potholes on the dirt road, but Matthew slept in the car all the way to the railroad station. While he slept, Tenzin confided in Thomas.

"I had strange dreams at the monastery, Thomas," said Tenzin.

"Uh huh. Me too," said Thomas, suppressing a yawn. At that moment, he envied Matthew.

"They were about a young man and his son. The young man will come to the center soon. I'm sure of it. Bad people are trying to destroy him and take control of his son. The boy has come into the world to do something important. He's the one. The dark power in the lower astral knows this, and wants to stop him before he grows up and can do his work."

"The one? What do you mean?" said Thomas, suddenly becoming more alert.

"The boy's come back to break the chains of darkness that are choking the world," Tenzin said. "I want you to watch for his father. If you're the first one to meet him, bring him to me, no matter what I'm doing."

"Sure," said Thomas. "But what's he look like?"

"Don't worry. You'll know him when he comes."

CHAPTER 43

Home Again

SANTA MONICA

Matthew insisted on wearing his robe when he walked down the jetway in Los Angeles.

When Alice saw her boy dressed as a monk, her jaw fell open. In his robe, he looked exactly like his father had as a young man, so handsome and irresistible. For a brief moment, she was sitting in the packed auditorium while Tenzin gave his first talk at UCLA. Her heart fluttered now as it had then. Her men were so beautiful!

"Hi, Mama," Matthew yelled. He burst into a run. Seconds later he was in her arms.

"My darling boy. I missed you so much."

"Do you like my robe, Mama? Nawang gave it to me. The Karmapa called me to the stage and made me a monk and invited me to come back. I met Dorjee, too."

"Who's Dorjee?" Alice asked.

"My cousin."

"Your cousin?" Alice's face registered complete shock.

At that moment Tenzin and Thomas reached her. Tenzin leaned over and kissed his wife.

She didn't return his kiss.

"Who's Dorjee?" she said.

"I missed you," said Tenzin, ignoring her question.

"I missed you, too. Now who's Dorjee?"

Tenzin sighed. So much for a little romance.

"My nephew. He was the only survivor of the attack on my village."

"I was killed there, Mama. I'm Dorjee's grandfather," he paused and giggled, "and Daddy's father."

"Is that right?" said Alice. A half smile flitted momentarily on her face. She thought of that night long ago when Tenzin had told her that he thought Matthew was the incarnation of Doezen and she had told him he was wrong. Well, it had taken some time, but events had proven her right. That part of it felt good, at least.

"I'll explain it all later," said Tenzin.

"I'm sure you will. Thomas, do you have anything miraculous to report?"

"Nope."

"Thank God."

She reached up and kissed Thomas's cheek. "Welcome home."

"Guess what, Mama," said Matthew excitedly.

"There's more?"

"I haven't had any headaches since we left the monastery."

"Oh, Matthew, that's wonderful news," she said, hugging him again.

"My whole head feels different, mama. You know the dull ache I always had? It's gone."

Alice looked over at Tenzin, searching his eyes.

"He saw what happened to him in his last life, and released the trauma. The headaches won't come back."

"Good."

"How are things here?"

"Fine. Three spoke his first words and Charlie did a great job with your classes."

"I knew he would. Let's go home. We're all dirty and exhausted. How about that kiss?"

Alice wrapped her arms around her husband's neck and kissed him deeply.

"I'm glad you're back," she said. "I missed you."

"I missed you more," said Tenzin smiling.

CHAPTER 44

An Important Lesson

LATER THAT NIGHT, when Tenzin and Alice were in bed, Tenzin took a small box that he had been hiding and put it in his wife's hand.

"What's this?" Alice asked.

"Open it."

Alice flipped on the lamp by the bed and opened the small white box. Inside was a pair of exquisite gold and jade earrings.

"They're beautiful!" Alice said.

"I thought you might like them," replied Tenzin.

"I love them!" she said, putting them on. "They're perfect!" She examined her reflection in the small gilt framed mirror that had belonged to her grandmother. "How did you know?"

"How does any man know? He guesses."

"You did not. You never guess. But thank you," she said, "for a wonderful gift." She kissed him happily and wrapped her arms around his neck.

"You're welcome," he said smiling, happy that he had pleased her.

Alice looked at him carefully, noting the dark circles under his eyes. Her expression became serious once more. "You're exhausted," she said. "We'd better get some sleep."

"Aren't you going to take off your earrings?"

"Not tonight."

Tenzin was soon asleep. Alice curled her body against his, feeling his warmth and strength seep into her. She sighed contentedly. She always slept better when he was there. She had missed him a great deal during his absence, more than she had let on. Their private time was so limited. Between the needs of the children and the demands of running the center, they had little time to themselves. Most of what they did have were the few moments before sleep.

Oh well, she thought, one day the children will be grown and we'll have more time to spend together. In the meantime, sleeping beside her husband, sharing his warmth and imbibing his scent would have to suffice. A moment later she too, was sound asleep.

In the dead of the night, she woke from a deep sleep. The room was pitch black, silent, and cold. The steady sound of Tenzin's breathing was missing. She reached out to touch him. He wasn't there. She looked around the room, her eyes gradually adjusting to the dark. Where had he gone, now? The man could be so exasperating. She reached for the clock on the bed table beside her. Ten minutes after three. She groaned. He knows better. He needs his sleep, especially tonight.

The balcony door was slightly ajar. No wonder the room was so chilly. She got out of bed and put on her robe, tying the sash tightly around her waist and raising the collar to cover the back of her neck.

Tenzin sat in his favorite chair on the balcony, deep in meditation, a heavy blanket over his shoulders. At least he's not freezing, she thought. She watched him for a moment, fluctuating between exasperation and concern. What was he doing there after returning from a grueling trip? Does he want to get pneumonia?

Tenzin felt the force of her presence, and left his meditation.

"Did I wake you?" he asked.

"Do you know what time it is?"

"I had a dream and couldn't get back to sleep."

"You're worse than the boys."

"I'm sorry."

"What did you dream?"

"A young man will come here soon. He's in trouble and needs our help."

"What's so unusual about that? It happens every day around here."

"The dark power from the astral world wants to destroy him and his young son. They're at great risk."

"In this world somebody's always after someone. Come back to bed. You're going to be exhausted if you don't get some sleep."

Tenzin knew better than to argue with his wife when she was like this. He took the blanket off his shoulders. "I'll be right there."

Charlie and Clare were eating breakfast when Tenzin entered the kitchen later that morning. Clare rose excitedly and kissed his cheek.

"It's good to have you home," she said.

"Thank you. It's good to be back."

"How was your trip?" said Charlie. "Everyone missed you in class."

Tenzin smiled broadly. "That's not what I heard."

"He was magnificent," said Clare. "You should have seen him. You would have been so proud. His war stories had everyone in tears, including me. I hadn't heard most of them. Charlie's so secretive."

"I was protecting you. Beside, they're not things I care to remember," said Charlie. "I want to separate myself from them as much as I can."

"Better to face them," said Tenzin. "Otherwise they will always haunt you. Telling your stories is therapeutic for you and educational for everyone else. I want you to lead the Tuesday night class from now on."

Clare clapped her hands and squealed with delight.

"But I have nothing more to say," protested Charlie. "I left it all on the podium."

"You have more to say than you know," said Tenzin. "Speak from your heart. One thing leads to another. The truth will flow effortlessly. You've been to war. You know what it is. Your generation needs you. Help them as I have helped you."

"I'm not sure that I'm the one to do that."

"Don't worry. It'll be fine. Now I have something for both of you."

"What?" asked Clare, her face flush with anticipation.

Tenzin reached into his pocket and pulled out two small boxes, one white, one gold. He handed the gold box to Clare, the white one to Charlie.

"What is it?" Clare asked.

"Open it."

Clare and Charlie opened their presents. The boxes contained matching gold and jade rings, beautifully crafted, with the symbol of the mystic dragon carved on the band.

"Oh, my God," said Clare, sliding the ring onto her right index finger. "It's so beautiful. What does the dragon represent?"

"Divine Union."

Clare rose and gave Tenzin another hug and kiss. "Thank you so much."

"I'm glad you like it," said Tenzin.

"Like it? I love it," said Clare.

Charlie hadn't taken his ring out. He stared at it instead. "Thanks, Tenzin," he said without much enthusiasm.

"You're welcome. I wear the medal you gave me proudly," he said. "Wear your ring the same way."

Charlie shook his head. "I can't. I haven't earned the right to yet."

"You're wrong," said Tenzin. "You've turned your wounds into wisdom. You're a better man because of what you've endured. You didn't sink into bitterness. You rose from the ashes of hell to heal your life. That makes you a teacher. The ring is a symbol of your achievement. You are now aligned with your soul. That is a big step in anyone's evolution. Wear it proudly."

Charlie nodded and slipped the ring on his finger. "Thanks," he said sheepishly.

"There's one more thing," said Tenzin.

"What's that?" asked Clare.

"A young man keeps appearing in my dreams. I believe he will come here soon. Bring him to me if you are the first to meet him."

"What does he look like?" asked Clare.

"In my dreams he has green eyes and curly, dark hair. He is very powerful but doesn't know it yet."

"He sounds cute," said Clare.

Charlie stared at her.

"Oh Charlie, I can look, can't I? You look at pretty girls all the time. I've seen you. It doesn't mean anything. At least it had better not. You're my one and only." She leaned over and kissed him.

The next Tuesday's class was filled with young people opposed to the war.

"How many of you have been drafted?" asked Charlie. Several hands shot up.

"I'm supposed to report on Thursday," said one particularly distraught young man. "What should I do?"

"There are no easy answers. Certainly no good ones," said Charlie, remembering his own dilemma. "It's a choice between bad and worse. Do you run or do you serve? War is hell. Many of my buddies died in my arms. But running puts you in a strange limbo. You have no country. There's no guarantee that you'll ever be allowed to return. So let's take a moment to get calm and centered. Then we'll talk."

"You're a wuss, dude," someone shouted. "The war took the backbone out of you. Where the hell is your sense of honor and country? You should be a patriot, not some sad-assed long-haired hippie protestor. You need to remember what your father and his father fought for. Sit the hell down if you can't!"

Charlie couldn't place the voice right away, but it was familiar. The large audience was becoming more agitated by the moment. Charlie scanned the crowd and finally spotted his accuser sitting in the back. His arms were folded across his chest; his face a smug mask. His light brown hair was close cropped in military style, and he wore a tight olive green t-shirt.

Wayne.

Charlie breathed deeply and took a moment to collect himself.

"You ever serve in Vietnam, Wayne?"

"Nope."

"Ever been in the military?"

Wayne shook his head.

"Ever seen your friends blown apart?"

Wayne stared straight ahead.

"Ever seen your friend's brain oozing out of his head or look into the eyes of the enemy as he was about to pull the trigger and end your life?"

Wayne's eyes turned into hard slits. He said nothing. His jaw pulsed with rage.

"Well, I have. You've never served, Wayne. You know nothing about war. You're just another armchair soldier and fake patriot. So shut the hell up or get out."

"No way, dude," Wayne said. "You may have been in 'Nam. So what? Pussies get drafted all the time. Just because my number didn't come up don't mean nothin'. You're just jealous."

"Of you?" said Charlie. He felt his sense of calm and self-control slipping away, but he pressed on. "I'll tell you what. You can stay if you apologize to Clare. Be a man, Wayne. Do the right thing for once."

Wayne looked around the room. "She ain't here."

"I'm here, Wayne. You can apologize to me. I'll tell her." His fists clenched. Color flushed his cheeks. He was powerless to stop it.

"I ain't apologizing for nothin'. I was standing up for your sorry ass, pardner. Protectin' your interest in the bitch while you were away."

"That's it," Charlie screamed. "Get out and don't ever come back. Our friendship is over. We're done."

"I got news for you, dude," said Wayne. "We weren't ever friends and I ain't movin'." He folded his arms across his chest again. "If you're so tough and brave, come down here and make me, soldier boy."

Charlie jumped off the dais and charged straight for Wayne. A collective gasp rose from the audience. Charlie didn't notice. His whole being was focused on getting to Wayne. A number of sharp, booming sounds in the back of the room broke the spell. Charlie came to an abrupt halt. Tenzin stood planted like an oak, pounding the floor with a thick wooden staff like a blacksmith beating his anvil with a hammer.

"Collect yourself, Charlie," Tenzin roared.

The excess heat drained from Charlie's face. He looked at the stunned faces around him, mortified at what he had been about to do. Boy, had he lost it. His shoulders slumped. He turned and walked dejectedly back to the podium.

"I always knew you were a coward," screamed Wayne. His face was beet red.

Tenzin strode up the aisle and stopped in front of Wayne.

"That was your last chance," said Tenzin. "Now leave."

"I don't think so. This is just gettin' interestin'."

"Suit yourself. I will have you arrested for trespassing and disturbing the peace. I hope you find that as interesting."

Wayne shrugged his shoulders. "Fine."

"I'll be happy to call the police," said a female voice from the back of the room.

All heads turned to see Clare standing there.

Tenzin nodded. Clare pivoted and left the room. Tenzin turned his back on Wayne and walked toward the dais.

A young man sitting near Wayne stood up. "No one wants you here, Wayne. You're a joke. Get out."

"Who the fuck are you?" said Wayne. He stood up and curled his hands into fists. Several other young men stood up and circled Wayne.

"No pal," said one of them, pointing his finger in Wayne's face. "Who the fuck are you?" They all edged closer.

Wayne hesitated. His eyes darted from one angry face to another. He hadn't planned on this. These guys were supposed to be pacifists. Sweat trickled down his neck. Finally, he pushed one of the men aside and ran toward the exit. When he felt safe, he turned back and raised his middle finger. "Fuck you all!" he screamed, then disappeared into the night.

The police arrived a moment later.

"Thank you for coming," said Tenzin to the two officers. "But the disturbance is over. The offender has fled."

"Do you want to press charges?" asked the lead officer.

"That won't be necessary," said Tenzin.

"If you want, you can file a report. That way, there'll be a record if he returns."

"Thank you. That won't be necessary."

"Here's my card, just in case," said the officer.

"Thank you," said Tenzin, taking the card.

The policemen nodded and left. Tenzin returned to the dais.

"It's been an interesting evening," said Tenzin. The audience murmured in agreement. "Dealing with the unexpected always tests our development. It exposes our weaknesses and shows us what we need to improve. That's always a good thing. Wayne tested Charlie on matters close to his heart. Any man would want to defend his wife. That kind of challenge would test anyone's character." He looked directly at Charlie. "In the short term, Charlie failed his test. He took the bait. But that's unimportant because in the long term this experience will benefit him. He won't repeat his mistake. The next time something like this happens, he'll be in control of his emotions. His humiliation happened in front of all of you. The lesson has been seared into his soul."

A woman in the audience spoke up. "We all have versions of Charlie's experience. What happened tonight helped me to realize that I'm not a bad person just because I've lost it before. Anyone would react like Charlie did. I tell you what. I wish I had a man like that to protect me." The women in the audience murmured their approval.

"You only fail when you don't learn from your errors," said Tenzin. "Wayne failed because he's learned nothing. He refuses to grow. That is why he is no longer welcome here. His negative side rules him." Tenzin thought again of the familiar shadow he had seen in Wayne's eyes and the extra measure of malevolence that had accompanied it. "That is the antithesis of spirituality. He has chosen to follow the dark side of his nature and to deny his soul. That's his right. But it is also my right to deny him entrance to this center, its programs and classes. Here we focus on getting better, not bitter. That's a journey he refuses to take."

After class was over, Tenzin asked Charlie and Clare to join him in the kitchen. He made tea and set a plate of oatmeal raisin cookies that Alice had baked that afternoon in front of them.

"Eat," said Tenzin. "You'll feel better."

"I really screwed up tonight, didn't I?" said Charlie.

"That depends on what you do with it," said Tenzin.

"I'm proud of what Charlie did," said Clare. "I'm not sorry about it at all. He stood up for me. Wayne had it coming. He's a creep."

"All true. However, that doesn't make it right," said Tenzin.

"What do you mean?" Clare asked.

"His response was purely emotional."

"It was justice," said Clare.

"Justice?" Tenzin said. "Do not confuse justice with revenge. Justice is not about hurting someone just because he hurt you. In the future, take the time to see the larger picture before you react, or you may do something that really brings harm to yourself. Charlie allowed Wayne to provoke him. If he had hit Wayne he could have been arrested and charged with assault and battery. If convicted he would have a criminal record. That would make him ineligible to be a doctor. Would that be justice? Is the short term emotional satisfaction of seeing Wayne bloodied worth sacrificing your husband's career and your future economic well-being?"

Clare hung her head. "I never thought about that."

"I know. Never get too emotional or you will lose perspective. When anger appears, sound judgment disappears. Don't do anything until you cool down and are clear and calm."

Clare covered her face and sobbed. This time, Tenzin ignored her.

"The spiritual path isn't easy, is it Charlie?"

"Hell, no."

"It's that way by design. Every time you take a step forward, the negative will test you to see if you are where you think you are. Wayne brought that test to you tonight. He was your teacher. An excellent one, by the way. You owe him a debt of gratitude."

"I owe him?"

"He revealed a weakness in your nature. Honor your teacher. He did more for your growth than a thousand compliments ever could."

"But..." Before Charlie could defend himself, Tenzin tapped him on the chest. Charlie's eyes widened with shock. He gasped and collapsed in tears.

"It's time to release your shame and self-loathing," said Tenzin. "Cry deeply and clear it all out."

He turned to go. Tonight had been powerful. Alice was waiting upstairs. He was looking forward to their time together. He took a final look at Clare and Charlie and smiled at what he saw. Clare held Charlie's hand. Tears streamed down both of their faces.

CHAPTER 45

The Man in the Dream

TENZIN SUMMONED CLARE and Charlie to his office the next morning. Their eyes were red, their faces puffy. Charlie hadn't bothered to shave or to comb his hair. His shirt was wrinkled.

Clare, at least, was well groomed. Her hair was brushed and pulled back in a ponytail. She wore a clean white blouse and jeans.

"Hard night?" Tenzin asked.

They both nodded.

"Did you sleep?"

"Not much," said Clare.

"Did the baby keep you awake?"

Clare shook her head.

"Is there anything you want to discuss?"

"I'm sorry," Clare blurted out.

"For what?"

"For only thinking about myself. For being an idiot. For wanting revenge. For not thinking about the consequences."

Tenzin smiled. "No one's perfect, Clare. Don't be too hard on yourself. What counts is learning from mistakes, not the mistakes themselves. Nothing happened last night that will have a negative impact on your future. No blows were struck. No arrests were made. You both learned important lessons that will serve you well going forward. It was a very good night."

"Not for me. Next to Charlie's going to war it was the worst night of my life."

"Later on, you will have a different view of it."

"Then you don't hate me?"

Tenzin couldn't help but laugh. "Quite the opposite."

"Thank God," said Clare, wiping her eyes.

"How are you, Charlie?"

"Okay."

"Really?"

"It wasn't the jungle. No one died. Worse things have happened."

"No questions?"

"You laid it out real good last night. Next time I'll step back first and think it through. I won't allow myself to be provoked like that again."

"Good. Now you'd better go study. Shower and shave before you do. The Tuesday night class is yours for the foreseeable future."

"Even after last night?"

"Especially after last night," said Tenzin. "One morning when Danny was little, he was sitting on a high stool in the kitchen. There was a plate of cookies on the counter nearby. He reached for one, lost his balance, and fell off the stool. When he hit the floor he was screaming. I picked him up and comforted him. After that, he calmed down and I put him back on the stool. I was not going to let his fear get the better of him. You're older. You don't need comforting, only correcting. The best time to go back to something is after you've failed at it. We learn from our mistakes and we move on. Don't ever let fear or shame stop you. Understood?"

"Yes, sir."

Two days later, on a quiet Friday afternoon, Clare was working at the reception desk when a young man she had never seen before walked in. He seemed hesitant, as if he wasn't sure that he had come to the right place. He took a folded piece of paper out of his pocket and handed it to Clare. It was a flyer with Tenzin's picture on it. "I'm sorry to bother you, but is this man here?"

"He is, but he's not available. You need an appointment to see him. There's a long waiting list."

"I see," he said, his shoulders sagging. He was obviously disappointed. "Would you mind if I sat down for a minute? I'm not feeling so good all of a sudden. The room is spinning."

"Sure," Clare said. A red flag popped up in her mind. What if this guy was another Wayne? He was clean, well-dressed and polite. But you never knew. Wayne had seemed nice too, until the moment that he wasn't. "Is there anything I can do for you?"

"Thanks. I just need a moment to collect myself. I'm sorry just to show up and impose myself on you. I'll leave in a minute. Promise."

"That's alright," she said. She pretended to busy her herself with the log book on the desk, but watched him from the corner of her eye. His head slowly tilted forward until it came to rest against his chest. His eyelids fluttered, opening and closing in rapid sequence.

Clare could not suppress her curiosity. "Why do you want to meet with Tenzin?"

The man forced his eyes open. "When I saw his picture on the flyer, something inside me knew I had to meet him. So I took a chance and came over."

You and every other Tom, Dick, and Harry, thought Clare. "How nice," she said.

"I never expected to feel like this, though. Guess it wasn't such a good idea, after all."

He turned his head and looked at her. His eyes were pools of light. She felt as though he were looking straight through her, that he knew her thoughts and could see through her lies.

Clare blushed and looked away. Oh, my God, had he really seen through me? If he knows what I've been thinking, he'll think I'm the worst person in the world. She cringed. Only one other man had ever made her feel like that-Tenzin. Where did this guy get that kind of power?

Oh my God, she thought, in a flash of insight. This was the man in Tenzin's dreams! She summoned her courage and studied him, seeing him for the first time. He had an athletic build, curly brown hair and green eyes. He fit the description that Tenzin had given her. Even though he looked awful at the moment, she could see he was a handsome man.

"Do you have a young son?" she asked.

"How did you know?"

"Just a guess," she said. "Don't leave. I'll be right back."

Clare hurried down the corridor and banged on Tenzin's door.

"Tenzin! Tenzin!" she said. "He's here."

Tenzin wasn't amused. He was preparing for an upcoming talk, and did not like having his concentration broken.

"Whatever it is will have to wait," he said.

Clare burst through the door. "Don't you remember? You told me to get you no matter what you were doing."

She's worse than Danny, thought Tenzin, now clearly exasperated. He dropped his pen in disgust. "What are you talking about?"

"The man in your dreams. He's here!"

"You're sure?"

"Come see for yourself."

Tenzin rose from his chair and strode down the hall, Clare trailing after him. The man had fallen asleep, his chin resting against his chest. Tenzin observed him carefully.

"His kundalini has been activated. The energy's overpowered him and knocked him out."

"Is it him?" Clare asked.

"Yes."

Tenzin tapped the young man on his stomach. Gold light leaped from Tenzin's fingers into the stranger's solar plexus. A wave of heat and electricity surged through his body. The man's eyes flew open in shock.

"You're the man on the flyer," he said when he saw Tenzin.

"What's your name?" said Tenzin.

"David Adams."

"What brings you here, David?"

"An old monk told me about you."

"What old monk?"

"You'll think I'm crazy."

"Not if you tell me the truth."

"My wife left me several months ago, while I was away on business. We lived in New Hampshire. She took our son, and went to live with a cult here in Malibu. She left a note on the kitchen table that said she was leaving to follow her spiritual path, but she would always be my best friend."

"Some friend," said Clare.

"I didn't sleep that night. The next morning I went downstairs and fell asleep on the sofa. When I woke up there was an unworldly brightness in the room. A group of monks was standing by the fireplace. Their bodies were made of light, not flesh." He paused for a moment, wiping his face with his hand. "It gets a lot stranger. Would you like me to stop?"

"Please continue."

"The leader came forward and spoke to me telepathically. I heard his voice in my head."

"What did he say?"

"That the dark side was after my son and we were both in danger. He told me to go to Los Angeles and save my boy. He said I would find an ally there, a monk like him."

"Did he say anything else?"

"That's it."

"Did he do anything else?"

"He put his hand through my forehead. When he did, my head was flooded with light and my pain disappeared. I was totally at peace. I fell into a deep sleep immediately afterward."

"That's amazing!" said Clare.

"That part of it was. But it get's a lot darker. Late that night, I woke up with a feeling of great danger all around me. My heart was beating rapidly. I looked around the room. There was a tall, black creepy lizard-looking thing at the foot of my bed."

"Did it have a tail?" said Tenzin.

"Yeah," said David.

The young man's story triggered a strand of remembrance in Tenzin. He recalled the night long ago when he had awakened in great fear from a terrible nightmare during his and Nawang's long trek over the Himalayas to escape the Chinese. In his nightmare, a big lizard had threatened to kill him unless he submitted to its power. The Lord of Darkness, it called itself. He remembered the deep shadow behind its flat reptilian eyes and the malevolence in the eyes themselves. It was a truly terrifying moment. That same shadow had appeared several times since then. It had flickered briefly in Thomas's eyes when he was consumed by the conspiracy; in the head of the latrine department at Rumtek when he was overwhelmed by hatred and charged after Dorjee; and recently, in Wayne, who was overome with envy.

Tenzin shuddered imperceptibly. Here was more proof. The Lord of Darkness and his minions were real and could attack anyone whenever they were consumed by negative emotion. Hate, fear, rage, resentment, revenge and retribution were all doors it could exploit with ease. What's more, these beings could appear in dreams, as astral entities in the physical world, and in extreme cases, possess the physical bodies of its victims. The enemy was flexible, adaptable, and multi-dimensional. The Lord of Darkness obviously commanded a large host. The danger that they posed was much greater than he had originally thought.

"Were you freaked out?" asked Clare.

"Yeah! The thing held my feet in its hands. Each of its hands had three long fingers. Blue and white energy oozed out of its hands into the soles of my feet. The energy was harsh and disruptive, and it scared the hell out of me. Somehow, I knew that it wanted to separate me from my soul and take possession of my body."

"What did you do?" asked Tenzin, collecting himself and returning to the present situation.

"I said the Lord's Prayer. After the first few lines, the creature disappeared."

Tenzin nodded. The young man had a strong intuition that would serve him well. Perhaps all was not lost. Prayer was one of the best ways to defeat them. "You did the right thing."

Tenzin left the room and returned a moment later with an old tin box. He took off the cover and sorted through several wrinkled and worn photographs.

"Here it is!" He handed the picture to David. "Do you recognize anyone?"

David studied the picture. It was an old photograph of a group of monks. "Him," he said. He pointed to a face in the middle of the picture. That's the man who spoke to me."

"Ishan!" said Tenzin.

"Who's that?" asked David.

"A senior rinpoche from my monastery. He was a great man. The Chinese executed him in 1950. How old is your son?"

"Five."

"The dark powers are aware of his destiny. They want to shut him down before he grows up. He's very evolved and has come back to help the world. He's a threat to their plans of planetary domination."

"Michael? A threat to plans of world domination? That's nuts!"

"Why?"

"He's a little kid! He's no threat to anyone."

"Look deeper. Go beyond his body and his physical age. See his soul. It is old and highly advanced. The dark side sees it, and fears it. You must see and protect it."

"How can you possibly know that?"

"I have learned to quiet my mind and view things from a clear space deep inside me. You must learn to do that, too. Nothing is what it seems on the surface."

"Maybe that explains what happened on the night he was conceived."

"What happened?" Clare asked. David's story had intrigued her.

"That night my wife was fertile and insisted we make love. The moment I ejaculated, she knew that she had conceived. While I slept, she had a strange vision. A bright golden sun settled in her womb. After it had settled inside her, several witchlike creatures appeared in the room. They were agitated, and screamed in high-pitched voices. She was terrified and woke me up. We heard their screams all night long. For the next three days, doors opened and slammed shut throughout the house on their own."

"The dark side has been after him from the beginning," said Tenzin. "It seems that they have succeeded with his mother. It is important that they don't succeed with you. You are his only hope."

"Then we're both in deep trouble. I'm not doing well right now. They're relentless. They make threatening phone calls at all hours. It's really gotten to me."

"Don't worry. I'll help you."

"Then what the old monk said was true," said David.

Tenzin nodded. "I was told in my dreams that you were coming."

"They set it all up?" said David.

"It would seem so. The different levels of reality are more interrelated than we know. Many events here are planned and coordinated in realities of which we are unaware. Is the leader of the cult a man or a woman?"

"A woman."

"Is she a surrogate mother figure for your ex-wife?"

"Yes."

"That's what I thought. Your former wife's need of nurturing and mothering is her weakness. The dark side has used it to control her. The cult leader projected herself as a kind and loving figure who understands your ex and wants to help her. It is a common seduction theme of the dark side. Those who fall into the trap don't understand the bargain that they've made until it's too late. It's easy to enter, but impossible to exit."

"She's hurt me badly, but I can't help hurting for her, too. Everyone loses in this situation, especially Michael."

"Broken people create havoc in the lives of those closest to them. Your wife has mistaken the negative for positive. The cult leader has deceived her. Your ex's openness to this woman makes her vulnerable to being programmed and mind- controlled."

"I want to hurt them for what they've done to my son."

"Think with your soul," said Tenzin. "Revenge is never the way. It makes you vulnerable to the dark side. Do you want another lizard from the dark side to show up in your bedroom late at night?"

"No."

"Then release your anger and practice forgiveness. Your anger only binds you to them, and helps them to hurt you again and again. Is that what you want?"

"Of course not."

"Then stop reacting. When you stop playing their game, they will have no more power over you. This is a spiritual war. You win by elevating your consciousness. That is the only way."

"How do I do that?"

Tenzin studied David's energy field for a moment. "You have several cracks in your energy field that allow them to get inside and steal your energy. That makes them stronger and you weaker. Are you aware of the transference of energy?"

"Every time Rayanne, the cult leader, calls up to threaten me, it feels as if a sword is piercing my stomach and ripping upward to my heart. It makes me fold over in pain. By the time I get off the phone, I'm wiped out and white as a ghost. It takes days to recover."

"Why do you answer the phone?"

"I'm afraid of what she'll do to my son if I don't."

"What can she do? Hang up on her from now on."

"That's what Michael told me to do."

Tenzin smiled. "He's very wise."

"One day we were driving to school and Michael said, 'Daddy, I hear Mummy and Rayanne talking about how to hurt you. Hang up when they call, Daddy. Don't let them hurt you.' I told him that I was worried what would happen to him if I did."

"What did he say?" Clare asked.

"He said they weren't going to hurt him."

"He's right," said Tenzin. "Hang up on them. Let the negative energy that they had intended to dump on you fester inside them. Have you met the cult leader?"

"Oh yeah."

"What does she look like?"

"Her face is cracked and lined. It looks like dried leather. She has cold gray eyes, and wears thick, wire-rimmed glasses that magnify her eyes and make her look like a bug. Her hair is a dull gray, but she dyes it black. She's wiry and wrinkled like a prune. Everything about her is severe and angry. She reminds me of a withered tree that's covered with knots."

"What does her energy feel like?"

"Cold and inhuman," he said, shivering at the recollection. "I've never felt anything like it before. It raises the hackles on the back of your neck."

"And your ex-wife thinks that this woman is going to save her?" said Clare.

"Apparently so," said David.

"Unbelievable," said Clare.

"Have you had much direct contact with her?" said Tenzin.

"More than I want."

"Does anything stand out about those encounters?"

"When I first came to L.A. she wouldn't let me see my son until I had met with her. The meeting took place in her room. She positioned me so that the sun was in my eyes. I couldn't see anything at first. When my eyes finally adjusted to the light, I saw several huge lizards standing in the room, just like the one who appeared in my room after my wife left me. The room was filled with them."

"Were they real?" said Clare, her eyes bulging.

"They kept shifting between being energetic and physical. It was very freaky."

"Were you scared?"

"I was freaked out of my mind."

"Did they do anything else?" asked Tenzin.

"Yeah. They threw their coarse bluish-white energy around the room. It crackled like lightning."

"She was letting you know that you were up against something you had never seen before, something that defies conventional explanation. She planned the meeting to make you cower and feel helpless, and conversely, to make her look omnipotent. She was telling you that you couldn't possibly win. What happened next?"

"She went into her usual rant that I was abusive, controlling, and manipulative, had a big ego, and was the worst man she had ever met. She said that she was the only person who dared to tell me the truth and it was her mission to break my ego and save my soul. No one else could do it. She said unless I changed, my son would grow up to be gay."

"Did you believe her?"

"No. But every time I talk to her or Sarah, my ex, they repeat their litany. It's exhausting."

"That's a standard mind-control technique. Repetition reprograms the subconscious. First we need to close the cracks in your energy field so that they can't get inside you and insert more programming in your subconscious."

"How can you do that?"

"Like this." Tenzin put one hand on David's stomach and the other on the base of his spine. A warm, pleasant stream of energy flowed into him. The energy was soothing and relaxing, very different from the reptilian energy he had encountered with the leader of the cult. He nodded off a moment later. When he woke Tenzin and Clare were smiling at him.

"How do you feel?" asked Tenzin.

David took a few seconds to get his bearings. He rolled his head back and forth. "Lighter, like a heavy weight has been removed."

"You seem surprised," said Tenzin.

"I am."

"They had opened your sexual center and your solar plexus center. An open sexual center combined with an open solar plexus center creates a direct pathway for programming to be inserted into your subconscious. That's why they always repeat the abusive, manipulative, controlling mantra. When the programming pathway is open, these programs are installed in your subconscious whether or not you try to resist them. They installed other programs to make you feel helpless, isolated, and depressed."

"I've felt that way since this nightmare began."

"I'm not surprised. I cleared the programming and closed your chakras. You'll be less vulnerable now. The sexual center needs to be excited and wide open for programming to be effectively installed. Don't ever forget this. Take precautions. Keep it closed."

"How?"

"Don't wear bright red. It stimulates and opens the sexual center. Try not to be sexually aroused too much. Meditate daily. Stay in balance."

"That's hard to do around here. L.A. is full of beautiful, sexy women."

Tenzin laughed. "Then find yourself a girlfriend. One who is emotionally stable, and loving. You'll be safe with a woman like that."

"Women like that still exist?"

A smile lit up Clare's face. "They do. If you know where to look," she said.

CHAPTER 46

More Than You Want to Know

DAVID WAS PREPARING to leave, when Thomas walked in later in the afternoon. His face was drawn and haggard from another grueling day in the UCLA library. He dropped his briefcase on the floor, slumped down in his favorite chair, stifled a yawn, and rubbed his eyes.

"Some tea, Thomas?" Tenzin said.

"Sure."

"You look worn out."

"I'd say that's an accurate observation of my current condition."

"Say hello to David."

"Hello, young man," said Thomas not even bothering to glance in his direction. New people were always dropping in. They came and went. There was nothing new in that.

"He's the young man I saw in my dreams."

"Really?" said Thomas. He turned and looked at David with renewed interest.

"David's in the middle of a difficult divorce."

"I see," said Thomas. "That can't be very pleasant."

"It's not," said David.

"He's had several disturbing encounters with reptilian entities from the dark side," said Tenzin. "They tried to separate him from his soul and possess his body."

"Seems your dreams were true then."

"Yes," said Tenzin without further elaboration.

"Well, you've come to the right place, young fellow," said Thomas, turning back to David. "There's nobody better than Tenzin to handle the pickle you've got yourself into."

"Ishan sent him," said Tenzin.

"Now that's a little farfetched, don't you think?" said Thomas. "Ishan's dead. He's been that way a long time."

"You know better than that. He appeared in his light body with a group of monks."

"Well, that figures. Those friends of yours get around."

"You can do a lot more when you're no longer bound to the earth plane by a body." Tenzin poured a steaming cup of green tea for Thomas. "What did you learn today?"

"Are you sure you want to delve into this now? We'll be going from the miraculous to the demonic in the blink of an eye."

Tenzin shrugged. "That's what we've been dealing with today. They're both connected, anyway.The dark power that controls the world is after David and his son. He needs to understand what he's up against. This is not your typical nasty divorce. It has much larger implications."

"All right. If that's what you want," said Thomas. "I learned what these guys call themselves today."

"That's good," Tenzin said. It was time to put names and faces on the conspiracy that reached by stealth into every nook and corner of the planet. "What's their name?"

"The Illuminati."

"What does that mean?" asked David, puzzled by all of this talk of dark powers and a hidden conspiracy.

"Keepers of the Light."

"Well, that can't be bad, right?" said David, grasping at the scrap of hope the definition implied. He looked first at Thomas, then at Tenzin.

"It depends on the kind of light you're talking about," said Thomas. "The light of the Illuminati is the light of Lucifer, not the Light of God. It originates in the astral plane, home to deception, duplicity, and evil. Black magic, sexual perversion, pedophilia, and blood sacrifice are the keystones of their religious practices. They engage in depraved rites and sexual rituals to gain power over the world. They exalt depravity and deride goodness and morality. To them, love and compassion are weaknesses, not virtues."

"Do you think there's a connection between the lizard entities that attacked me and the Illuminati?" David asked.

"I think," said Thomas picking his words carefully, "that the Illuminati on earth serve the agenda of the dark power on the astral plane. The entities you saw are probably foot soldiers in the army of darkness. The conspiracy is multi-dimensional and hierarchical. The line of command is strictly enforced from the astral plane to the physical world."

"What do they want?" said David, his mind spinning from the shock of these revelations. Blood sacrifice? Pedophilia? Black magic? He hadn't enlisted to deal with any of this. Damn Sarah! She had opened the gates of hell. He didn't care if she knew what she was doing or not. Her self-absorption, unstable nature, and lack of judgment had put Michael in grave danger. A normal divorce was hard enough. But normal didn't exist in this scenario. His life had become a science-fiction movie filled with demonic creatures, supernatural occurrences, twisted people, and bizarre events in which he had been cast unwillingly in the role of hero. He hadn't chosen it, didn't want it, and would gladly give the part away to anyone foolish enough to take it. He rued the day when he had first laid eyes on Sarah and been taken by her beauty. She had looked angelic then, so pure and glowing. That had proven to be a mirage, a deception replete with terrible consequences. The next time he became interested in a woman, he would look deeper. A good heart was more important than a beautiful face. Beauty fades, goodness grows.

"What do they want?" said Thomas. The sound of his voice returned David from his descent into hell. "It's pretty simple, I think. They want to control the world and everyone in it. They want to make Satanism the New World Religion and enslave humanity. They want to replace democracy with some combination of communism and fascism. They want to destroy our intelligence and our ability to think critically, ruin our health, and reduce the world's population by eighty to ninety percent."

"This just keeps getting worse," said David. "It's like a Nazi concentration camp, or one of Stalin's gulags, only on a larger scale."

"That's not far off the truth," Thomas said. "Those were experiments, forerunners of the future that they have planned for us. They fluoridated the water in those camps, just as they now do throughout America as government policy."

"But fluoride protects teeth from cavities."

"More propaganda. Remember the principle, nothing is what it seems. The fluoride they put in the water supply is a highly toxic industrial waste product. It makes teeth brittle, causes bone cancer, destroys the thyroid gland, calcifies the pineal gland, causes lesions in the brain, lowers IQ and makes the masses docile and easy to control. Population control is why they use it. After the Nazis fluoridated the water in the concentration camps, they only needed a quarter of the number of guards. Fluoridation means it takes fewer of them to control more of us."

"You're saying that if they succeed, the world will be plunged into darkness," said David. "There'd be no hope and no freedom. We'd be reduced to robots on an assembly line."

"Exactly," said Thomas. "That's the Luciferian ideal. Robots do what they're programmed to do. They don't rebel. Everything is orderly and predictable. Outcomes are not left to chance. Totalitarianism is control over everything. Freedom and democracy are not predictable. Human beings with free will and minds of their own are not predictable; they are difficult to control. The Illuminati intend to replace our free will with their mind-control."

"Exactly who are the Illuminati? Do you know their names?" asked David.

"I'm just beginning to unravel that part of it. They don't make it easy. They've been entrenched behind the scenes for millennia. Thirteen dynastic families sit at the top of the hierarchy; they control the world and have for ages. I suspect that most royal families are part of it, but I'm not absolutely sure yet. Thirteen is an important number to them. Take the United States. There were thirteen original American colonies. The eagle on the seal of the United States has thirteen arrows in its talon. There are thirteen stripes on our flag. None of that's by coincidence. Each of the thirteen families controlled a colony."

"Damn," said David. "It gets stranger and stranger."

"That's the nature of conspiracies," said Thomas. "The more you unravel them, the stranger they get. Below the thirteen dynastic families at the top of the pyramid there's a larger group called the Committee of 300 made up of three hundred supporting families that work under the control of the thirteen major families. The Committee of 300 has several organizations that develop and implement strategies to further their agenda of a new world order. These groups include the Council on Foreign Relations, the Royal Institute for International Affairs, the Bilderburgers, the Club of Rome, the Federal Reserve, the International Monetary Fund, the United Nations, the CIA, Interpol, and the Mafia, among others. All told, the Illuminati make up one to two percent of the world's population, but they control the major centers of power and influence in government and politics, the military, the media, all major newspapers, Hollywood, TV, music, medicine, religion, and banking. Secrecy, discipline, and organization are keys to their success."

"The Mafia?" said David. "They're criminals."

Thomas cracked a tight smile. "And the others aren't? They wrap themselves in the guise of respectability, that's all. Don't you love how our politicians wear an American flag on their lapels? They think it makes them patriots, hides their hypocrisy, and makes them immune to criticism. As far as I'm concerned, anyone who wraps himself in the American flag is suspect. In America, everything's for sale. Politicians sell their votes to corporate interests. Whoever has the most money owns the country. And that's the Illuminati."

David's jaw tightened noticeably. His face grew pale.

"These guys are long-term planners," Thomas continued. "What they don't achieve in their lifetimes, their sons and grandsons will achieve in theirs. In 1820 the Russian Czar kicked the Rothschild banking cartel out of his country. The Rothschilds were incensed and pledged that they would assassinate the Czar and his entire family. Almost one hundred years later, on July 18, 1918, the Communists, who were created and funded by the Rothschilds, murdered Czar Nicholas and his family. These guys keep their promises. Never underestimate them. They never stop."

David's jaw twitched. "Everything I ever learned about history is a damn lie," he said. "And I majored in history."

"Unfortunately, education is another form of mind-control. The purpose of education, and religion for that matter, is to instill conformity and prevent you from thinking critically."

"We're surrounded," sighed David. "Evil is everywhere."

"We're fighting an enemy that we can't see," said Thomas. "The noose keeps tightening around us and most people don't even know that it exists. It's taken years of research to learn what I know. Most people don't have the time or inclination to do it. Now, maybe your boy really does represent a threat to the Illuminati. Tenzin says he does, so I believe him. From what you've said, it would seem that the Illuminati and their agents have been aware of him since he was conceived. We also know that emissaries from the spiritual planes have been watching over him, too. That suggests that both sides know your boy's potential and his future mission. Obviously, he's special. Otherwise, why bother with him?"

"They're using the boy's mother to control him," said Tenzin. "The cult leader is an expert in the art of deception. She knows how to present herself as a spiritual teacher and a loving mother figure while hiding her real agenda. David's ex has fallen for it. She's completely mind-controlled. David is all that stands in their way."

"Well, he has us now. That's a beginning."

"Can you tell me more, Thomas?" said David.

"I will, as long as you understand that there's a danger in knowing too much."

"What's that?" said David.

"It's easy to get overwhelmed. The public has no idea this exists. We're pretty alone in what we know."

"They can't keep it quiet forever," said David.

"They've managed to do so for thousands of years."

"Thousands of years? That's not possible."

"Unfortunately, it is. The Illuminati New World Order conspiracy goes all the way back to ancient Sumer, some seven thousand years ago. You're aware of the crown on the Statue of Liberty?"

"Sure. Who isn't?"

"Ever seen a crown like that before?"

"No."

"That didn't come out of the artist's mind. It's the crown of Semiramis, hybrid Goddess of the ancient Sumerians. Semiramis was half human, half reptilian. A Freemason Lodge in France gave The Statue of Liberty to America. Semiramis is a major Goddess of the Illuminati. The Illuminati control the higher levels of Freemasonry. Most Masons above the twenty-ninth degree are members of the Illuminati. The Statue of Liberty represents freedom, hope, and opportunity to most Americans but it symbolizes something quite different to the Illuminati."

"Like what?"

"That they are the true owners of America; that its wealth and resources belong to them."

David frowned, but was otherwise silent.

"In the Illuminati hierarchy," said Thomas, "the President of the United States is nothing more than a foot soldier. He is told what to do and does it. He has no freedom to make decisions. He doesn't act in the interests of America, but in the interests of the Illuminati. The Illuminati's long-term plan is to destroy the American economy, gut the middle class, undermine the moral values and integrity of the people, destroy respect and trust between men and women, weaken the family, degrade love with pornography, revoke the constitution, destroy our health, take away our freedoms, and introduce martial law."

"That's one hell of an agenda," said David. "What you're really saying is that the government of the United States is the enemy of the American people. That its function is not to protect our freedoms and way of life but to revoke them."

"An excellent summary. What does it look like to you?"

David was quiet for a moment. "I don't know anything, anymore."

"Believe me," said Thomas. "I would take great comfort in being wrong. It's what I pray for every night. Then, every day I discover more disturbing evidence to support my conclusions. They've done a great job of obscuring the truth. When you do encounter it, you're shocked and unprepared to handle it. It flies in the face of everything that you've been programmed to think and to believe. The Illuminati are betting that the masses will never open their minds to the truth, and will always be easy to dupe. I'm betting that they're wrong. The American people are a sleeping giant. Not so long ago they woke up and defeated Hitler and fascism. One day, when they're pushed into a corner, they'll wake up again and defeat the Illuminati and the New World Order."

"I hope you're right."

A faint smile appeared on Thomas's face. "Me too," he said.

David leaned back in his chair and stared out the window. The sunset was a pink blaze; soft clouds shimmered like cotton candy in the darkening sky. The truth was shocking, each revelation another arrow through his heart. The gears in his mind spun ever faster. These guys did whatever they wanted. They assassinated Presidents and kings and suffered no consequences. Given their political, financial, and military might; their superior organization; their talent for long-term strategic planning; and the web of mind-control that they had spun, where was hope to come from? What chance did his son have of leading a safe and fulfilling life? What chance did other parents have to give the American dream to their children? How could he ever hope to defeat the vast forces arrayed against him? They could come in and go out of physical reality at will. They were expert at this kind of warfare. David was a novice in the multi-dimensional war for his child's soul. He had never felt such despair.

Somewhere, there had to be hope, he reminded himself. No problem was without a solution. His job was to find it. Unfortunately, whenever he thought that he had found safety, the ground shifted under his feet. Terra firma turned to quicksand. Tenzin had given him hope. Thomas's revelations had taken it away. The forces of darkness seemed too well-organized and in control of the world for hope to ever prevail. He sighed, and focused on the beauty in the back yard. The last light of the day danced on the dappled leaves of the oleander. The grass was a deep, healthy green, thick and freshly mowed. The flower beds were full of blue, red and yellow tulips in full bloom. Who would have ever guessed that so much evil was so close at hand?

Tenzin had spoken little during their conversation. He noted David's slumping shoulders, observed the growing despair that had stolen the light from his eyes and felt the sense of doom that had taken control of his mind.

"You know," he said at last. "It's easy to feel hopeless in your circumstances. Especially with this added knowledge. Despair is the path most men take when they come face to face with overwhelming opposition. They give up, lie down and wilt under the pressure. They either die slowly or make the best deal that they can with the enemy, often surrendering their power and ending up enslaved. The hero chooses the opposite path, the path of most resistance. He strengthens his mind and spirit. He knows that the real enemy lives inside himself. If he defeats his fear and hopelessness, then he will have the power and creativity to defeat his external enemy. He knows that when you align your mind with your soul, it doesn't matter how long the odds are or how vast the forces arrayed against you. Mind and soul are one. That spiritual connection is the strongest force in the universe. Remember Buddha defeating Mara and the armies of evil under the Bodhi tree. One man in silent meditation defeated a vast multitude. Do you understand, David? You must never forget that."

"I think so."

"Who benefits when you fall into hopelessness?"

"My enemies."

"That's right. Your hopelessness empowers those who want to extinguish your light. Right now, that's the leader of the cult, and your former wife. Your despair is their ally and your enemy. Don't do their work by letting them turn your mind against you. If the Illuminati keep us from discovering our spiritual potential and connecting with our soul, they win. If we overcome their mind control programming and regain our soul connection, we win. Feeling hopeless and defeated is only a choice. It's never a good one. It helps your enemies. Choose something that expands you, instead of something that diminishes you."

"Like what?'"

"What do you need most right now?"

"Strength and confidence."

"Good. Close your eyes. Inhale violet light. Let it flow down your spine into your hips. As you exhale, send the violet light up your spine, and out through the top of your head. When it exits your head see it flowing into a big bright golden sun a few inches above your head. As the violet light rises up your spine and flows into the sun, let your feelings of hopelessness and negativity rise with it. The sun, which represents your soul, will transform the negative energy and turn it back into pure light. Repeat this process until you feel free of negativity. Your soul will hold the transformed energy until you need it back."

David closed his eyes and did as instructed. When he felt free of the negative energy, he opened his eyes and looked around.

"How do you feel?" asked Tenzin.

"Clear. Peaceful."

"And your hopelessness?"

"It's gone."

"You sound surprised."

"I am."

"You see? It's easier to rise above your negativity than you thought. Do this exercise daily. With practice, maintaining your balance and clarity will become second nature."

"That would be a welcome relief."

"We grow stronger by facing adversity. Most people have little tolerance for reality. They wear blinders to shield themselves from seeing what they can't accept. They'd rather remain ignorant than realize the truth. They find more comfort in self-delusion than in self-realization. By maintaining their ignorance, they do the Illuminati's work for them. The refusal by most people to face the truth adds another level to the conspiracy. The first level, of course, is the Illuminati agenda to establish a New World Order. The second level is the masses who have no idea what the New World Order is or how they're being led blindly down the path to destruction. The Illuminati level concerns clear, conscious, and focused intention. The level of the masses is about unconscious avoidance. The two levels are partners in a great dance. One leads, the other follows. The future depends on the masses waking from their trance and leaving the dance."

"I wish I could change my dance partners. I'm still dancing with Rayanne and my ex, and I know it."

"Don't worry. You will. It's a matter of clearing your negative programming and opposing them consciously, not reactively. Your ex's mind is broken. I think that it's always been broken and unfortunately always will be, unless she seeks specialized help. You just never saw it until it was too late. She's been taken over, mind- controlled and entranced by the cult leader. That couldn't have happened unless her mind had been fractured and programmed previously. If you stay centered and balanced, the negative energy they send will bounce off you and return to them. That's how you will break out of the dance with them. Your mind and soul are united now. You're neither broken nor entranced, and that's why you will win."

"What do you think broke your ex-wife?" Thomas asked. "These things usually start in childhood."

David grew thoughtful for time. "I think that she was sexually abused as a young girl," said David. "But she's completely suppressed it."

"Why do you think that?" asked Thomas.

"She always complained about being sexually blocked and unable to feel anything when we made love. She also never made a sound during sex. Until I came along her pattern was to run whenever a male expressed interest in her. She also said she was angry at God. She felt God had abandoned her."

"Hmm," said Thomas, rubbing his chin. "Do you think her abuser might have threatened her to keep her silent while he abused her?" asked Thomas.

"Perhaps. I don't know. It's all pretty speculative."

"It probably always will be," answered Thomas. "But it does suggest why she's easy to program. Sexual abuse is a favorite tool of the Illuminati to break a child's mind. They do it to their own children. The Illuminati are all programmed. What color are your ex's hair and eyes, by the way?"

"Blond and blue. Why?"

"I assume that she's attractive."

"She's gorgeous."

"Do you know what traumatic mind-control is?" asked Thomas.

"No," answered David.

"Traumatic mind-control is a calculated and systematic campaign of brutality against a targeted individual. In most cases it begins in infancy. They use ongoing rape, electric shock, drugs, beatings, constant threats, psychological torture, and emotional deprivation to shatter a subject's mind. The subject eventually disassociates, and the mind fragments into a cube containing 2197 compartments, 13 deep, 13 wide, 13 high. Skilled programmers then program each compartment with a different function, ability, and personality. The programmed compartments, or alter personalities, remain unknown to the core personality. Alters stay in the background until triggered by a phrase, a song, a cartoon, a color, or a movie, or any trigger they want to use. When an alter comes forward and takes control, the core personality recedes into in the background and has no memory of what has transpired. The Illuminati install many programs and personalities in their victims. These programs include moonchild programming, stalking and assassin programs, destroyer programs, new age programs, cult programs, monarch sex slave programs, sexual ritual magick programs, end time programs, and ritual sacrifice programs, to list a few. The list is long. Traumatic mind control is the main cause of multiple personality disorder."

"And you think my ex is a victim of traumatic mind control?" David said.

"Possibly. Blue-eyed, blonde-haired people have an enzyme in their DNA that makes them especially susceptible to programming. From what you've said, your ex appears to be a highly programmed individual. What changes have you noticed in her since she's become affiliated with Rayanne and her cult?"

"She's become hard, nasty, and vicious. I don't know her anymore. Hurting me is her mission. She even looks different."

"How?"

"Her face has lost its softness. It's become hard and severe, more like Rayanne's than the woman I married. There's no hint of gentleness or kindness. Her eyes are filled with hatred."

"What was she like before the change?"

"She was thoughtful, kind and sweet. She loved animals. It's hard to adjust to the fact that someone I trusted and thought I could count on has become my mortal enemy. Her goodness has completely disappeared. She blames me for all her problems."

"It sounds like she has shifted into an alter personality. Programmed people always play the victim. They find it easier to blame others for their failings than to take responsibility for them," said Thomas. "I call this condition Courage Deficit Disorder. CDD."

"It has a certain ring to it," said David.

"It does, doesn't it?" said Thomas, laughing. "If you don't heal your problems, you'll draw them to you repeatedly. Distance is no escape from yourself. Your ex went three thousand miles only to be dominated and diminished by a tyrant posing as a loving mother. She might blame you, but her choices are clear evidence to the contrary. She's reliving her childhood imprinting. You're not the problem. The problem is her. Neurotic people always project their problems onto others."

"She'll never stop blaming me."

"Let's hope that she'll get the help she needs," said Tenzin. "You solve your problems by closing the distance with your shadow, not by widening it, as she's done. It's elementary physics. Clear the darkness and more space opens for the light. If the darkness persists, it will expand until there's no room for the light. Sooner or later, we all stand before life's major crossroad and must choose between darkness and light, between a self-imposed prison or self-realization and freedom."

"At least I know which way I'm going," said David. "That's a start, at least."

"There are two keys to victory, David," said Tenzin, who had been listening quietly. "Release your anger and bitterness. Then forgive your enemies. Do so, and you are no longer a victim, but a warrior. That will place you on a different energetic plane from them, and they will not be able to hurt you. That's what Rayanne and her allies in the astral world fear. Don't react to their attempts to goad you. Ignore them. Stay centered in your soul. Surround yourself in violet light for protection. Buddha defeated an armed multitude. All you have to do is to beat back Rayanne. Is it so impossible?"

"Not when you put it like that."

Tenzin permitted himself a brief smile. "Context," he said, "is everything."

CHAPTER 47

The Challenge

At three a.m., David's phone rang. He fumbled for the phone before finally raising the receiver to his ear.

"Yeah," he said, not awake enough to realize who was on the other end.

"You're a snake!" Rayanne screamed in her shrill voice. "How dare you try to turn Michael against his mother! I'm going to send your wife and son into hiding where you'll never find them. You're evil and abusive. You're a bully. You've destroyed your wife. I'm not going to let you destroy your son, too. Someone has to protect them. I'm the strongest person you've ever met. You don't scare me at all."

David's eyes were now wide open. His heart pounded as wave after wave of adrenaline shot through his body. Rayanne had caught him with his guard down, but this time he was determined to recover and hurl her toxic energy back at her. It was hers. Let her deal with it. The time when she could hurt him without fear of reprisal was over. There would be no more listening to her threats, letting her energy get inside him and wreak havoc in his mind. No more being a victim—ever. She was still screaming, but he wasn't listening. He dropped the phone and let her screams and threats sink harmlessly into the thick carpet on the floor.

Instead of falling into fear and anxiety, he sat up and meditated as Tenzin had taught him to do. Inhale. Exhale. Focus the mind on the breath. Remember that the breath controls the mind. If you slow the breath, you clear the mind. Within minutes his mind became quiet and his heartbeat normalized. Now centered and calm, he visualized a violet light around him. Around the violet light, he imagined a global mirror reflecting all negative energy back to the sender.

With his protection firmly in place, he visualized a slippery black ooze and sent it back to Rayanne. Let her confront her own slime. When he was finished, he felt light and clear and fell into a deep sleep.

Meanwhile, Rayanne was furious that David wasn't responding to her threats. The male ego was so obvious and easy to defeat. She had spent a good deal of time working on her latest tactic to unhinge him and turn him into a pathetic creature with his tail tucked firmly between his legs. How dare he ignore her! She'd show that pathetic excuse of a man exactly with whom he was dealing. He thought he had his balls back and could walk away from her, did he?

At that moment, a wall of dark energy slammed into her. Her heart began racing; she gasped for air. A chronic asthmatic, she realized at once that she was having a serious, perhaps life-threatening attack. Starved for oxygen and rasping like a rusty bellows, she dropped the phone and reached for the bell near her bed. She rang it twice before her strength ebbed and the bell fell to floor with a dull thud. Her hand trembled as she sprayed her inhaler into her mouth. It helped some, but not nearly enough. Her weathered face, full of harsh lines and lacking color in the best of times, had turned a bluish gray. If she didn't get help soon, she would die.

Please God, she begged, let someone hear the bell. It was her last thought before she lost consciousness.

Moments later, two of her male followers burst into the room. These men, like the rest of Rayanne's followers, thought of themselves as superior spiritual beings. In reality, she had transformed them into eunuchs. Their belief in their superiority was an essential part of their programming, true in their minds, but not in fact. To them, she was an enlightened master and being allowed to serve her was a demonstration of their superior status in the cult. To her, they were pathetic slaves, donating their income to the cult and doing as she commanded. All she had had to do to extract those things from them was to flatter their egos and make them feel special. That it had been so easy was a source of constant amusement to her. It made *her* feel special.

The two eunuchs took one look at her face, wrapped her robe about her and carried her to the car. When they reached the hospital twenty minutes later, Rayanne was rushed into the critical-care unit. Her face had darkened to ashen gray; her pulse was barely detectable. The doctor put an oxygen mask over her face and administered a large dose of prednisone. The steroid took effect quickly. Her bronchial passages opened and she began to breathe normally again. The gray cast to her face gradually turned to a pale pink. As dawn broke she fell into a light sleep.

CHAPTER 48

Breakthrough

CLARE ANSWERED THE phone when David called later that morning. "Santa Monica Tibetan Center," she said.

"Hi Clare, it's David. Is Tenzin available?"

"I'll check. By the way, are you dating anyone?"

"You've got to be kidding."

"I wouldn't have asked if I was."

"Who would want to date me? My life is a mess. No woman in her right mind needs this kind of trouble."

"You'd be surprised. I told a friend about you. It's not easy to find a good partner. There's a lot of great women out there are looking for someone like you."

"Good men can't be that hard to find."

"You're a guy. How would you know?"

"Is your friend smart?"

"Of course."

"Well, if she's smart, she'll stay away."

"God, you're impossible!" said Clare. "Annie's willing to give you the benefit of the doubt. The least you could do is meet her."

"I'm in a war, Clare. I never know what's coming next. It's an unstable and volatile environment. I couldn't put a woman in the middle of all that. It wouldn't be fair to her."

"Are you a good father?"

"You bet."

"Well, any man who has made the kind of sacrifices you've made for your son has the kind of character a woman wants."

"That's not what my ex thinks."

"Who cares what that she thinks? I once read that hell is believing what other people think of you. You need to remember that."

"You're good, Clare. Too bad you're not available. I'll meet your friend. But don't expect anything to come of it."

Clare laughed. "If I were unattached I'd think about it. But I've got my two guys. They're my life. I never knew I could love anyone like I love them."

"Your two Charlies are lucky dudes."

"You're gonna be lucky, too. You'll see. Now hold on. I'll buzz Tenzin."

A short silence followed before the familiar voice came on the line. "David?"

"Hi, Tenzin."

"How are you?"

"Good. I got attacked by Rayanne last night but I returned her energy to her. I have no idea if anything happened to her, but I fell back asleep and feel great today. That's good enough for me."

"You see how easy it is when you use your mind to your advantage and not let them use it against you?" said Tenzin. "You didn't go into fear. You held your center. When you do that, your mind has unlimited power. The wise man focuses that power to his advantage. He knows that when he loses self-control, he loses his power. You're learning to remain stable despite the dark power's attempts to intimidate you, knock you off balance, make you doubt yourself, and steal your energy. Rayanne and your ex use what you love the most against you, your son. But now the tide has turned. You're using their energy against them. Can you bring Michael over Saturday afternoon and stay for dinner? We'd all love to meet him. He can play with Matthew and Danny. Does he play sports?"

"Soccer's his game."

"Danny, too. The kids will have a great time together."

"Thanks. We'll be there."

"Thomas will be home on Wednesday. My last counseling session is at two. Can you come by after that? We can continue our conversation then."

"You bet."

Clare was sitting at the reception desk when David arrived on Wednesday afternoon. "Did you think more about what we talked about?" she said.

"About meeting your friend?"

"Uh huh."

"Not really. I've got a lot of other things on my mind. Are Thomas and Tenzin here?"

"Hold on a minute. I've got something to show you." Clare rummaged through her purse. "God, I've got to get this thing organized." She finally gave up and dumped the contents on the desk. "Here it is," she said, handing David a photo.

David's jaw fell open when he saw the face in the photo. The woman smiling at him was beyond beautiful. She was angelic. "Is she as good as she looks?"

Clare smiled triumphantly. "Better."

David shook his head. "I'm not in her league. She could have anyone she wants. Why bother with me?"

Clare rolled her eyes and shook her head. "Because I told her about you. Men have no idea how difficult beauty can be for a woman. Every psychopathic predator in the world hits on you, and the ones that you want to meet are often too shy to try. She wants to meet you. Don't you dare blow it. Here's her number. Call her."

"She knows my situation?"

"She knows everything."

"And she still wants to meet me?"

"How many times do I have to answer that stupid question?" she said.

"Sorry," said David sheepishly.

"Look," said Clare. "Annie's very perceptive. She'll see who you are right away. Just be yourself. Now go away. They're waiting for you in the kitchen and I've got work to do." God, she muttered to herself, he can be such a pain in the ass. But he is so damn irresistible. Annie is going to love him. His ex-wife was an idiot to let him go.

Thomas was sitting at the kitchen table, his notebooks open in front of him. Files were scattered around the table. He was scribbling furiously on the margins of a yellow legal pad when David entered the room.

"What's all this?" asked David.

Thomas looked up. "Want some tea?"

"No thanks."

"I suggest you get some anyway. We've got a lot of ground to cover. You'll need it."

"Okay," David said. He got his tea and sat down at the table.

"First, let me summarize a few major points from our last conversation. They're important to keep in mind. All mind-control programming has a sexual basis. They use repeated rapes to fracture the mind. It starts when children are very young."

"How young?"

"Sometimes just a few months old. Sometimes a few years old. Sometimes it starts in the womb. They have techniques by which they can attach a demonic entity to a fetus in the womb. They call that one Moon Child programming. Your ex may be a victim of it."

"That's appalling."

"It certainly is. Sexual trauma opens the sex chakra at the base of the spine. When the sexual center is open, it creates a direct pathway to the mind. An overly stimulated and opened sex chakra is bright red. A normal sexual center is a pale red. The Illuminati want to keep everyone's sexual center open and constantly aroused. That's why they use sexual images to sell everything. They created the sexual revolution and put drugs on the street to encourage deviant behavior. Drugs make it easier to install programming in the mind, and keep it operational. If people are drugged, and in a state of constant sexual arousal, they are easy to control. Think any of this keeps a culture strong and healthy?"

"Obviously not."

"If you can turn women against men and portray marriage as undesirable to today's liberated woman, it's just a matter of time until the culture is bankrupt and the country destroyed. In the coming decades, pornography and promiscuity will replace love, commitment, and fidelity. You can see it happening already. The divorce rate will accelerate. The goal is to subvert the family, destroy its role as a support system, and make the individual dependent on the state. That's ultimate control and an essential tenet of Communism."

"I can't imagine all that happening. A Communist takeover in America? C'mon."

"Communism has been here for a long time. It's just hidden. From what I've read, Roosevelt's administration was infiltrated with communists."

"That's not possible. Roosevelt was a great President."

"FDR was a 33rd degree Mason and an Illuminist. The Delanos were his mother's family. They made their fortune in the opium trade in China, a favorite Illuminati business. In 1933 Roosevelt declared America a bankrupt corporation and handed our paper over to the international banking cartel in the City of London. America is a free and sovereign country in name only."

"That's ridiculous."

"Why? Because you can't accept it? Remember our operating principle. Nothing is what it seems. Don't forget what we talked about yesterday. These boys move slowly, one small step at a time, but they never stop moving toward their goal. We adapt to the changes they introduce with little or no resistance, never connecting the dots and seeing where we're headed. This stuff doesn't just happen. It's planned. War, cultural upheaval, the assault on the family, the growing conflict between men and women, drugs, all of it. It's called social engineering. It won't be long before America is overwhelmed with debt and the most enduring contribution of our educational system is illiteracy."

"That's much too pessimistic. We're the richest country on earth and our universities are the envy of the rest of the world."

"For how long?"

David didn't reply. What if Thomas was right? A chill slithered down his spine.

"If we know their agenda," Thomas continued, "we can fight it. There's a hell of a lot more of us than them. Emily woke me up, and I'm not going back to sleep. You either wrap yourself in the illusion that all is well in the world or you face the cold hard truth. I've made my choice."

"That's obvious."

"Now let's get back to your ex," said Thomas. "We've taken enough of a detour for now." He opened another file. His bifocals slipped down the bridge of his nose while he scanned the pages. "Here's a list of some of the major attributes of cult programming."

"What are they?"

"People with cult programming gravitate toward groups with authoritarian leaders. They give total obedience to the leader; they lack an independent will and the ability to think critically; they separate themselves from friends and family; they adopt the cult lingo; the cult becomes their new family. They are generally meek, but become hostile when challenged. They are passive-aggressive, usually unemotional and robotic. Their eyes are glazed as if they're entranced."

"Sarah has all those traits," said David. "But what you've described also seems to be the goal the Illuminati have for all of us."

"It is. Cult programming is a specific application of their larger programming goals."

David looked down. "Months before she left me, Sarah said that she felt lost in my shadow and had to find herself."

"She wasn't lost in your shadow," said Thomas. "She was lost in her own. Remember, highly programmed people never take responsibility for their problems, particularly those with monarch programming. They always blame others. They are archetypal victims."

"When she first connected with the cult leader she went to visit her in L.A. for a couple of weeks to find herself. Her visit turned into a few months."

"She left her son for all that time?"

"Yeah. He felt abandoned. His pre-school teachers were worried about him. He always wanted to sit in their laps."

"How old was he?"

"Four."

Thomas frowned and shook his head, remembering the loneliness of his own childhood.

"When she returned, she had a book of photos that Rayanne and her followers had given her. It had pictures of the cult members and their frequent parties. They had all written sweet things about her, urging her to come back to L.A. and live with them. She took that book everywhere she went and shared it with friends and colleagues. That book was her bible and the cult in Malibu was her new family. From then on, she treated me with contempt. In her mind, I was beneath her. She was now the superior being. I think that's what she was really after."

"If that's not cult programming," said Thomas, "then what is?"

"But she's not unemotional. She flies into a rage whenever she doesn't get what she wants."

Thomas nodded and tapped his index finger on the page. "Hostile when challenged. How does she act otherwise?"

"Emotionally shut down, sort of robot-like. Her eyes have a glazed look. She can be nice on the surface and fool everyone. But go down a level and you'll find a sociopath waiting to attack and destroy."

"There it is then."

"She's an entirely different person since she's come under Rayanne's spell. I don't recognize her at all. When we were together we had a dog, four cats and horses. She doted on them all. After she met Rayanne she abandoned them, just as she abandoned me. She didn't care about her family, her home, her responsibilities, anything to do with her former life. All that mattered was her new "family" and doing whatever Rayanne told her to do. She exists to serve her, not to raise Michael. His needs are secondary, at best."

Strong hands rested unexpectedly on David's shoulders.

"Hi Tenzin," said David without turning his head.

"Shall we do a little emotional work?"

The heat pouring out of Tenzin's hands made his chest ache. Every time Tenzin touched him it seemed that he returned to his grief. How was that possible? He had been fine seconds ago.

The pain in his heart suddenly cut deeper. His eyelids fluttered. His arms and legs trembled. A moment later, a terrifying wail rose from the depths of his soul.

Clare turned her head toward the corridor and gasped. She wanted to run down the corridor and come to David's aid, but resisted her impulse. Tenzin knew what he was doing. She herself had screamed like that when she had relived her past life rape and murder. David would be fine, she told herself, actually better than fine, once he had gotten through this.

The kindness and warmth in David's nature drew people to him, and Clare was no exception. The mother in her wanted to protect him, but she was smart enough to know that that's exactly what he didn't need. He needed to be opened and raw so he could feel and release his grief. She picked up Three and held him to her breast while he slept, peacefully unaware of the commotion down the hall or the turmoil in his mother's heart.

CHAPTER 49

The Mala

AT BREAKFAST ON Saturday morning, David told Michael that they were going to meet new friends that afternoon. Michael had been happily wolfing down his buckwheat and blueberry pancakes drenched in real maple syrup, the special breakfast that his father made for him only on weekends. During the school week it was always the same boring eggs and toast. He took a sip of juice to clear his throat, then looked over at his father.

"No way, Dad," Michael said. "I'm gonna play with Marie and Zack today."

"Just give it a chance. You'll have fun. If not, we'll leave early. Promise."

"That's not fair, Daddy. I only get to be with my friends every other weekend. I'm not here every day like you are."

"You're the guest of honor, Michael. They're all looking forward to meeting you."

"I don't care."

"They have two boys who love soccer."

"It won't be only boring adults?"

"Not at all."

"We'll leave early if I don't like it?"

"Yep."

"Promise?"

"Promise."

That afternoon, Michael clung to his father's hand as they walked up the drive to the center. He still wasn't sure about this and he really didn't want to meet new people. His life hadn't been the same since his mother had dragged him to Los Angeles to live with all those strange people. People came and went from the big house in Malibu all the time. There was always some new stranger to whom he had to be nice. And they were all weird. He hated it, and he hated what Rayanne had done to his mother. He wanted to go to bed in his own room in his own home with both of his parents happily together. He wanted his mother to be a good mother again. But he was smart enough to know that this would never happen. Even at his young age, Michael had learned that most dreams die disappointing deaths.

"What do you think of this place?" said David. "Pretty neat, huh?"

"It's okay, I guess," said Michael.

At that moment, two boys burst through the front door. Each had tousled hair, copper skin, and green eyes. The taller of the two was slight, but built to be as swift and agile as a deer. The shorter one was stocky and muscled.

"Give me the ball, Danny!" screamed Matthew, the taller of the two boys.

"No way!"

"It's mine!"

"Then take it," said Danny, pausing to torment his brother. "If you can!"

Matthew reached in to punch the ball out of his brother's hands. Danny turned away to protect it. They abruptly halted when they saw Michael and David. Danny stared at Michael.

"Can you play?" said Danny. It was more of a challenge than a question.

Michael nodded.

"Prove it," said Danny. He dropped the ball and kicked it at Michael. Michael dropped his father's hand, let the ball bounce off his chest and trapped it with his feet. He looked at his target, gauged the distance, and kicked the ball back. The ball curled swiftly toward its target, low, hard, and heavy with back spin. Danny trapped it against his chest, but the velocity and spin on the ball stung him.

"Where'd you learn to do that?" he asked. Michael's power and skill shocked him.

Michael shrugged.

"You're left-footed," said Matthew, missing nothing. "What's your name?"

"Michael."

"I'm Matthew. That jerk you just kicked my ball to is Danny."

"Shut up, Matthew. You're the jerk."

"No I'm not!"

Danny turned away from his brother, ignoring him. "You wanna play with us, Michael? We're meeting some buddies at the park. You can be on my team."

"Danny's not really my brother," said Matthew. "He's adopted."

Michael laughed. They obviously had the same parents.

"Our Dad told us you were coming," said Danny. "We've been waiting to see if you were as good as he said you are. He says some pretty weird stuff. We think he's nuts most of the time."

"I don't think he's nuts!" said Matthew. "Don't listen to him, Michael. Our dad's awesome."

Danny rolled his eyes and smirked at his younger brother. "You coming? We're going to be late if we don't get going."

"Can I, Dad?" Michael asked.

"Sure."

A big smile creased Michael's face. The three boys turned in unison and ran past him, racing down the drive before disappearing behind the yellow stucco wall bordering the property.

David shook his head. Well, that sure was fast. One minute Michael's begging to stay home. The next he's best buddies with kids older than him. Go figure.

Alice was tidying up the reception desk when he entered. "I thought you were bringing Michael," she said.

"I did."

"Then where is he?"

"With your boys."

"Danny let him go with them?" she asked.

"Danny invited him."

She closed the log book. "Well, I'll be. Michael must be very talented. Danny's a big star, at least in his mind. He leads his league in scoring. He's at that age where girls call him all the time. He thinks he's Don Juan. It's gone to his head. I can't stand it."

"It'll pass. And believe it or not, it'll do him more good than harm. Boys need to know that they're attractive, just like girls do."

"Thanks for saying that. I worry about him. Matthew is sensitive and thoughtful. There's more of his father in him. Danny's a steamroller. He's a lot to handle."

David smiled. "I wouldn't worry about it. Danny will turn out just fine. He's got great parents as role models."

Alice smiled. "I hope you're right. Charlie's here today. He's looking forward to meeting you. He's upstairs studying, but he'll be down soon. Tenzin and Thomas are in the kitchen. Clare's out. She'll be home a little later. She can't wait to meet your son."

"Alright then," said David, turning to go into the kitchen to see Tenzin and Thomas.

"David," said Alice, stopping him in his tracks.

"Yeah?"

"Clare's spoken for."

"I'm well aware of that," said David, a puzzled look on his face. "She has a friend she wants me to meet."

"There's energy between the two of you. I know that Clare likes you and wants to help. Just don't misinterpret her kindness. Men hunt beauty like rabid wolves. Clare had some bad experiences while Charlie was in Vietnam. That's why I'm surprised she's been as open with you as she has."

"Don't worry. I've got enough to deal with," said David. "I have no romantic interest in Clare or anyone else."

"You do have a lot on your plate. That's for sure."

"Beauty is a double-edged sword, Alice. It cuts both ways. My ex is also beautiful. But she uses her beauty as a weapon. There are predatory men who hunt beauty, but there are also predatory women who use their beauty to hurt and destroy."

"Point well taken," said Alice. "I suppose I'm overreacting. God knows, it wouldn't be the first time. I'm just protective of everyone here. That includes you, by the way. You've become part of our family and it's important to me that my family is harmonious and happy. I hope you understand that. I'm just being a big old mama bear."

"No offense taken, big mama," said David. "It's an honor to be considered part of your family."

But as he walked toward the kitchen another line of thought entered his mind, one he couldn't easily dismiss. Ever since this nightmare began, every woman he met seemed to question his motives. Why? It had never happened before. It didn't matter if the women were in the dark or in the light; if they were evil or good; if they were loving or hateful. Was his experience an isolated event, or were all men subjected to endless suspicion? Was this a new development in the culture or was it an issue as old as time? One thing he knew for certain: anger and hostility distort everything. Solutions become impossible to find, and if found, impossible to implement. Angry women were unhappy women and unhappy men were angry men. What better way to destroy a country than to pit its men against its women?

Families were being torn apart. Children were growing up depressed and emotionally stunted. Over time, more and more people would end up isolated and alone. Lonely people without a family to sustain and support them were easy to control. Thomas was absolutely right. The only winner would be the New World Order. The country's future was in peril and no one knew it. America was slipping away, drip by drip. An irrevocable slide into darkness was under way, imperceptible to most, but obvious to those whose eyes had been opened. It was only a matter of time before isolated events coalesced into a toxic tide that would submerge everyone and everything. No wonder Thomas was so focused and serious. The search for the truth was a lonely occupation. He opened the door and entered the kitchen.

"Why the long face?" asked Tenzin. He was enjoying a cup of tea and a good laugh with Thomas.

"You look like you saw a ghost," said Thomas, grinning.

"It's that obvious?"

"Yeah," they answered together.

"I saw the future."

"Ah," said Thomas, understanding at once where David was. "Turns your world upside down, doesn't it? Don't worry. You'll adjust. In the end, the truth will make you stronger."

"Maybe so. But I've already got a long, hard road ahead of me. I hardly needed another."

"You have to face what's confronting you," said Tenzin. "There's no other way. In your case the personal and the political are woven from the same cloth."

"Lucky me," said David. "Is any place on earth really free?"

Thomas shook his head. "There are only places where the illusion of freedom persists."

"That's what I thought."

"Freedom is in your mind, David. That's the only place it really exists."

"But what about all the evil in the world?"

"Liberate the Self. The rest will follow."

"What good will liberating my Self do if the powers of darkness control the world?"

"Light cures darkness," said Tenzin. "People want freedom. Nobody wants to live in fear and terror. One day a great spiritual awakening will come to the world. Humanity will see the great deception and overthrow its oppressors."

"That's hard to believe. The masses are easily manipulated. They want security, not freedom. Scare them enough and they'll give up their freedom for a false security that enslaves them more. If I hadn't met you, I'd still believe what the media told me to believe. I'd still believe what the government says. I'd believe we live in a representative democracy. I'd believe we're the freest country in the world. Now I know none of that's true. It's a bitter pill to swallow."

"Be patient. Change will come. The light will prevail. There are many who will come after us, Michael among them. Where is he, by the way? I thought you were bringing him with you."

"He's gone with Danny and Matthew."

The kitchen door creaked open. Charlie walked in, face unshaven, hair askew, eyes blurry and unfocused. He massaged his temples with his fingertips.

"How's the studying, Charlie?" said Thomas.

"Organic chemistry is impossible. I'll never get it."

"A familiar complaint."

"I don't think I'm cut out to be a doctor."

"Organic chemistry is the curse of premeds," said Thomas. "Persevere. You'll get it."

"Charlie, say hello to David," said Tenzin.

"Sorry, man. I didn't mean to ignore you. Clare's told me all about you. Sorry about the divorce and all that. How you doin'?"

"I've been better. But organic chemistry is easier than going through a nasty divorce and dealing with a cult full of crazies. Be thankful for what you have."

"You've got a point there," said Charlie. He smiled for the first time since he entered the kitchen and offered his hand. The two young men shook hands.

"You've got a great wife and kid," said David. "That was me, once upon a time."

"Man, I couldn't deal if Clare left me and took Three, I know that."

"If the war didn't destroy you, nothing will," said David.

"Believe me, if anything happened to Clare or Three, that would kill me. They're my life, man."

"I hear you. I'd like my life back, but that's not going to happen."

Charlie stared directly into David's face, his piercing blue eyes now clear as the cloudless sky. "I've got a feeling about you, man."

"What's that?" asked David.

"One day your life's going to be better than ever. Just hang in there and do whatever Tenzin says. I wouldn't be here without him. I wouldn't be with Clare without him. And I wouldn't be going to med school without him. The only thing I did without him was make Clare pregnant."

Everyone laughed.

"Glad you could do something by yourself, Charlie," Thomas said.

The door creaked open again. This time, Alice entered the kitchen.

"Tenzin, when are you going to oil the hinges on that door?"

"Soon."

"That's what you always say," said Alice. "I see you two have finally met."

"Yep," said Charlie. "I'll oil the hinges tomorrow for you, Alice. Do you know where Clare is?"

"Thanks Charlie. That'd be just great. Tenzin's useless around the house. Clare said to start without her. She had to go out for a bit. Tenzin, get the salad and cold cuts out of the fridge, will you. I'll heat the soup."

"Are we eating without the boys?" asked Tenzin.

"They'll be back when they're hungry. I don't expect that will be very long, do you?"

Tenzin laughed. "I'll get the salad."

"Thomas, would you set the table, please?"

"Sure."

They had just sat down at the kitchen room table when the boys charged in, sweaty and in high spirits.

"Hi Mom, we're starving," Danny bellowed.

"Wash your hands."

"But Mom," Danny said.

"Don't argue with me, young man."

The boys rushed out of the kitchen and returned a minute later with dripping hands.

Danny raised his hands. "See," he said.

"Very nice," said Alice.

Matthew and Danny took their usual seats. Michael sat between his father and Tenzin.

"How was your game?" said Tenzin. The boys ripped into their sandwiches.

"Good," said Matthew. Danny was too busy eating his dinner to bother replying.

"Michael?" asked David.

"Good," he said. Like the other boys he was too engrossed in eating his food to bother with the adults.

Tenzin leaned back in his chair, a broad smile on his face. His eyes gleamed with satisfaction. Alice ate slowly, observing the scene around the table. The energy in the kitchen pulsed with possibility. Something big's about to happen, she thought. I can feel it.

"What's for dessert, Mom?" Danny asked.

"Clare baked chocolate chip cookies this morning."

"Her's are the best!" said Danny. He was up in a flash, followed by Matthew and Michael.

"You better not eat them all, Danny," Matthew screamed.

Danny ignored his brother. He pulled the cloth napkin off the plate of cookies and helped himself to several. Fortunately, Clare had anticipated the frenzy her cookies would create and had made an extra-large batch. Matthew followed on his brother's heels and grabbed a bunch of his own. Michael was more restrained. He looked over at his father before taking his share.

"Dad?"

"Go ahead. Just save some for the rest of us."

Michael selected a handful and returned to the table. Tenzin poured each of the boys a glass of milk.

"You can't eat cookies without a glass of cold milk," he said. He rubbed Michael's head affectionately. When Tenzin touched his head, Michael's mind began to buzz, faintly at first, then the sound grew much louder, like the roar of waves crashing on the shore. He looked at Tenzin with eyes full of wonder. Tenzin returned Michael's gaze with a smile.

When Tenzin smiled, a vision appeared in Michael's mind. He was in a stone building high in the mountains. Strong winds blew across a bleak landscape of sand and stones. Only an occasional bush or a lonely tree punctuated the barren terrain. He sat behind a wooden desk, an older man with a bald head and wire-rimmed glasses. A boy, not much older than he, stood before him. Then the vision faded as quickly as it had come. Michael shook his head and bit into his cookie. The sweet taste of chocolate anchored him in this time and place, at the kitchen table with his new friends.

"How do you like the cookies, Michael?" asked Tenzin.

"Good."

"How was your game, Danny?"

"Good."

"I'm glad you let Michael play."

"He's really good, Dad."

"What did your friends think about playing with someone much younger than them?"

"Michael's better than all of 'em. They had nothing to say."

"Is that true, Matthew?"

"Uh huh."

"I have a surprise," Tenzin said. "I'll be right back."

Tenzin returned shortly with a dark wooden jewelry box. He took out two exquisite turquoise and silver bracelets and put them on the table. Then he removed the worn mala that he wore around his neck. He laid it on the table between the two bracelets.

"Michael, please take one of these. Whichever one you choose is yours."

"Tenzin, that's way too generous," David said. "You've given us so much already."

Tenzin waved him off. "Choose, Michael."

Michael studied the objects in front of him. Everyone was silent, their eyes focussed on him, waiting to see which one he would choose. His hand had just begun to inch forward when the sounds of feet beyond the kitchen door broke his concentration. A second later the door creaked opened and Clare walked in. She was not alone.

"Are we interrupting something important?" she asked.

"Your timing couldn't be worse," said Charlie.

David could not take his eyes off the woman with Clare. She was far more beautiful in person than in her picture. Her radiance and warmth exceeded what any camera could capture. Beyond her obvious beauty, there was something nebulous he couldn't define; a feeling that seemed to connect them in ways he didn't understand. A stream of sweat trickled down his spine. He turned away, overwhelmed by what he felt. It was too much, too soon.

Annie felt him withdraw his energy and wondered if she had done something wrong. He was a lovely looking man and she felt herself attracted to him as soon as she saw him. She was sure that he felt the same way. Had she been mistaken? She did her best to hide her disappointment, but Clare wasn't fooled. She touched Annie's forearm.

"Don't worry," she whispered. "He'll come around." Annie nodded bravely, but her confidence had been shaken.

"Which one do you want, Michael?" Tenzin asked Michael again, bringing everyone's focus back to Michael and the drama surrounding his decision.

This time Michael didn't hesitate. He seized the mala, kissed it, and put it around his neck. A collective gasp rose from the table. Everyone but Tenzin was stunned.

"Why did you choose the mala, Michael?" asked Alice. "The bracelets are far more beautiful."

"Because it's mine," he said without hesitation.

A broad smile illuminated Tenzin's face. Light shone from his eyes.

"What do you mean "it's yours", Michael?" David said.

"Is he saying what I think he's saying?" said Thomas.

Tenzin nodded. "When I left Tibet, Doezen gave me his mala. In all the years since then, I've never taken it off. The time has finally come to return it to its rightful owner."

"Michael is the incarnation of Doezen?" said David. His mouth hung open.

"I'll be," said Alice. Her eyes filled with tears.

Everyone was silent, even Danny.

"Do you remember anything from your last life?" Tenzin asked Michael.

"A room in a stone building," he said. "You were young. And I was old. I was sitting at a desk."

"I remember that moment as if it were yesterday," said Tenzin. "Do you remember how you died?"

A sudden pain in Michael's chest caused him to double over. Disturbing images flashed through his mind. Soldiers. A stone wall. Raised rifles. The flash of gunfire. A sudden silence, then stillness. Rising rapidly out of his body. Moving at great speed through a tunnel of light. Ecstasy at the other end.

Michael nodded. "I was shot," he said. "By the Chinese."

Tenzin embraced Michael. There were no dry eyes in the room.

David's head was swimming. The revelations were overwhelming. Michael was the incarnation of an enlightened master? Tenzin and Michael had been brothers in another life? Michael had been Tenzin's teacher? How do I deal with that along with everything else? He rose and left the kitchen. He needed time to think it through. He collapsed on a sofa in the living room, leaned his head back and closed his eyes, his forehead throbbing.

The afternoon shadows grew longer. How long he had sat there by himself, he didn't know. He felt someone sit down next to him. A soft hand rested atop his. It was warm and comforting. He opened his eyes to see Annie looking at him.

"A lot to handle, isn't it?" she said.

David tried to answer, but he couldn't speak. The next thing he knew, he was sobbing in her arms. She held his head against her breast and stroked his hair. It was dark and thick and wavy. She loved the feel of it and the smell of him.

When he regained a measure of control, he sat up and wiped his eyes. What a beginning, he thought. I'm pathetic.

"Sorry," he said. "I don't know what happened."

"You've had a big shock. Better a good cry than a stroke."

"That's all I ever seem to do whenever I'm around Tenzin."

"Everyone cries around him. We're all wounded. His light releases our pain," said Annie.

"You too?" said David.

"Sure."

"I'm certain you've got better things to do than wasting your time watching me cry," he said. He had a hard time facing her.

"Why would you say that?" She hadn't expected to be rejected so soon again.

"My life's a mess."

"So what? It happens to everyone sooner or later."

"You want to stay here after my display of weakness?"

"No. Because of it."

"Why?" It was David's turn to be shocked.

"It takes courage to be vulnerable. Most people can't do it." She pressed her soft hand to his cheek. "Particularly, men."

"I never thought of it like that."

Annie leaned over and kissed him on the cheek. "We should go back in. They'll be wondering what happened to us."

"You're beautiful," he said. The words slipped out before he even knew he was speaking.

Annie blushed. "Thank you."

"I'd like to see you again," said David.

"I was hoping you'd ask me that."

When they returned to the kitchen, Michael was sitting in Alice's lap. Clare was clearing the table. She looked over at Annie, a question in her eyes. Annie smiled. Clare picked up another plate and allowed herself a faint smile. She had been right about these two. Michael jumped out of Alice's lap when his Dad walked in. He ran to him and wrapped his arms around his waist.

"Where were you Daddy? I missed you."

"In the living room."

"I want to go home now. I'm tired."

"Me, too."

On the way home, a crowd had gathered on the corner of Wilshire and 13th St.. Sirens were blaring. An ambulance and several police cars were parked by the curb.

"Stop, Dad."

"The police are taking care of it, Michael."

"No, Dad. Stop. Please."

"Okay." David slowed the van and pulled over. Michael shot out the door before they had stopped. By the time David located him, Michael had wormed his way through the large crowd and was standing next to an older woman laying on a stretcher. She was unconscious, her face gray. She wasn't breathing. Two emergency medical techs worked furiously on her. An oxygen mask covered her nose.

"What do you think, Bill?" said one of the techs.

"Not good, partner," said Bill, shaking his head.

"She ain't gonna make it, is she?"

"Let's give it our best shot, anyway. I don't wanna go to bed thinking I didn't do everything I could to save her. It could be our moms laying there, for chrissakes."

"Yeah."

Despite the cool evening, their brows were covered with sweat. Michael watched the unfolding drama like a hawk, looking for the moment to strike. When one of the techs went to the emergency vehicle for more equipment, Michael seized his chance. He reached out and touched the woman's left hand. The contact was brief, but long enough to allow a burst of gold light to leap from his hand to hers. Almost immediately, the woman's energy field began to glow. David saw it, but no one else seemed to notice. No one noticed Michael's presence either. Strange, thought David. With his mission accomplished, Michael slipped back into the crowd. The woman groaned then coughed several times and opened her eyes. The two EMT's stared at one another in amazement.

"Damn!"

"I could swear she was done for."

"Me too. Hell, you never know what's going to happen in this job."

They wiped the sweat from their foreheads.

A moment later, Michael climbed back into the van. "Let's go, Dad."

"How did you do that, Michael? That was amazing."

"I don't know. I just did it. Let's go, Dad. I'm really tired."

Michael fell asleep as soon as his head hit the pillow, but not David. He tossed and turned for a long time. The ground had opened under his feet several more times tonight. Nothing in his life was stable, that was certain. What would happen when Rayanne found out who Michael really was? She would. He was sure of it. He couldn't keep something like this from her for long. The mala would be a giveaway. Was Michael in even greater danger now?

And what about Annie? What was going to happen between them? Would it be a good thing, or the start of another nightmare? His relationship with Sarah had started on a high note, and look where that had gone. Everything in his life was a question. There were no answers.

CHAPTER 50

The Lord's Prayer

The world will not be saved by acts of God but by acts of men representing God.
Henry Makow

LATE THAT NIGHT, Tenzin and Alice lay in bed enjoying a few precious minutes of privacy.

"How does it feel to have your teacher back?" asked Alice. "Even if this time he's a little American boy with blond hair and blue eyes?"

"The body doesn't matter," said Tenzin. "The fact that his soul has returned does. But I'm worried. I'd be lying if I said I weren't."

"Why?" said Alice.

"The evil pursuing Michael and David will stop at nothing to achieve its ends. It's organized, disciplined, and relentless."

"Michael is a beautiful boy. Rayanne and Sarah would never hurt him."

"Rayanne and Sarah are the least of our problems."

"What do you mean?"

"Rayanne and Sarah opened their souls to the dark power in the astral plane, invited it into their bodies and allowed it to possess them. Non-physical evil like that is difficult to defeat. That's the real problem."

"But you know how to defeat evil. And you're teaching David, too."

"We're not just facing vicious people. This evil isn't human. You can't kill it with bullets or put it in prison. Few people understand it. Even fewer have the eyes to see it. Most people think it only exists in movies. The dark power uses disturbed, dysfunctional people with an axe to grind, to serve its ends. Psychopathic personalities like Rayanne are a perfect fit for it. People like her have little empathy for others. They enjoy inflicting pain. She has remade Sarah in her image. David's ex is a chameleon without a core self. That's an indication of a highly programmed person. She becomes whatever she attaches herself to. She's putty in Rayanne's hands."

"Are you saying that David's ex is a clone of the cult leader?"

"Exactly," said Tenzin.

"That's awful. I feel so badly for Michael that he has to be subjected to that."

"Did you know that the same dark power that controls Rayanne once controlled Hitler?"

"What? Are you sure?"

"I'm very sure. The dark power is a huge octopus. Its tentacles reach into every dimension of life and every part of this planet. Humanity writhes in its clutches without knowing it. Evil is the plague that never ends. Even though the Nazis were destroyed, the evil behind Nazism wasn't. It's still here. It never left. We have to find a way to stop it, so that what happened to Doezen in Tibet won't happen to him here. The Light must prevail on this planet. There will be no freedom without it. Politics and spirituality are crucially linked."

Alice reached out and touched her husband's arm. "You'll find a way to protect Michael."

"It depends more on David now than it does on me."

"You've prepared him well. He'll be ready."

"I've done my best. I hope it's enough."

"It will be. You never lose."

"I lost everything once, remember? In one day, the Chinese took my whole life away from me."

"Yes, but you built a new one, found me, and are raising a family. You've changed the lives of thousands of people you never would have met otherwise. In trying to destroy you, the evil brought you out of obscurity and put you before the world."

"That was not its intention."

"No, Tenzin. That was your intention. The light inside you was stronger than the darkness chasing you. It will be that way for David and Michael, too. You'll see."

"I hope you're right. David is only beginning to come into his power and discover who he is. He was once a great warrior king. Michael is very young. His soul will flash on from time to time, but his physical vehicle has to mature. He must gather important life experience before his wisdom and spiritual power will be consistently available to him. They are most vulnerable at present. The evil knows that now is its best chance to strike."

"But you have leveled the playing field."

"Only to a degree."

"David's a fast learner. Something inside him is unbreakable, despite what he has been through. He will stop at nothing to save his son. That little boy is precious. I know you'll do everything in your power to protect them both."

"That goes without saying."

"It will end differently this time."

"I hope so. But I also know what we're facing. People die. Evil doesn't. It moves on to other willing hosts and sows trouble elsewhere. Its goal is to keep conflict and hatred eternally alive. Its intent is to block humanity from ever finding peace and realizing its spiritual potential. Fear is it's greatest weapon. It has always been that way in this world."

"I know. But that cycle is weakening. One day, the light will shine in people's minds. Love will replace fear. Humanity will no longer be unwitting victims. The dark power will have no more access here."

"That kind of transformation takes a long time."

"I know," Alice whispered. She kissed him softly on the cheek. "We're the pioneers. But one day others will take the torch and follow your example. Look to that time. You've always been a champion of the Light. You always will be. You've been my hero from the first moment I saw you. You'll find a way to save your teacher and prepare your friend. The evil won't take Michael this time. There must be others who know what you know. We can't be alone."

"There are a few with the knowledge scattered here and there. Not enough for us to change the tide. Not yet. You're right about the future, though. One day a critical mass of humanity will wake to the danger. Then there will be a huge outcry, a great awakening, and a worldwide movement toward the Light. The satanic cabal that controls the world will be exposed, and those who do its bidding will be flushed from their lairs and held accountable."

"When will that be?"

"When?" Tenzin grew silent as he pondered the question, his mind flowing easily down the corridors of time, sifting through future time lines and alternate realities. "When Michael is in the White House."

Alice's eyes bulged. Her jaw went slack. "Michael? President? But, he's just a boy."

"An awakening people need an awakened leader."

"You're not serious."

"I'm very serious. But first, David must win this war. The future will be very different if he fails."

Alice shuddered. "Then I will pray for his success."

"The fate of the world is riding on his shoulders. But David must not know that. It's too big a burden for anyone to bear. You must say nothing about it to anyone, even Thomas."

"Of course not. When is David bringing Michael back?"

"Thursday, for dinner."

"But you have class that night."

"Exactly."

The next morning, Clare and Alice lingered in the kitchen over coffee. Three slept soundly in his stroller next to Clare.

"What did you think of Michael?" asked Clare.

"He's precious," said Alice.

"He's the most beautiful boy I've ever seen," said Clare.

Alice laughed. "More beautiful than Three?"

"He's older. His features are more fully formed."

"True."

"Do you really think he's the incarnation of Doezen?" asked Clare.

"Tenzin thinks so."

"Do you think Tenzin can be objective when it comes to Doezen? Maybe he wants it too much," said Clare.

"Did you know that Michael saved a woman's life last night?"

"What do you mean?" said Clare.

"Last night, David and Michael drove by an auto accident on the way home. Michael insisted on stopping. When David pulled over, Michael raced out of the car and resuscitated an older woman who had suffered a heart attack and wasn't breathing."

"How'd he do that?"

"He touched her."

"He touched her?" Clare's eyes were wide as saucers.

"David said he saw a burst of gold light shoot out from Michael's hand when he touched her. The woman's energy field began to glow right away. She coughed and started breathing a moment later."

Clare took a sip of her tea. "Maybe he really is Doezen."

"It's something Doezen would do. I've rarely known Tenzin to be wrong. Have you?"

"Never. But you've known him longer than I have."

"In all the years we've been together I can count on three fingers the times that he's been wrong."

"That's impressive."

"What did Annie think of David?" said Alice. "She followed him into the living room. They were gone quite a while."

"She likes him."

"I'm not surprised."

"You're not?"

"You were falling for him."

Clare blushed. "Was it that obvious?"

"That young man has a lot of power and charisma. That combination draws women like the light on the porch draws moths. You were coming unglued around him."

"But I never would have allowed anything to happen," said Clare. She was mortified that Alice had guessed her secret.

"Self-restraint separates the wise woman from the foolish one. You're nobody's fool, Clare. And don't worry about having a crush on someone now and then. It happens."

"Have you had crushes on anyone since you've been married?"

Alice laughed. "I've only had one hero and I married him."

"You're so lucky."

"So are you. But being lucky doesn't mean it's easy, does it? Every marriage has its challenges. I've had to be Tenzin's gatekeeper. Everybody wants something from him. I'm the one who has to say no. It's not enjoyable. I protect him as best I can, but he still works too hard. I worry about the strain on him. It's taken a big toll. And look what you had to go through with Charlie, not hearing from him or knowing if he was alive or dead for over a year."

"Or if he still loved me. Without you and Tenzin, there'd be no me and Charlie. I'd be alone and unlucky. You're my hero."

Clare reached over to hug Alice.

"And you're the daughter I never had."

On Thursday evening, David brought Michael to dinner at the center. This time, Michael was eager to go.

"Do you think there'll be enough light to play soccer after supper, Dad?"

"Should be."

"Will you come and watch?"

"Sure."

"Danny said I can be on his team."

"That's great."

"His friends suck, Dad."

"They're older than you. They must be bigger and faster."

"Yeah, but they don't have any ball skills. That soccer camp you sent me to really helped. I got to play with college guys. They taught me a lot."

"I'm glad you liked it."

"That's where I learned to use both feet. None of Danny's friends can."

Michael sat with Danny and Matthew at dinner. The boys wolfed down their food, intent on getting out of the house as soon as they could.

"I understand you saved a woman's life the other night, Michael," said Alice.

"Uh huh," said Michael as he swallowed a big bite of spaghetti and meatballs. "Your meatballs are really good."

"I'm glad you like them," said Alice, smiling.

"Can we be excused, Mom?" asked Danny.

"Are you done?"

"Yep," the three boys answered in unison.

Alice sighed. "Go ahead then."

"Let's go guys," Danny shouted. The boys charged out the kitchen door.

"Not so fast," said Tenzin, breaking their charge. "Be back by seven. Matthew, remember?"

"Sure, Dad," said Matthew. "Seven. I won't forget. Don't worry."

"Not a minute later or you'll both be grounded this weekend."

"But I have a big game on Saturday," said Danny.

"Then make sure you're not late."

"Oh, okay," said Danny. "Let's go. We've only got an hour."

"You'll stay for class tonight?" Tenzin asked David.

"I'd like to, but I've got to get Michael bathed and in bed. He's got school tomorrow."

"Class won't go late."

"Don't you think Michael's a bit young for that?"

"Matthew and Danny will be there."

"That's nice, but Michael needs his sleep."

"Annie's coming," said Clare.

"Well," David said, trying not to show his excitement, "I guess we could stay for a little while."

Everybody laughed. David's face turned bright red.

"I wish I could come, but I've got to study," sighed Charlie.

"Take Three with you," said Clare. "I'm going to class."

"But I won't get anything done."

"Three's tired. He'll go right to sleep."

"He never sleeps when he's with me," said Charlie. "He'll cry the whole time."

"Then hold him until he falls asleep. Some bonding time will be good for both of you."

"C'mon, Clare," said Charlie. "This is about our future. Organic chemistry is hard enough without having diaper duty, too."

"No. You c'mon, Charlie. Three is our future. Don't you care about your son?"

"That's not fair. You know I do."

Clare stared hard at him. "Charlie."

Charlie sighed. He knew when he was beat. "Okay, okay. I'll keep Three with me."

Clare smiled and kissed him on the cheek. "I knew you'd understand. Thanks, honey."

"Sure," said Charlie seeing his medical career vanish before his eyes.

"I'll help you clear the table, Alice." Clare rose to help collect the dirty dishes.

Tenzin leaned toward Charlie. "Don't worry about Three," he whispered. "He'll sleep the whole time. You'll get your studying done."

"He never sleeps with me, Tenzin. I just don't have the touch."

"He will tonight."

Three was crying for his mother. Tenzin touched him on the forehead with his index finger. Pink light shot out of his finger. Seconds later, Three was sleeping peacefully.

"You'll be able to study, now."

"Thanks, Tenzin. I owe you one," said Charlie.

Clare finished clearing the table and went over to her husband and son, her eyes soft and glowing, the flare-up between them forgotten.

"I love you, Charlie," she said.

"I love you more."

"Don't you ever stop."

"I couldn't if I wanted to," he said. He kissed her while holding Three in his arms.

"David," said Clare, her eyes on Charlie and Three as they went through the kitchen door. "Save two seats, will you?"

Class started at seven-thirty sharp. By seven fifteen the room was packed. David sat in the back with Michael and Danny. Matthew was with Tenzin in the study. Clare and Annie joined them a few minutes later.

"Hi," David said, smiling.

"Hi," Annie said, smiling back.

"Do you know why there's an extra chair on the dais, Clare?" said David.

Clare looked toward the front of the room. Two solid black wooden chairs with padded arms and gold cushions sat on the dais. One of the chairs was positioned several inches higher than the other.

"I've never seen that before," answered Clare.

Tenzin entered the room with Matthew at his side. Matthew was wearing the robe that the Karmapa had given him. He carried a golden box in his arms. Alice and Thomas slid into their seats behind David and Clare as Matthew and Tenzin climbed onto the dais.

"Thank you all for coming tonight," said Tenzin. He looked out at the audience. "It is always good to have a full house. Every speaker craves one."

Laughter rippled through the audience.

"I believe you all know my son, Matthew."

The crowd nodded.

"I have a special surprise for you, tonight. But before we get to that I'd like to share some thoughts with you."

"What surprise?" whispered David to Clare. "He didn't say anything about a surprise at dinner."

Clare shrugged. "I don't know any more than you do."

David turned to Alice. She shook her head. David's stomach tensed. He didn't have a good feeling about this.

"The goal of life is growth. To grow, we must confront our challenges, using them as a springboard for transformation. Our mission is to convert the darkness hidden in us into light. If we succeed, our journey will be rewarding, regardless of how difficult the tests we face may be. Lao Tzu, the great Taoist sage, put it this way: *Because the sage confronts his difficulties, he never experiences them.*

"All of us are called to this great work. But we are also given free will. We must each make the choice to walk the path. Most people aren't ready yet. That is why I am grateful that you are all here tonight. Over time, many more will answer the call of their soul and begin their journey home to the Light. Eventually, a critical mass will form. Then, a new era will begin. The world will turn from greed and materialism to spirituality and compassion; from negative to positive; from fear to love; from separation and hostility to peace and unity.

"You are pioneers in this great work, a vanguard for the future. Even now, people are watching you. When your light and radiance expand, they will want to know how you changed your life. They are hungry for growth, even if they don't yet realize it. The work you do on yourself, you do not do for yourself alone. Your growth will also bear fruit in the lives of those you touch. When enough of us change, the world will change. Never doubt that."

Tenzin paused and looked out over the audience. Every face seemed hungry for growth. Good. It was crucial that there would be like-minded people to support Michael when the time came.

"Life on earth is temporary. Our real home is in the Light, beyond the suffering that accompanies the duality of the physical plane. Our true home is in the Oneness and the bliss that it confers. We are multi-dimensional beings, not limited to our bodies with their cycles of growth, decline, and death. The wise man knows this, and does not cling to his body when the time comes for him to depart. He does not feel terror at the approaching dissolution of his form, but a deepening sense of peace. The release of his body brings freedom to his soul. It is no longer tethered to the material world nor burdened by its limitations. Nothing is final, not even death. There is no end to consciousness. Growth is the eternal condition of life.

"There is no limit to how bright your soul can shine in this life. That decision is in your hands, and yours alone. Use your time in this world to maximum advantage. Let go of the negatives that corrode the soul: selfishness, greed, hurt, hatred, resentment, bitterness, jealousy, and anger. Do not waste your time blaming others. Blame is just another way to be a victim and give your power away to those who would hurt you. Nothing will change until you take full responsibility for your life. Acting from negative emotions creates karmic problems and future complications that must be faced before you can move forward to freedom. Why suffer avoidable delays? Negative emotions are a waste of time. Nursing grievances is the province of fools.

"Learn to love unconditionally and you will realize your Self. The Oneness created you in love. You will realize your destiny through love. Open the doors of your heart. Let love out so you can let love in. In this way you become love itself. The purpose of life is to reunite with the Oneness. The truth is you never really left it.

"Everything else is an illusion. Separation is the disease of the mind. Love gives. It nurtures; it nourishes; it heals; it makes us one. It doesn't judge or condemn or act in self-interest. It has no ego. It knows no fear. It is limitless. It is who you are."

Tenzin paused momentarily to allow the audience to absorb his message.

"Now, for the surprise I promised you. There is a special young man that I want you to meet. Michael, would you please stand up."

Michael was hesitant to do so, but finally stood. All heads turned toward him. Uncomfortable with the attention, he reached down to grasp his father's hand.

"Why, he's just a little boy," whispered a woman.

"Yes, but look at those eyes," said her friend. "They're so pure. He's an angel."

"That's true," said the first woman.

"Come up here, Michael," said Tenzin.

Michael looked to his father.

"Go ahead," said David.

Michael let go of his father's hand and walked slowly to the dais. When he reached it, Tenzin bent down over and took his hand. "Come," he said. Michael climbed the three steps to the dais and faced the large group. Tenzin put his arm around Michael's shoulder.

"Michael is the incarnation of my teacher, Doezen Rinpoche," said Tenzin.

The room went stone silent.

"Matthew," said Tenzin.

Matthew came forward with the golden box that Tenzin had entrusted to his care. Inside was a new red and yellow monk's robe. Tenzin held it up so the audience could see it, then put it around Michael's shoulders, helping him to slide his arms through its sleeves.

"As the incarnation of Doezen Rinpoche, the highest chair on the dais belongs to you."

Tenzin pointed to the empty chair that sat higher than his.

"That seat is now yours. Please take it."

When Michael had taken his seat, Tenzin and Matthew turned toward him and bowed.

"An enlightened soul has returned to help humanity," said Tenzin. "When the time is darkest, the emissaries of the Supreme Truth return. It has always been so."

David looked around. The audience was very moved. Tears moistened Annie's cheeks. She wasn't the only one. Where's this going, he asked himself. The sirens in his head screamed louder. He's just a kid and the war with Sarah and Rayanne is far from over. He might be an enlightened soul and a Bodhisattva and all that, but right now he was also a boy who loved soccer, chocolate chip cookies, buckwheat pancakes, and wanted his father to read to him before he went to sleep. He wasn't ready to liberate anyone of anything. As a matter of fact, he needed protection more than anyone else in the room. Please God, grant me the strength and wisdom to provide it, prayed David, his head bowed slightly.

There was danger ahead, lots of it. He knew it and was in no mood to join the celebration. A harsh wind nipped at his back, silently gathering strength and biding its time. He shuddered to think what disasters lay ahead. Annie saw the tension in his face and put her hand on his. He looked over at her, his face grim, eyes clouded by doubt. Would she still be there when the darkness came after him? How could she be? It was more than any normal person could bear. He was wrong to hope for it. If she were smart, she'd run now.

He returned his gaze to his son. Michael's energy field had expanded, filling the dais with gold light. For the moment, his soul had revealed his true power. Not many possessed that kind of light. Tenzin certainly, but no one else that he had ever seen. There was great beauty, but also grave danger in its manifestation. The darkness would want to extinguish it as soon as possible. His boy was a threat. He couldn't deny it anymore. Tenzin had been right again. He took a deep breath and steeled himself for the hard road ahead. The way forward was sure to be long and twisted, full of surprising turns, sharp descents and dark passages. He sighed. The future would be far more difficult than the present. The Lord's Prayer rose silently from his lips.

Our Father, who art in heaven,

hallowed be thy name.

Thy Kingdom come,

Thy will be done,

on earth as it is in heaven. Give

us this day our daily bread. And

forgive us our trespasses,

as we forgive those who trespass against us.

And lead us not into temptation,

but deliver us from evil.

For thine is the kingdom,

the power and the glory,

forever and ever.

The Lord's Prayer had banished the darkness once before. Would it work as well in the days to come?

Join Alan Mesher's forum on Facebook. Ask questions and join the discussion.
Alan will answer questions and reply to comments.
http://www.facebook.com/thetenzintrilogy

Read more about Alan Mesher's work and follow his appearance schedule at:
www.alanmesher.com or www.oversoulcommunications.com

BOOK TWO OF THE TENZIN TRILOGY

Coming in 2014

CPSIA information can be obtained at www.ICGtesting.com
Printed in the USA
LVOW06s2232110813

347350LV00002B/17/P

9 780966 029543